John Byrne's NEXT MEN ™

Book One

Story and art by John Byrne
Colors by Matt Webb

Mike Richardson • publisher
Neil Hankerson • vice president of operations
Randy Stradley • creative director
Barbara Kesel • managing editor
Ronnie Noize • marketing director
Bob Schreck • special projects director
Andy Karabatsos • controller
Mark Anderson • general counsel
Cece Cutsforth • design director
Jerry Prosser • editorial coordinator
Jeff Gillis • shipping manager

Collections Editor: Kij Johnson   Collections Design: Brian Gogolin

Jennie Bricker, Debbie Byrd, Chris Chalenor, Bob Cooper, Brian Gogolin, Kij Johnson,
Edward Martin III, Diana Schutz, Monty Sheldon, Suzanne Taylor, Dan Thorsland,
Chris Warner, John Weeks, Ryder Windham • editorial staff

Randy Bowen • product development

Theresa Fogel, Pamela Fricker, Scott Fuentes, Adam Gallardo, Cary Grazzini, Heather
Hale, Evelyn Harris, Jim Johns, Diane Kintrea-Wassman, Todd Knight, Debra Koch,
Todd McAllister, Perry McManne, Jay Moreau, David Nestelle, Brian Neubauer, Cara
Niece, Cary Porter, Rich Powers, Professoruss, Meleah Rutherford, James Sinclair,
Carolyn Stinson, Kai Thomasian, Scott Tice, Sean Tierney, Marty Todd, Tim Tran •
production staff

John Dennett, Ray Gruen, Joe Kamei, Mark Pedersen, Egon Selby, David Weigel, Kris
Young • marketing staff

Lorrie Flaschner, Tod Borleske, Charissa Butler, Kimberly Chandler, Chris Creviston,
Raylene Dusenberry, Jeff Gillis, Tia Guile, Kim Haines, Kristy Hamilton, Dale
LaFountain, Sue Ostermann, Rebecca Rautenberg, Mike Van Horn • operations staff

Published by Dark Horse Comics, Inc.
10956 SE Main Street
Milwaukie, OR 97222

ISBN: 1-878574-70-1
First edition: March 1993
10 9 8 7 6 5 4 3 2 1
Printed in Canada.

Introduction by John Byrne

In "I, Claudius," the mad emperor Caligula describes his "metamorphosis" into a living god as being "like a birth, in which the mother delivers herself." The "birth" of the Next Men was not quite so painful — or dramatic. It's been my experience that the important things that happen in my life are rarely accompanied by moments of great drama. Usually they are the culmination of a string of circumstance which, viewed through the eagle eye of retrospect, invariably proves quite logical. Things happen because they were meant to happen. Because there was not a whole lot else that could happen.

So it was with the Next Men, although at the time I would have been the last person on Earth to see it.

To begin at the beginning, first a moment to dispel a popular misconception: *John Byrne's Next Men* is not a failed or rejected Marvel project. Never was. Confusion rises from the fact that my first Dark Horse project, the *2112* graphic novel, was created from material which I originally prepared for a Marvel project, and since *2112* has been installed into the Next Men canon it is only logical, albeit erroneous, to think the two had the same genesis.

What actually happened was this: *2112* was created originally as a "pilot" for Marvel's "Futureverse" project, initiated by Stan Lee. Stan asked me if I would like to create the future of the Marvel Universe, and my reaction was "If I don't, somebody else will." Call it ego, but I felt I was better qualified than most to project the future timelines of the universe with which I had been so intimately involved for so many years. So I took a number of different notions which had been percolating through my head for some time, and shuffled them into a package which would seem a reasonably logical extrapolation of Marvel's timeline. Unfortunately, as it turned out, things were not quite what I had been led to believe, and ultimately I found myself in a position in which I could only maintain artistic integrity — pretentious term, but there you are — if I took back that part of the work which was exclusively mine, as distinguished from the elements which I had mixed in in order to make the story fit into Marvel continuity. The problem, though, was that this left me with some sixty-four pages of original material which, at that moment, had no home. I received a tentative offer from DC Comics, one of their editors expressing an interest in publishing the work, but I felt that what I really needed to do was go "independent" with this. I needed to find a company which would be willing to publish the work while allowing me to retain full rights to the property. As memory serves, it was my longtime friend and sometime collaborator, Roger Stern, who suggested I try Dark Horse. So I called Bob Schreck, Dark Horse's Special Projects Director, and sort of tiptoed around the idea of what I wanted to do. By the end of the conversation I was tiptoeing no longer: I had offered *2112* to Dark Horse, and Dark Horse, through Bob, had accepted, cheerfully girding their loins for a confrontation with Marvel which, happily, never came.

There's an old saying: In for a penny, in for a pound. Having taken this first tentative step into the realms of creator-owned material, I began to think I should go ahead and shoot the works: create a whole series which I would completely own and control. This was the birth of the Next Men, as I set about constructing a matrix which would serve two important purposes: firstly, to assemble in one place all those elements which I knew my fans liked best about my work, and secondly to create something I could have a lot of fun with. One of the most frustrating things about working for Marvel and DC, despite all the wonderful toys such work allows one to play with, was an unavoidable fact that those toys are all quite old. Superman, Batman, the X-Men, the Fantastic Four — they all have long and well-established histories, as do the universes in which their stories unfold. It is impossible, for example, to do a First Alien Contact story at either Marvel or DC. At DC it has been impossible since Day One, since Superman is himself an alien. At Marvel it has been impossible since Day Two, since the villains the Fantastic

Four encountered in their second issue were marauding aliens. Space flight, time travel, lost civilizations — all these familiar staples of comic books have a heavy weight of chain attached to them in all the established "universes." That chain is continuity, the allegiance to what has gone before. So I felt the need for a "virgin" universe, and in *Next Men* I would have just that.

But there was still something bristling in the back of my mind as I set to work on the first few pages of the first chapter of Next Men. At that point I was still scripting and lettering *2112*, and the further along I got into the story, the more I realized there was one element of its conception from which I would never be able to completely divorce it: no matter what I did, it still felt and read as a pilot, as the introduction to an ongoing storyline. Then it occurred to me, if *2112* was the future of a universe — or, at this point, a planet, Earth — why shouldn't it be the future of the Next Men's universe? All I needed to do was have the characters in *2112* make some passing remarks which indicated their awareness of the Next Men as part of their history, and voilà, a cohesive whole was formed out of two separate parts. More than that, since *2112* was still scheduled for publication before them, the Next Men were able thereby to lay claim to a unique bit of comic-book history, becoming the first title ever to debut with a sequel.

This also allowed me to turn my nascent Next Men storyline into a time travel story, and I was in puppy heaven. Time travel stories are far and away my favorite.

Ah, but I bet there's one question the more astute among you — or, at least, those who have already read what follows — will be asking yourselves: "If *2112* was originally conceived as a separate entity, and only subsequently installed as a part of the Next Men timeline, how does it happen that the main bad guy from *2112* plays such a significant role in *Next Men*?"

Good question. Maybe it was always in the back of my mind that *2112* should be a part of the Next Men canon. Certainly I can no longer remember what I was planning to do with the Next Men's ongoing saga before I connected them to *2112*. It is a curious thing about the way my mind works that — unlike some writers I know, who in some ways I envy — once I have abandoned or modified a storyline the original simply evaporates from my memory. As if I'd dragged its little icon across my brain's desktop and dumped it into the trash. I have no idea where I would have gone with the Next Men had the end of issue 2 (the third issue herein collected) been different from what it is. Not so much as a single wisp of those stories remains in my brain — which is indeed unfortunate, since, being completely separate now from the Next Men, they might have been something I could have used elsewhere.

And, after all, isn't that where we started, with me using something that had begun one place in an entirely different place?

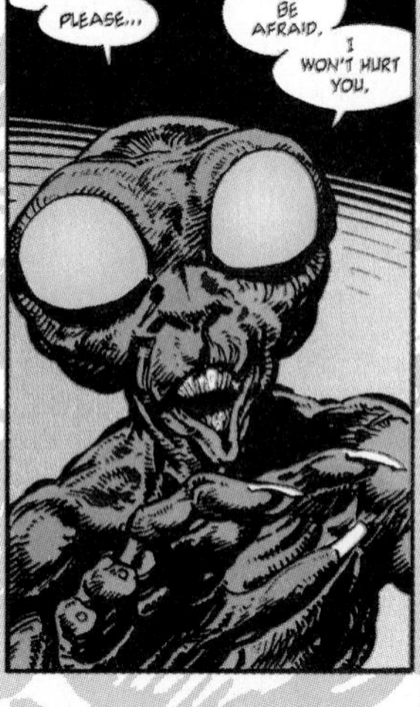
NO...
PLEASE...
DON'T BE AFRAID.
I WON'T HURT YOU.

-John Byrne

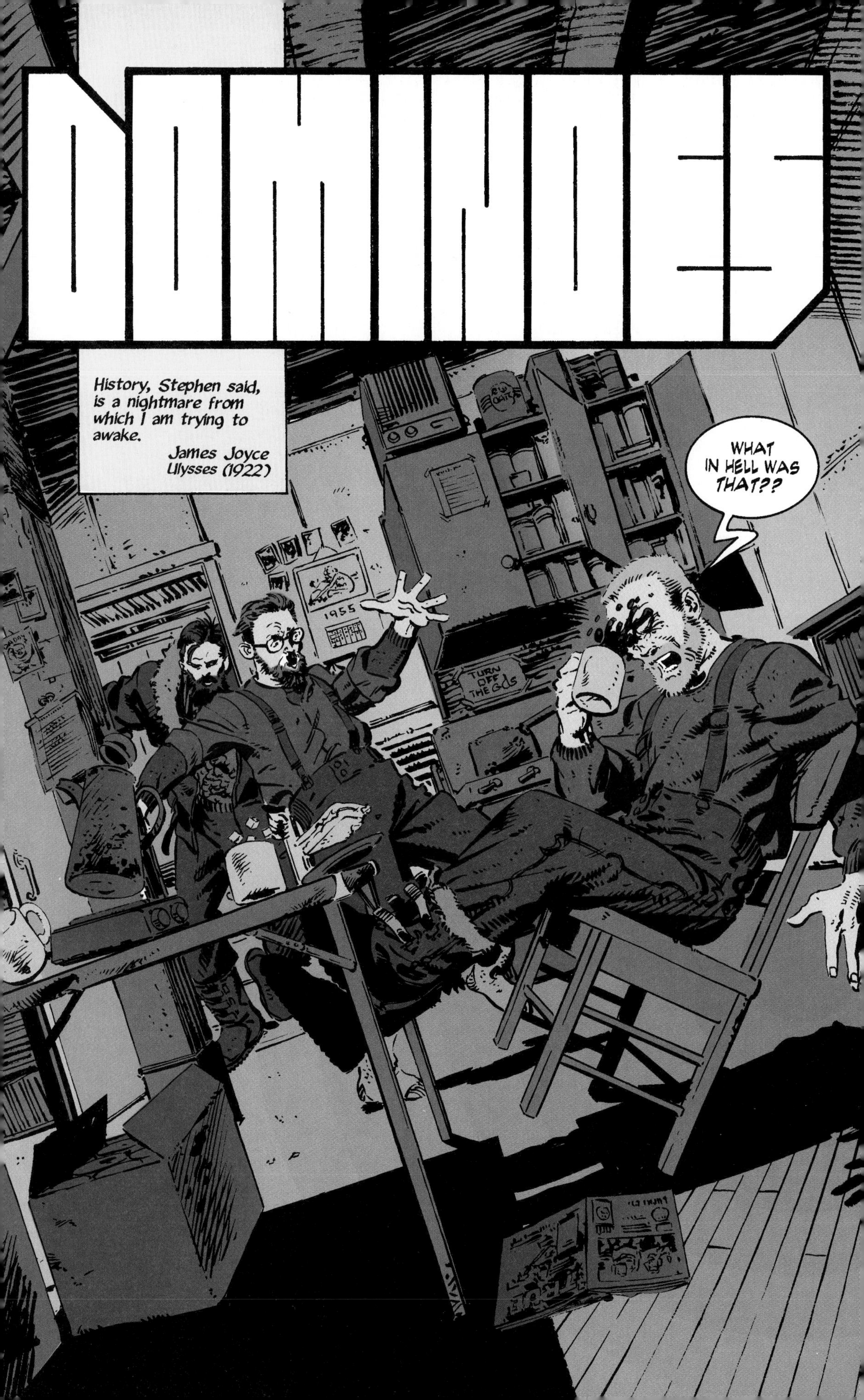
DOMINOES
History, Stephen said, is a nightmare from which I am trying to awake.
James Joyce Ulysses (1922)
WHAT IN HELL WAS THAT??
1955
TURN OFF THE GAS

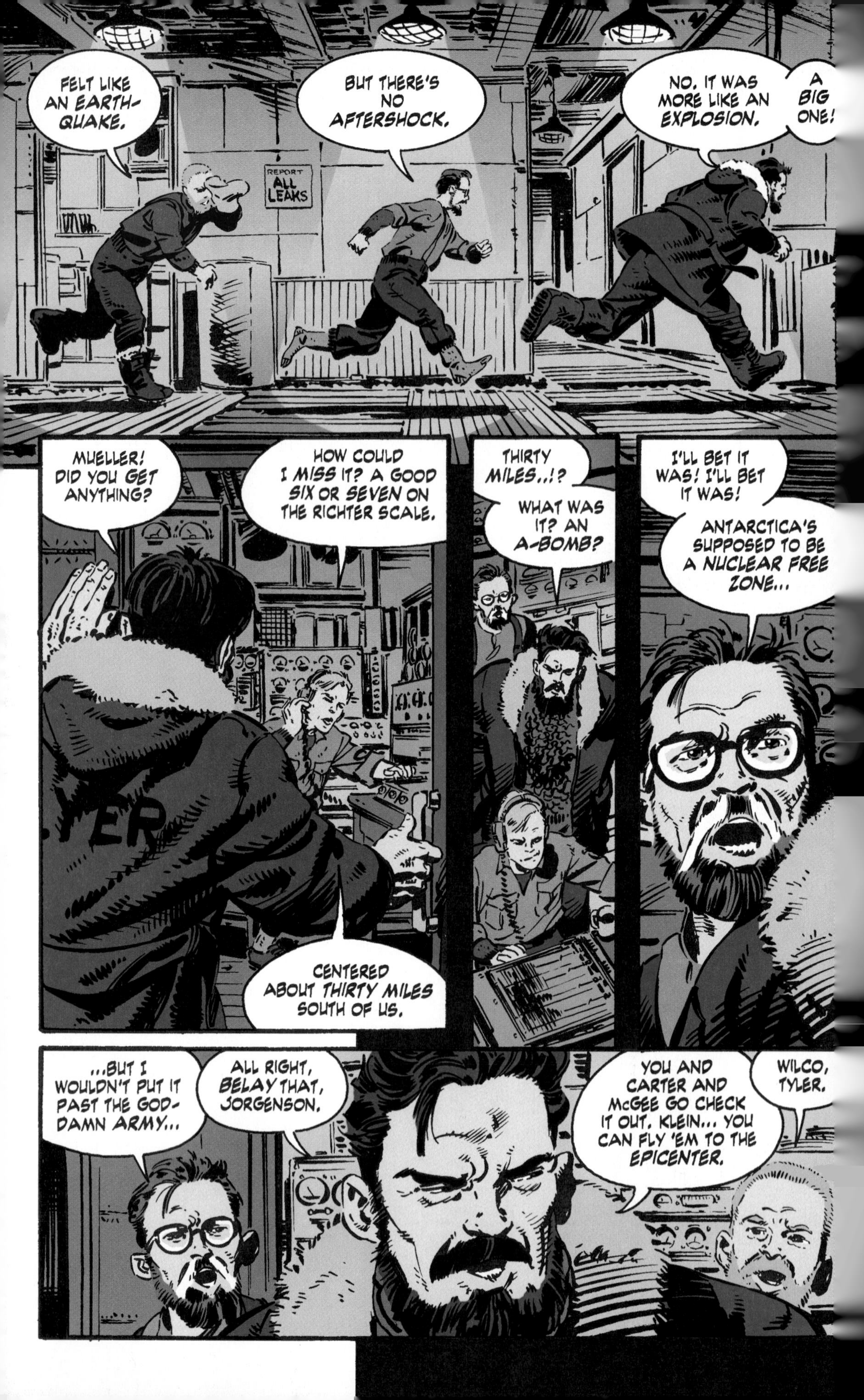
FELT LIKE AN EARTH-QUAKE.
BUT THERE'S NO AFTERSHOCK.
NO. IT WAS MORE LIKE AN EXPLOSION.
A BIG ONE!
REPORT ALL LEAKS
MUELLER! DID YOU GET ANYTHING?
HOW COULD I MISS IT? A GOOD SIX OR SEVEN ON THE RICHTER SCALE.
CENTERED ABOUT THIRTY MILES SOUTH OF US.
THIRTY MILES..!?
WHAT WAS IT? AN A-BOMB?
I'LL BET IT WAS! I'LL BET IT WAS!
ANTARCTICA'S SUPPOSED TO BE A NUCLEAR FREE ZONE...
...BUT I WOULDN'T PUT IT PAST THE GOD-DAMN ARMY...
ALL RIGHT, BELAY THAT, JORGENSON.
YOU AND CARTER AND McGEE GO CHECK IT OUT. KLEIN... YOU CAN FLY 'EM TO THE EPICENTER.
WILCO, TYLER.

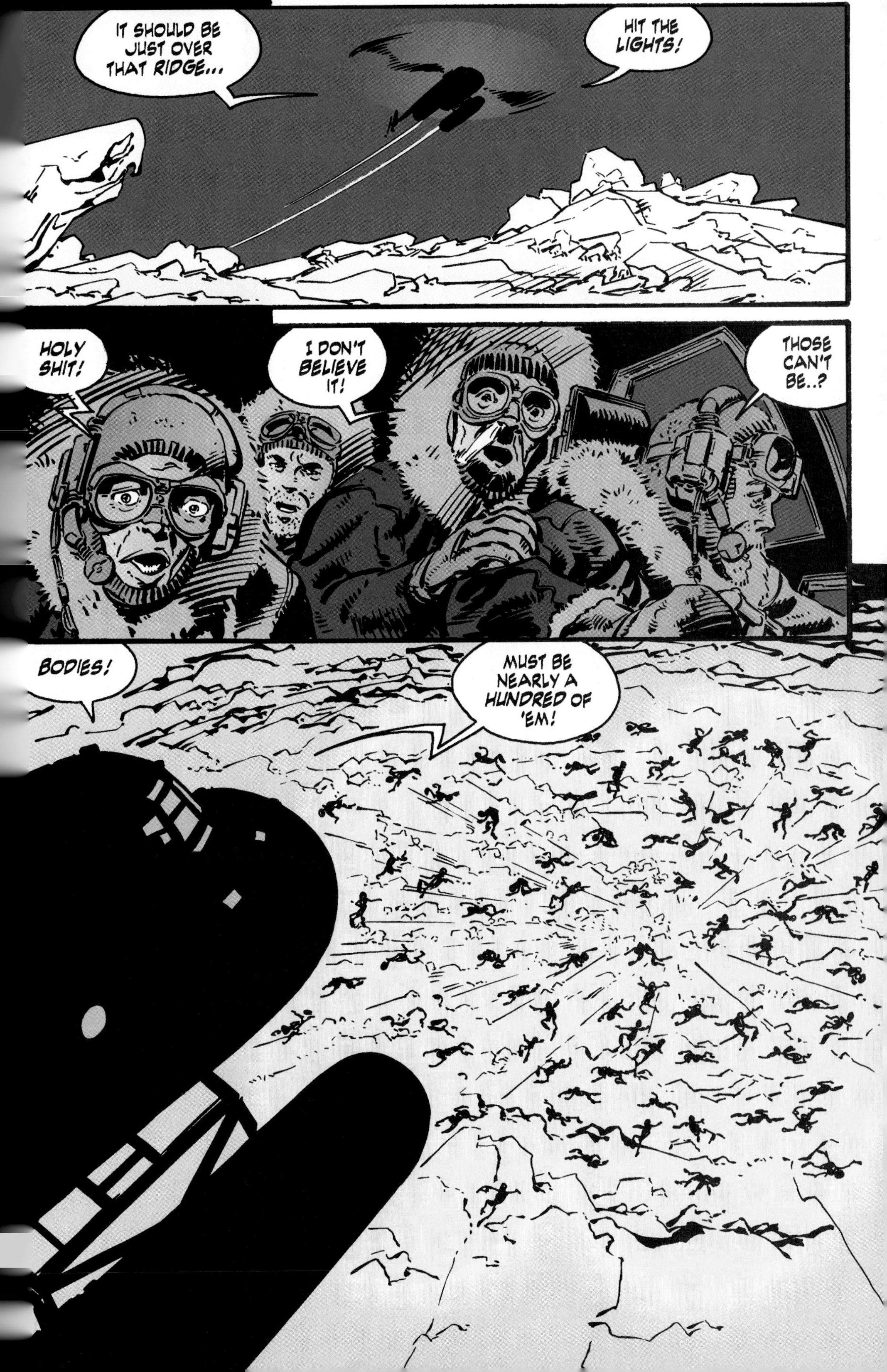
IT SHOULD BE JUST OVER THAT RIDGE...
HIT THE LIGHTS!
HOLY SHIT!
I DON'T BELIEVE IT!
THOSE CAN'T BE..?
BODIES!
MUST BE NEARLY A HUNDRED OF 'EM!

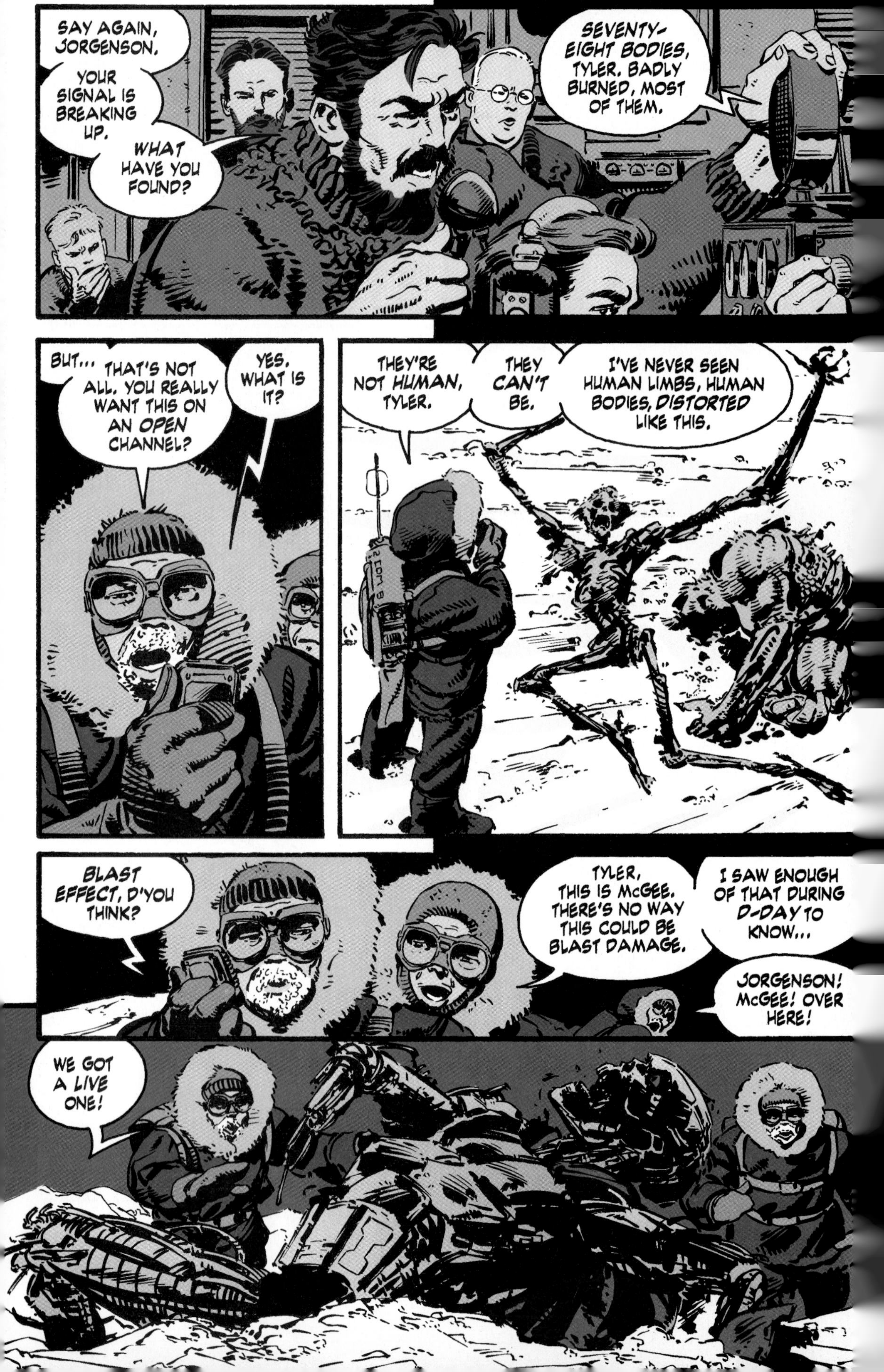
SAY AGAIN, JORGENSON.
YOUR SIGNAL IS BREAKING UP.
WHAT HAVE YOU FOUND?
SEVENTY-EIGHT BODIES, TYLER. BADLY BURNED, MOST OF THEM.
BUT... THAT'S NOT ALL. YOU REALLY WANT THIS ON AN OPEN CHANNEL?
YES. WHAT IS IT?
THEY'RE NOT HUMAN, TYLER.
THEY CAN'T BE.
I'VE NEVER SEEN HUMAN LIMBS, HUMAN BODIES, DISTORTED LIKE THIS.
BLAST EFFECT, D'YOU THINK?
TYLER, THIS IS McGEE. THERE'S NO WAY THIS COULD BE BLAST DAMAGE.
I SAW ENOUGH OF THAT DURING D-DAY TO KNOW...
JORGENSON! McGEE! OVER HERE!
WE GOT A LIVE ONE!

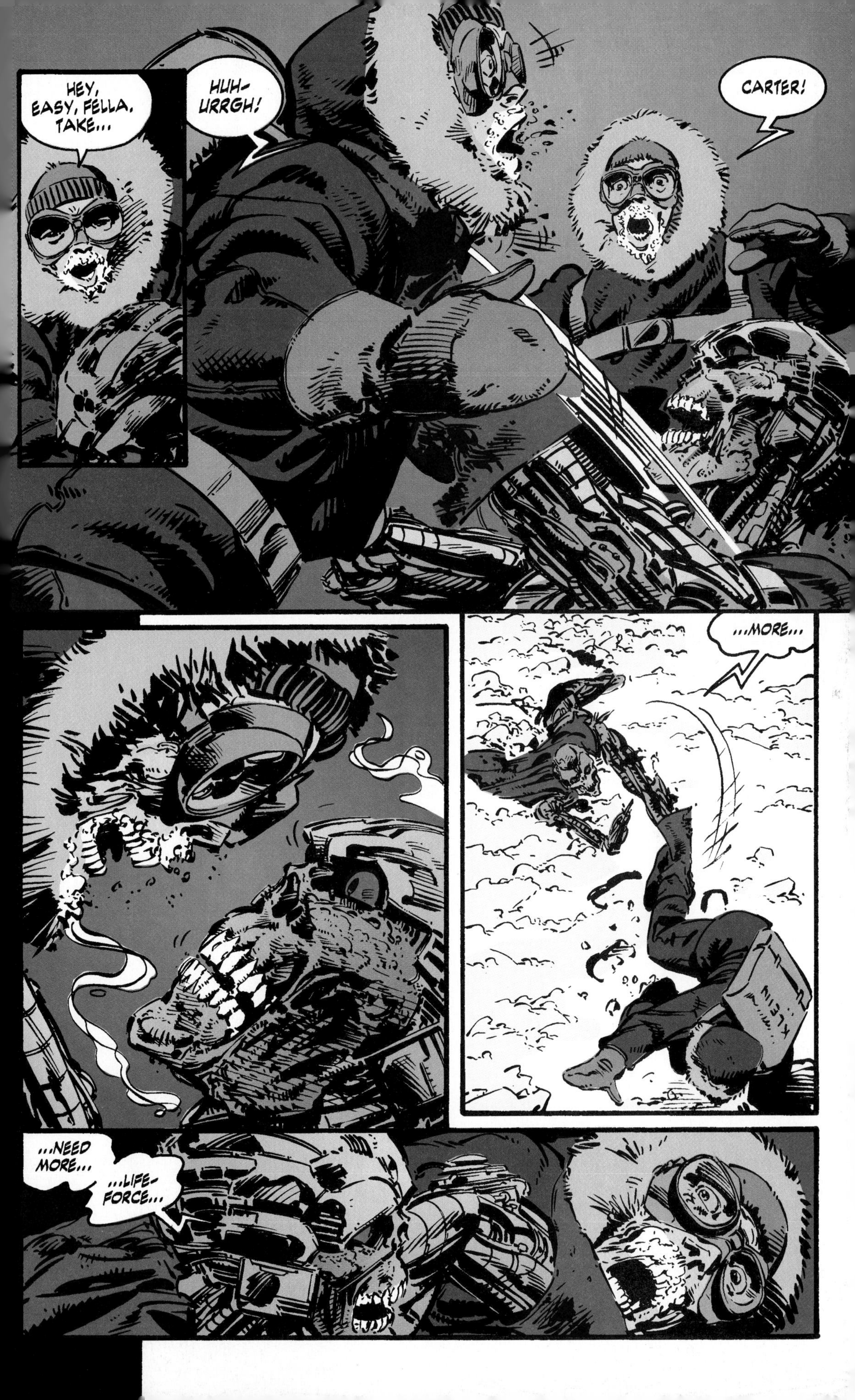
HEY, EASY, FELLA. TAKE...
HUH-URRGH!
CARTER!
...MORE...
KLEIN
...NEED MORE...
...LIFE-FORCE...

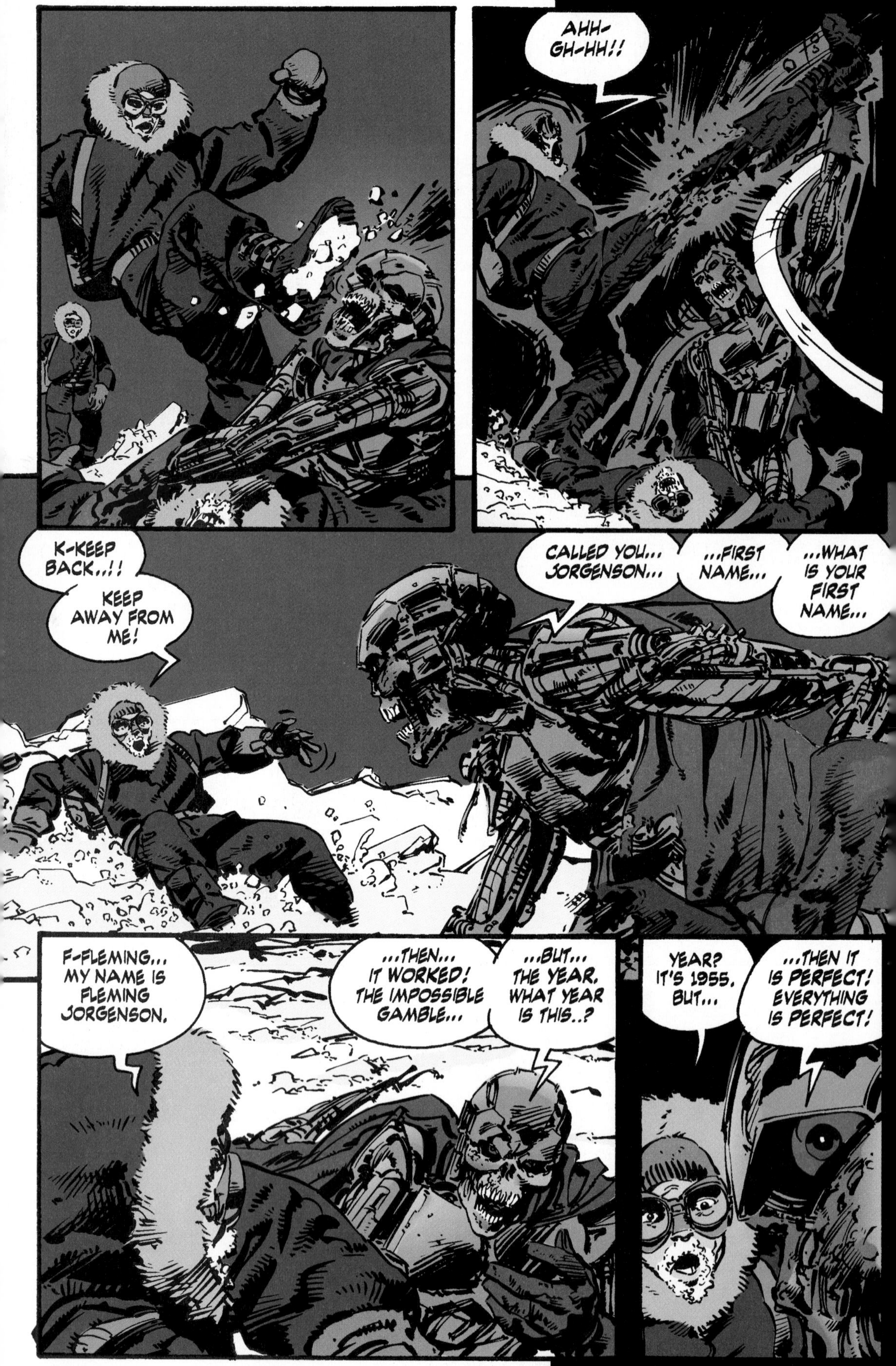
AHH-GH-HH!!
K-KEEP BACK..!!
KEEP AWAY FROM ME!
CALLED YOU... JORGENSON...
...FIRST NAME...
...WHAT IS YOUR FIRST NAME...
F-FLEMING... MY NAME IS FLEMING JORGENSON.
...THEN... IT WORKED! THE IMPOSSIBLE GAMBLE...
...BUT... THE YEAR. WHAT YEAR IS THIS..?
YEAR? IT'S 1955. BUT...
...THEN IT IS PERFECT! EVERYTHING IS PERFECT!

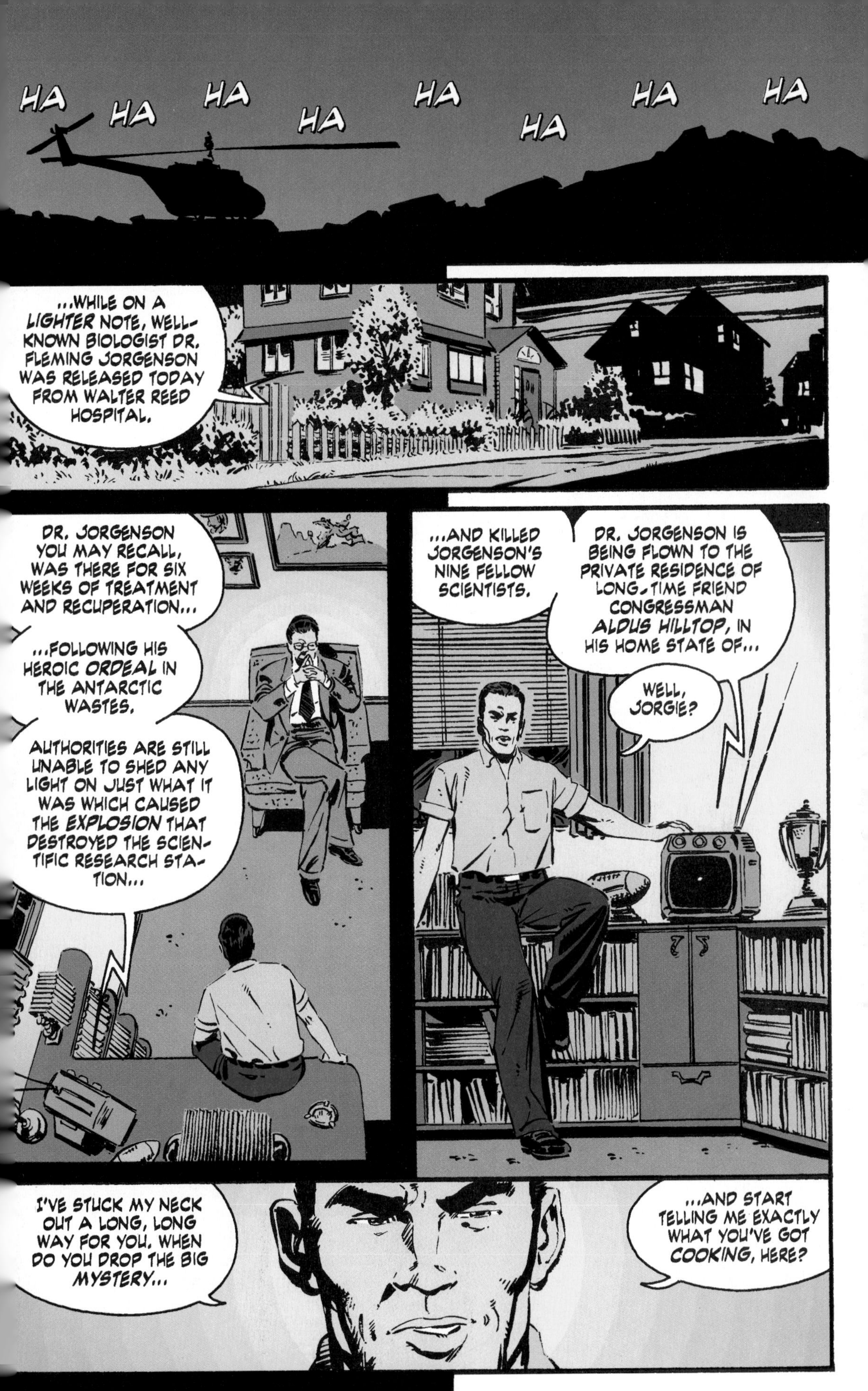
HA HA HA HA HA HA HA HA
...WHILE ON A LIGHTER NOTE, WELL-KNOWN BIOLOGIST DR. FLEMING JORGENSON WAS RELEASED TODAY FROM WALTER REED HOSPITAL.
DR. JORGENSON YOU MAY RECALL, WAS THERE FOR SIX WEEKS OF TREATMENT AND RECUPERATION...
...FOLLOWING HIS HEROIC ORDEAL IN THE ANTARCTIC WASTES.
AUTHORITIES ARE STILL UNABLE TO SHED ANY LIGHT ON JUST WHAT IT WAS WHICH CAUSED THE EXPLOSION THAT DESTROYED THE SCIENTIFIC RESEARCH STATION...
...AND KILLED JORGENSON'S NINE FELLOW SCIENTISTS.
DR. JORGENSON IS BEING FLOWN TO THE PRIVATE RESIDENCE OF LONG-TIME FRIEND CONGRESSMAN ALDUS HILLTOP, IN HIS HOME STATE OF...
WELL, JORGIE?
I'VE STUCK MY NECK OUT A LONG, LONG WAY FOR YOU. WHEN DO YOU DROP THE BIG MYSTERY...
...AND START TELLING ME EXACTLY WHAT YOU'VE GOT COOKING, HERE?

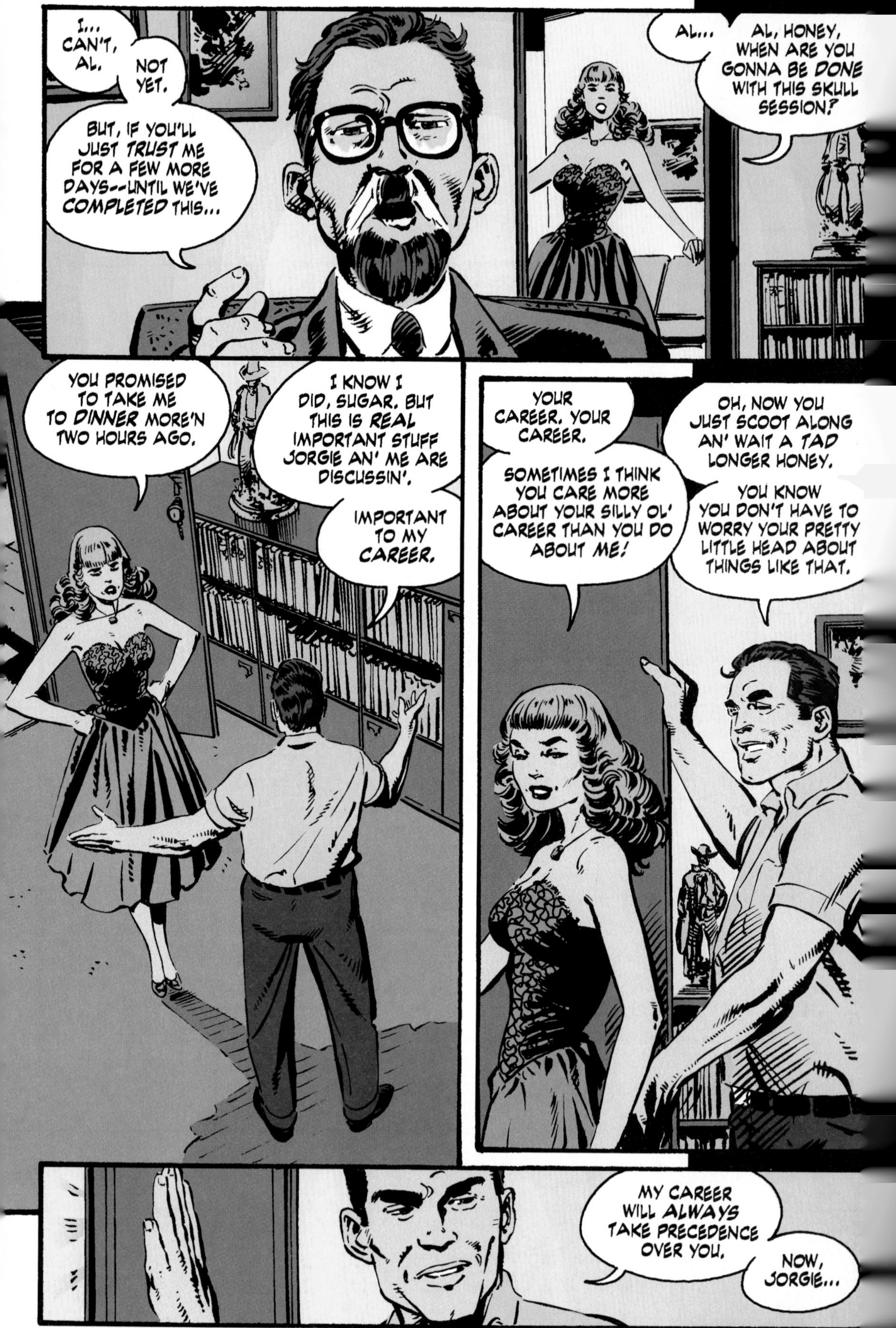
I... CAN'T, AL.
NOT YET.
BUT, IF YOU'LL JUST TRUST ME FOR A FEW MORE DAYS--UNTIL WE'VE COMPLETED THIS...
AL...
AL, HONEY, WHEN ARE YOU GONNA BE DONE WITH THIS SKULL SESSION?
YOU PROMISED TO TAKE ME TO DINNER MORE'N TWO HOURS AGO.
I KNOW I DID, SUGAR. BUT THIS IS REAL IMPORTANT STUFF JORGIE AN' ME ARE DISCUSSIN'.
IMPORTANT TO MY CAREER.
YOUR CAREER. YOUR CAREER.
SOMETIMES I THINK YOU CARE MORE ABOUT YOUR SILLY OL' CAREER THAN YOU DO ABOUT ME!
OH, NOW YOU JUST SCOOT ALONG AN' WAIT A TAD LONGER HONEY.
YOU KNOW YOU DON'T HAVE TO WORRY YOUR PRETTY LITTLE HEAD ABOUT THINGS LIKE THAT.
MY CAREER WILL ALWAYS TAKE PRECEDENCE OVER YOU.
NOW, JORGIE...

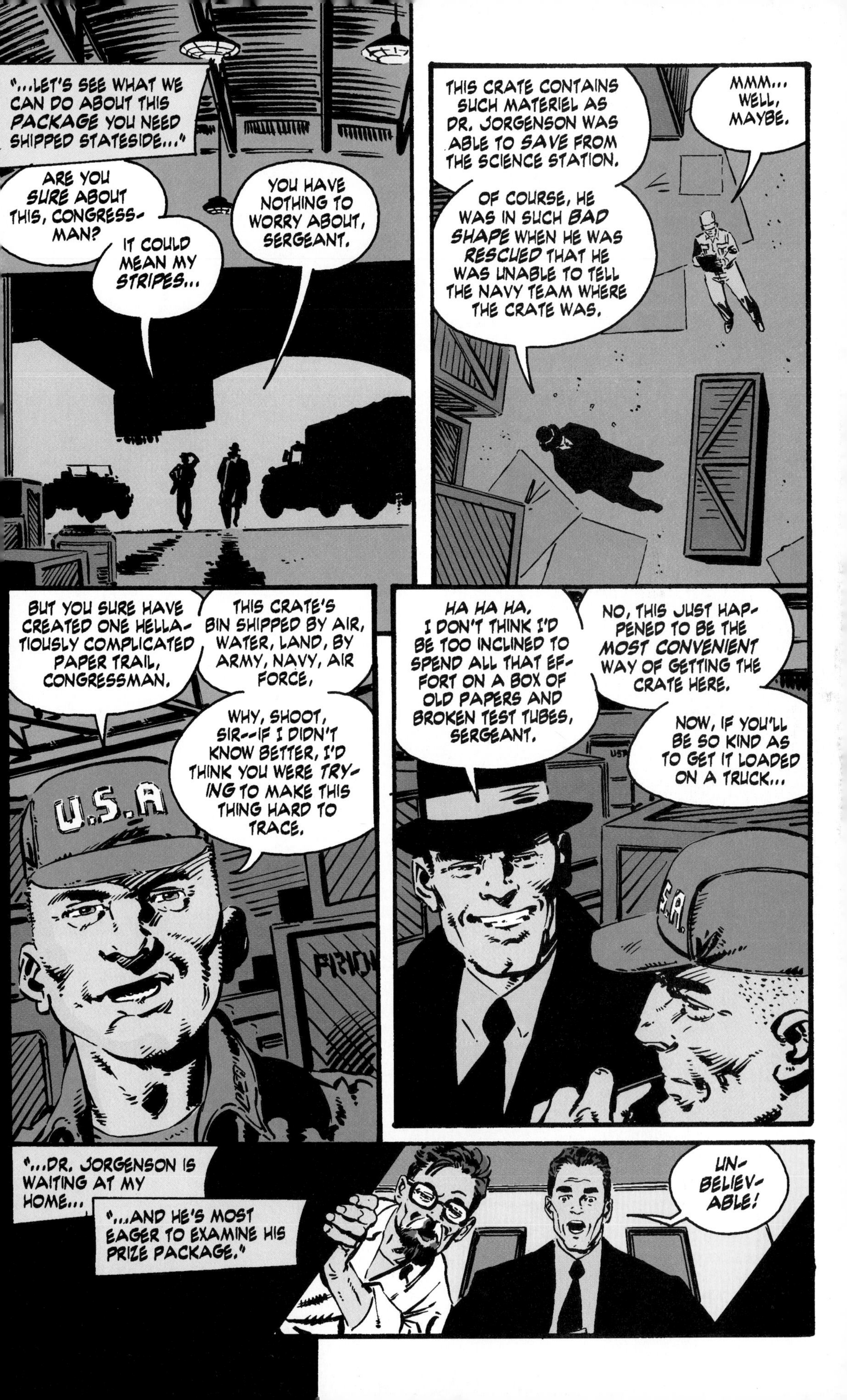
"...LET'S SEE WHAT WE CAN DO ABOUT THIS PACKAGE YOU NEED SHIPPED STATESIDE..."
ARE YOU SURE ABOUT THIS, CONGRESS-MAN?
IT COULD MEAN MY STRIPES...
YOU HAVE NOTHING TO WORRY ABOUT, SERGEANT.
THIS CRATE CONTAINS SUCH MATERIEL AS DR. JORGENSON WAS ABLE TO SAVE FROM THE SCIENCE STATION.
MMM... WELL, MAYBE.
OF COURSE, HE WAS IN SUCH BAD SHAPE WHEN HE WAS RESCUED THAT HE WAS UNABLE TO TELL THE NAVY TEAM WHERE THE CRATE WAS.
BUT YOU SURE HAVE CREATED ONE HELLA-TIOUSLY COMPLICATED PAPER TRAIL, CONGRESSMAN.
THIS CRATE'S BIN SHIPPED BY AIR, WATER, LAND, BY ARMY, NAVY, AIR FORCE.
WHY, SHOOT, SIR--IF I DIDN'T KNOW BETTER, I'D THINK YOU WERE TRY-ING TO MAKE THIS THING HARD TO TRACE.
U.S.A
HA HA HA. I DON'T THINK I'D BE TOO INCLINED TO SPEND ALL THAT EF-FORT ON A BOX OF OLD PAPERS AND BROKEN TEST TUBES, SERGEANT.
NO, THIS JUST HAP-PENED TO BE THE MOST CONVENIENT WAY OF GETTING THE CRATE HERE.
NOW, IF YOU'LL BE SO KIND AS TO GET IT LOADED ON A TRUCK...
"...DR. JORGENSON IS WAITING AT MY HOME...
"...AND HE'S MOST EAGER TO EXAMINE HIS PRIZE PACKAGE."
UN-BELIEV-ABLE!

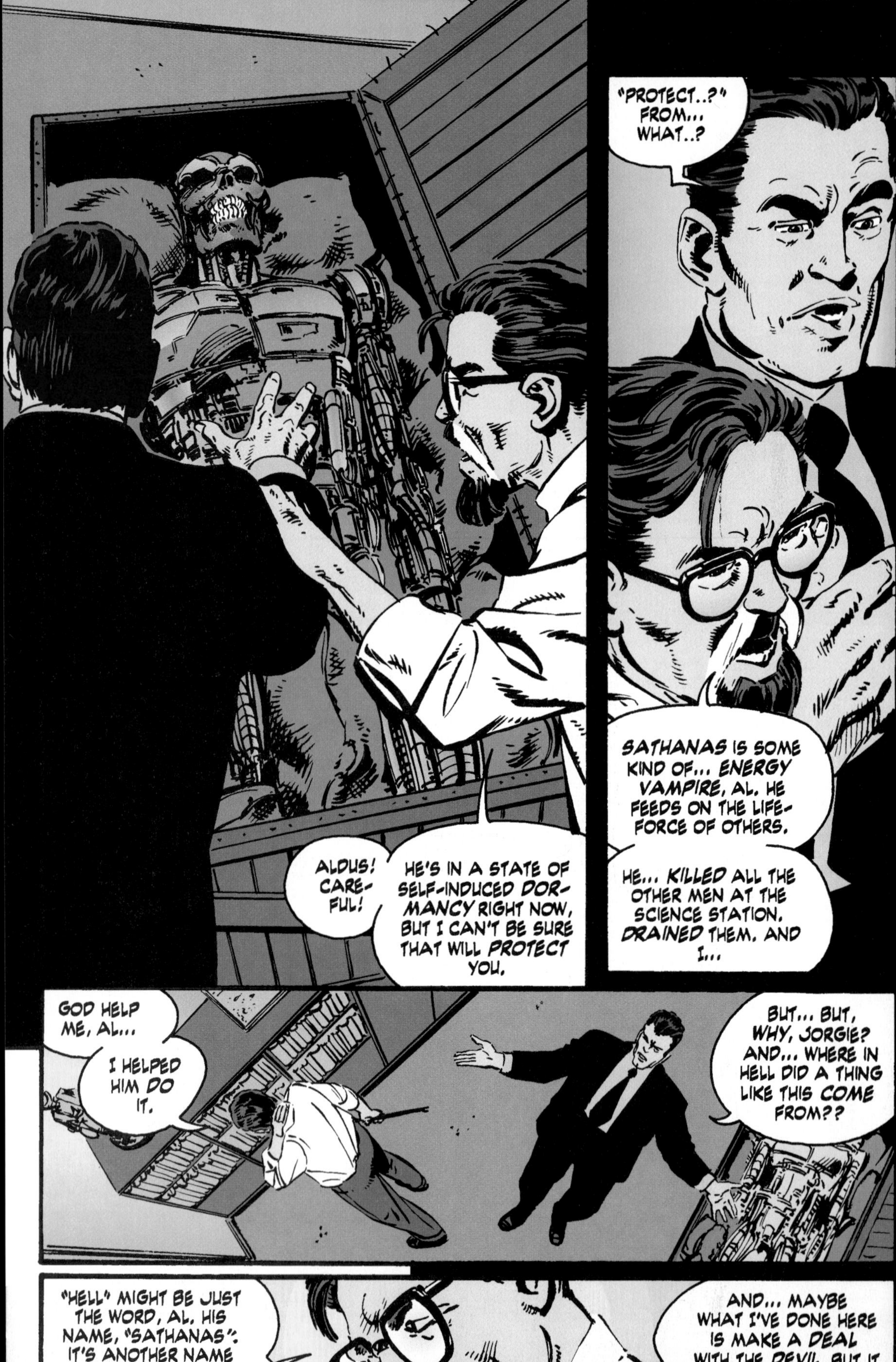
"PROTECT..?" FROM... WHAT..?
ALDUS! CARE-FUL!
HE'S IN A STATE OF SELF-INDUCED DOR-MANCY RIGHT NOW, BUT I CAN'T BE SURE THAT WILL PROTECT YOU.
SATHANAS IS SOME KIND OF... ENERGY VAMPIRE, AL. HE FEEDS ON THE LIFE-FORCE OF OTHERS.
HE... KILLED ALL THE OTHER MEN AT THE SCIENCE STATION. DRAINED THEM. AND I...
GOD HELP ME, AL...
I HELPED HIM DO IT.
BUT... BUT, WHY, JORGIE? AND... WHERE IN HELL DID A THING LIKE THIS COME FROM??
"HELL" MIGHT BE JUST THE WORD, AL. HIS NAME, "SATHANAS". IT'S ANOTHER NAME FOR SATAN.
AND... MAYBE WHAT I'VE DONE HERE IS MAKE A DEAL WITH THE DEVIL. BUT IT WAS WORTH IT!

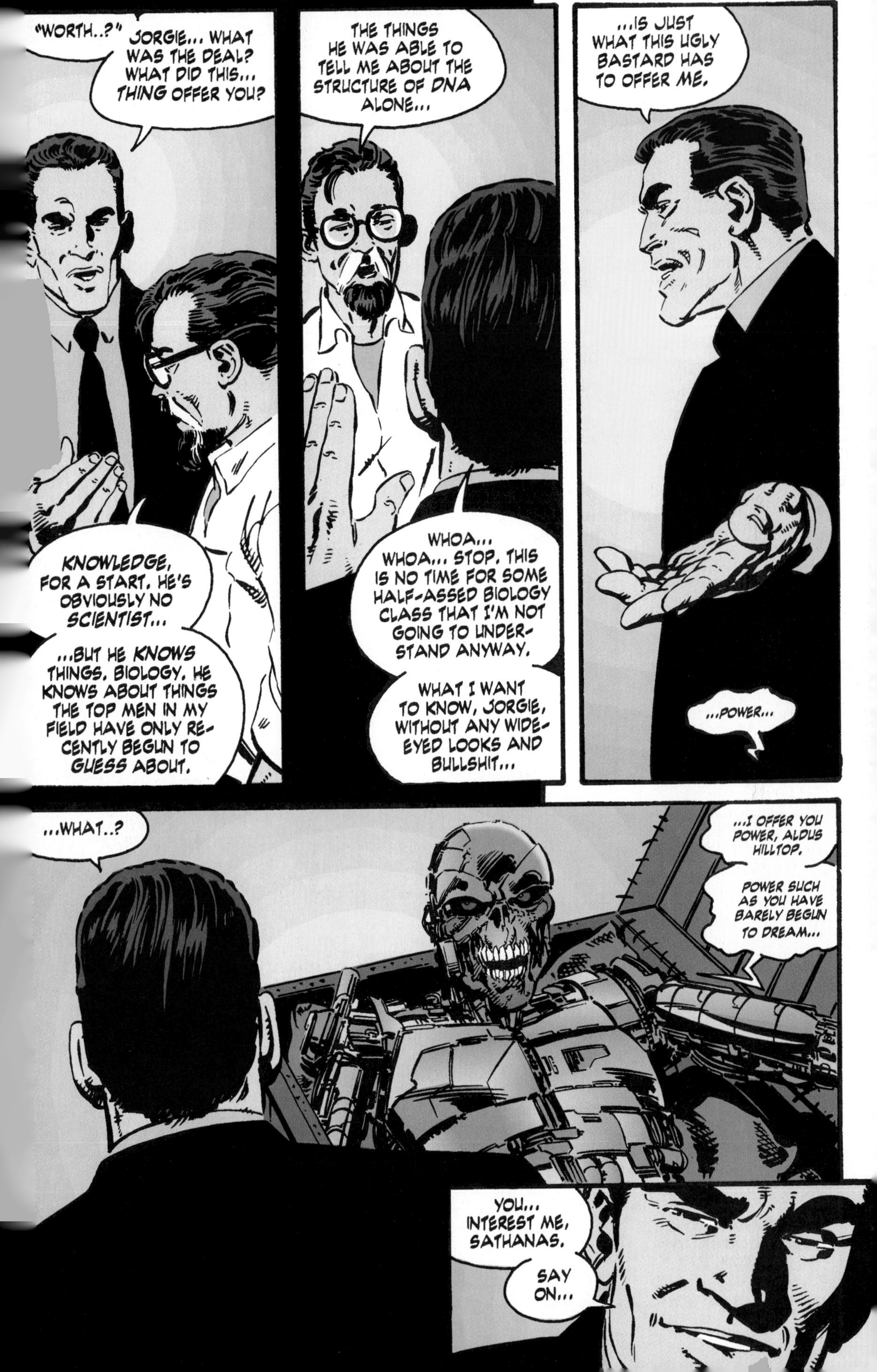
"WORTH..?" JORGIE... WHAT WAS THE DEAL? WHAT DID THIS... THING OFFER YOU?
KNOWLEDGE, FOR A START. HE'S OBVIOUSLY NO SCIENTIST...
...BUT HE KNOWS THINGS. BIOLOGY. HE KNOWS ABOUT THINGS THE TOP MEN IN MY FIELD HAVE ONLY RECENTLY BEGUN TO GUESS ABOUT.
THE THINGS HE WAS ABLE TO TELL ME ABOUT THE STRUCTURE OF DNA ALONE...
WHOA... WHOA... STOP. THIS IS NO TIME FOR SOME HALF-ASSED BIOLOGY CLASS THAT I'M NOT GOING TO UNDERSTAND ANYWAY.
WHAT I WANT TO KNOW, JORGIE, WITHOUT ANY WIDE-EYED LOOKS AND BULLSHIT...
...IS JUST WHAT THIS UGLY BASTARD HAS TO OFFER ME.
...POWER...
...WHAT..?
...I OFFER YOU POWER, ALDUS HILLTOP.
POWER SUCH AS YOU HAVE BARELY BEGUN TO DREAM...
YOU... INTEREST ME, SATHANAS.
SAY ON...

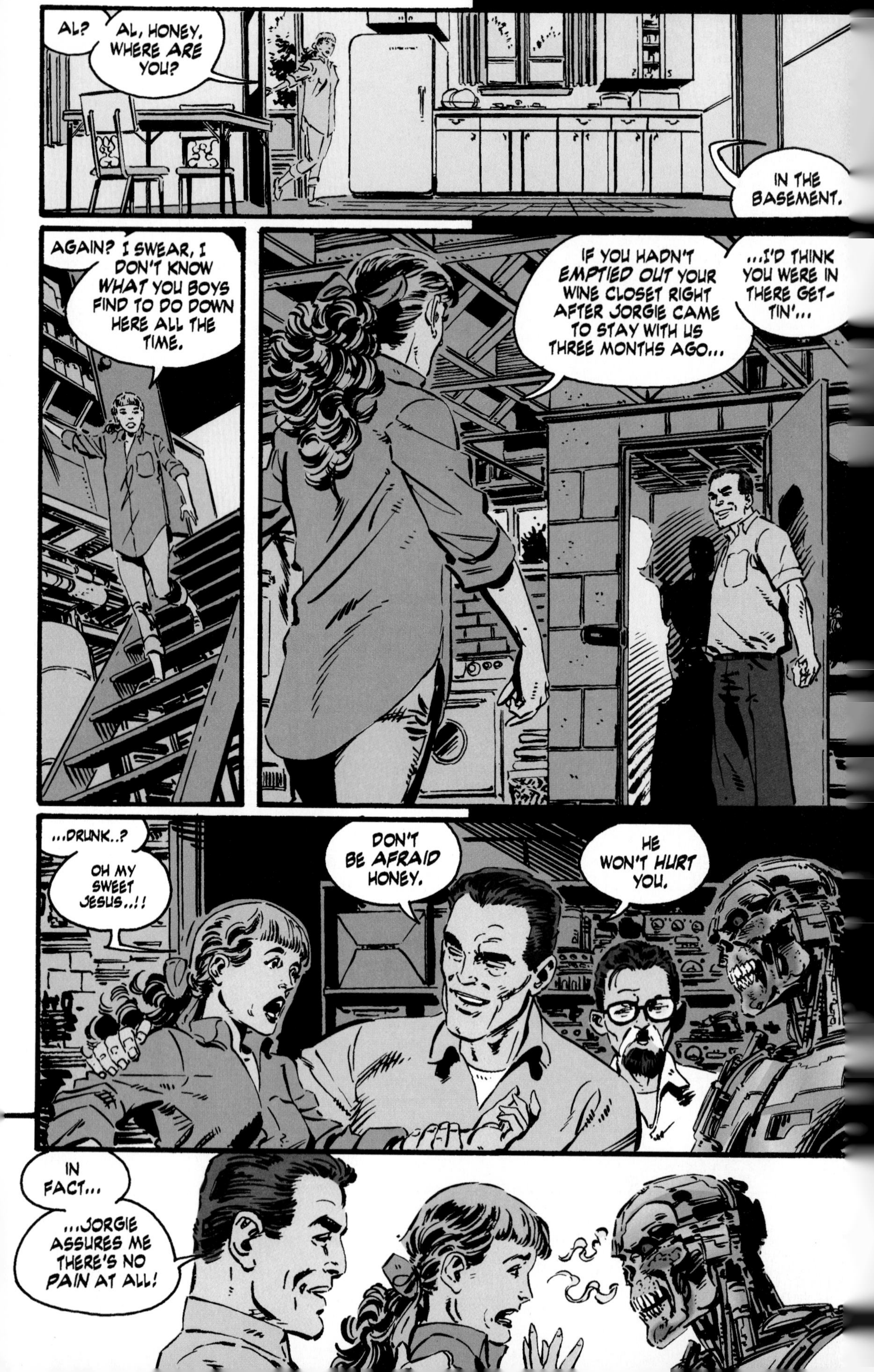
AL?
AL, HONEY. WHERE ARE YOU?
IN THE BASEMENT.
AGAIN? I SWEAR, I DON'T KNOW WHAT YOU BOYS FIND TO DO DOWN HERE ALL THE TIME.
IF YOU HADN'T EMPTIED OUT YOUR WINE CLOSET RIGHT AFTER JORGIE CAME TO STAY WITH US THREE MONTHS AGO...
...I'D THINK YOU WERE IN THERE GET-TIN'...
...DRUNK..?
OH MY SWEET JESUS..!!
DON'T BE AFRAID HONEY.
HE WON'T HURT YOU.
IN FACT...
...JORGIE ASSURES ME THERE'S NO PAIN AT ALL!

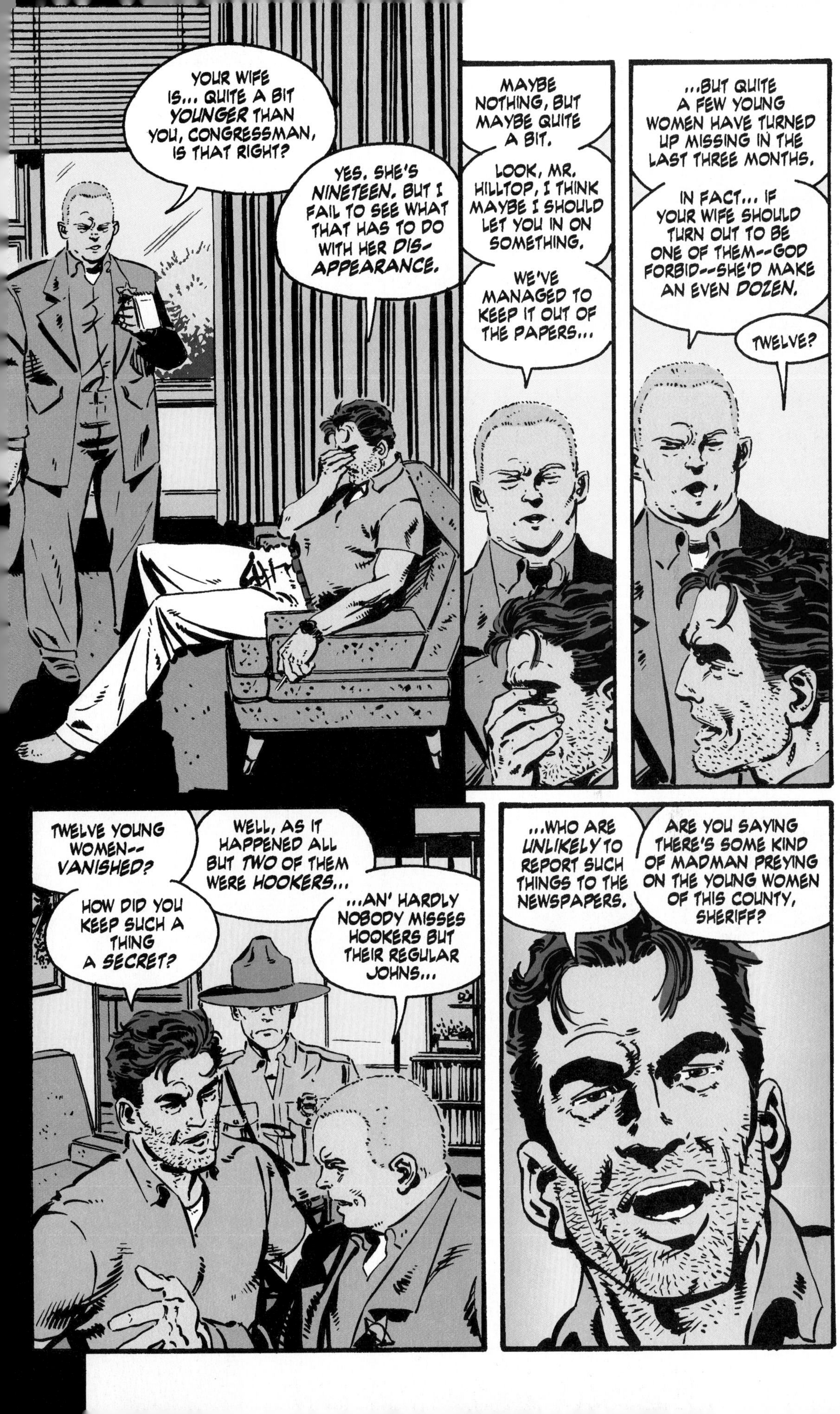
YOUR WIFE IS... QUITE A BIT YOUNGER THAN YOU, CONGRESSMAN, IS THAT RIGHT?
YES. SHE'S NINETEEN. BUT I FAIL TO SEE WHAT THAT HAS TO DO WITH HER DIS-APPEARANCE.
MAYBE NOTHING, BUT MAYBE QUITE A BIT.
LOOK, MR. HILLTOP, I THINK MAYBE I SHOULD LET YOU IN ON SOMETHING.
WE'VE MANAGED TO KEEP IT OUT OF THE PAPERS...
...BUT QUITE A FEW YOUNG WOMEN HAVE TURNED UP MISSING IN THE LAST THREE MONTHS.
IN FACT... IF YOUR WIFE SHOULD TURN OUT TO BE ONE OF THEM--GOD FORBID--SHE'D MAKE AN EVEN DOZEN.
TWELVE?
TWELVE YOUNG WOMEN--VANISHED?
HOW DID YOU KEEP SUCH A THING A SECRET?
WELL, AS IT HAPPENED ALL BUT TWO OF THEM WERE HOOKERS...
...AN' HARDLY NOBODY MISSES HOOKERS BUT THEIR REGULAR JOHNS...
...WHO ARE UNLIKELY TO REPORT SUCH THINGS TO THE NEWSPAPERS.
ARE YOU SAYING THERE'S SOME KIND OF MADMAN PREYING ON THE YOUNG WOMEN OF THIS COUNTY, SHERIFF?

IT'S MORE'N THAT, CONGRESSMAN. *TELL* HIM, BILL. TELL HIM TH' WHOLE STORY.

"WHOLE STORY..?"

ER... YEAH, WELL, ZACH HERE HAS AN IDEA THIS MIGHT ALL BE MIXED IN WITH A NASTY BIT OF BUSINESS THEY'VE GOT GOIN' OVER IN CREEK COUNTY.

SEE... TH' FUNNY THING IS, WE'VE GOT TWELVE GIRLS KNOWN TO BE MISSING, INCLUDIN' YOUR LADY WIFE...

...AN' AS OF YESTERDAY THEY'VE GOT TWELVE DEAD OLD LADIES THAT NOBODY SEEMS TO KNOW.

...OLD... LADIES..?

YESSIR. THEY'VE BIN BUSTIN' THEIR HUMPS TO KEEP THAT ONE OUT'N THE PAPERS, LET ME TELL YOU!

IT GOT AROUND THAT OLD LADIES WAS TURNIN' UP STARK NAKED AND STONE COLD DEAD...

SHERIFF...

LOOK, I'M NATURALLY DISTRESSED TO HEAR ALL THIS IS HAPPENING IN MY DISTRICT...

...BUT MY SOLE CONCERN RIGHT NOW IS LOCATING MY WIFE. AND UNTIL SUCH TIME AS YOU HAVE A CLEAR LINK BETWEEN ALL THIS AND HER DISAPPEARANCE...

I UNDERSTAND, CONGRESSMAN. I'M SORRY I EVEN BROUGHT IT UP. WE'LL TREAT YOUR WIFE AS A SPECIAL, SEPARATE CASE.

AND DON'T YOU WORRY, SIR. WE'LL FIND HER, RIGHT AS RAIN, TOO, I'LL BET.

THANK YOU, SHERIFF. YOU DO MY HEART GOOD.

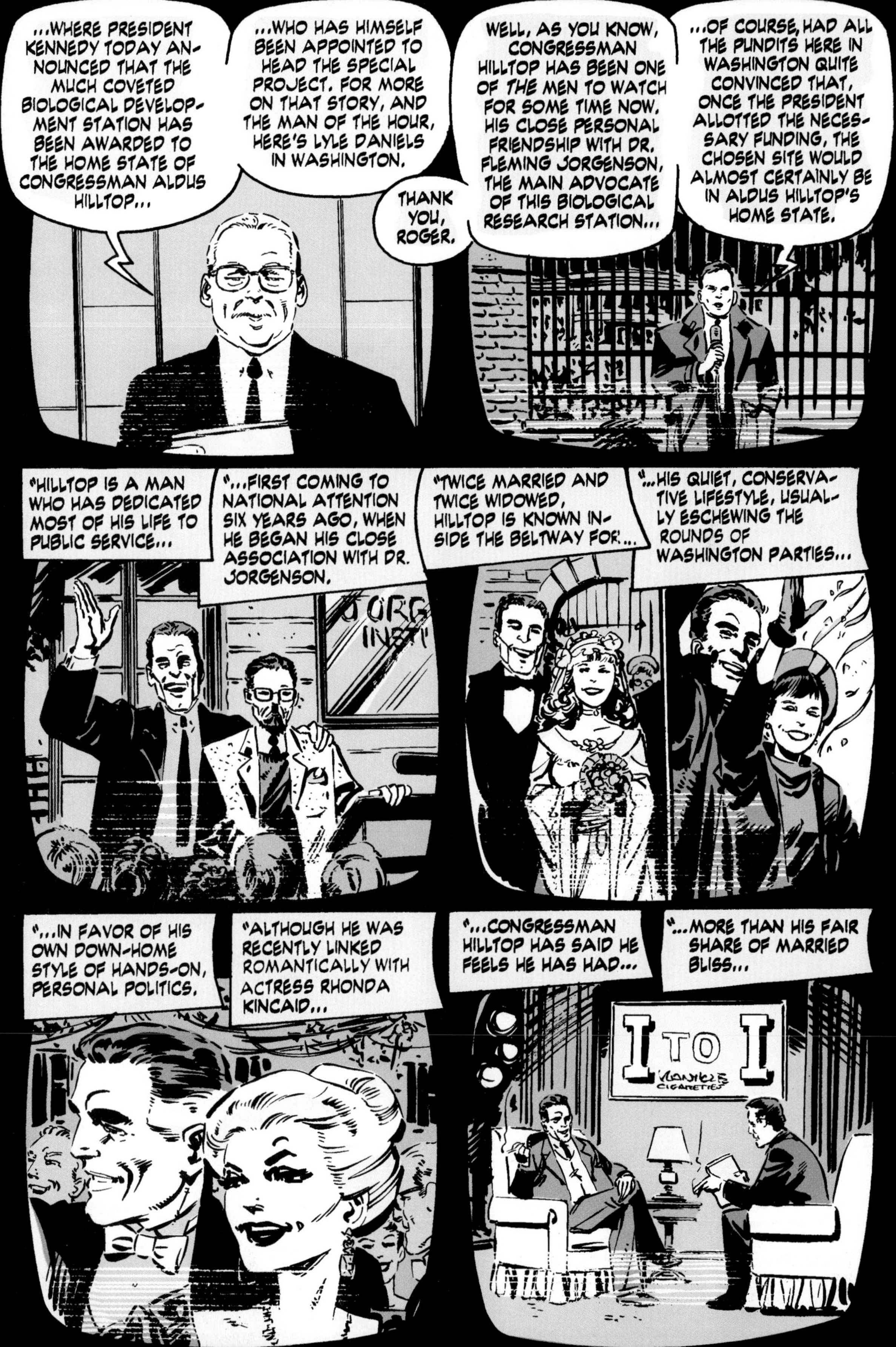
...WHERE PRESIDENT KENNEDY TODAY AN-NOUNCED THAT THE MUCH COVETED BIOLOGICAL DEVELOP-MENT STATION HAS BEEN AWARDED TO THE HOME STATE OF CONGRESSMAN ALDUS HILLTOP...
...WHO HAS HIMSELF BEEN APPOINTED TO HEAD THE SPECIAL PROJECT. FOR MORE ON THAT STORY, AND THE MAN OF THE HOUR, HERE'S LYLE DANIELS IN WASHINGTON.
THANK YOU, ROGER.
WELL, AS YOU KNOW, CONGRESSMAN HILLTOP HAS BEEN ONE OF THE MEN TO WATCH FOR SOME TIME NOW. HIS CLOSE PERSONAL FRIENDSHIP WITH DR. FLEMING JORGENSON, THE MAIN ADVOCATE OF THIS BIOLOGICAL RESEARCH STATION...
...OF COURSE, HAD ALL THE PUNDITS HERE IN WASHINGTON QUITE CONVINCED THAT, ONCE THE PRESIDENT ALLOTTED THE NECES-SARY FUNDING, THE CHOSEN SITE WOULD ALMOST CERTAINLY BE IN ALDUS HILLTOP'S HOME STATE.
"HILLTOP IS A MAN WHO HAS DEDICATED MOST OF HIS LIFE TO PUBLIC SERVICE...
"...FIRST COMING TO NATIONAL ATTENTION SIX YEARS AGO, WHEN HE BEGAN HIS CLOSE ASSOCIATION WITH DR. JORGENSON.
"TWICE MARRIED AND TWICE WIDOWED, HILLTOP IS KNOWN IN-SIDE THE BELTWAY FOR...
"...HIS QUIET, CONSERVA-TIVE LIFESTYLE, USUAL-LY ESCHEWING THE ROUNDS OF WASHINGTON PARTIES...
"...IN FAVOR OF HIS OWN DOWN-HOME STYLE OF HANDS-ON, PERSONAL POLITICS.
"ALTHOUGH HE WAS RECENTLY LINKED ROMANTICALLY WITH ACTRESS RHONDA KINCAID...
"...CONGRESSMAN HILLTOP HAS SAID HE FEELS HE HAS HAD...
"...MORE THAN HIS FAIR SHARE OF MARRIED BLISS...
I TO I
CIGARETTES

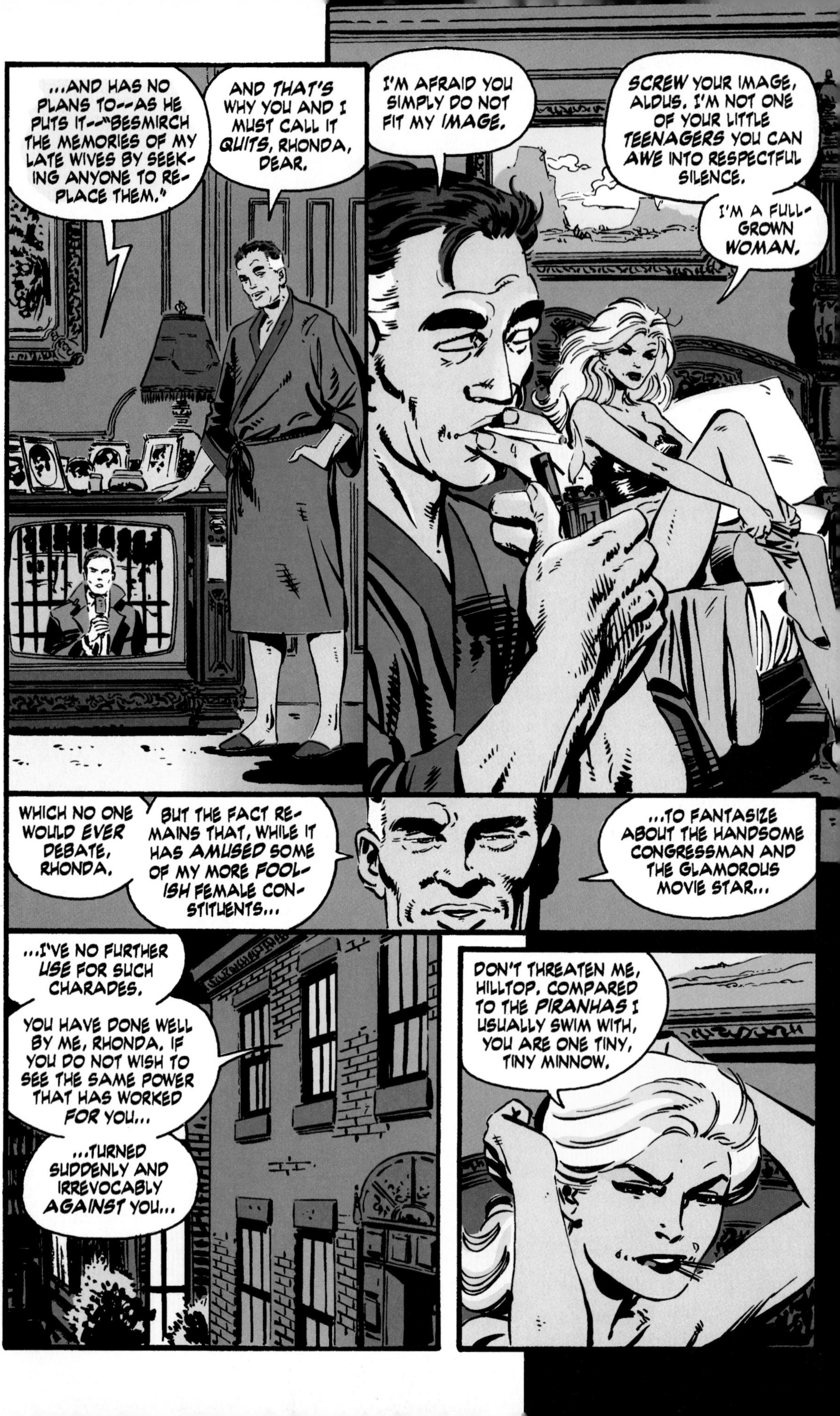

...AND HAS NO PLANS TO--AS HE PUTS IT--"BESMIRCH THE MEMORIES OF MY LATE WIVES BY SEEKING ANYONE TO REPLACE THEM."
AND THAT'S WHY YOU AND I MUST CALL IT QUITS, RHONDA, DEAR.
I'M AFRAID YOU SIMPLY DO NOT FIT MY IMAGE.
SCREW YOUR IMAGE, ALDUS. I'M NOT ONE OF YOUR LITTLE TEENAGERS YOU CAN AWE INTO RESPECTFUL SILENCE.
I'M A FULL-GROWN WOMAN.
WHICH NO ONE WOULD EVER DEBATE, RHONDA.
BUT THE FACT REMAINS THAT, WHILE IT HAS AMUSED SOME OF MY MORE FOOLISH FEMALE CONSTITUENTS...
...TO FANTASIZE ABOUT THE HANDSOME CONGRESSMAN AND THE GLAMOROUS MOVIE STAR...
...I'VE NO FURTHER USE FOR SUCH CHARADES.
YOU HAVE DONE WELL BY ME, RHONDA. IF YOU DO NOT WISH TO SEE THE SAME POWER THAT HAS WORKED FOR YOU...
...TURNED SUDDENLY AND IRREVOCABLY AGAINST YOU...
DON'T THREATEN ME, HILLTOP. COMPARED TO THE PIRANHAS I USUALLY SWIM WITH, YOU ARE ONE TINY, TINY MINNOW.

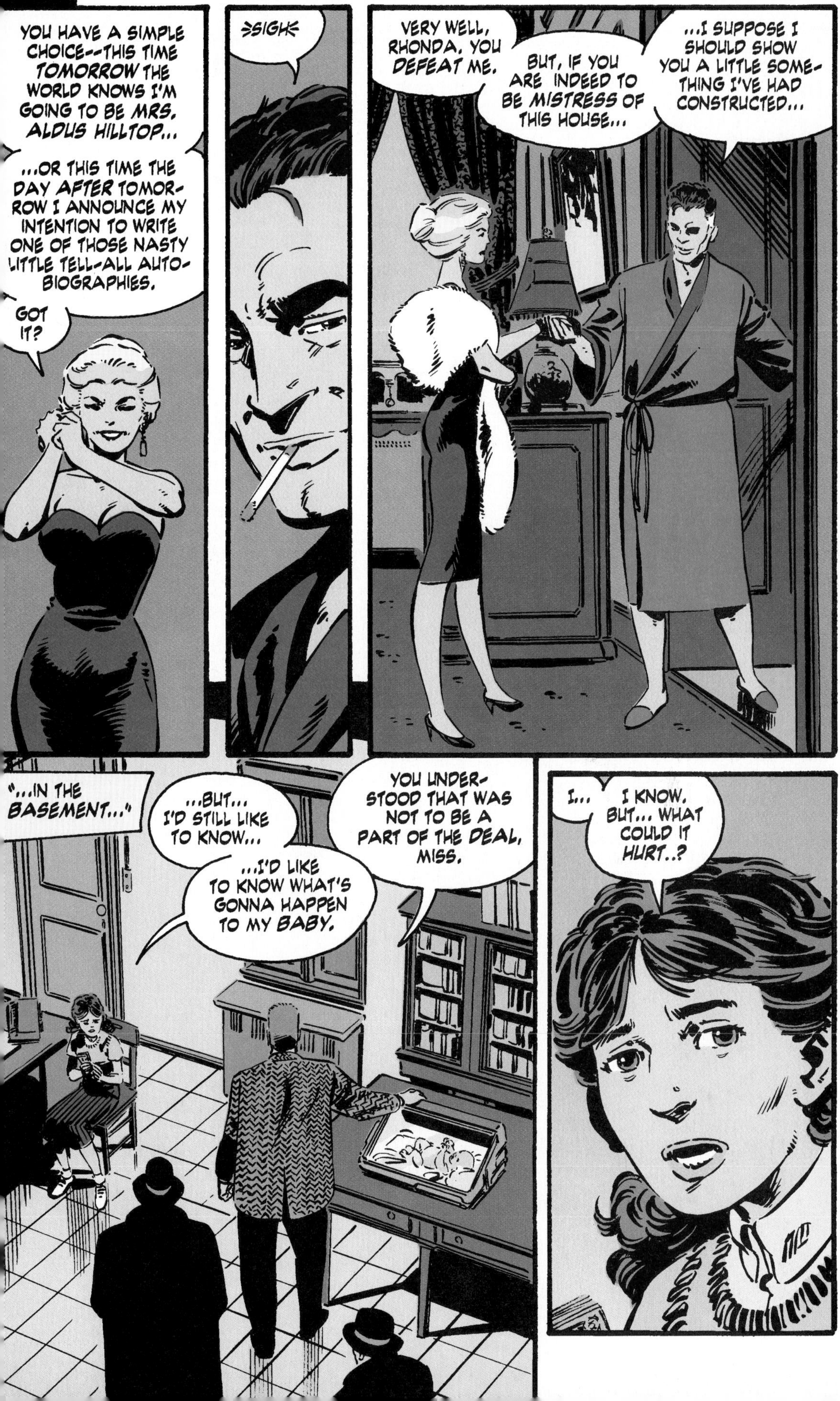

YOU HAVE A SIMPLE CHOICE--THIS TIME TOMORROW THE WORLD KNOWS I'M GOING TO BE MRS. ALDUS HILLTOP...
...OR THIS TIME THE DAY AFTER TOMORROW I ANNOUNCE MY INTENTION TO WRITE ONE OF THOSE NASTY LITTLE TELL-ALL AUTOBIOGRAPHIES.
GOT IT?
>SIGH<
VERY WELL, RHONDA. YOU DEFEAT ME.
BUT, IF YOU ARE INDEED TO BE MISTRESS OF THIS HOUSE...
...I SUPPOSE I SHOULD SHOW YOU A LITTLE SOMETHING I'VE HAD CONSTRUCTED...
"...IN THE BASEMENT..."
...BUT... I'D STILL LIKE TO KNOW...
...I'D LIKE TO KNOW WHAT'S GONNA HAPPEN TO MY BABY.
YOU UNDERSTOOD THAT WAS NOT TO BE A PART OF THE DEAL, MISS.
I...
I KNOW. BUT... WHAT COULD IT HURT..?

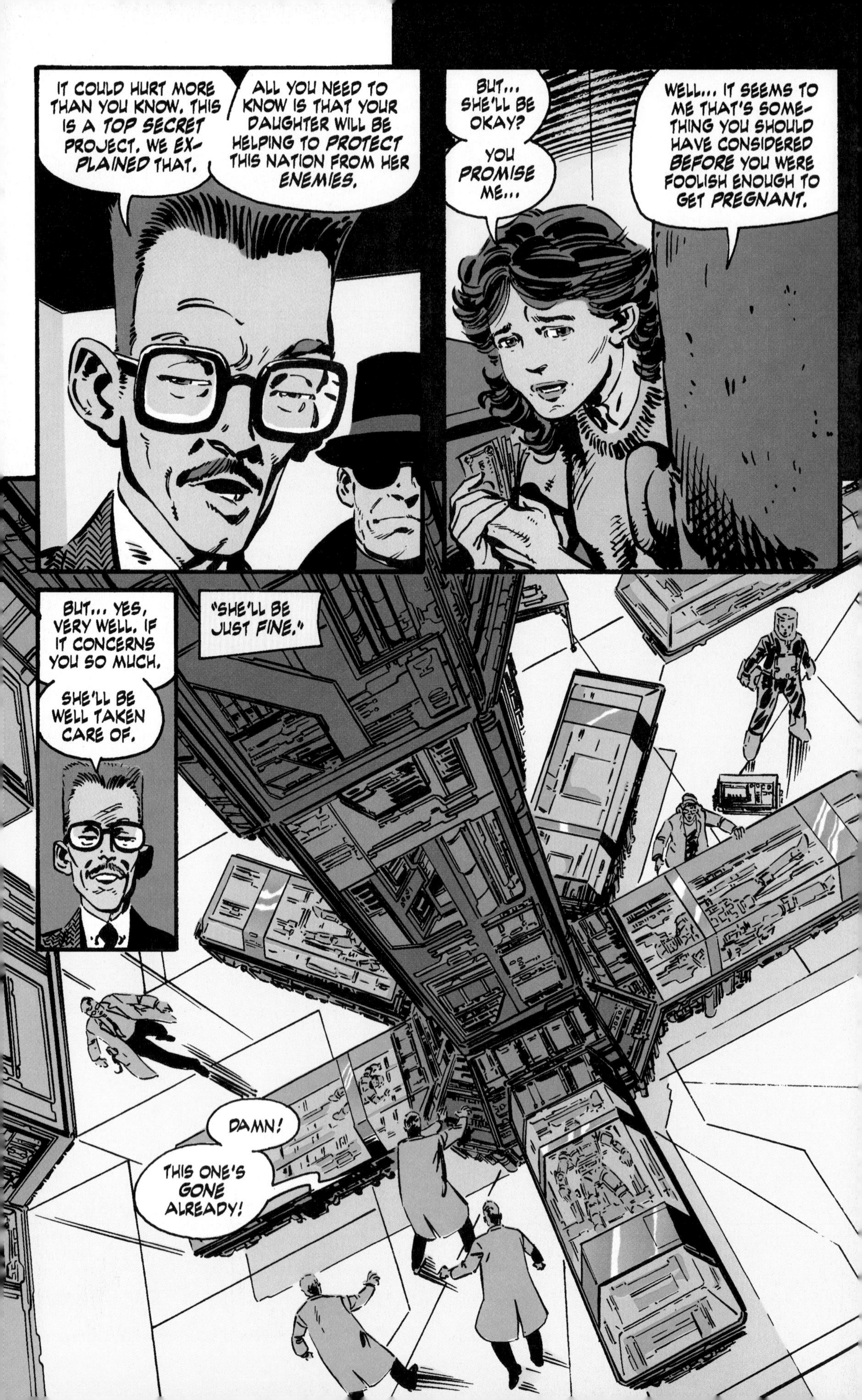
IT COULD HURT MORE THAN YOU KNOW. THIS IS A TOP SECRET PROJECT. WE EXPLAINED THAT.
ALL YOU NEED TO KNOW IS THAT YOUR DAUGHTER WILL BE HELPING TO PROTECT THIS NATION FROM HER ENEMIES.
BUT... SHE'LL BE OKAY?
YOU PROMISE ME...
WELL... IT SEEMS TO ME THAT'S SOMETHING YOU SHOULD HAVE CONSIDERED BEFORE YOU WERE FOOLISH ENOUGH TO GET PREGNANT.
BUT... YES, VERY WELL. IF IT CONCERNS YOU SO MUCH.
SHE'LL BE WELL TAKEN CARE OF.
"SHE'LL BE JUST FINE."
DAMN!
THIS ONE'S GONE ALREADY!

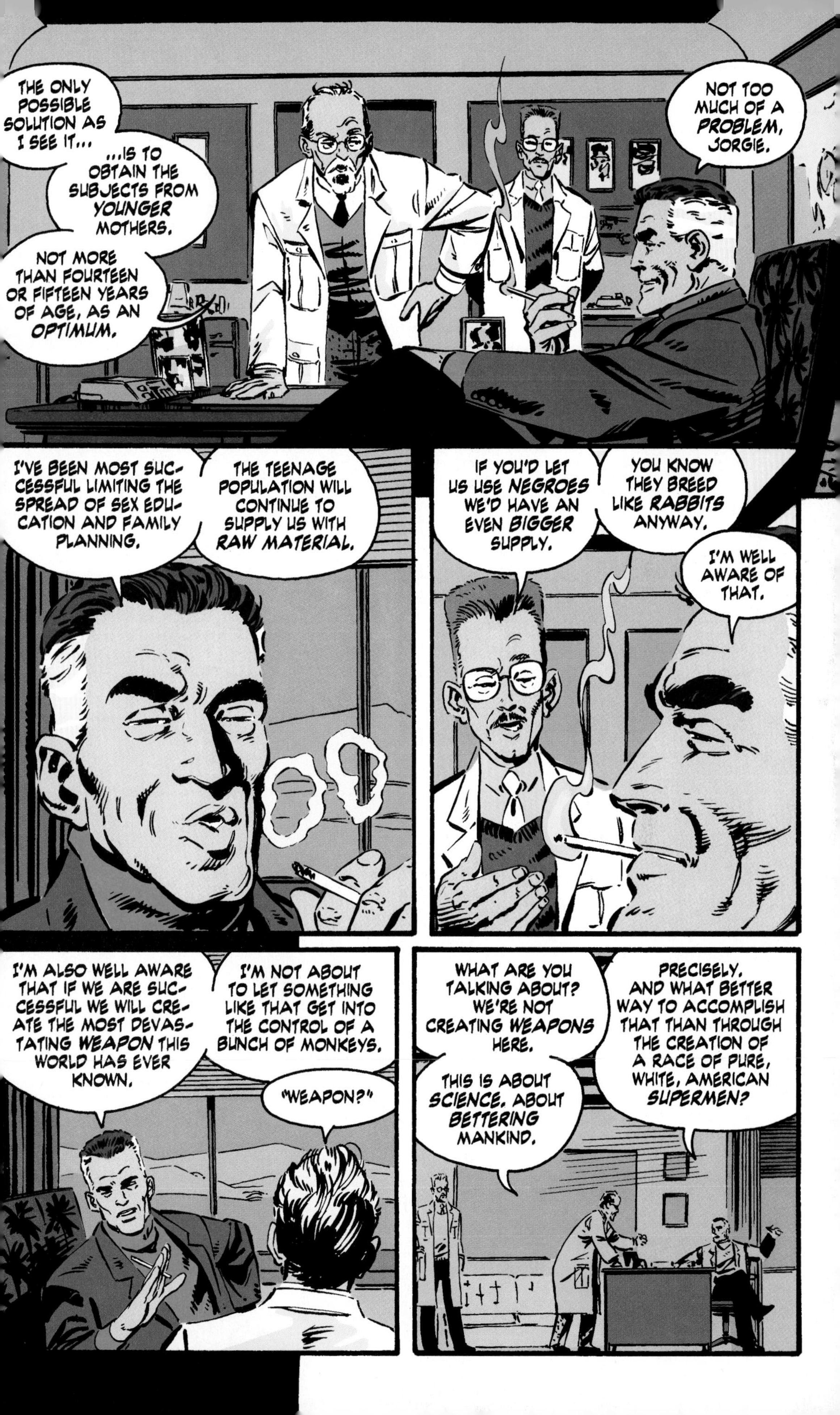
THE ONLY POSSIBLE SOLUTION AS I SEE IT...
...IS TO OBTAIN THE SUBJECTS FROM YOUNGER MOTHERS.
NOT MORE THAN FOURTEEN OR FIFTEEN YEARS OF AGE, AS AN OPTIMUM.
NOT TOO MUCH OF A PROBLEM, JORGIE.
I'VE BEEN MOST SUCCESSFUL LIMITING THE SPREAD OF SEX EDUCATION AND FAMILY PLANNING.
THE TEENAGE POPULATION WILL CONTINUE TO SUPPLY US WITH RAW MATERIAL.
IF YOU'D LET US USE NEGROES WE'D HAVE AN EVEN BIGGER SUPPLY.
YOU KNOW THEY BREED LIKE RABBITS ANYWAY.
I'M WELL AWARE OF THAT.
I'M ALSO WELL AWARE THAT IF WE ARE SUCCESSFUL WE WILL CREATE THE MOST DEVASTATING WEAPON THIS WORLD HAS EVER KNOWN.
I'M NOT ABOUT TO LET SOMETHING LIKE THAT GET INTO THE CONTROL OF A BUNCH OF MONKEYS.
"WEAPON?"
WHAT ARE YOU TALKING ABOUT? WE'RE NOT CREATING WEAPONS HERE.
THIS IS ABOUT SCIENCE. ABOUT BETTERING MANKIND.
PRECISELY. AND WHAT BETTER WAY TO ACCOMPLISH THAT THAN THROUGH THE CREATION OF A RACE OF PURE, WHITE, AMERICAN SUPERMEN?

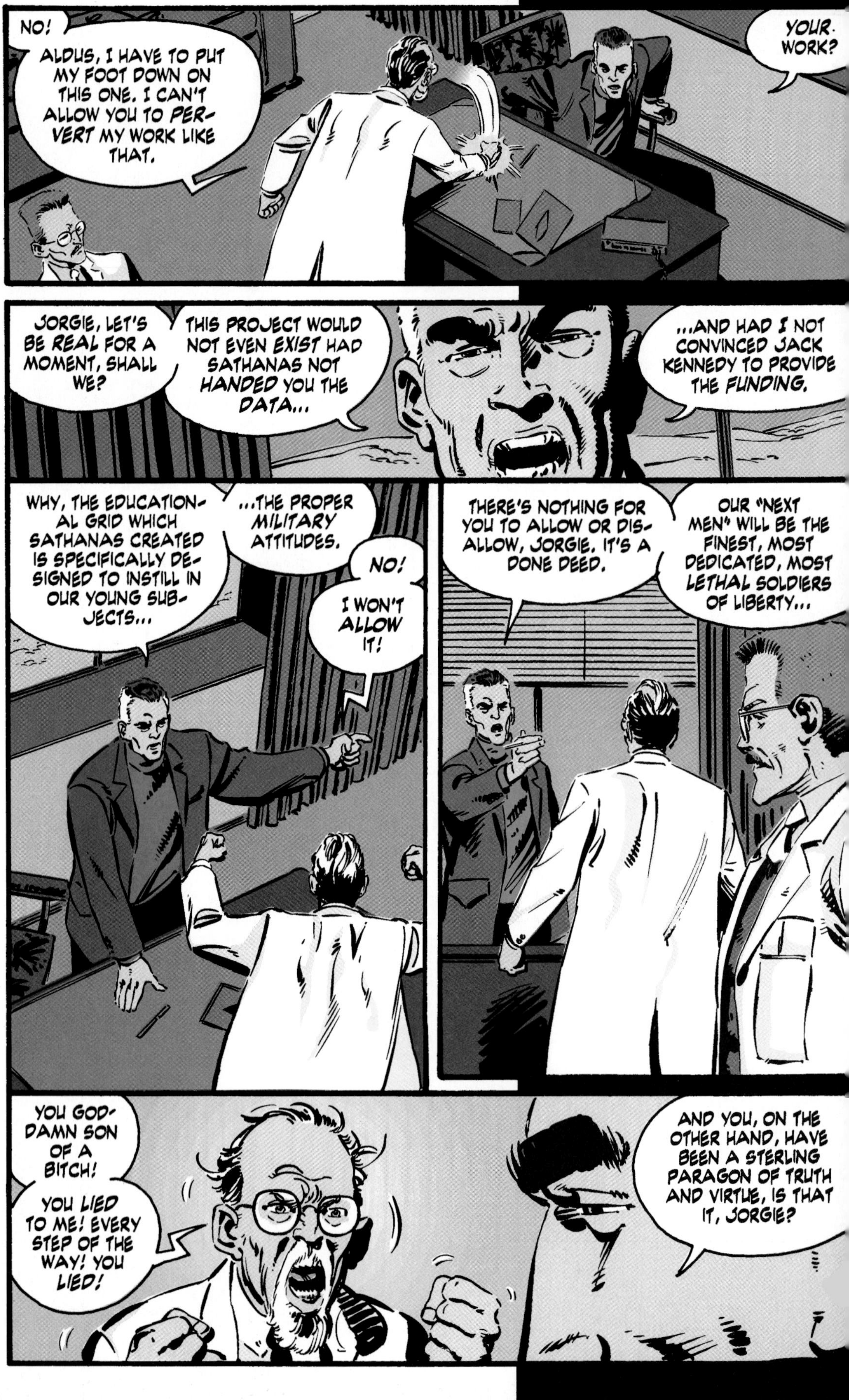
NO!
ALDUS, I HAVE TO PUT MY FOOT DOWN ON THIS ONE. I CAN'T ALLOW YOU TO PER-VERT MY WORK LIKE THAT.
YOUR. WORK?
JORGIE, LET'S BE REAL FOR A MOMENT, SHALL WE?
THIS PROJECT WOULD NOT EVEN EXIST HAD SATHANAS NOT HANDED YOU THE DATA...
...AND HAD I NOT CONVINCED JACK KENNEDY TO PROVIDE THE FUNDING.
WHY, THE EDUCATION-AL GRID WHICH SATHANAS CREATED IS SPECIFICALLY DE-SIGNED TO INSTILL IN OUR YOUNG SUB-JECTS...
...THE PROPER MILITARY ATTITUDES.
NO!
I WON'T ALLOW IT!
THERE'S NOTHING FOR YOU TO ALLOW OR DIS-ALLOW, JORGIE. IT'S A DONE DEED.
OUR "NEXT MEN" WILL BE THE FINEST, MOST DEDICATED, MOST LETHAL SOLDIERS OF LIBERTY...
YOU GOD-DAMN SON OF A BITCH!
YOU LIED TO ME! EVERY STEP OF THE WAY! YOU LIED!
AND YOU, ON THE OTHER HAND, HAVE BEEN A STERLING PARAGON OF TRUTH AND VIRTUE, IS THAT IT, JORGIE?

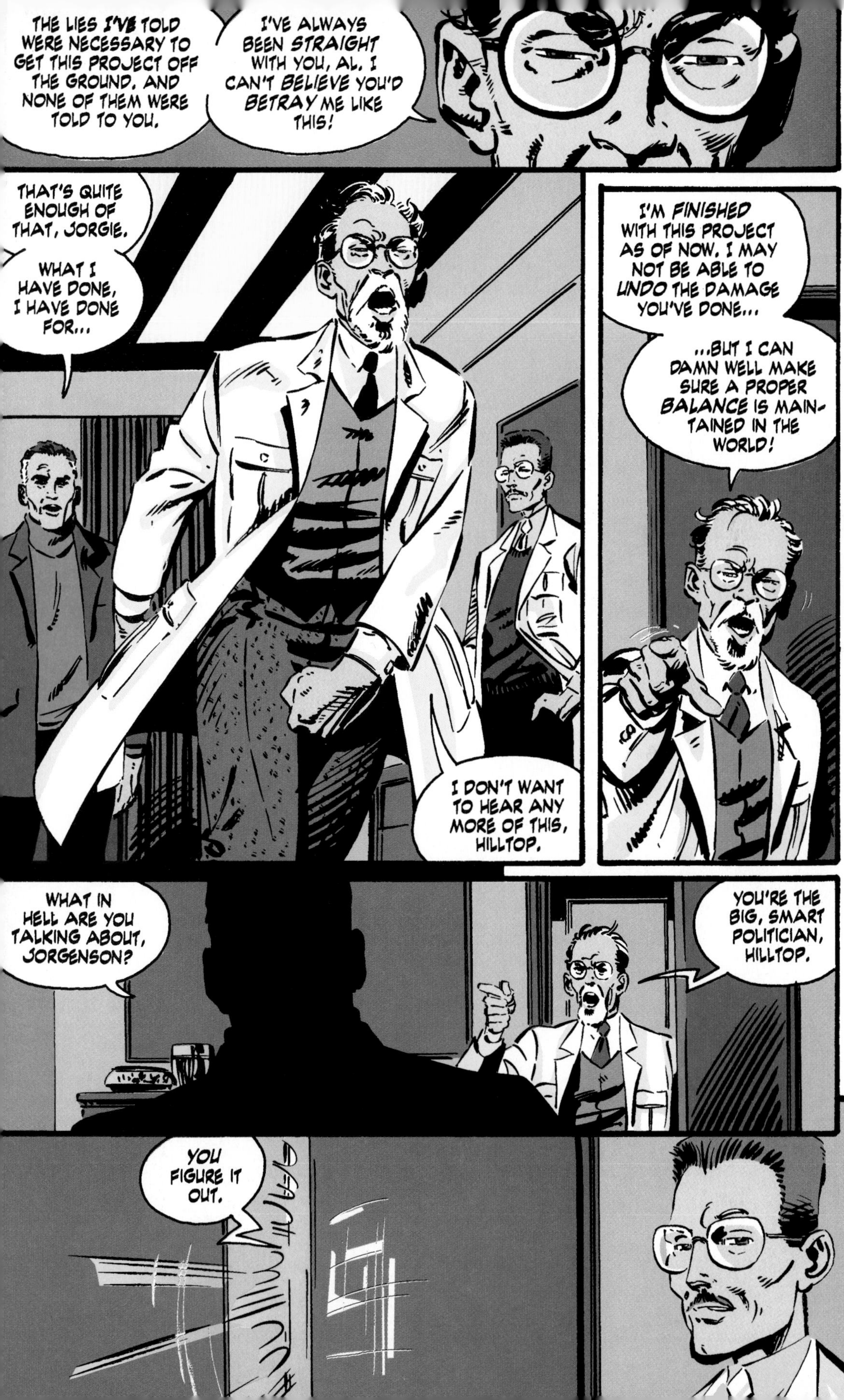

THE LIES I'VE TOLD WERE NECESSARY TO GET THIS PROJECT OFF THE GROUND. AND NONE OF THEM WERE TOLD TO YOU.
I'VE ALWAYS BEEN STRAIGHT WITH YOU, AL. I CAN'T BELIEVE YOU'D BETRAY ME LIKE THIS!
THAT'S QUITE ENOUGH OF THAT, JORGIE.
WHAT I HAVE DONE, I HAVE DONE FOR...
I DON'T WANT TO HEAR ANY MORE OF THIS, HILLTOP.
I'M FINISHED WITH THIS PROJECT AS OF NOW. I MAY NOT BE ABLE TO UNDO THE DAMAGE YOU'VE DONE...
...BUT I CAN DAMN WELL MAKE SURE A PROPER BALANCE IS MAIN-TAINED IN THE WORLD!
WHAT IN HELL ARE YOU TALKING ABOUT, JORGENSON?
YOU'RE THE BIG, SMART POLITICIAN, HILLTOP.
YOU FIGURE IT OUT.

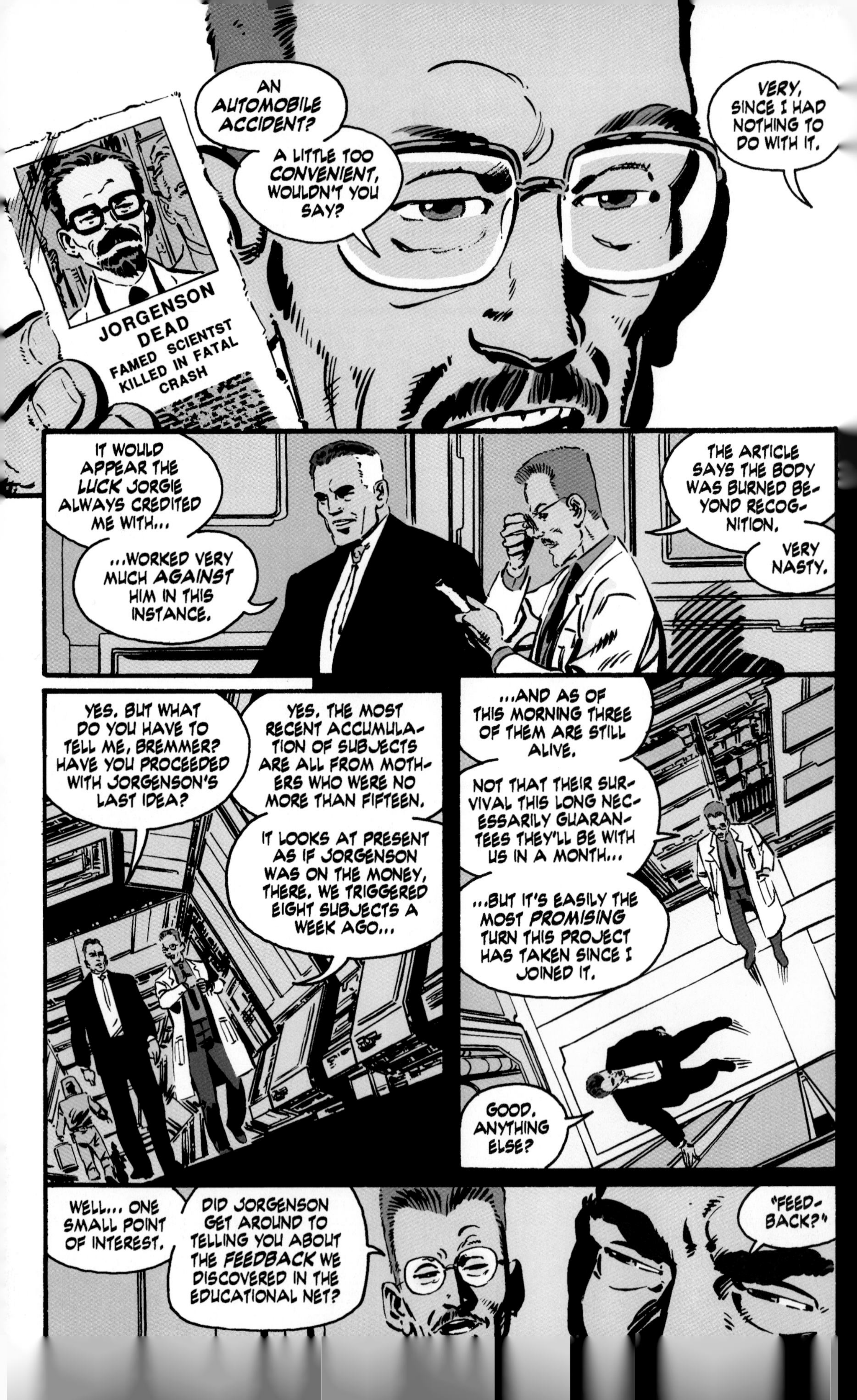

JORGENSON DEAD
FAMED SCIENTST KILLED IN FATAL CRASH
AN AUTOMOBILE ACCIDENT?
A LITTLE TOO CONVENIENT, WOULDN'T YOU SAY?
VERY, SINCE I HAD NOTHING TO DO WITH IT.
IT WOULD APPEAR THE LUCK JORGIE ALWAYS CREDITED ME WITH...
...WORKED VERY MUCH AGAINST HIM IN THIS INSTANCE.
THE ARTICLE SAYS THE BODY WAS BURNED BE-YOND RECOG-NITION.
VERY NASTY.
YES. BUT WHAT DO YOU HAVE TO TELL ME, BREMMER? HAVE YOU PROCEEDED WITH JORGENSON'S LAST IDEA?
YES. THE MOST RECENT ACCUMULA-TION OF SUBJECTS ARE ALL FROM MOTH-ERS WHO WERE NO MORE THAN FIFTEEN.
IT LOOKS AT PRESENT AS IF JORGENSON WAS ON THE MONEY, THERE. WE TRIGGERED EIGHT SUBJECTS A WEEK AGO...
...AND AS OF THIS MORNING THREE OF THEM ARE STILL ALIVE.
NOT THAT THEIR SUR-VIVAL THIS LONG NEC-ESSARILY GUARAN-TEES THEY'LL BE WITH US IN A MONTH...
...BUT IT'S EASILY THE MOST PROMISING TURN THIS PROJECT HAS TAKEN SINCE I JOINED IT.
GOOD, ANYTHING ELSE?
WELL... ONE SMALL POINT OF INTEREST.
DID JORGENSON GET AROUND TO TELLING YOU ABOUT THE FEEDBACK WE DISCOVERED IN THE EDUCATIONAL NET?
"FEED-BACK?"

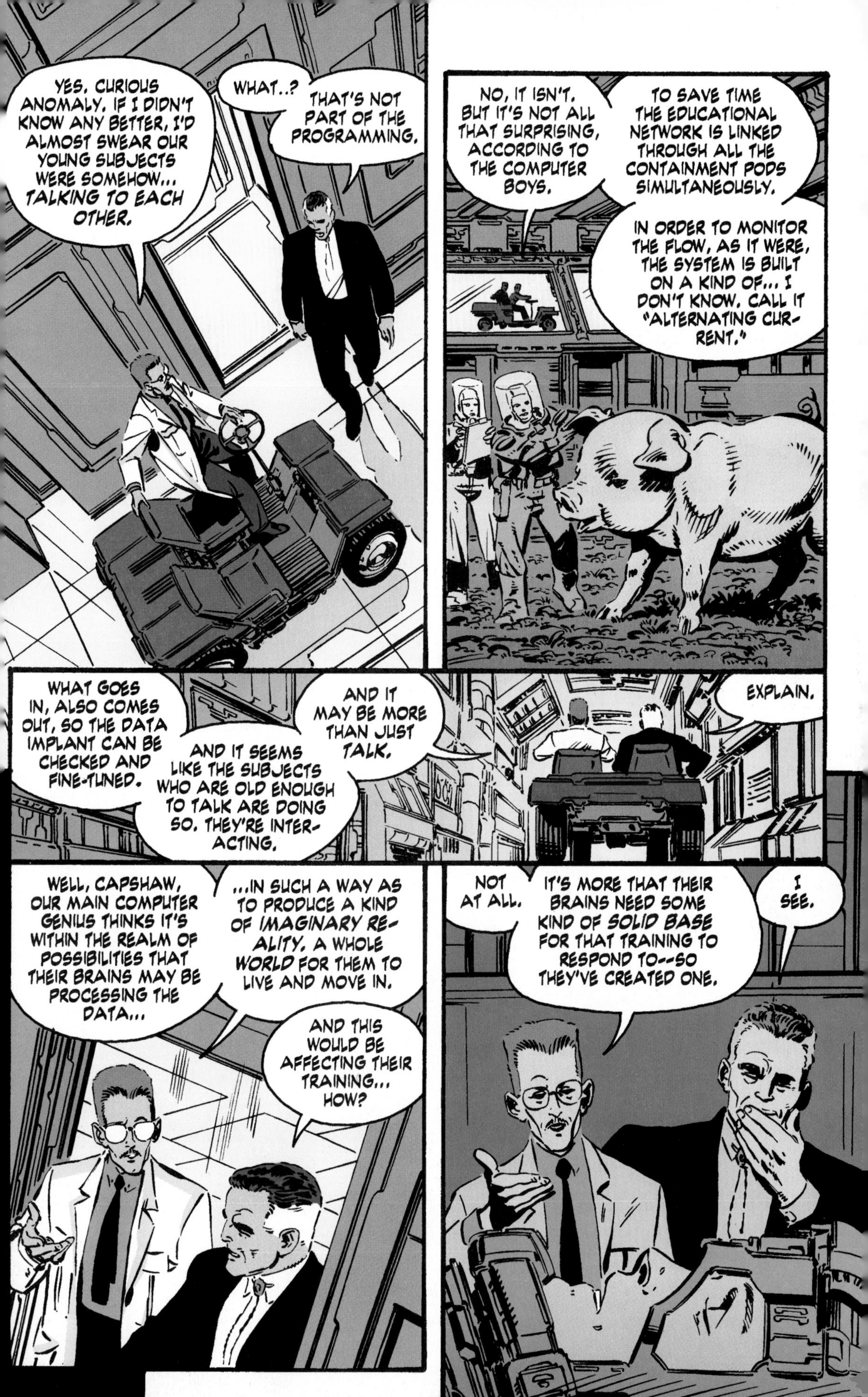
YES. CURIOUS ANOMALY. IF I DIDN'T KNOW ANY BETTER, I'D ALMOST SWEAR OUR YOUNG SUBJECTS WERE SOMEHOW... TALKING TO EACH OTHER.
WHAT..?
THAT'S NOT PART OF THE PROGRAMMING.
NO, IT ISN'T. BUT IT'S NOT ALL THAT SURPRISING, ACCORDING TO THE COMPUTER BOYS.
TO SAVE TIME THE EDUCATIONAL NETWORK IS LINKED THROUGH ALL THE CONTAINMENT PODS SIMULTANEOUSLY.
IN ORDER TO MONITOR THE FLOW, AS IT WERE, THE SYSTEM IS BUILT ON A KIND OF... I DON'T KNOW. CALL IT "ALTERNATING CURRENT."
WHAT GOES IN, ALSO COMES OUT, SO THE DATA IMPLANT CAN BE CHECKED AND FINE-TUNED.
AND IT SEEMS LIKE THE SUBJECTS WHO ARE OLD ENOUGH TO TALK ARE DOING SO. THEY'RE INTERACTING.
AND IT MAY BE MORE THAN JUST TALK.
EXPLAIN.
WELL, CAPSHAW, OUR MAIN COMPUTER GENIUS THINKS IT'S WITHIN THE REALM OF POSSIBILITIES THAT THEIR BRAINS MAY BE PROCESSING THE DATA...
...IN SUCH A WAY AS TO PRODUCE A KIND OF IMAGINARY REALITY. A WHOLE WORLD FOR THEM TO LIVE AND MOVE IN.
AND THIS WOULD BE AFFECTING THEIR TRAINING... HOW?
NOT AT ALL.
IT'S MORE THAT THEIR BRAINS NEED SOME KIND OF SOLID BASE FOR THAT TRAINING TO RESPOND TO--SO THEY'VE CREATED ONE.
I SEE.

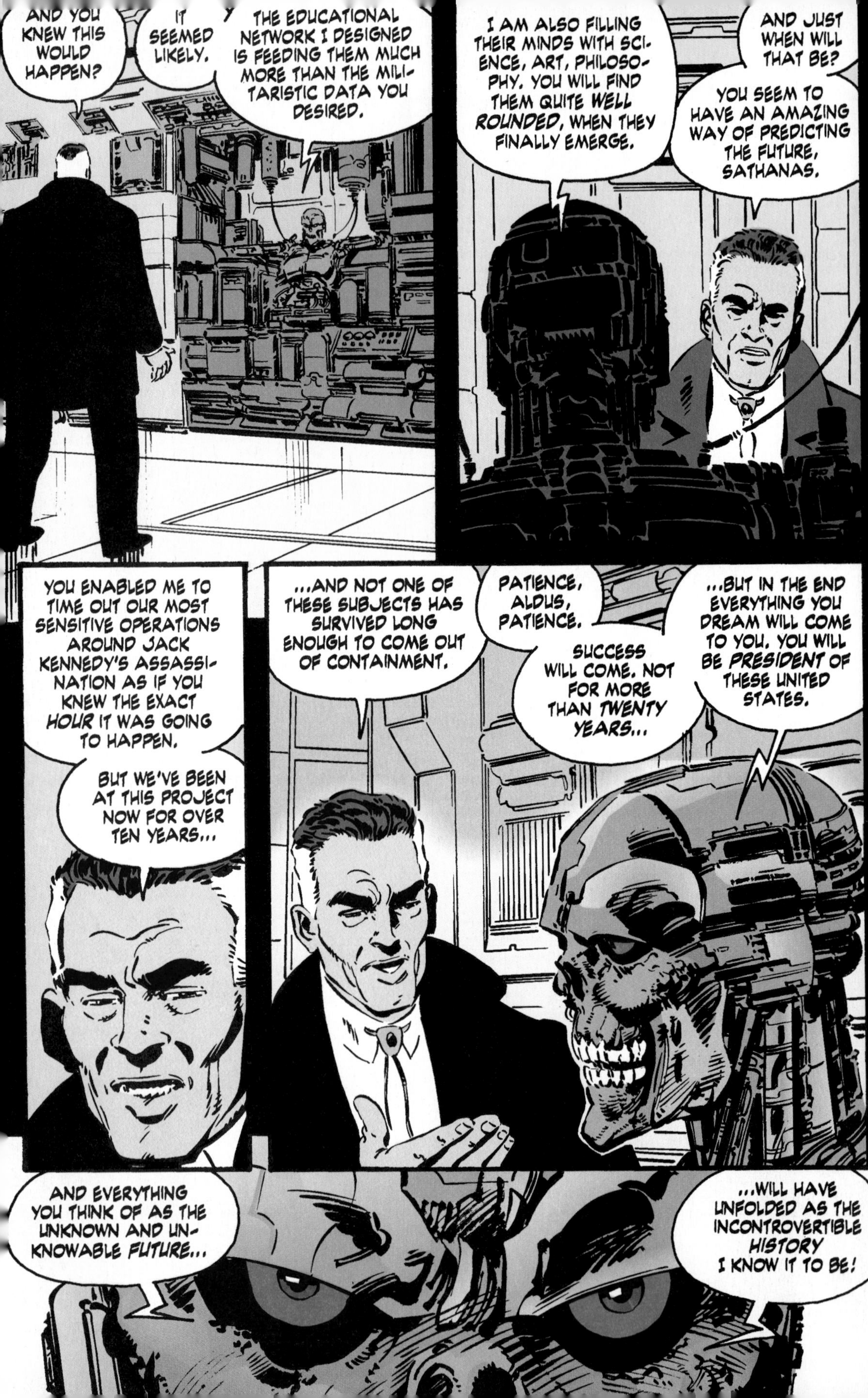

AND YOU KNEW THIS WOULD HAPPEN?
IT SEEMED LIKELY.
THE EDUCATIONAL NETWORK I DESIGNED IS FEEDING THEM MUCH MORE THAN THE MILITARISTIC DATA YOU DESIRED.
I AM ALSO FILLING THEIR MINDS WITH SCIENCE, ART, PHILOSOPHY. YOU WILL FIND THEM QUITE WELL ROUNDED, WHEN THEY FINALLY EMERGE.
AND JUST WHEN WILL THAT BE?
YOU SEEM TO HAVE AN AMAZING WAY OF PREDICTING THE FUTURE, SATHANAS.
YOU ENABLED ME TO TIME OUT OUR MOST SENSITIVE OPERATIONS AROUND JACK KENNEDY'S ASSASSINATION AS IF YOU KNEW THE EXACT HOUR IT WAS GOING TO HAPPEN.
BUT WE'VE BEEN AT THIS PROJECT NOW FOR OVER TEN YEARS...
...AND NOT ONE OF THESE SUBJECTS HAS SURVIVED LONG ENOUGH TO COME OUT OF CONTAINMENT.
PATIENCE, ALDUS, PATIENCE.
SUCCESS WILL COME. NOT FOR MORE THAN TWENTY YEARS...
...BUT IN THE END EVERYTHING YOU DREAM WILL COME TO YOU. YOU WILL BE PRESIDENT OF THESE UNITED STATES.
AND EVERYTHING YOU THINK OF AS THE UNKNOWN AND UNKNOWABLE FUTURE...
...WILL HAVE UNFOLDED AS THE INCONTROVERTIBLE HISTORY I KNOW IT TO BE!

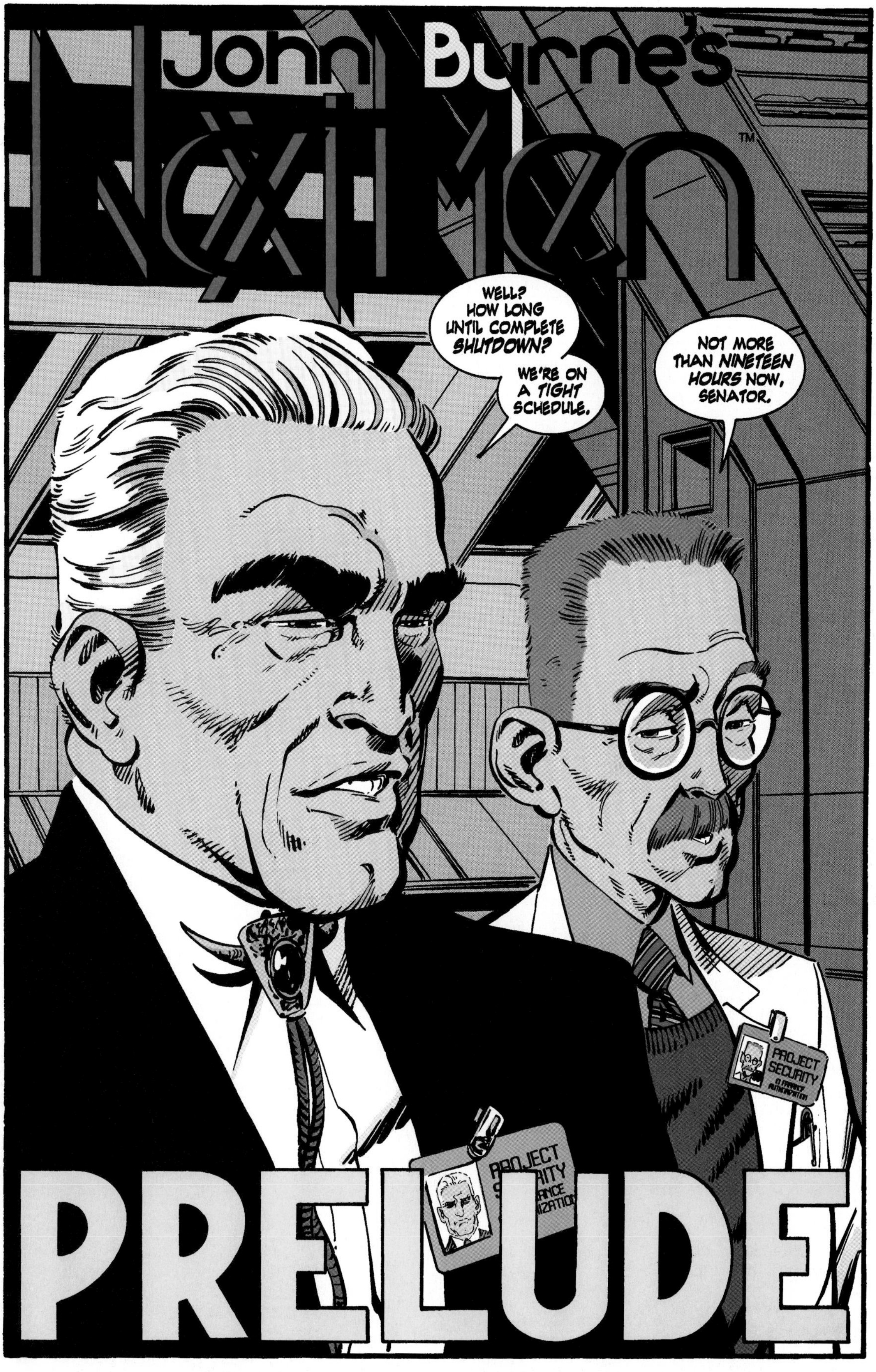
John Byrne's
Next Men™
WELL? HOW LONG UNTIL COMPLETE SHUTDOWN?
WE'RE ON A TIGHT SCHEDULE.
NOT MORE THAN NINETEEN HOURS NOW, SENATOR.
PROJECT SECURITY
PRELUDE

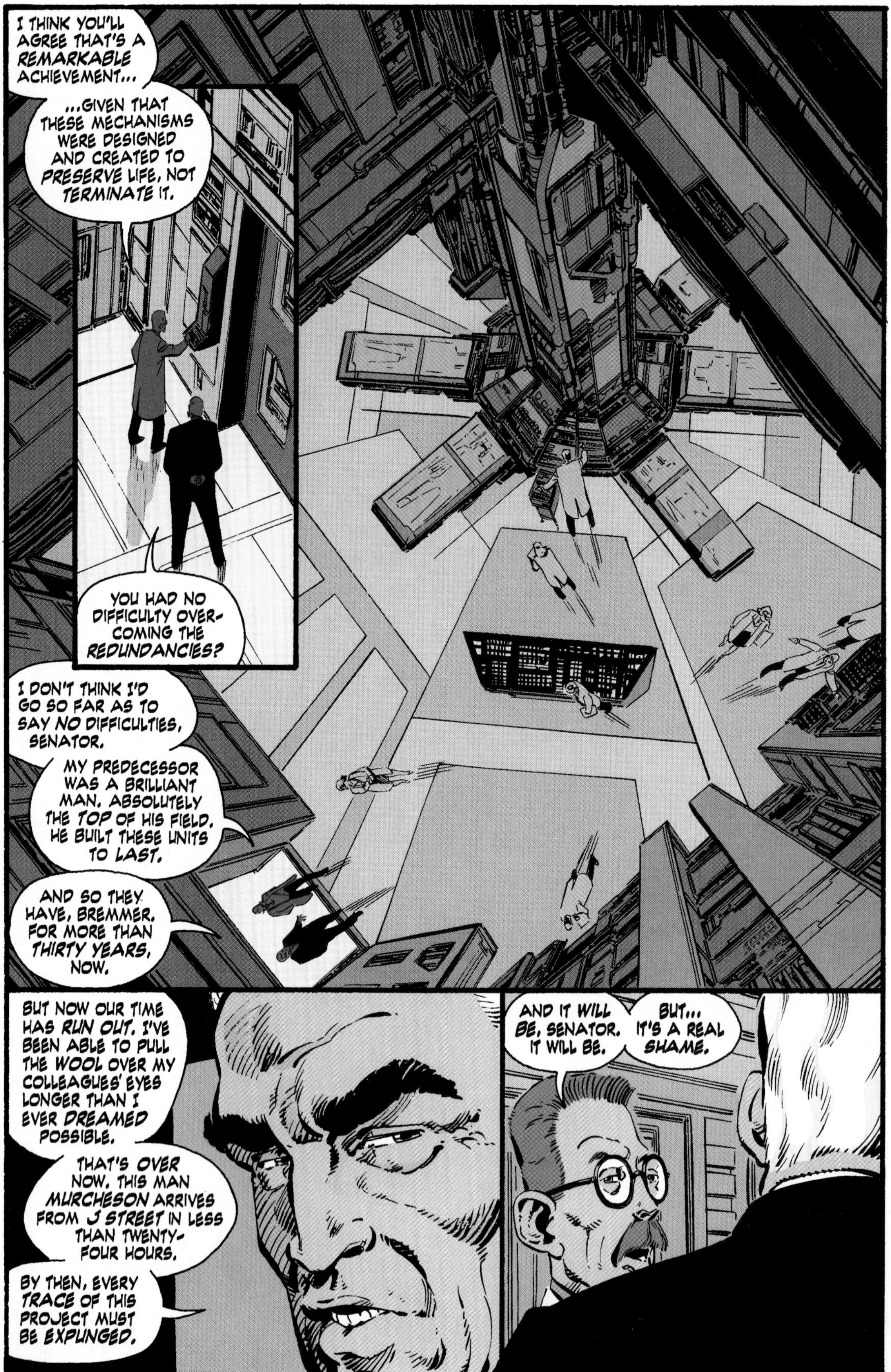
I THINK YOU'LL AGREE THAT'S A *REMARKABLE* ACHIEVEMENT...
...GIVEN THAT THESE MECHANISMS WERE DESIGNED AND CREATED TO *PRESERVE* LIFE, NOT *TERMINATE* IT.
YOU HAD NO DIFFICULTY OVER-COMING THE *REDUNDANCIES?*
I DON'T THINK I'D GO SO FAR AS TO SAY *NO* DIFFICULTIES, SENATOR.
MY PREDECESSOR WAS A BRILLIANT MAN. ABSOLUTELY THE *TOP* OF HIS FIELD. HE BUILT THESE UNITS TO *LAST.*
AND SO THEY HAVE, BREMMER. FOR MORE THAN *THIRTY YEARS,* NOW.
BUT NOW OUR TIME HAS *RUN OUT.* I'VE BEEN ABLE TO PULL THE *WOOL* OVER MY COLLEAGUES' EYES LONGER THAN I EVER *DREAMED* POSSIBLE.
THAT'S *OVER* NOW. THIS MAN *MURCHESON* ARRIVES FROM *J STREET* IN LESS THAN TWENTY-FOUR HOURS.
BY THEN, EVERY *TRACE* OF THIS PROJECT MUST BE *EXPUNGED.*
AND IT *WILL BE,* SENATOR. IT WILL BE.
BUT... IT'S A REAL *SHAME.*

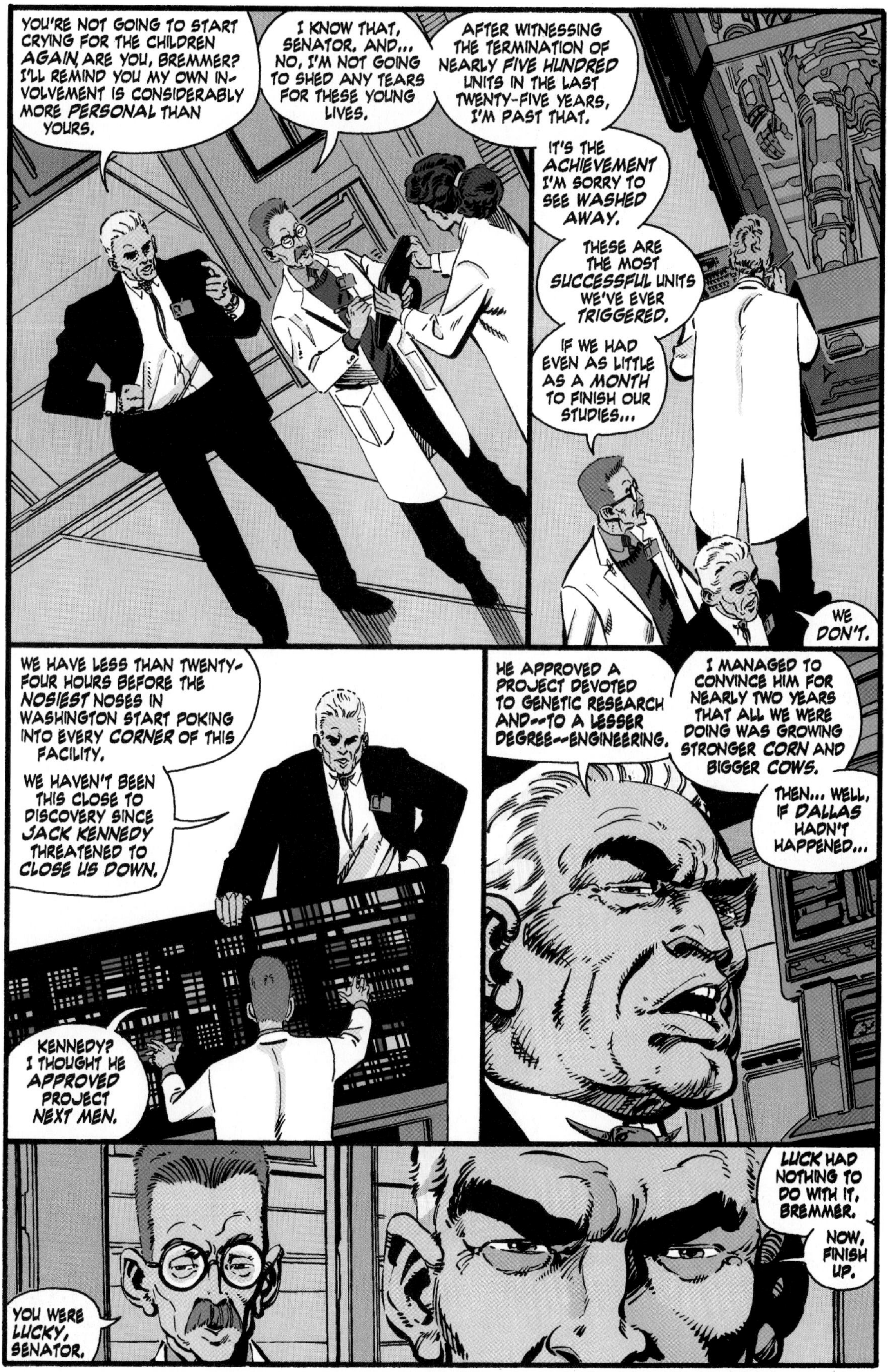
YOU'RE NOT GOING TO START CRYING FOR THE CHILDREN AGAIN, ARE YOU, BREMMER? I'LL REMIND YOU MY OWN INVOLVEMENT IS CONSIDERABLY MORE PERSONAL THAN YOURS.
I KNOW THAT, SENATOR. AND... NO, I'M NOT GOING TO SHED ANY TEARS FOR THESE YOUNG LIVES.
AFTER WITNESSING THE TERMINATION OF NEARLY FIVE HUNDRED UNITS IN THE LAST TWENTY-FIVE YEARS, I'M PAST THAT.
IT'S THE ACHIEVEMENT I'M SORRY TO SEE WASHED AWAY.
THESE ARE THE MOST SUCCESSFUL UNITS WE'VE EVER TRIGGERED.
IF WE HAD EVEN AS LITTLE AS A MONTH TO FINISH OUR STUDIES...
WE DON'T.
WE HAVE LESS THAN TWENTY-FOUR HOURS BEFORE THE NOSIEST NOSES IN WASHINGTON START POKING INTO EVERY CORNER OF THIS FACILITY.
WE HAVEN'T BEEN THIS CLOSE TO DISCOVERY SINCE JACK KENNEDY THREATENED TO CLOSE US DOWN.
KENNEDY? I THOUGHT HE APPROVED PROJECT NEXT MEN.
HE APPROVED A PROJECT DEVOTED TO GENETIC RESEARCH AND--TO A LESSER DEGREE--ENGINEERING.
I MANAGED TO CONVINCE HIM FOR NEARLY TWO YEARS THAT ALL WE WERE DOING WAS GROWING STRONGER CORN AND BIGGER COWS.
THEN... WELL, IF DALLAS HADN'T HAPPENED...
YOU WERE LUCKY, SENATOR.
LUCK HAD NOTHING TO DO WITH IT, BREMMER.
NOW, FINISH UP.

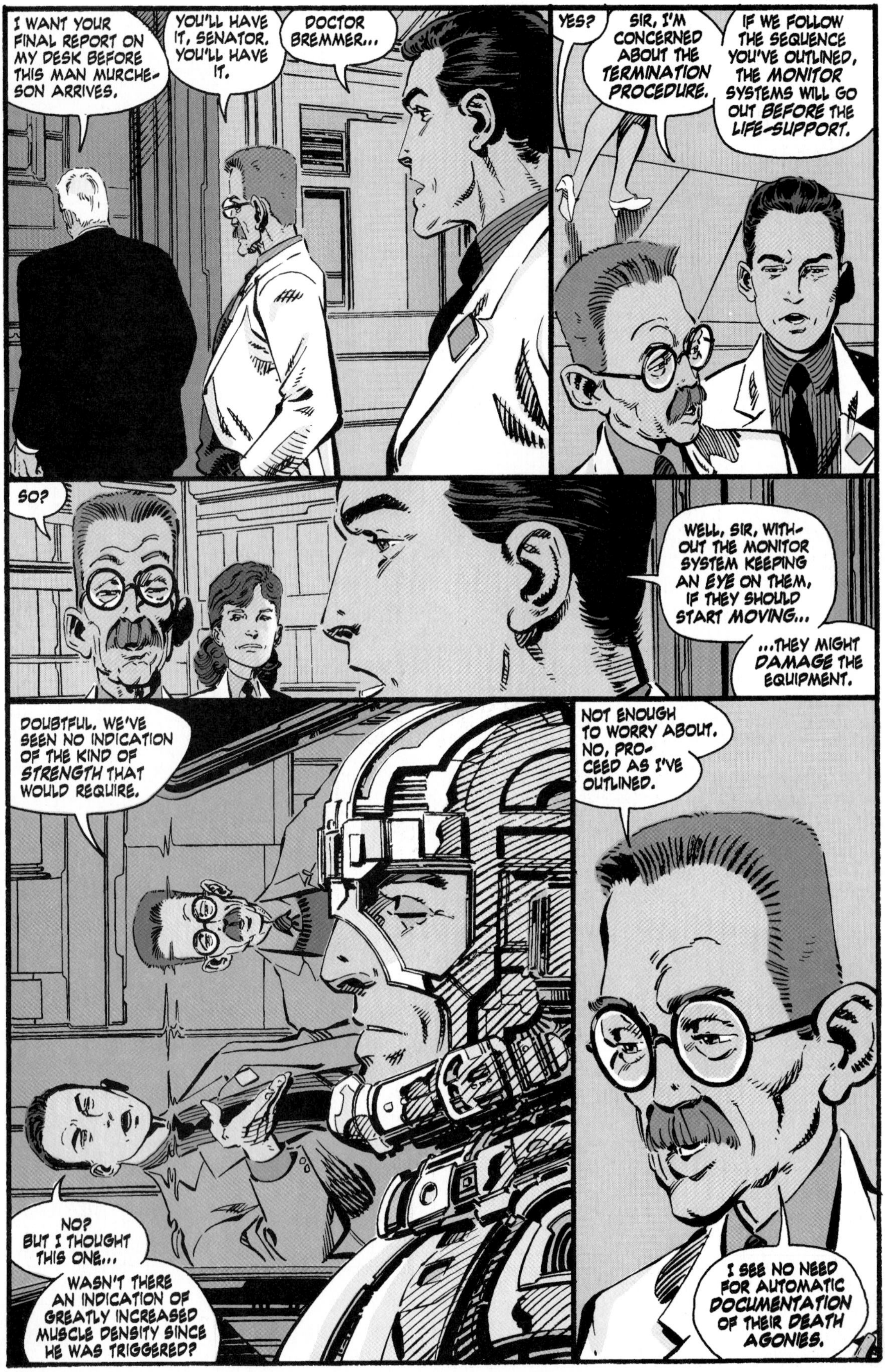
I WANT YOUR FINAL REPORT ON MY DESK BEFORE THIS MAN MURCHESON ARRIVES.
YOU'LL HAVE IT, SENATOR. YOU'LL HAVE IT.
DOCTOR BREMMER...
YES?
SIR, I'M CONCERNED ABOUT THE TERMINATION PROCEDURE.
IF WE FOLLOW THE SEQUENCE YOU'VE OUTLINED, THE MONITOR SYSTEMS WILL GO OUT BEFORE THE LIFE-SUPPORT.
SO?
WELL, SIR, WITHOUT THE MONITOR SYSTEM KEEPING AN EYE ON THEM, IF THEY SHOULD START MOVING...
...THEY MIGHT DAMAGE THE EQUIPMENT.
DOUBTFUL. WE'VE SEEN NO INDICATION OF THE KIND OF STRENGTH THAT WOULD REQUIRE.
NO? BUT I THOUGHT THIS ONE...
WASN'T THERE AN INDICATION OF GREATLY INCREASED MUSCLE DENSITY SINCE HE WAS TRIGGERED?
NOT ENOUGH TO WORRY ABOUT. NO, PROCEED AS I'VE OUTLINED.
I SEE NO NEED FOR AUTOMATIC DOCUMENTATION OF THEIR DEATH AGONIES.

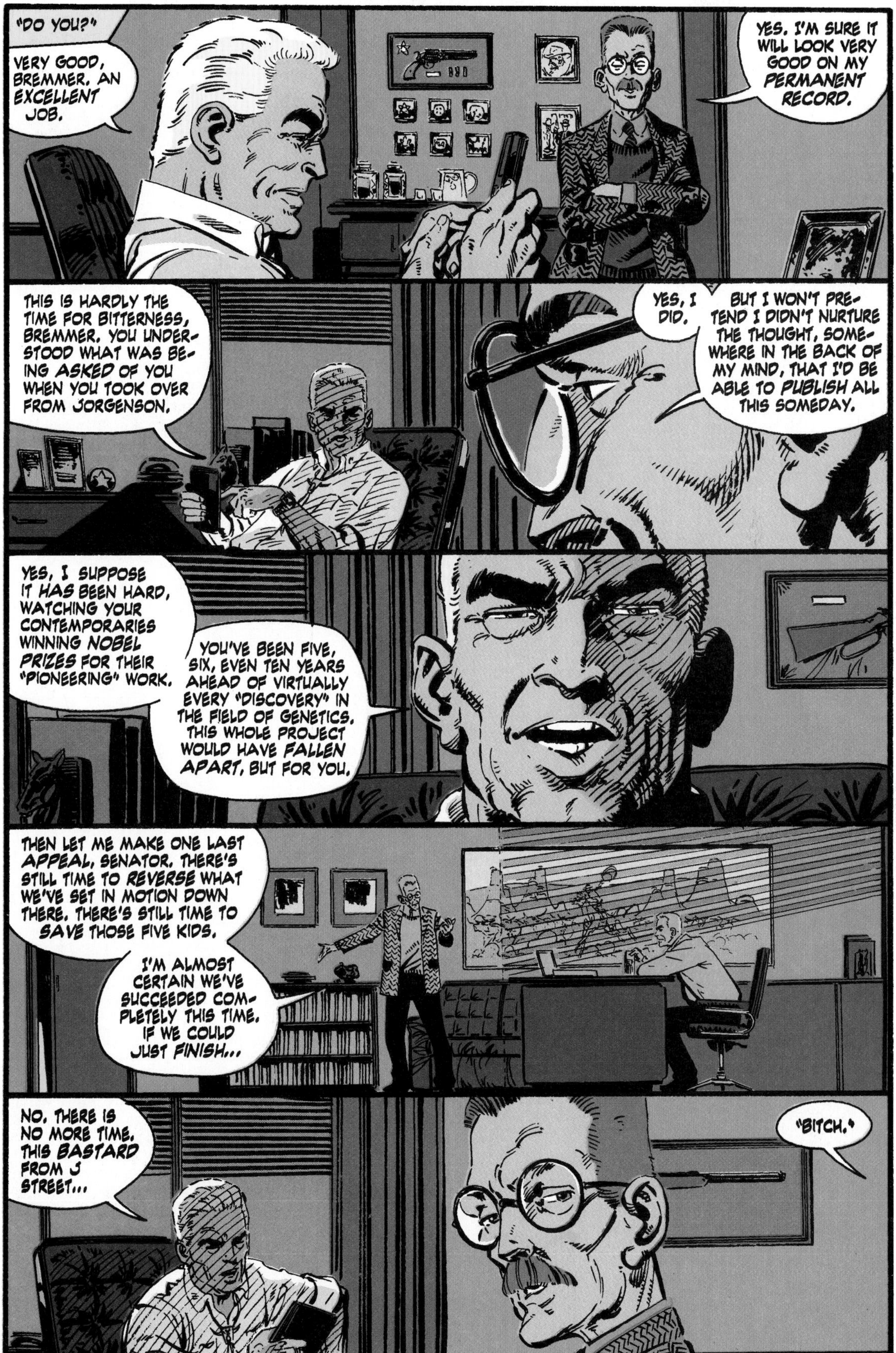
"DO YOU?"
VERY GOOD, BREMMER. AN EXCELLENT JOB.
YES. I'M SURE IT WILL LOOK VERY GOOD ON MY PERMANENT RECORD.
THIS IS HARDLY THE TIME FOR BITTERNESS, BREMMER. YOU UNDERSTOOD WHAT WAS BEING ASKED OF YOU WHEN YOU TOOK OVER FROM JORGENSON.
YES, I DID.
BUT I WON'T PRETEND I DIDN'T NURTURE THE THOUGHT, SOMEWHERE IN THE BACK OF MY MIND, THAT I'D BE ABLE TO PUBLISH ALL THIS SOMEDAY.
YES, I SUPPOSE IT HAS BEEN HARD, WATCHING YOUR CONTEMPORARIES WINNING NOBEL PRIZES FOR THEIR "PIONEERING" WORK.
YOU'VE BEEN FIVE, SIX, EVEN TEN YEARS AHEAD OF VIRTUALLY EVERY "DISCOVERY" IN THE FIELD OF GENETICS. THIS WHOLE PROJECT WOULD HAVE FALLEN APART, BUT FOR YOU.
THEN LET ME MAKE ONE LAST APPEAL, SENATOR. THERE'S STILL TIME TO REVERSE WHAT WE'VE SET IN MOTION DOWN THERE. THERE'S STILL TIME TO SAVE THOSE FIVE KIDS.
I'M ALMOST CERTAIN WE'VE SUCCEEDED COMPLETELY THIS TIME. IF WE COULD JUST FINISH...
NO. THERE IS NO MORE TIME. THIS BASTARD FROM J STREET...
"BITCH."

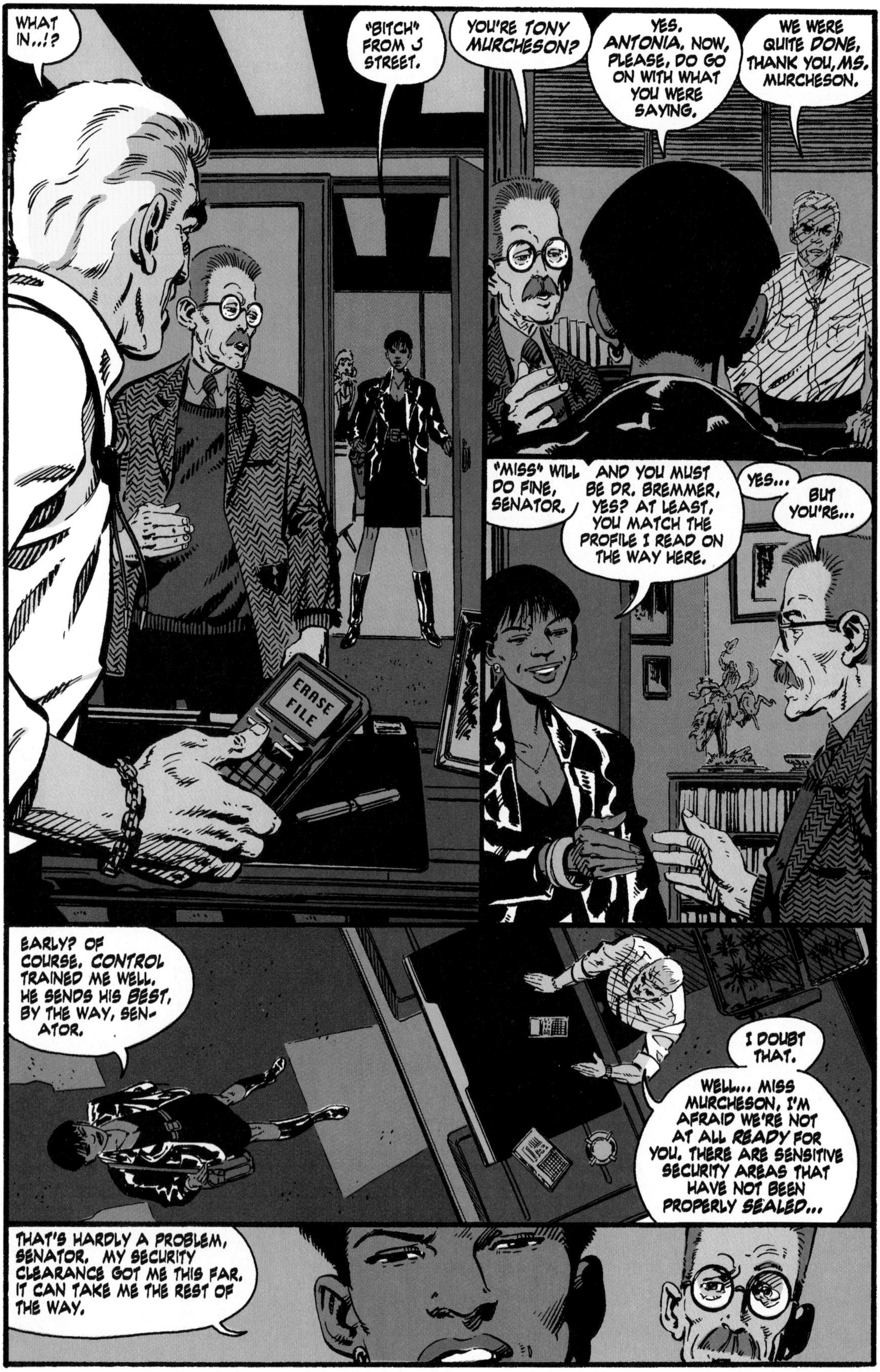
WHAT IN..!?
"BITCH" FROM J STREET.
YOU'RE TONY MURCHESON?
YES. ANTONIA. NOW, PLEASE, DO GO ON WITH WHAT YOU WERE SAYING.
WE WERE QUITE DONE, THANK YOU, MS. MURCHESON.
ERASE FILE
"MISS" WILL DO FINE, SENATOR.
AND YOU MUST BE DR. BREMMER, YES? AT LEAST, YOU MATCH THE PROFILE I READ ON THE WAY HERE.
YES...
BUT YOU'RE...
EARLY? OF COURSE. CONTROL TRAINED ME WELL. HE SENDS HIS BEST, BY THE WAY, SEN-ATOR.
I DOUBT THAT.
WELL... MISS MURCHESON, I'M AFRAID WE'RE NOT AT ALL READY FOR YOU. THERE ARE SENSITIVE SECURITY AREAS THAT HAVE NOT BEEN PROPERLY SEALED...
THAT'S HARDLY A PROBLEM, SENATOR. MY SECURITY CLEARANCE GOT ME THIS FAR. IT CAN TAKE ME THE REST OF THE WAY.

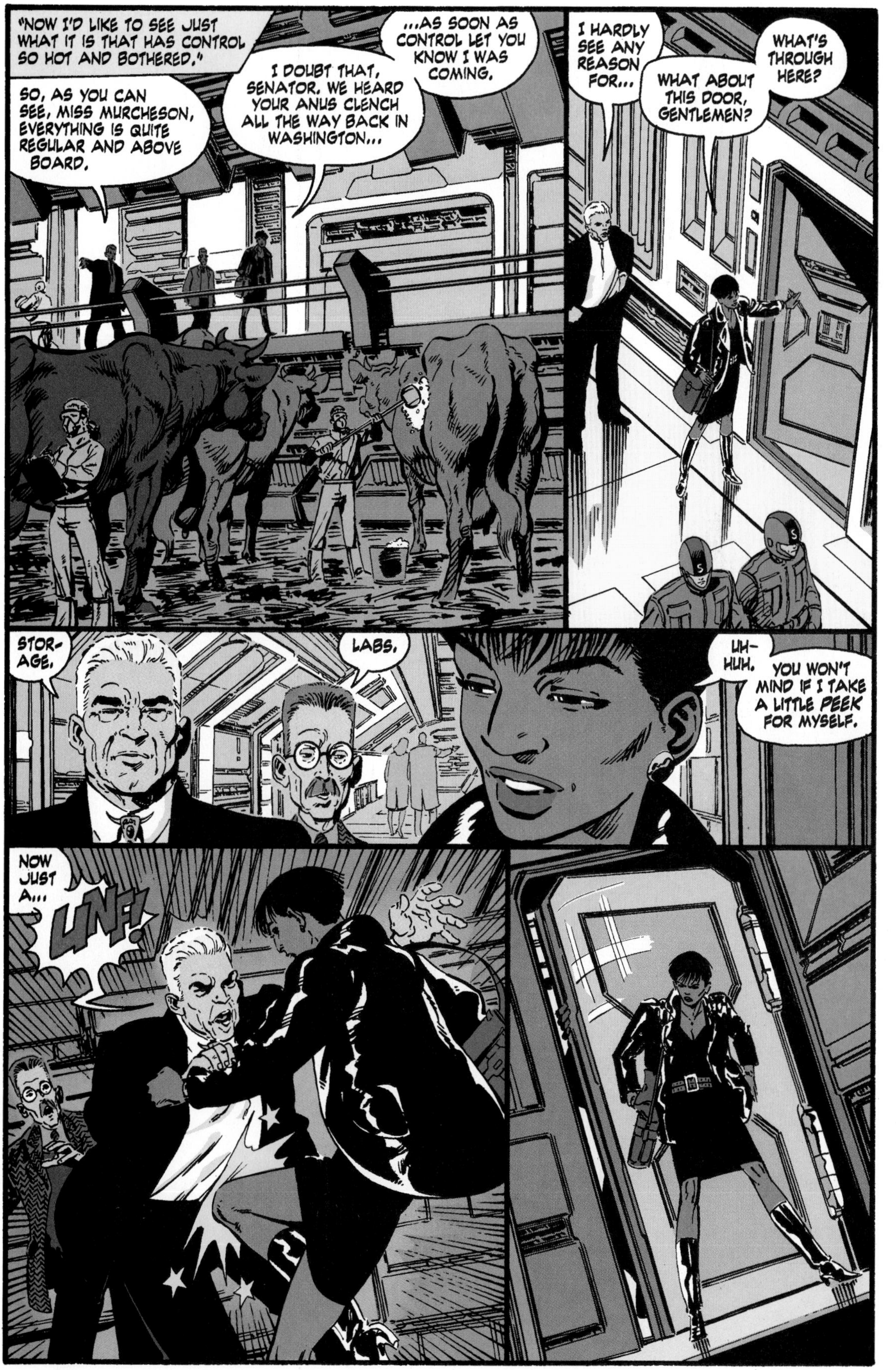
"NOW I'D LIKE TO SEE JUST WHAT IT IS THAT HAS CONTROL SO HOT AND BOTHERED."
SO, AS YOU CAN SEE, MISS MURCHESON, EVERYTHING IS QUITE REGULAR AND ABOVE BOARD.
I DOUBT THAT, SENATOR. WE HEARD YOUR ANUS CLENCH ALL THE WAY BACK IN WASHINGTON...
...AS SOON AS CONTROL LET YOU KNOW I WAS COMING.
I HARDLY SEE ANY REASON FOR...
WHAT ABOUT THIS DOOR, GENTLEMEN?
WHAT'S THROUGH HERE?
STOR-AGE.
LABS.
UH-HUH.
YOU WON'T MIND IF I TAKE A LITTLE PEEK FOR MYSELF.
NOW JUST A...
UNF!

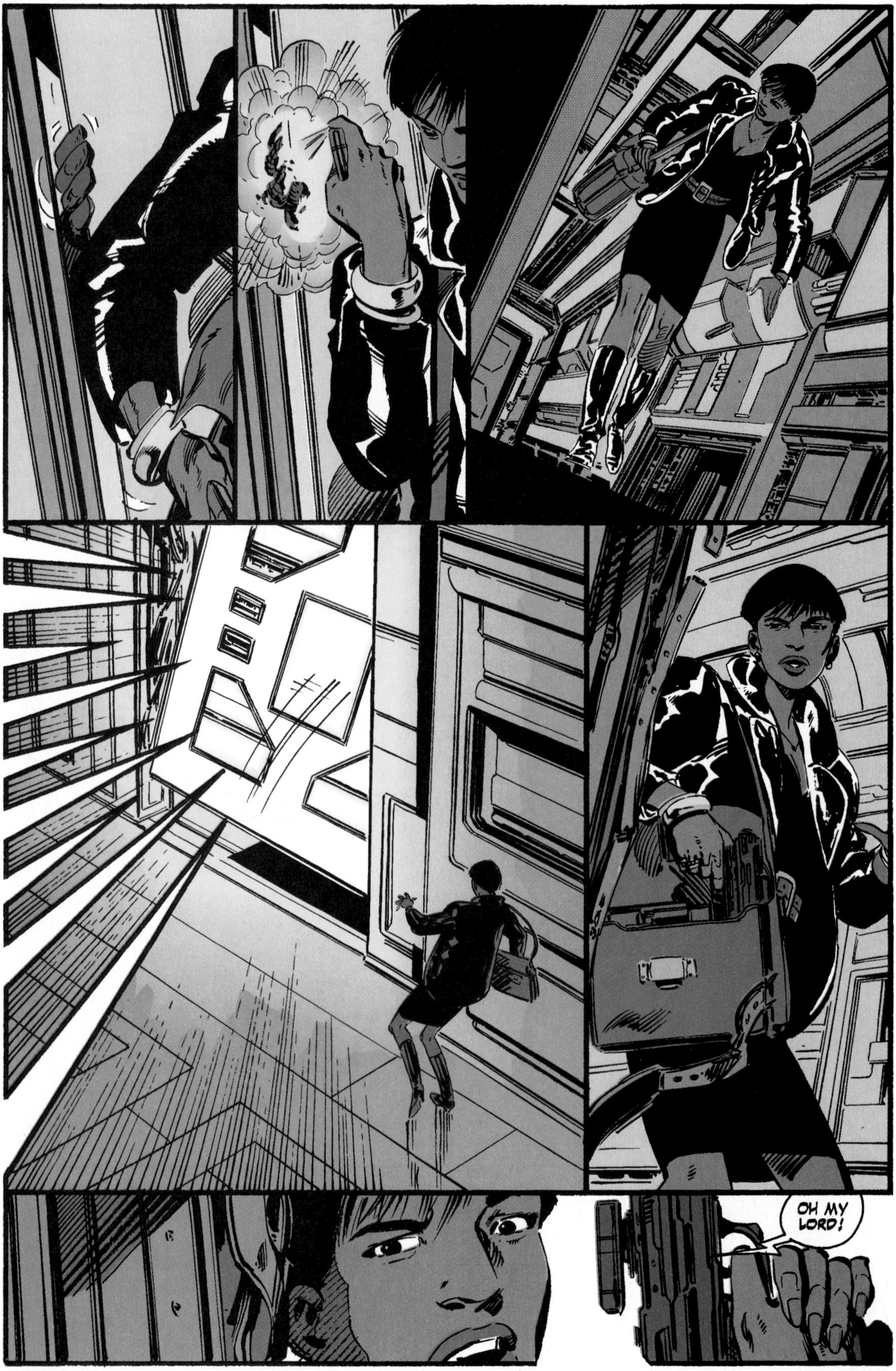
OH MY LORD!

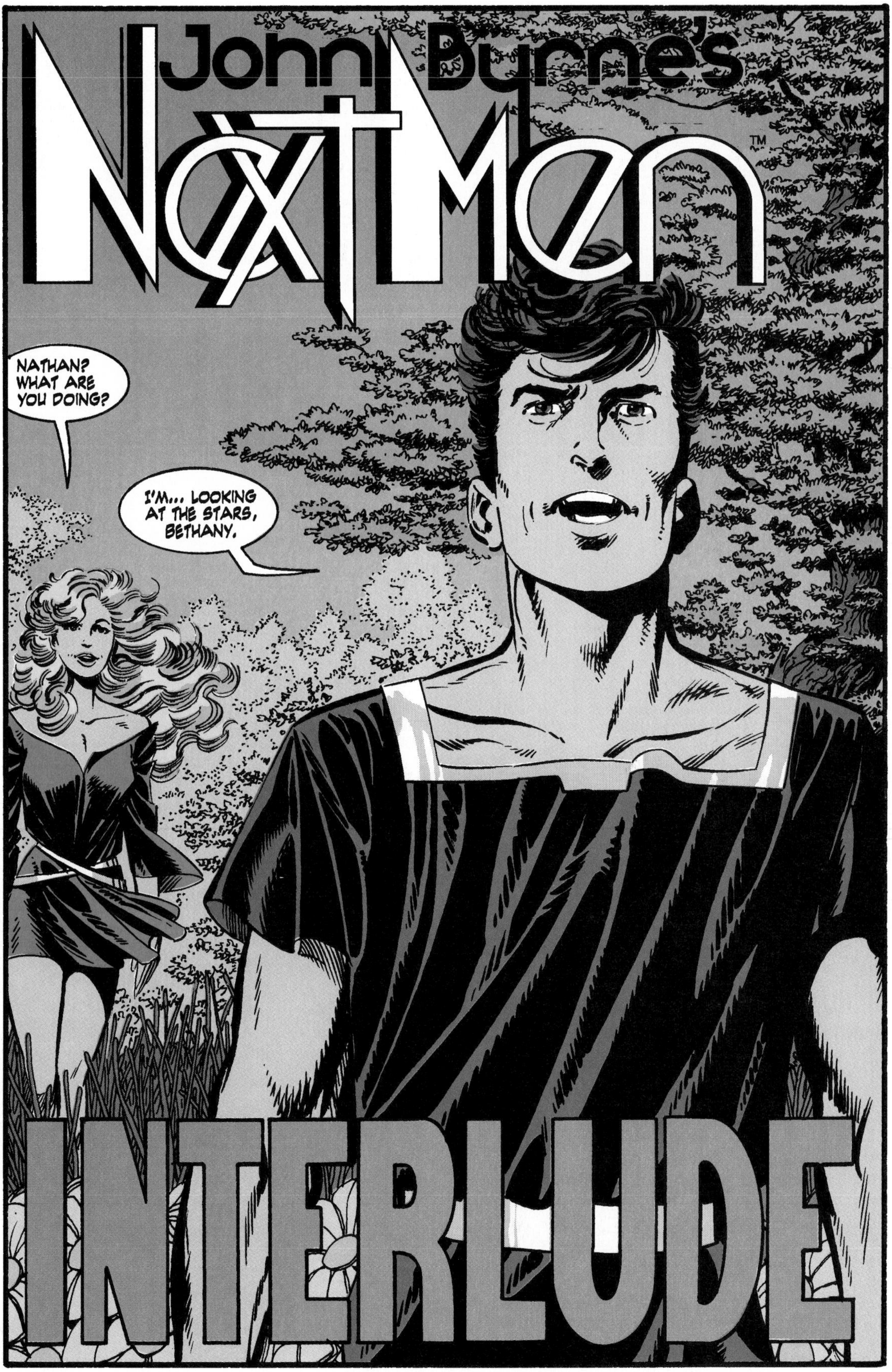
John Byrne's
Next Men™
NATHAN? WHAT ARE YOU DOING?
I'M... LOOKING AT THE STARS, BETHANY.
INTERLUDE

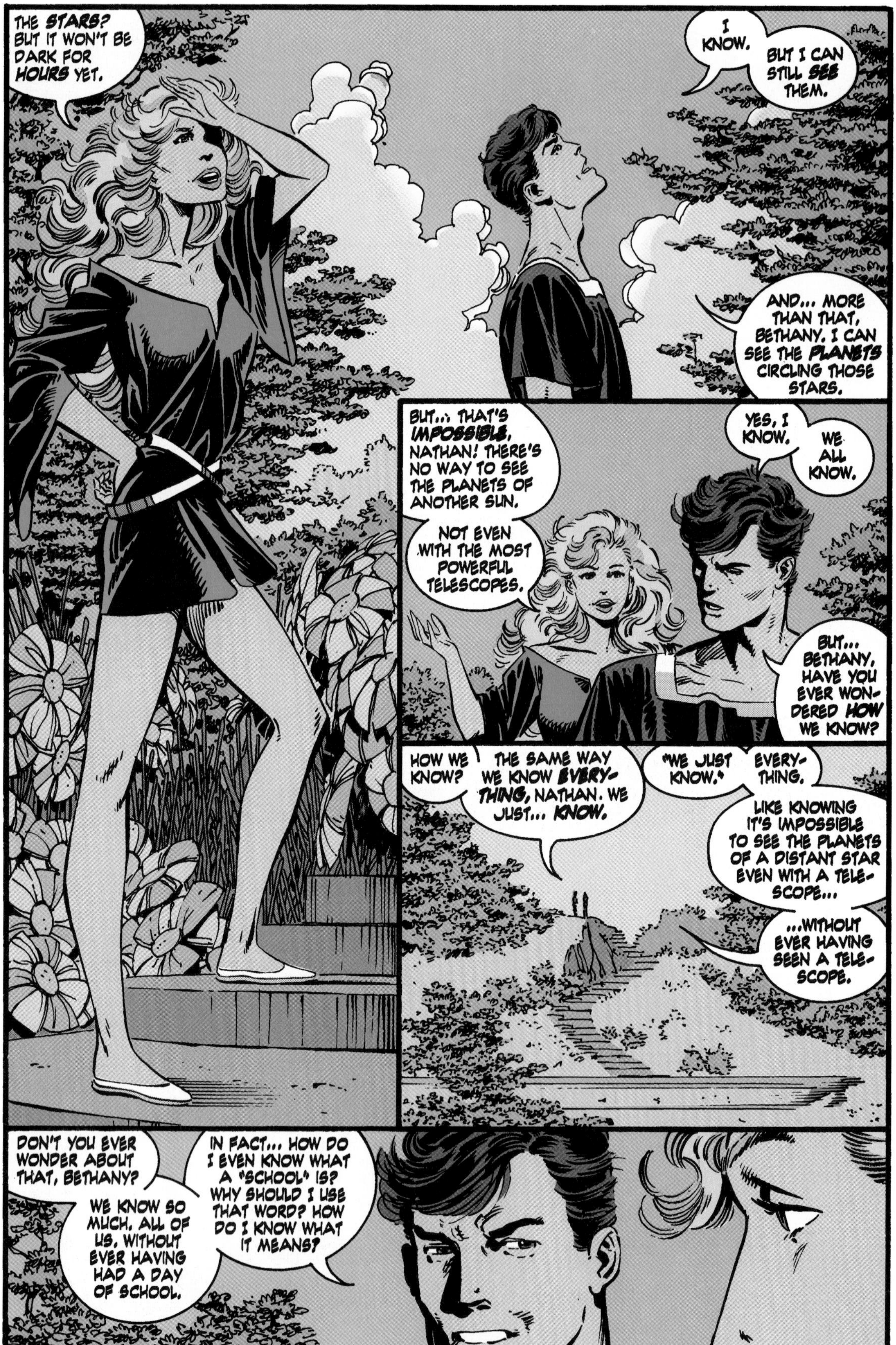
THE STARS? BUT IT WON'T BE DARK FOR HOURS YET.
I KNOW.
BUT I CAN STILL SEE THEM.
AND... MORE THAN THAT, BETHANY. I CAN SEE THE PLANETS CIRCLING THOSE STARS.
BUT... THAT'S IMPOSSIBLE, NATHAN! THERE'S NO WAY TO SEE THE PLANETS OF ANOTHER SUN.
NOT EVEN WITH THE MOST POWERFUL TELESCOPES.
YES, I KNOW.
WE ALL KNOW.
BUT... BETHANY, HAVE YOU EVER WONDERED HOW WE KNOW?
HOW WE KNOW?
THE SAME WAY WE KNOW EVERYTHING, NATHAN. WE JUST... KNOW.
"WE JUST KNOW."
EVERYTHING.
LIKE KNOWING IT'S IMPOSSIBLE TO SEE THE PLANETS OF A DISTANT STAR EVEN WITH A TELESCOPE...
...WITHOUT EVER HAVING SEEN A TELESCOPE.
DON'T YOU EVER WONDER ABOUT THAT, BETHANY?
WE KNOW SO MUCH, ALL OF US, WITHOUT EVER HAVING HAD A DAY OF SCHOOL.
IN FACT... HOW DO I EVEN KNOW WHAT A "SCHOOL" IS? WHY SHOULD I USE THAT WORD? HOW DO I KNOW WHAT IT MEANS?

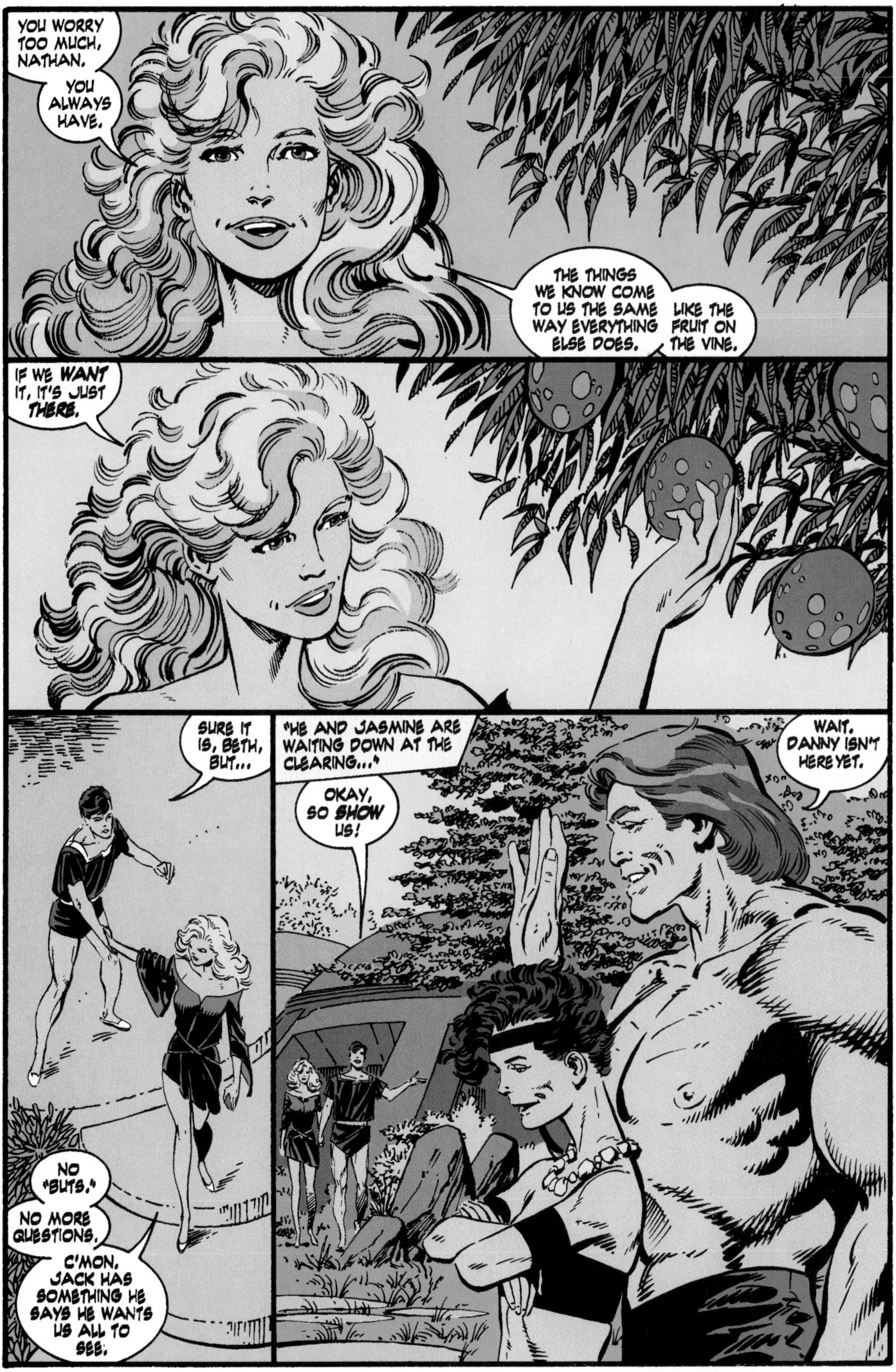
YOU WORRY TOO MUCH, NATHAN.
YOU ALWAYS HAVE.
THE THINGS WE KNOW COME TO US THE SAME WAY EVERYTHING ELSE DOES.
LIKE THE FRUIT ON THE VINE.
IF WE WANT IT, IT'S JUST THERE.
SURE IT IS, BETH, BUT...
NO "BUTS."
NO MORE QUESTIONS.
C'MON, JACK HAS SOMETHING HE SAYS HE WANTS US ALL TO SEE.
"HE AND JASMINE ARE WAITING DOWN AT THE CLEARING..."
OKAY, SO SHOW US!
WAIT. DANNY ISN'T HERE YET.

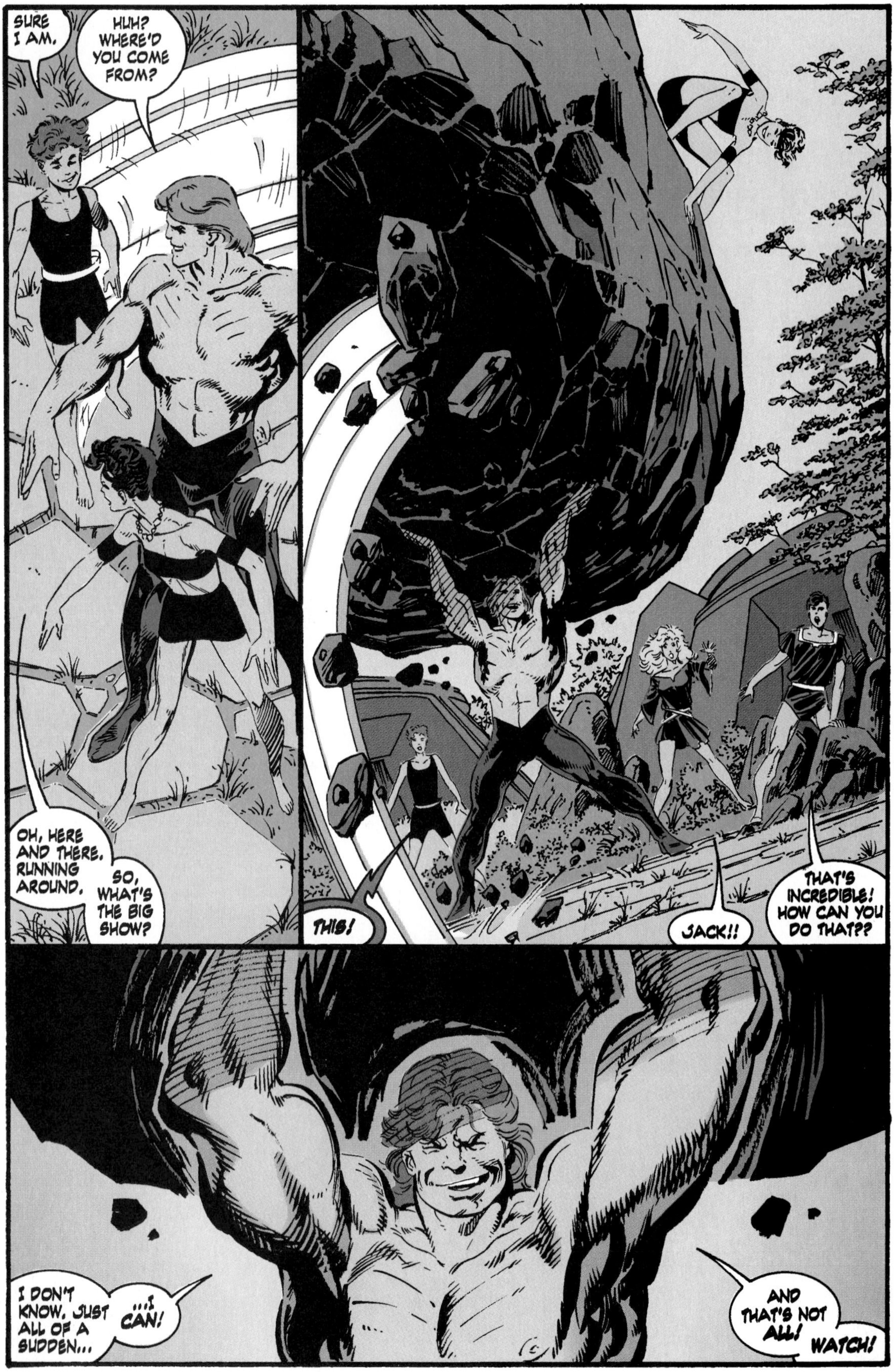
SURE I AM.
HUH? WHERE'D YOU COME FROM?
OH, HERE AND THERE. RUNNING AROUND.
SO, WHAT'S THE BIG SHOW?
THIS!
JACK!!
THAT'S INCREDIBLE! HOW CAN YOU DO THAT??
I DON'T KNOW, JUST ALL OF A SUDDEN...
...I CAN!
AND THAT'S NOT ALL!
WATCH!

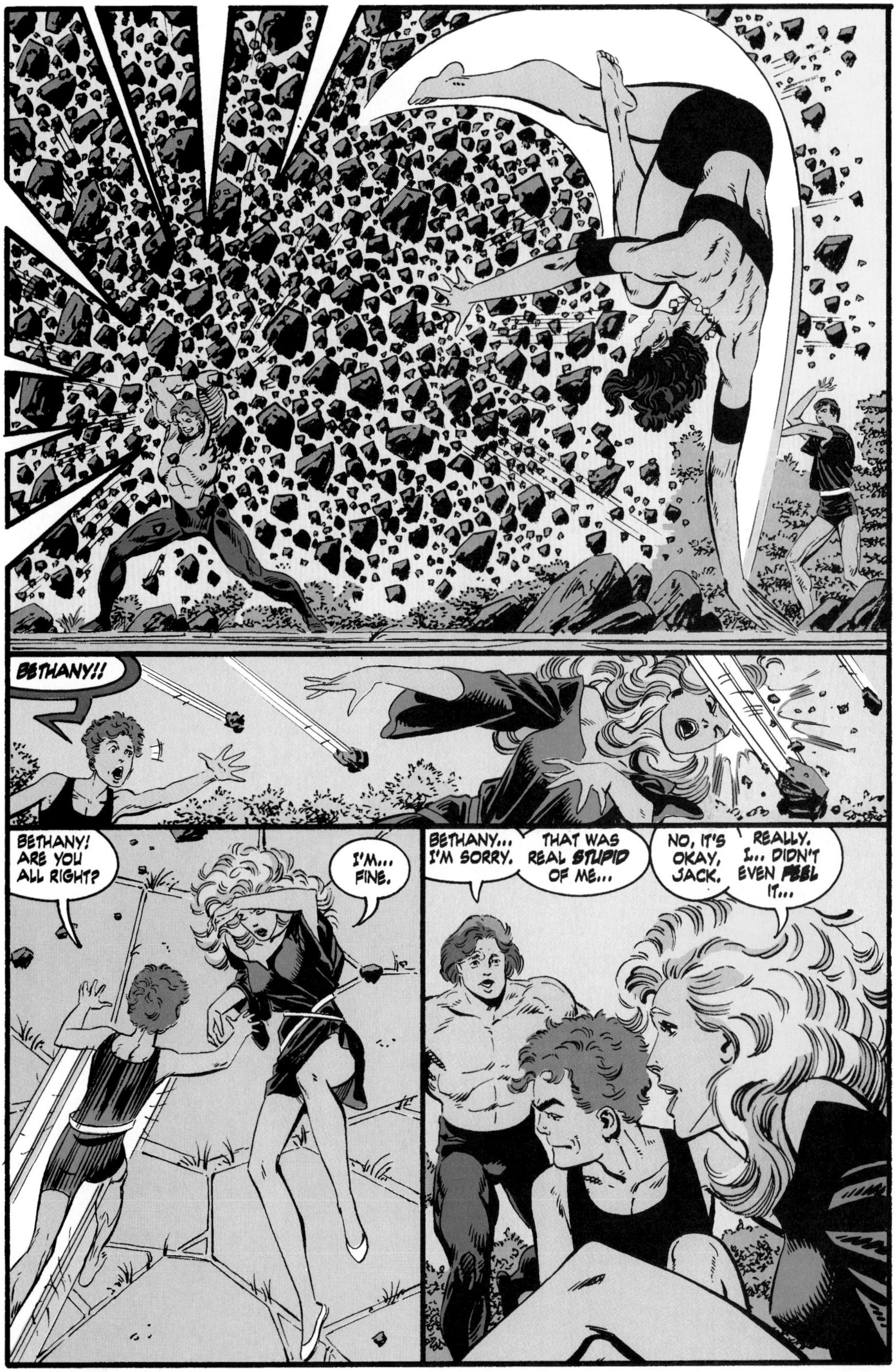
BETHANY!!
BETHANY! ARE YOU ALL RIGHT?
I'M... FINE.
BETHANY... I'M SORRY.
THAT WAS REAL STUPID OF ME...
NO, IT'S OKAY, JACK.
REALLY. I... DIDN'T EVEN FEEL IT...

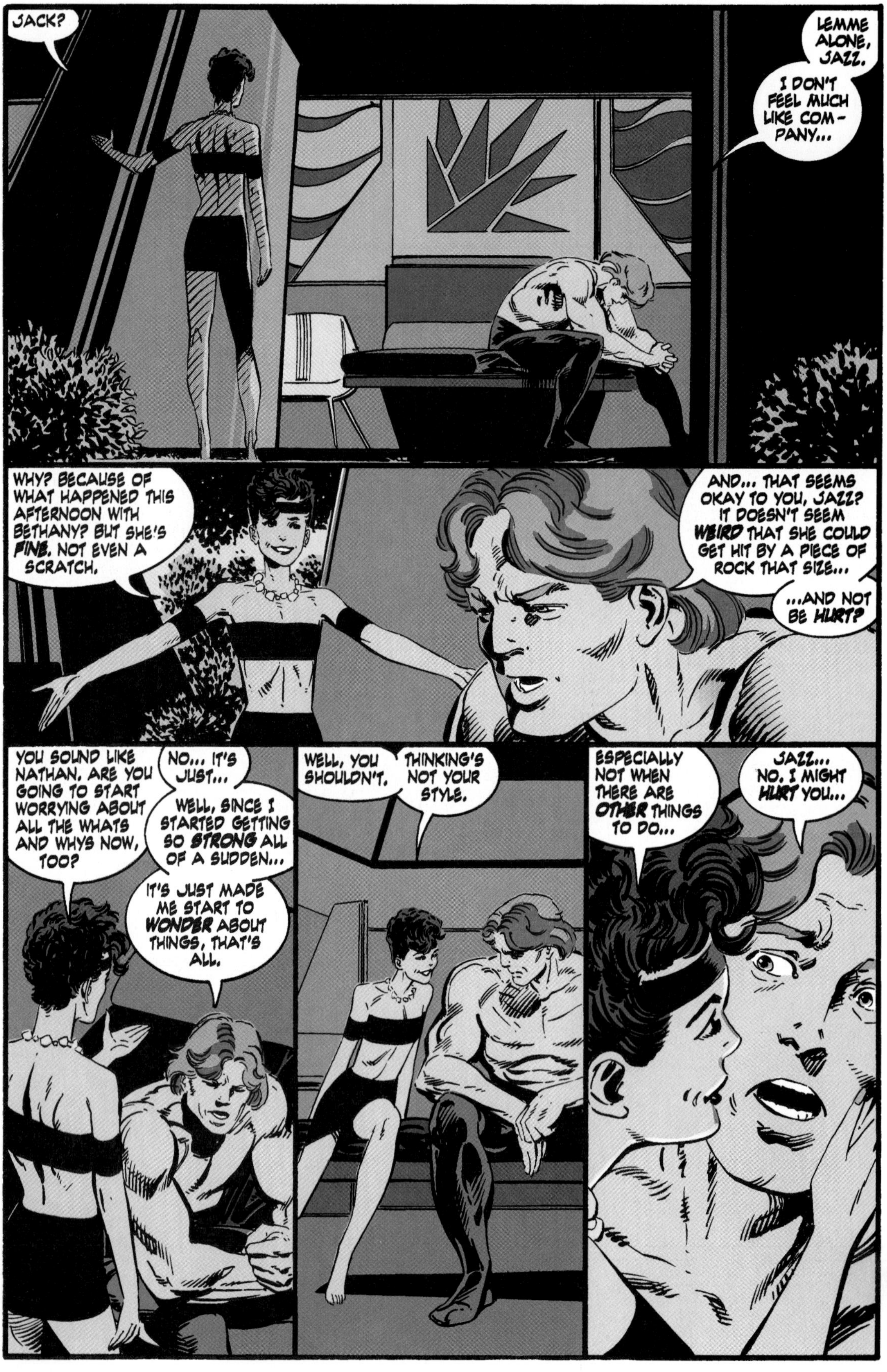
JACK?
LEMME ALONE, JAZZ.
I DON'T FEEL MUCH LIKE COM-PANY...
WHY? BECAUSE OF WHAT HAPPENED THIS AFTERNOON WITH BETHANY? BUT SHE'S FINE. NOT EVEN A SCRATCH.
AND... THAT SEEMS OKAY TO YOU, JAZZ? IT DOESN'T SEEM WEIRD THAT SHE COULD GET HIT BY A PIECE OF ROCK THAT SIZE...
...AND NOT BE HURT?
YOU SOUND LIKE NATHAN. ARE YOU GOING TO START WORRYING ABOUT ALL THE WHATS AND WHYS NOW, TOO?
NO... IT'S JUST...
WELL, SINCE I STARTED GETTING SO STRONG ALL OF A SUDDEN...
IT'S JUST MADE ME START TO WONDER ABOUT THINGS, THAT'S ALL.
WELL, YOU SHOULDN'T.
THINKING'S NOT YOUR STYLE.
ESPECIALLY NOT WHEN THERE ARE OTHER THINGS TO DO...
JAZZ... NO. I MIGHT HURT YOU...

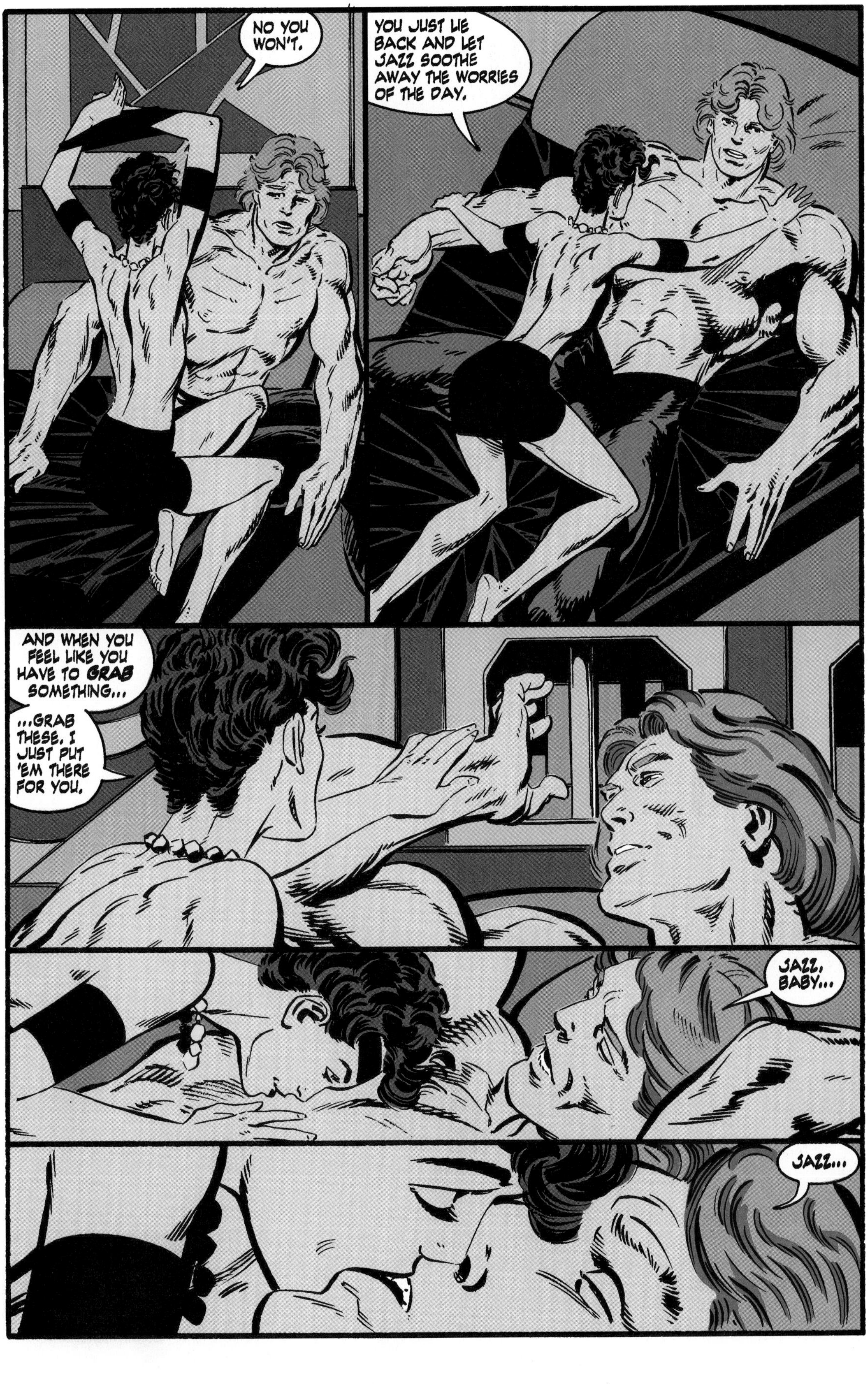
NO YOU WON'T.
YOU JUST LIE BACK AND LET JAZZ SOOTHE AWAY THE WORRIES OF THE DAY.
AND WHEN YOU FEEL LIKE YOU HAVE TO GRAB SOMETHING...
...GRAB THESE. I JUST PUT 'EM THERE FOR YOU.
JAZZ, BABY...
JAZZ...

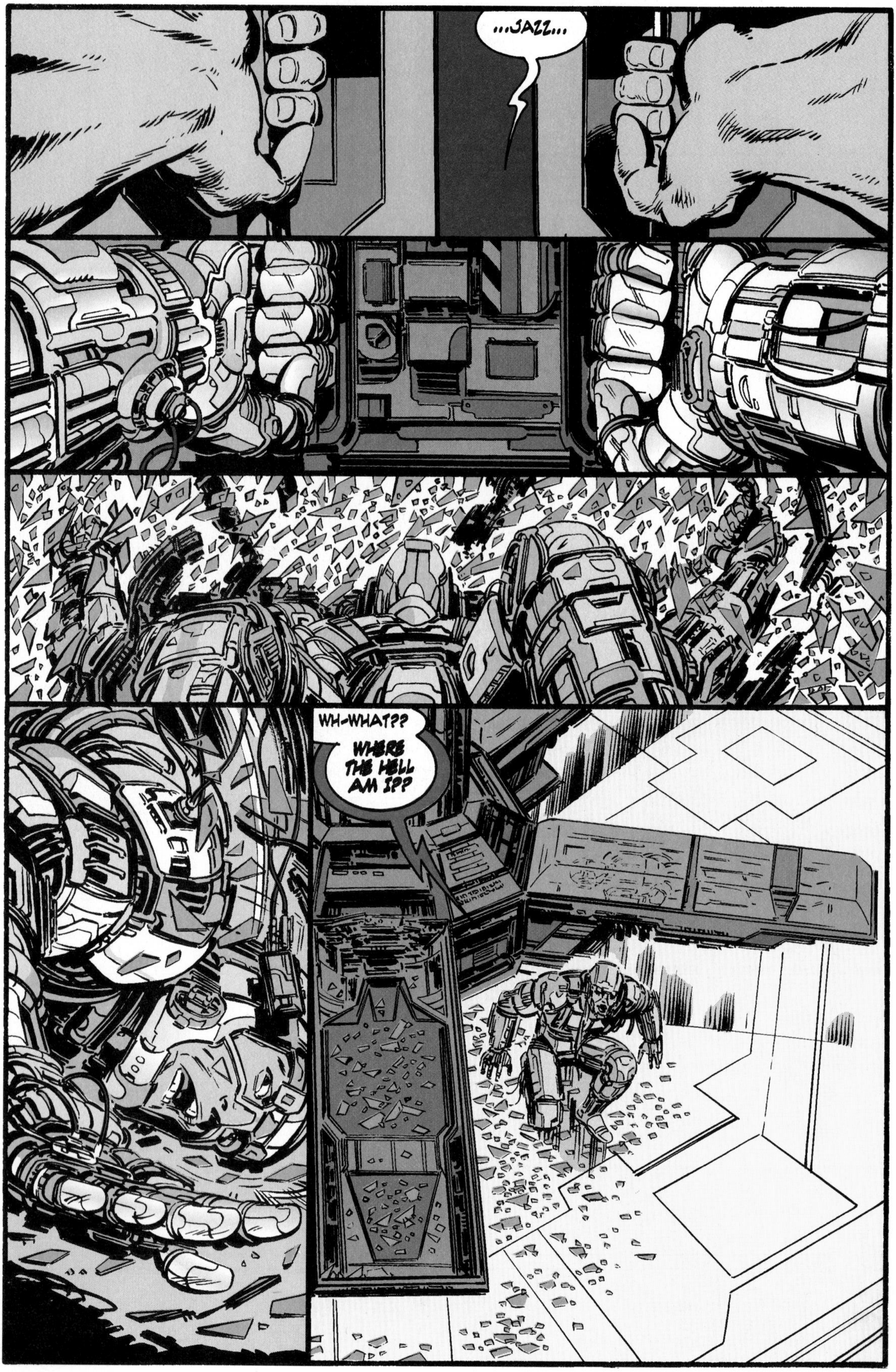
...JAZZ...
WH-WHAT??
WHERE THE HELL AM I??

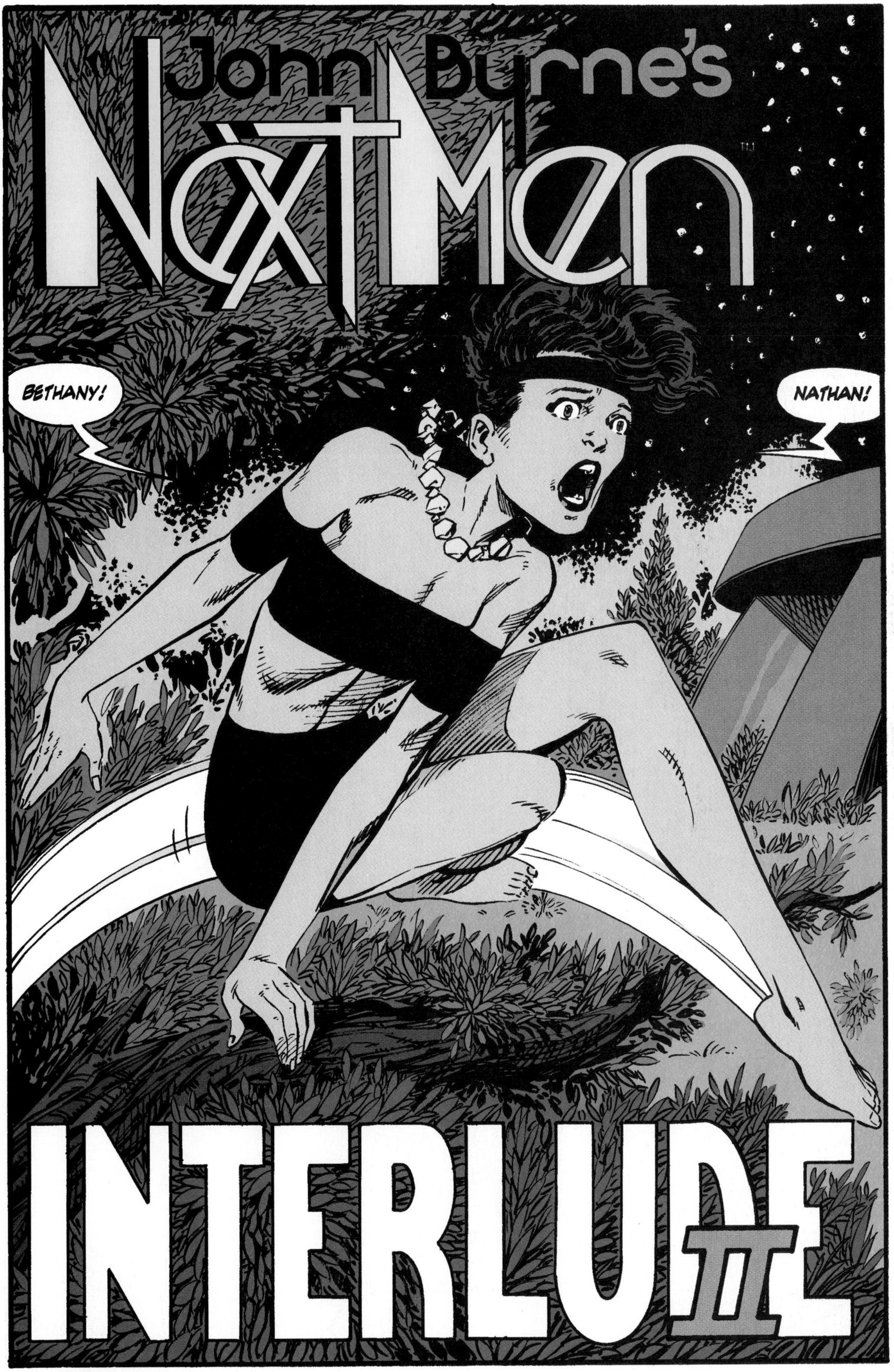
John Byrne's
NextMen
BETHANY!
NATHAN!
INTERLUDE II

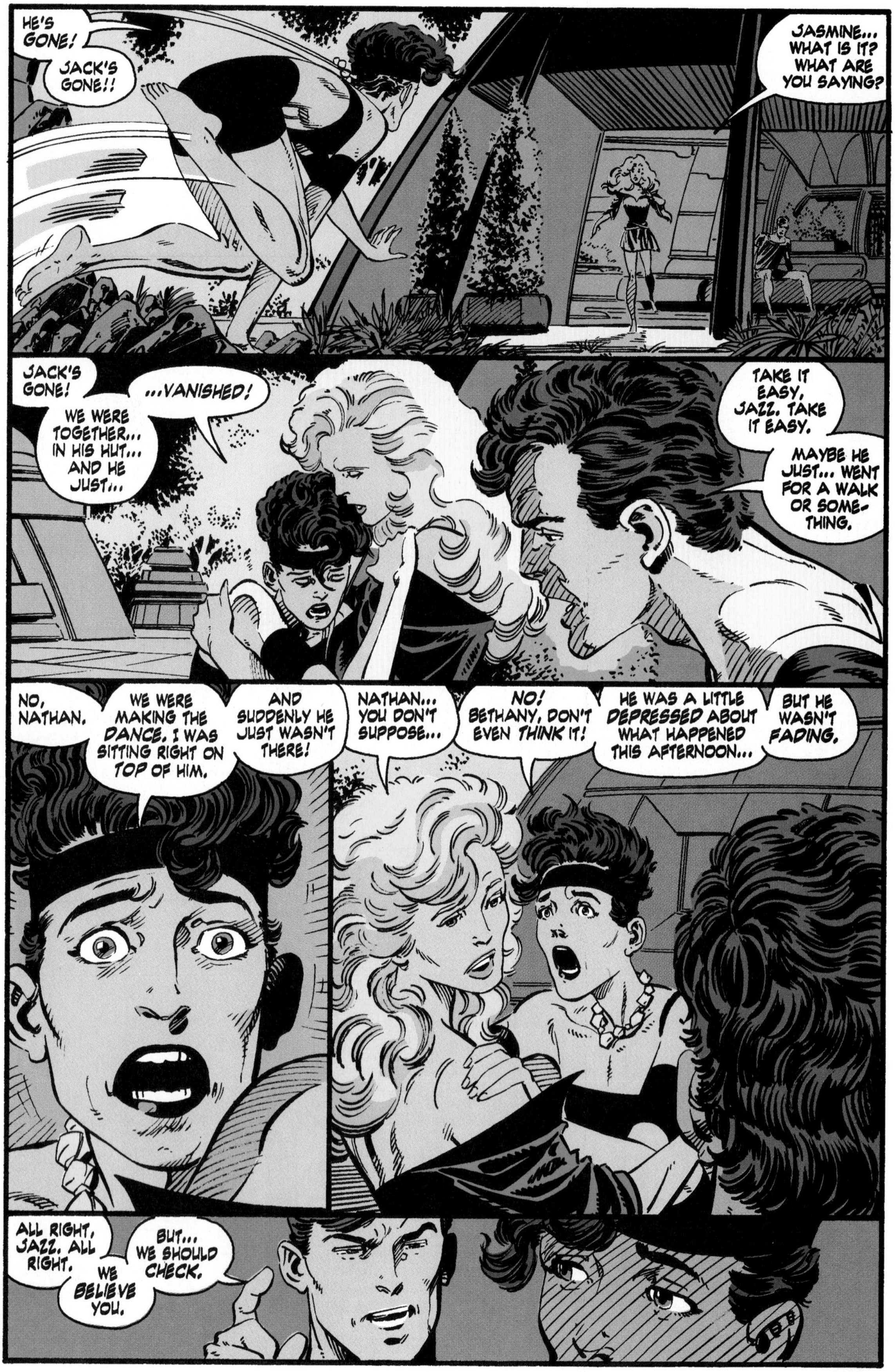
HE'S GONE!
JACK'S GONE!!
JASMINE... WHAT IS IT? WHAT ARE YOU SAYING?
JACK'S GONE!
...VANISHED!
WE WERE TOGETHER... IN HIS HUT... AND HE JUST...
TAKE IT EASY, JAZZ. TAKE IT EASY.
MAYBE HE JUST... WENT FOR A WALK OR SOME-THING.
NO, NATHAN.
WE WERE MAKING THE DANCE. I WAS SITTING RIGHT ON TOP OF HIM.
AND SUDDENLY HE JUST WASN'T THERE!
NATHAN... YOU DON'T SUPPOSE...
NO! BETHANY, DON'T EVEN THINK IT!
HE WAS A LITTLE DEPRESSED ABOUT WHAT HAPPENED THIS AFTERNOON...
BUT HE WASN'T FADING.
ALL RIGHT, JAZZ. ALL RIGHT.
WE BELIEVE YOU.
BUT... WE SHOULD CHECK.

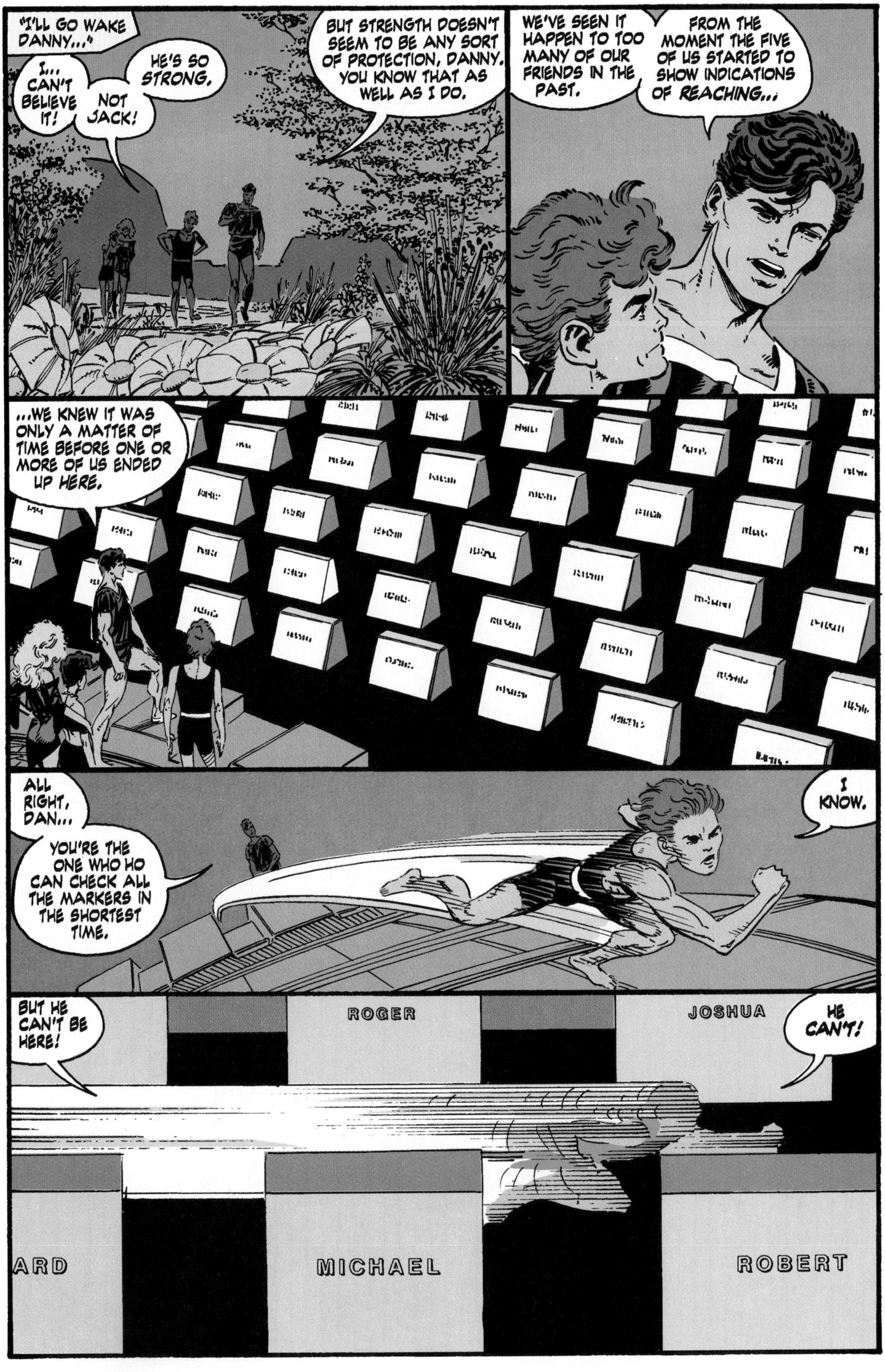

"I'LL GO WAKE DANNY..."
I... CAN'T BELIEVE IT!
NOT JACK!
HE'S SO STRONG.
BUT STRENGTH DOESN'T SEEM TO BE ANY SORT OF PROTECTION, DANNY. YOU KNOW THAT AS WELL AS I DO.
WE'VE SEEN IT HAPPEN TO TOO MANY OF OUR FRIENDS IN THE PAST.
FROM THE MOMENT THE FIVE OF US STARTED TO SHOW INDICATIONS OF REACHING...
...WE KNEW IT WAS ONLY A MATTER OF TIME BEFORE ONE OR MORE OF US ENDED UP HERE.
ALL RIGHT, DAN...
YOU'RE THE ONE WHO HO CAN CHECK ALL THE MARKERS IN THE SHORTEST TIME.
I KNOW.
BUT HE CAN'T BE HERE!
ROGER
JOSHUA
HE CAN'T!
ARD
MICHAEL
ROBERT

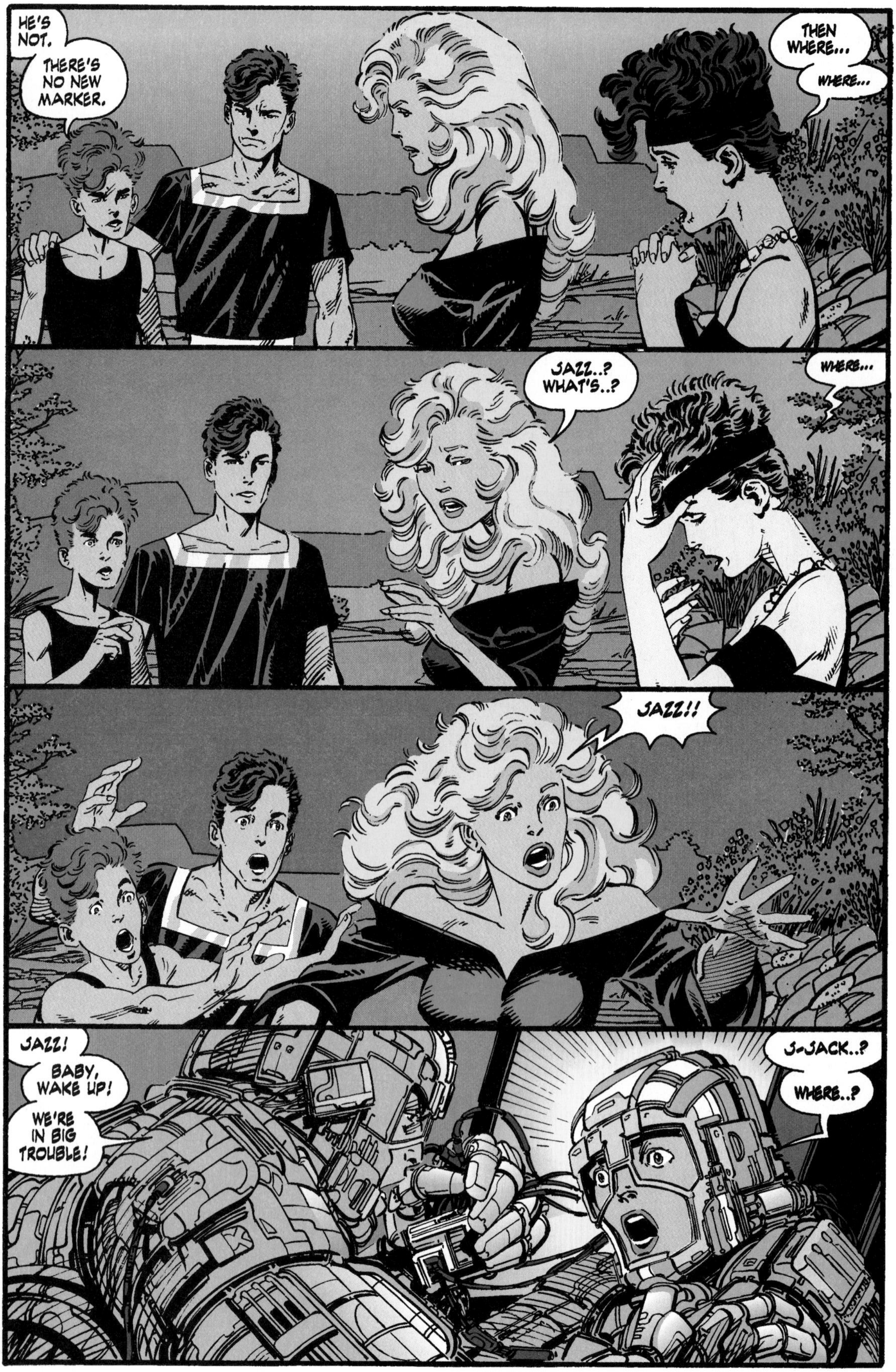
HE'S NOT.
THERE'S NO NEW MARKER.
THEN WHERE...
WHERE...
SAZZ..? WHAT'S..?
WHERE...
SAZZ!!
SAZZ!
BABY, WAKE UP!
WE'RE IN BIG TROUBLE!
J-JACK..?
WHERE..?

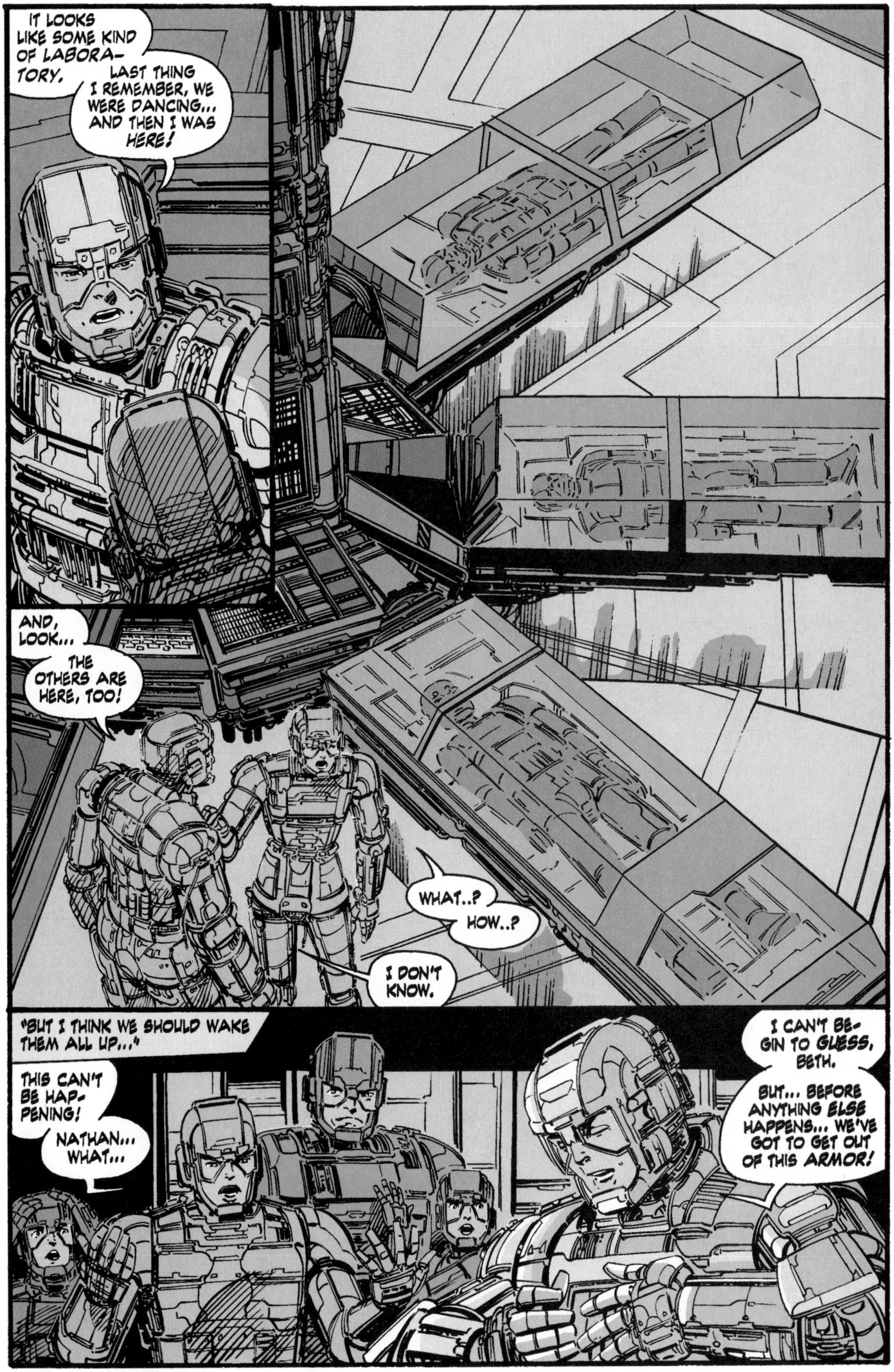
IT LOOKS LIKE SOME KIND OF LABORA-TORY.
LAST THING I REMEMBER, WE WERE DANCING... AND THEN I WAS HERE!
AND, LOOK...
THE OTHERS ARE HERE, TOO!
WHAT..?
HOW..?
I DON'T KNOW.
"BUT I THINK WE SHOULD WAKE THEM ALL UP..."
THIS CAN'T BE HAP-PENING!
NATHAN... WHAT...
I CAN'T BE-GIN TO GUESS, BETH.
BUT... BEFORE ANYTHING ELSE HAPPENS... WE'VE GOT TO GET OUT OF THIS ARMOR!

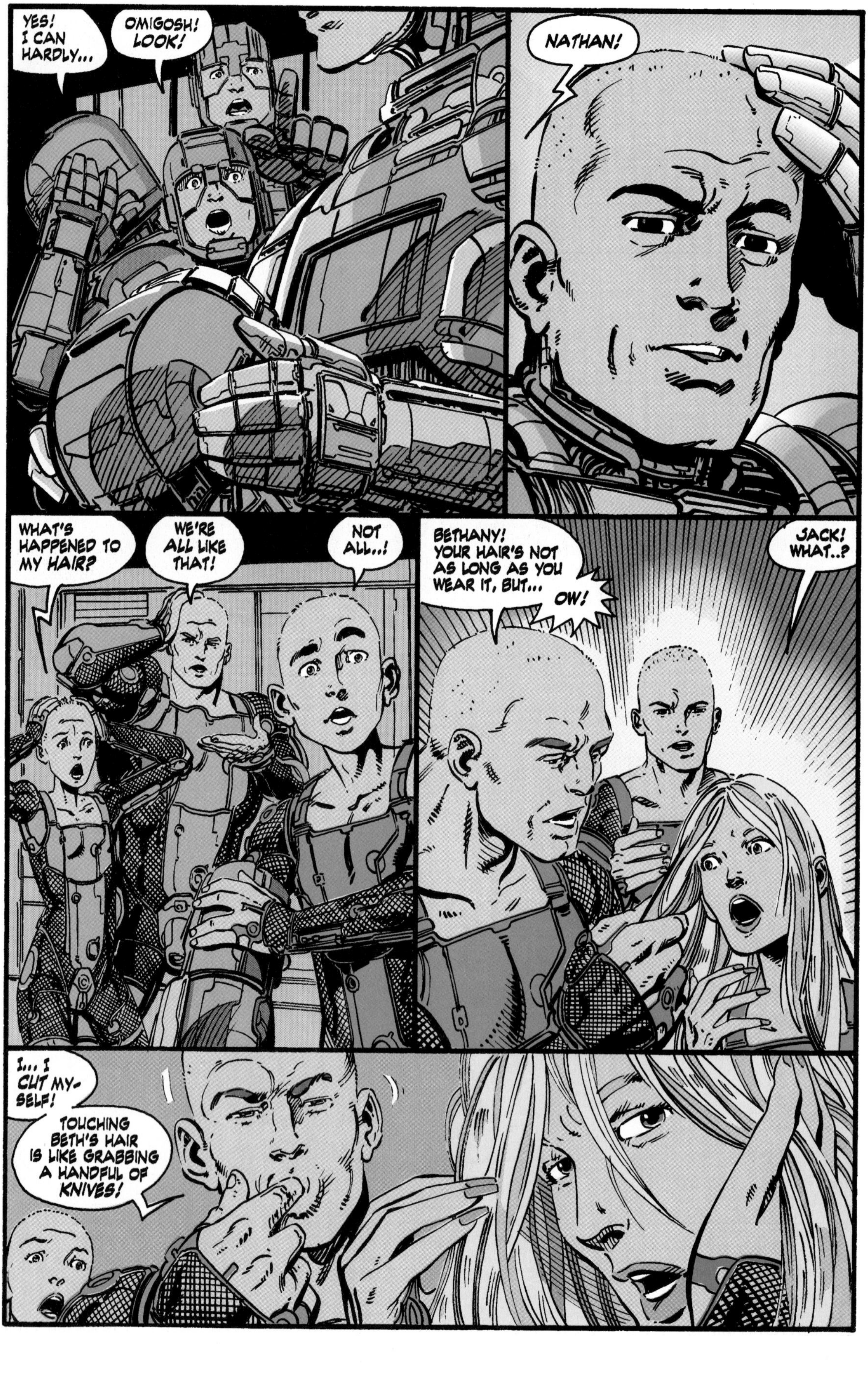
YES! I CAN HARDLY...
OMIGOSH! LOOK!
NATHAN!
WHAT'S HAPPENED TO MY HAIR?
WE'RE ALL LIKE THAT!
NOT ALL...!
BETHANY! YOUR HAIR'S NOT AS LONG AS YOU WEAR IT, BUT...
OW!
JACK! WHAT..?
I... I CUT MY-SELF!
TOUCHING BETH'S HAIR IS LIKE GRABBING A HANDFUL OF KNIVES!

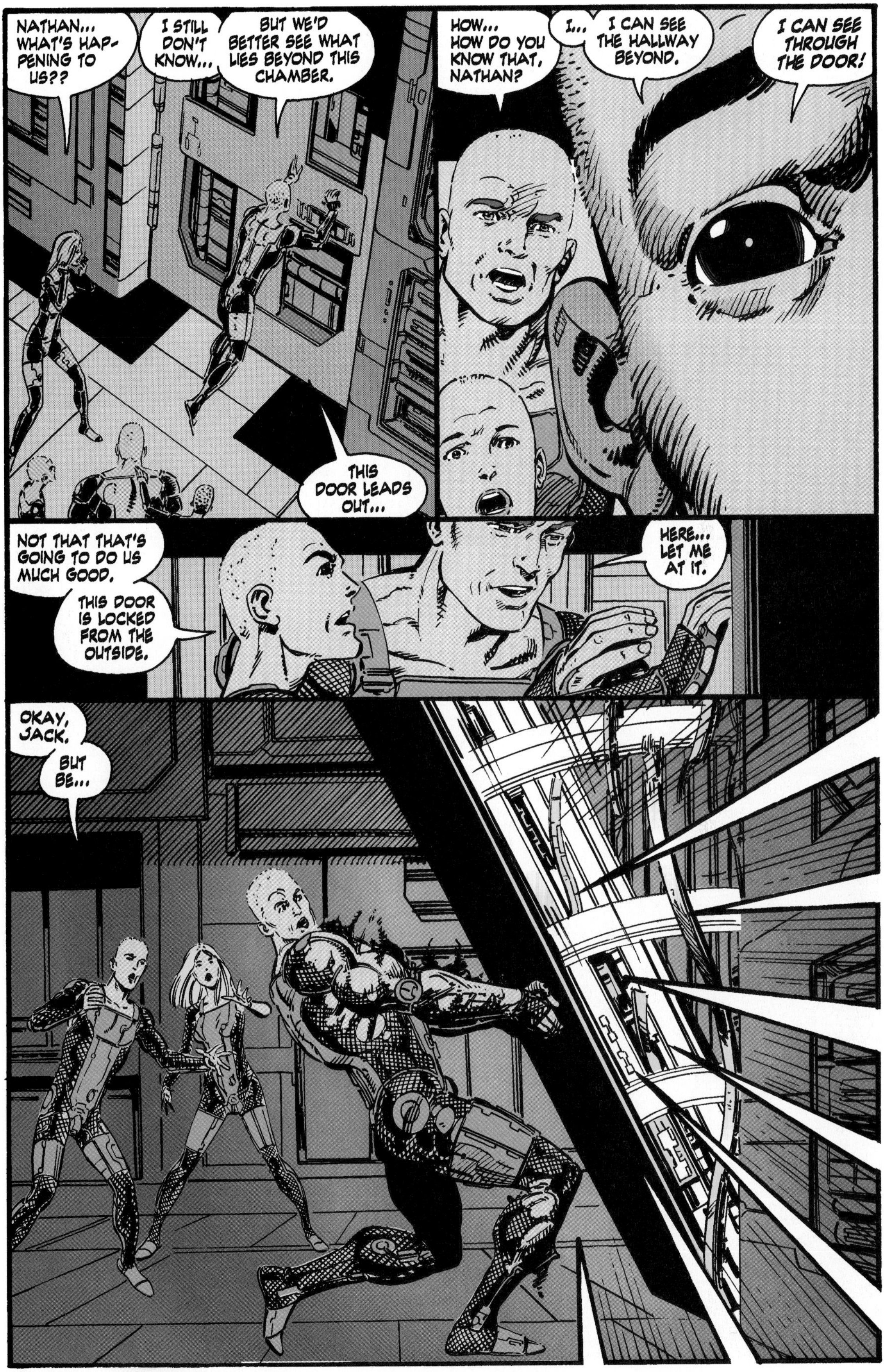
NATHAN... WHAT'S HAP-PENING TO US??
I STILL DON'T KNOW...
BUT WE'D BETTER SEE WHAT LIES BEYOND THIS CHAMBER.
THIS DOOR LEADS OUT...
HOW... HOW DO YOU KNOW THAT, NATHAN?
I...
I CAN SEE THE HALLWAY BEYOND.
I CAN SEE THROUGH THE DOOR!
NOT THAT THAT'S GOING TO DO US MUCH GOOD.
THIS DOOR IS LOCKED FROM THE OUTSIDE.
HERE... LET ME AT IT.
OKAY, JACK.
BUT BE...

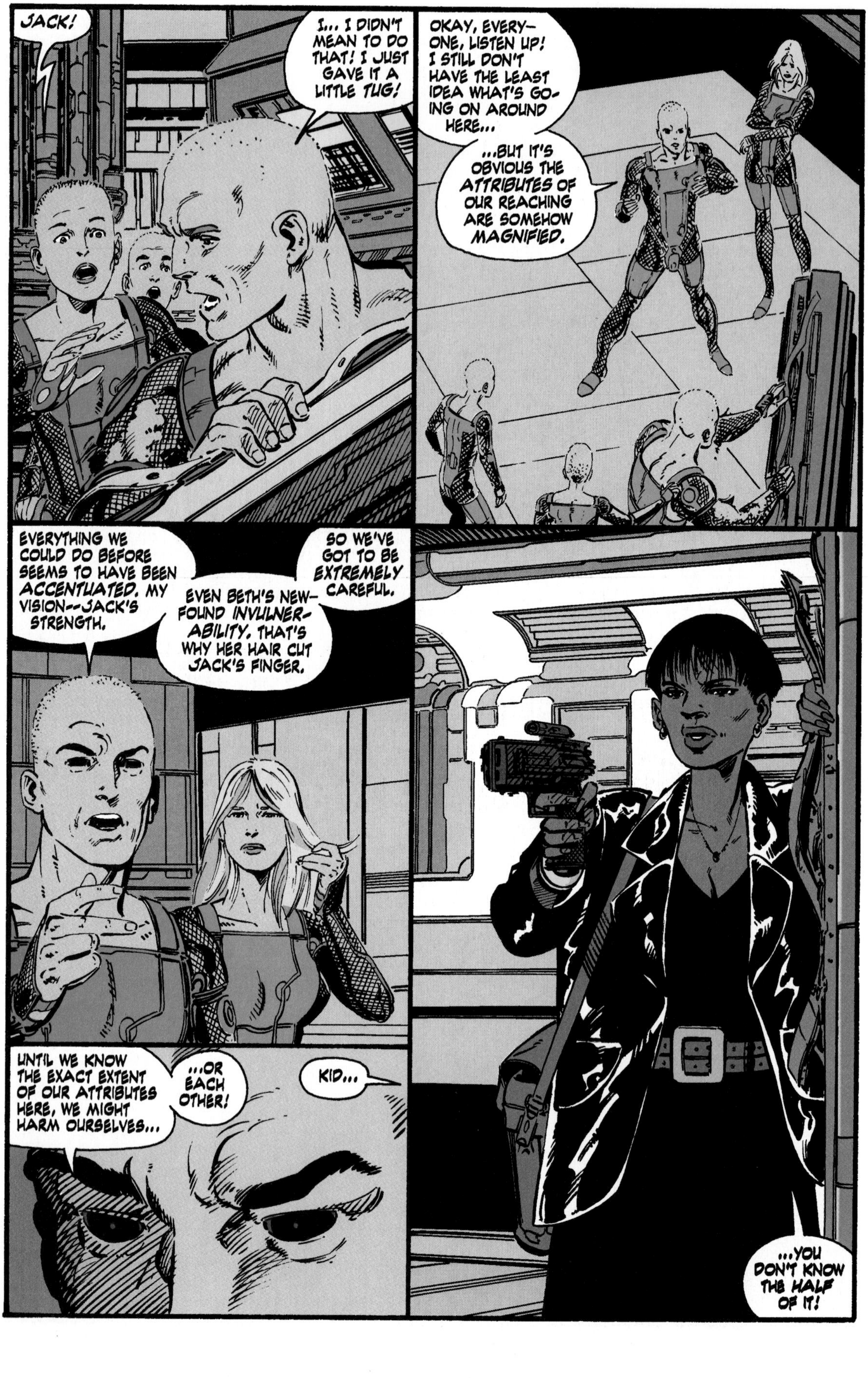
JACK!
I... I DIDN'T MEAN TO DO THAT! I JUST GAVE IT A LITTLE TUG!
OKAY, EVERY-ONE, LISTEN UP! I STILL DON'T HAVE THE LEAST IDEA WHAT'S GO-ING ON AROUND HERE...
...BUT IT'S OBVIOUS THE ATTRIBUTES OF OUR REACHING ARE SOMEHOW MAGNIFIED.
EVERYTHING WE COULD DO BEFORE SEEMS TO HAVE BEEN ACCENTUATED. MY VISION--JACK'S STRENGTH.
EVEN BETH'S NEW-FOUND INVULNER-ABILITY. THAT'S WHY HER HAIR CUT JACK'S FINGER.
SO WE'VE GOT TO BE EXTREMELY CAREFUL.
UNTIL WE KNOW THE EXACT EXTENT OF OUR ATTRIBUTES HERE, WE MIGHT HARM OURSELVES...
...OR EACH OTHER!
KID...
...YOU DON'T KNOW THE HALF OF IT!

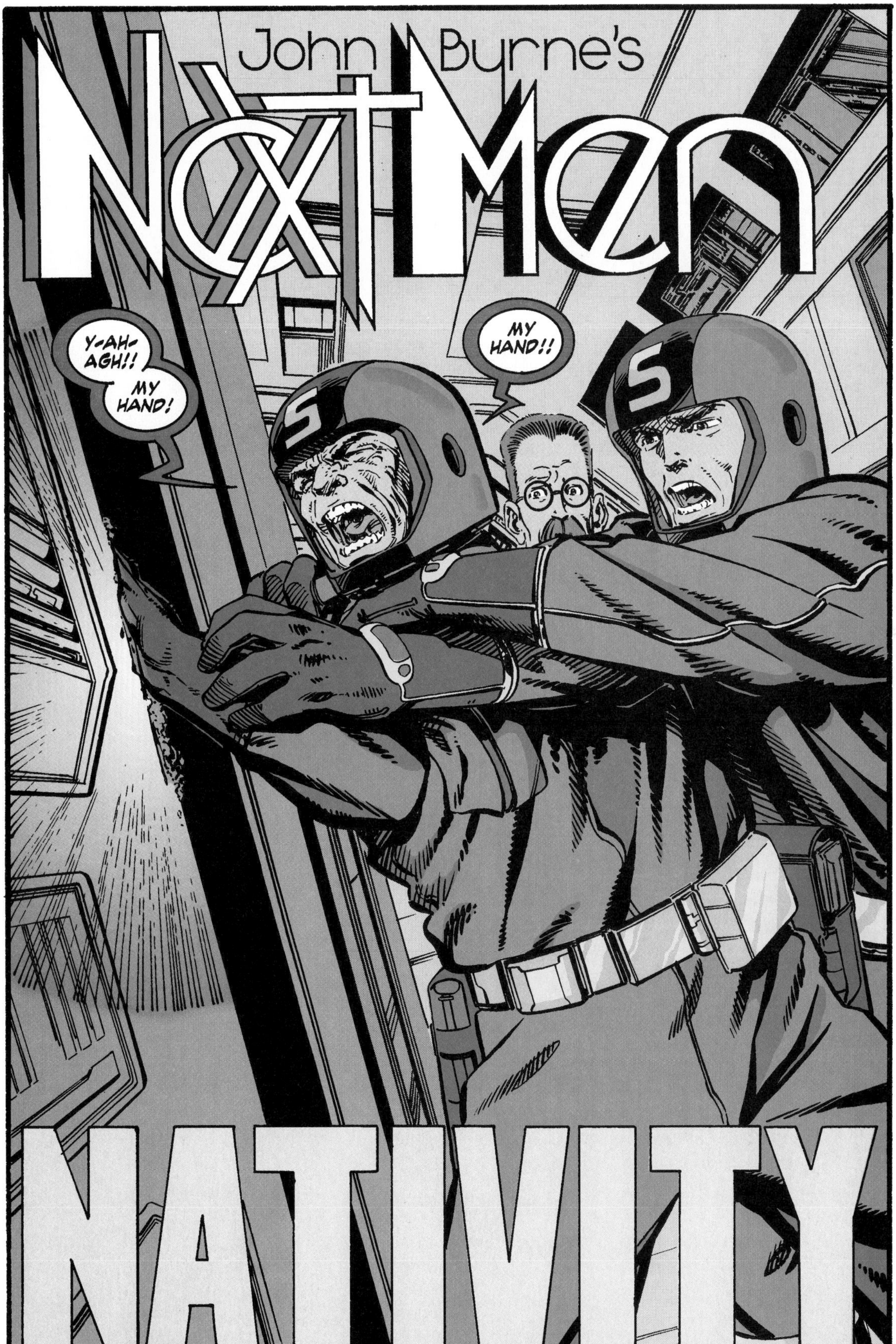
John Byrne's
Next Men
Y-AH-AGH!! MY HAND!
MY HAND!!
NATIVITY

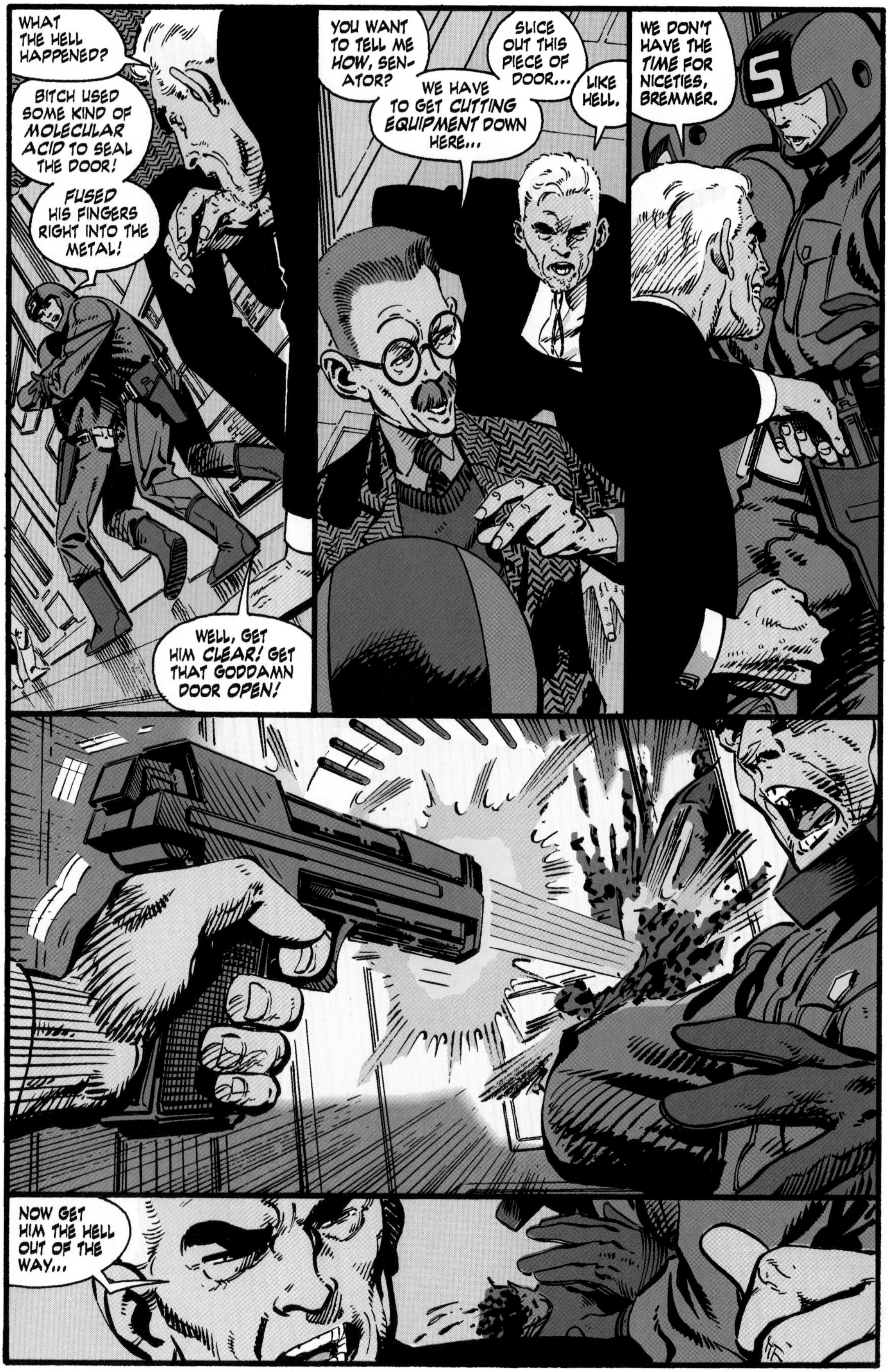
WHAT THE HELL HAPPENED?
BITCH USED SOME KIND OF MOLECULAR ACID TO SEAL THE DOOR!
FUSED HIS FINGERS RIGHT INTO THE METAL!
WELL, GET HIM CLEAR! GET THAT GODDAMN DOOR OPEN!
YOU WANT TO TELL ME HOW, SEN-ATOR?
WE HAVE TO GET CUTTING EQUIPMENT DOWN HERE...
SLICE OUT THIS PIECE OF DOOR...
LIKE HELL.
WE DON'T HAVE THE TIME FOR NICETIES, BREMMER.
NOW GET HIM THE HELL OUT OF THE WAY...

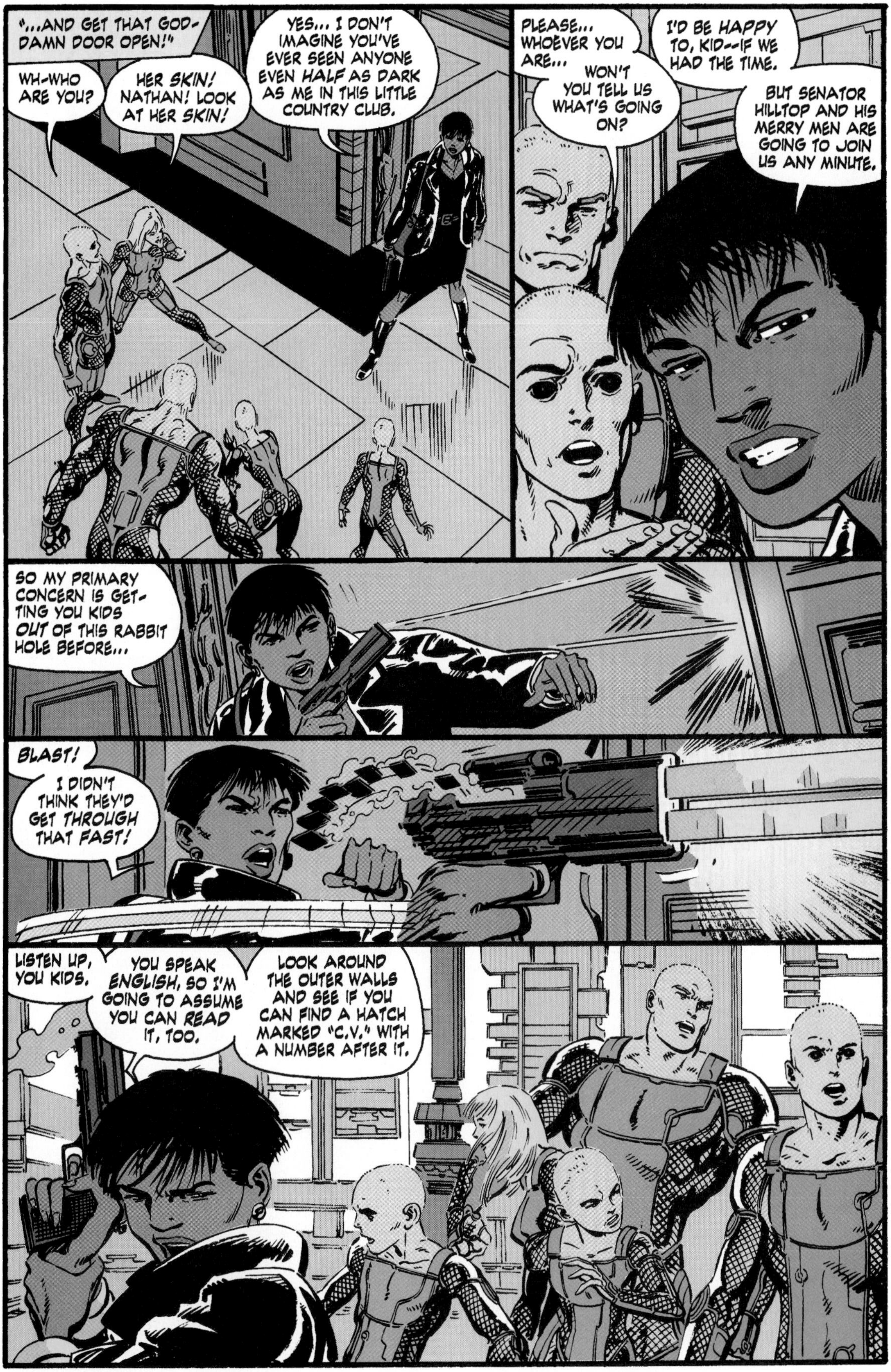
"...AND GET THAT GOD-DAMN DOOR OPEN!"
WH-WHO ARE YOU?
HER SKIN! NATHAN! LOOK AT HER SKIN!
YES... I DON'T IMAGINE YOU'VE EVER SEEN ANYONE EVEN HALF AS DARK AS ME IN THIS LITTLE COUNTRY CLUB.
PLEASE... WHOEVER YOU ARE...
WON'T YOU TELL US WHAT'S GOING ON?
I'D BE HAPPY TO, KID--IF WE HAD THE TIME.
BUT SENATOR HILLTOP AND HIS MERRY MEN ARE GOING TO JOIN US ANY MINUTE.
SO MY PRIMARY CONCERN IS GETTING YOU KIDS OUT OF THIS RABBIT HOLE BEFORE...
BLAST!
I DIDN'T THINK THEY'D GET THROUGH THAT FAST!
LISTEN UP, YOU KIDS.
YOU SPEAK ENGLISH, SO I'M GOING TO ASSUME YOU CAN READ IT, TOO.
LOOK AROUND THE OUTER WALLS AND SEE IF YOU CAN FIND A HATCH MARKED "C.V." WITH A NUMBER AFTER IT.

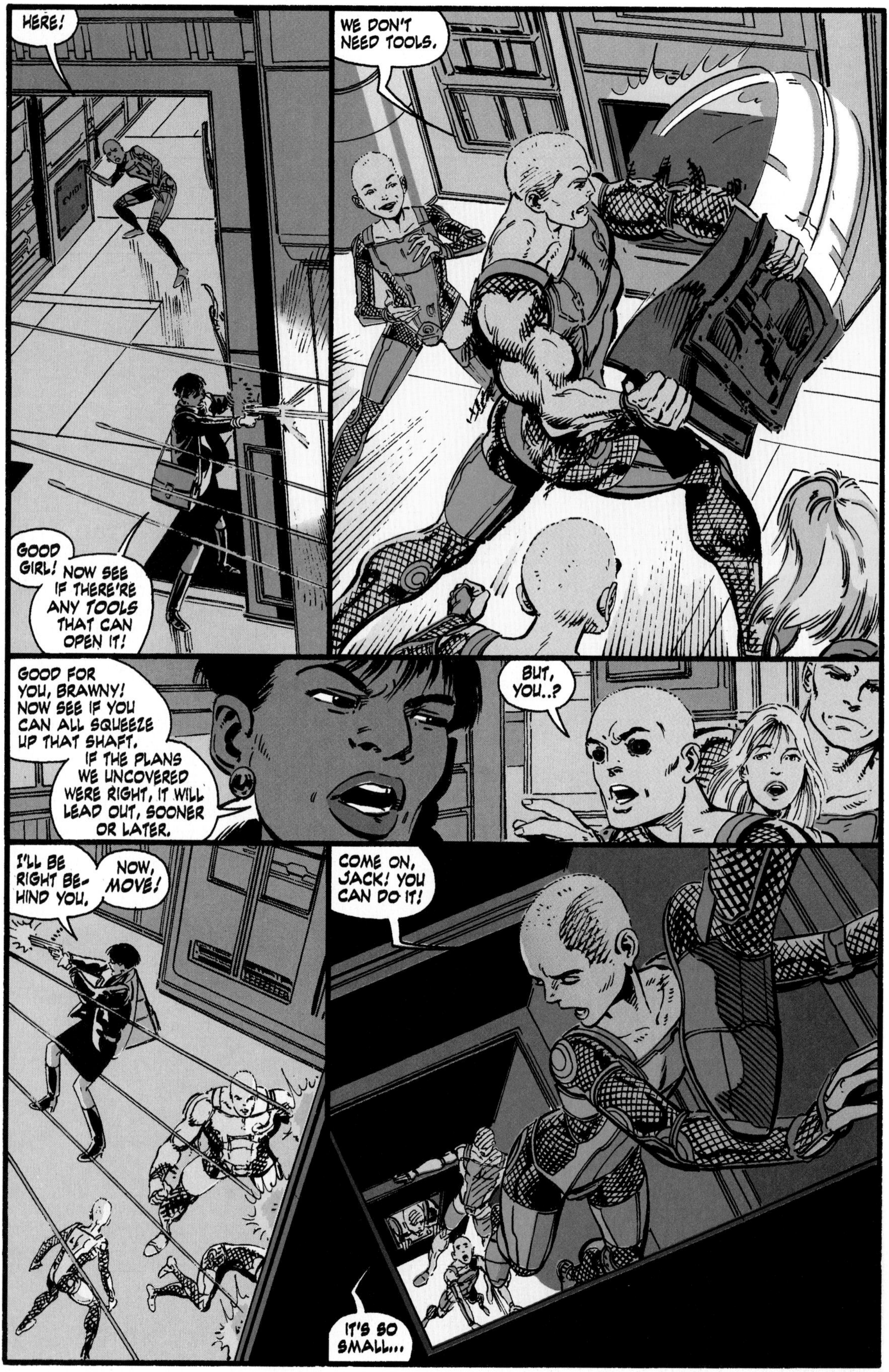
HERE!
GOOD GIRL!
NOW SEE IF THERE'RE ANY TOOLS THAT CAN OPEN IT!
WE DON'T NEED TOOLS.
GOOD FOR YOU, BRAWNY! NOW SEE IF YOU CAN ALL SQUEEZE UP THAT SHAFT.
IF THE PLANS WE UNCOVERED WERE RIGHT, IT WILL LEAD OUT, SOONER OR LATER.
BUT, YOU..?
I'LL BE RIGHT BEHIND YOU.
NOW, MOVE!
COME ON, JACK! YOU CAN DO IT!
IT'S SO SMALL...

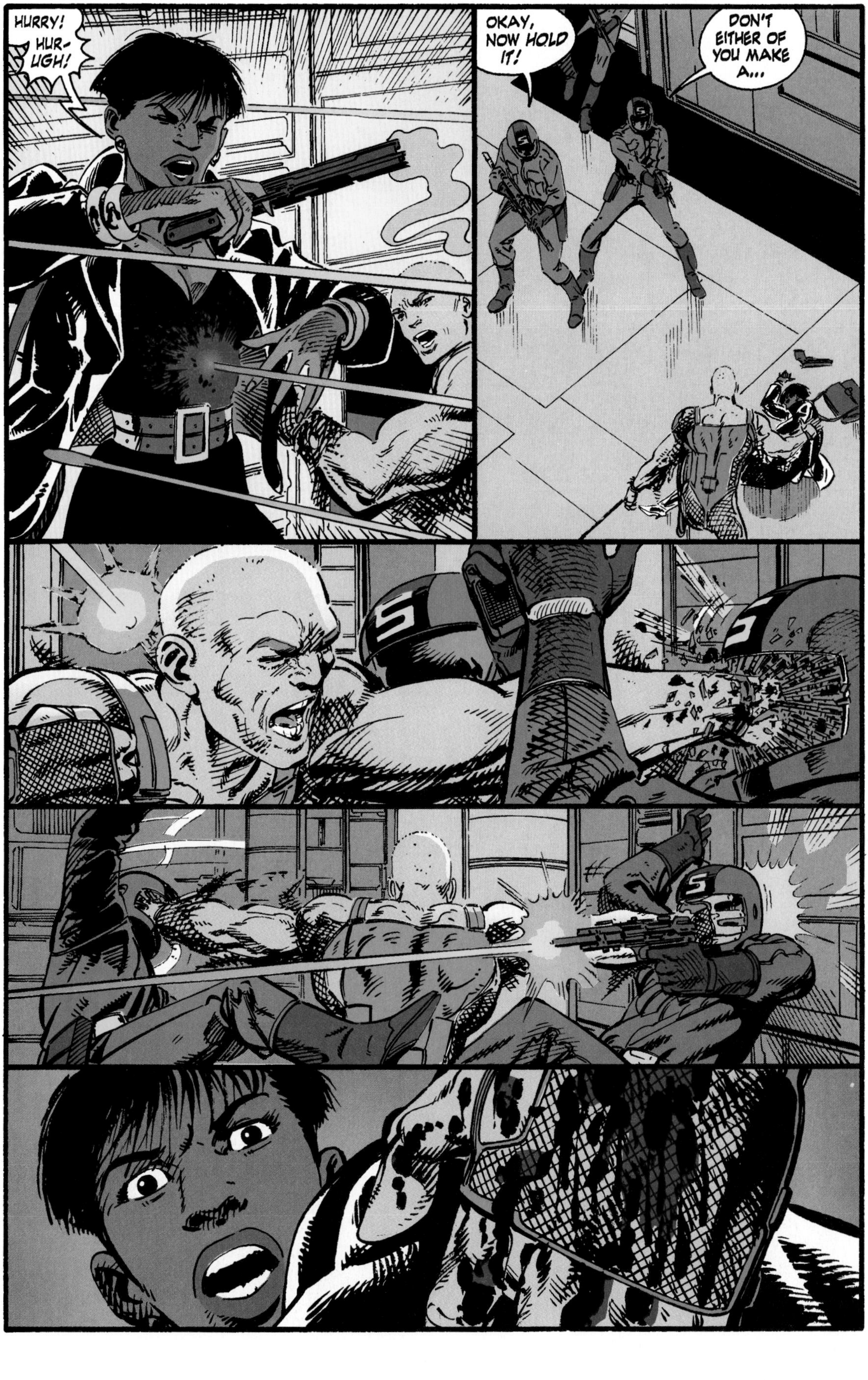
HURRY! HUR-UGH!
OKAY, NOW HOLD IT!
DON'T EITHER OF YOU MAKE A...

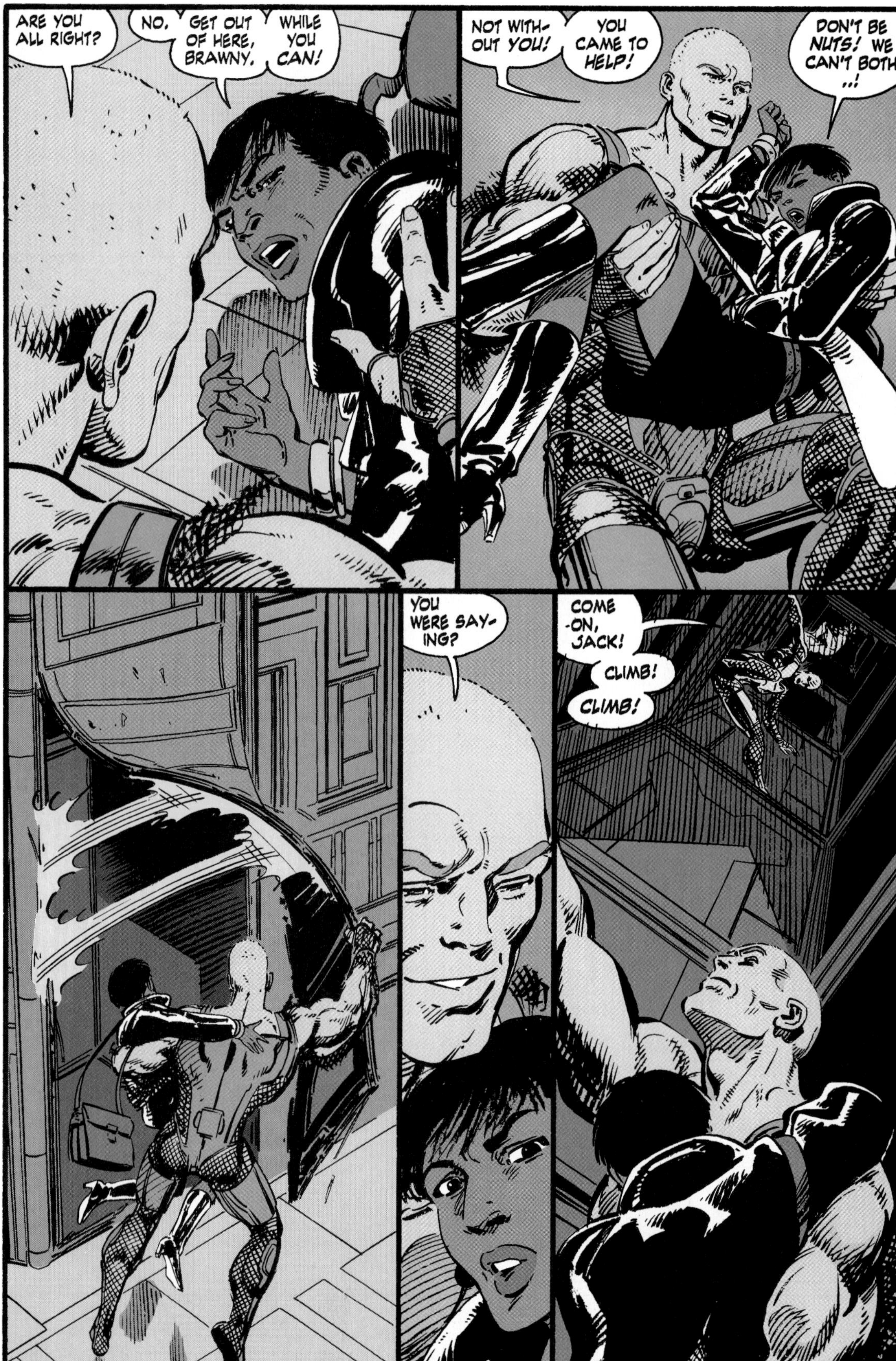
ARE YOU ALL RIGHT?
NO.
GET OUT OF HERE, BRAWNY.
WHILE YOU CAN!
NOT WITH-OUT YOU!
YOU CAME TO HELP!
DON'T BE NUTS! WE CAN'T BOTH ..!
YOU WERE SAY-ING?
COME -ON, JACK!
CLIMB!
CLIMB!

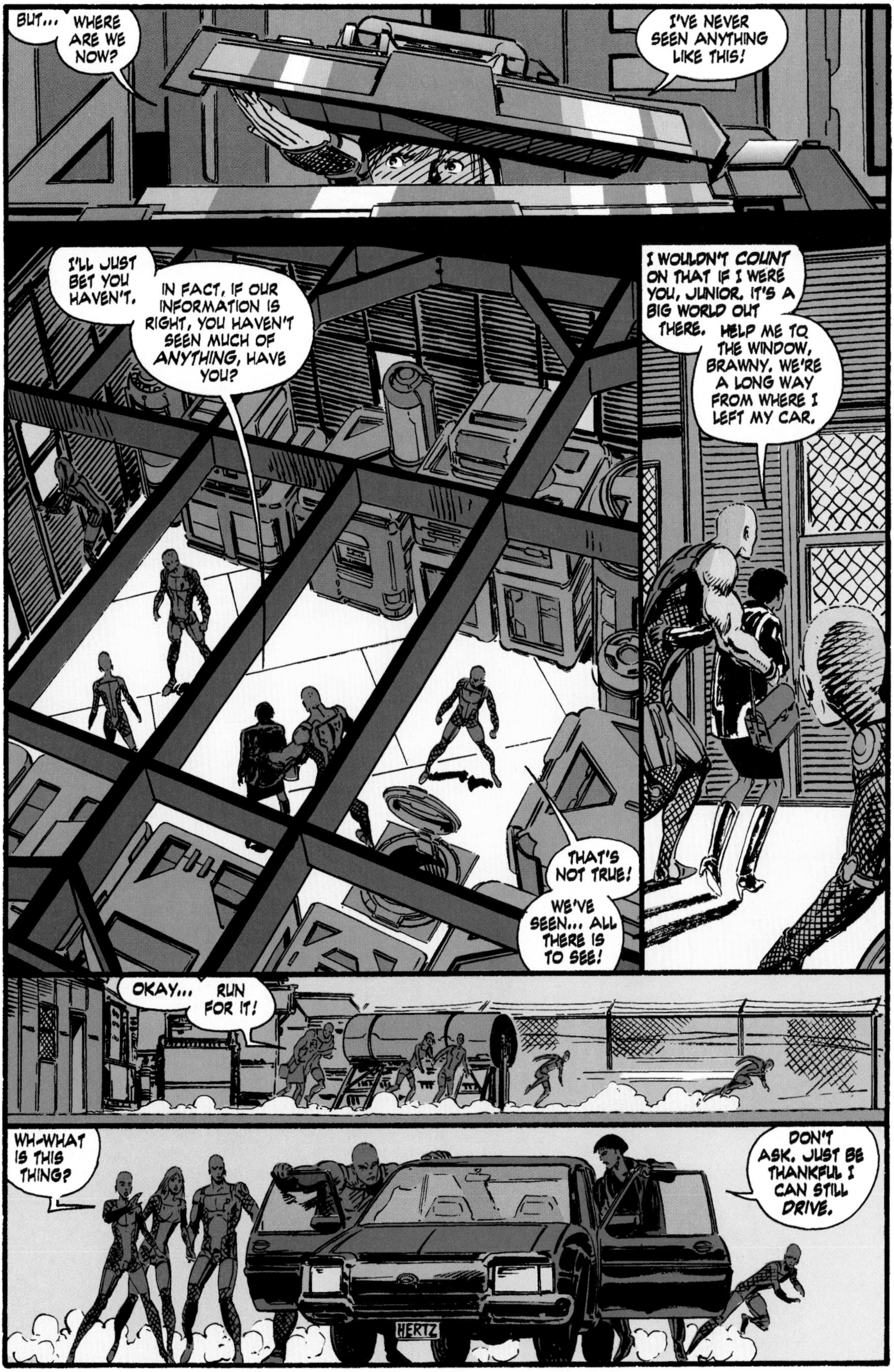

BUT... WHERE ARE WE NOW?
I'VE NEVER SEEN ANYTHING LIKE THIS!
I'LL JUST BET YOU HAVEN'T.
IN FACT, IF OUR INFORMATION IS RIGHT, YOU HAVEN'T SEEN MUCH OF ANYTHING, HAVE YOU?
THAT'S NOT TRUE!
WE'VE SEEN... ALL THERE IS TO SEE!
I WOULDN'T COUNT ON THAT IF I WERE YOU, JUNIOR. IT'S A BIG WORLD OUT THERE.
HELP ME TO THE WINDOW, BRAWNY. WE'RE A LONG WAY FROM WHERE I LEFT MY CAR.
OKAY...
RUN FOR IT!
WH-WHAT IS THIS THING?
DON'T ASK. JUST BE THANKFUL I CAN STILL DRIVE.
HERTZ

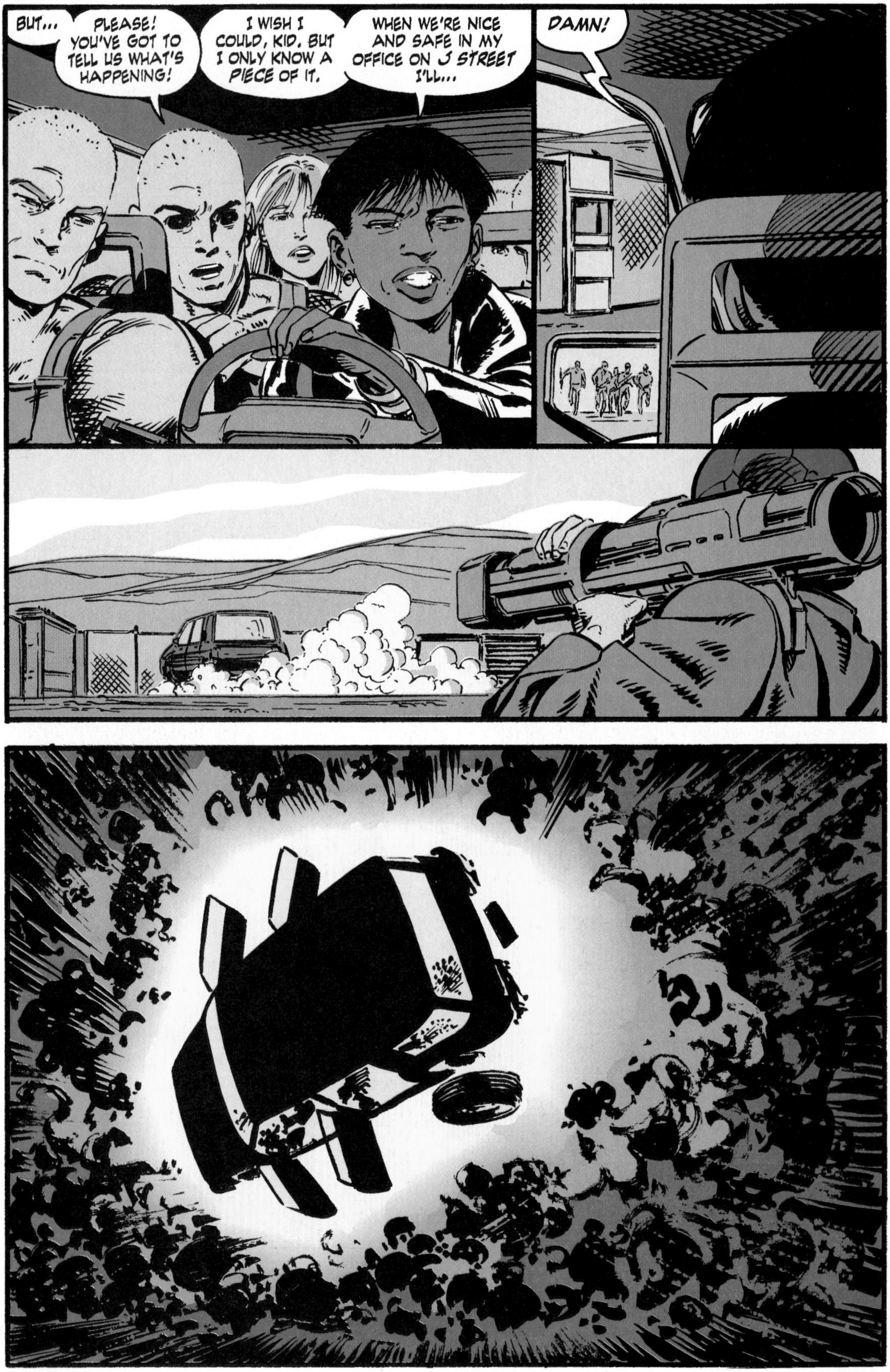
BUT...
PLEASE! YOU'VE GOT TO TELL US WHAT'S HAPPENING!
I WISH I COULD, KID. BUT I ONLY KNOW A PIECE OF IT.
WHEN WE'RE NICE AND SAFE IN MY OFFICE ON J STREET I'LL...
DAMN!

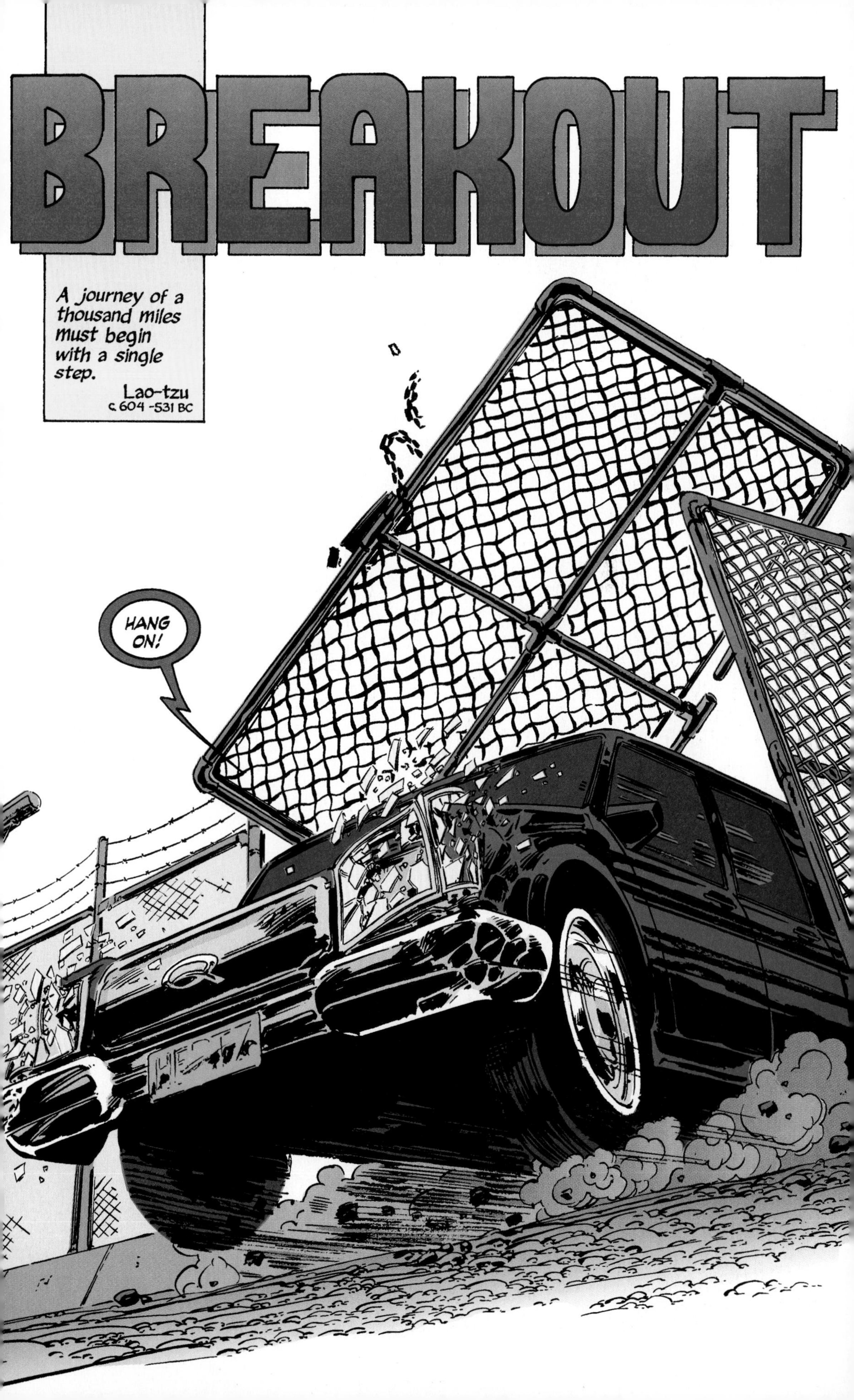
BREAKOUT
A journey of a thousand miles must begin with a single step.
Lao-tzu
c. 604 -531 BC
HANG ON!

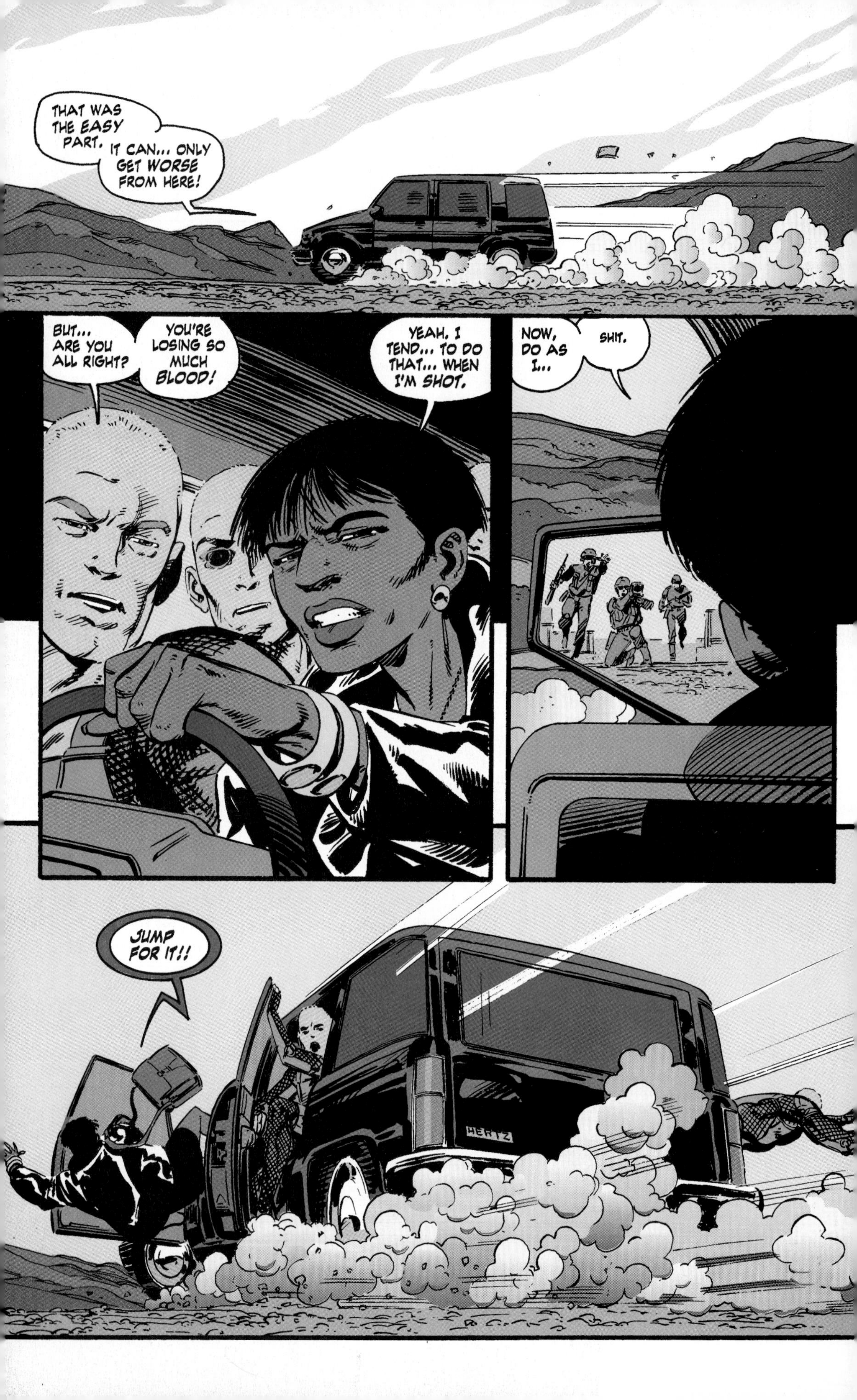
THAT WAS THE EASY PART.
IT CAN... ONLY GET WORSE FROM HERE!
BUT... ARE YOU ALL RIGHT?
YOU'RE LOSING SO MUCH BLOOD!
YEAH, I TEND... TO DO THAT... WHEN I'M SHOT.
NOW, DO AS I...
SHIT.
JUMP FOR IT!!
HERTZ

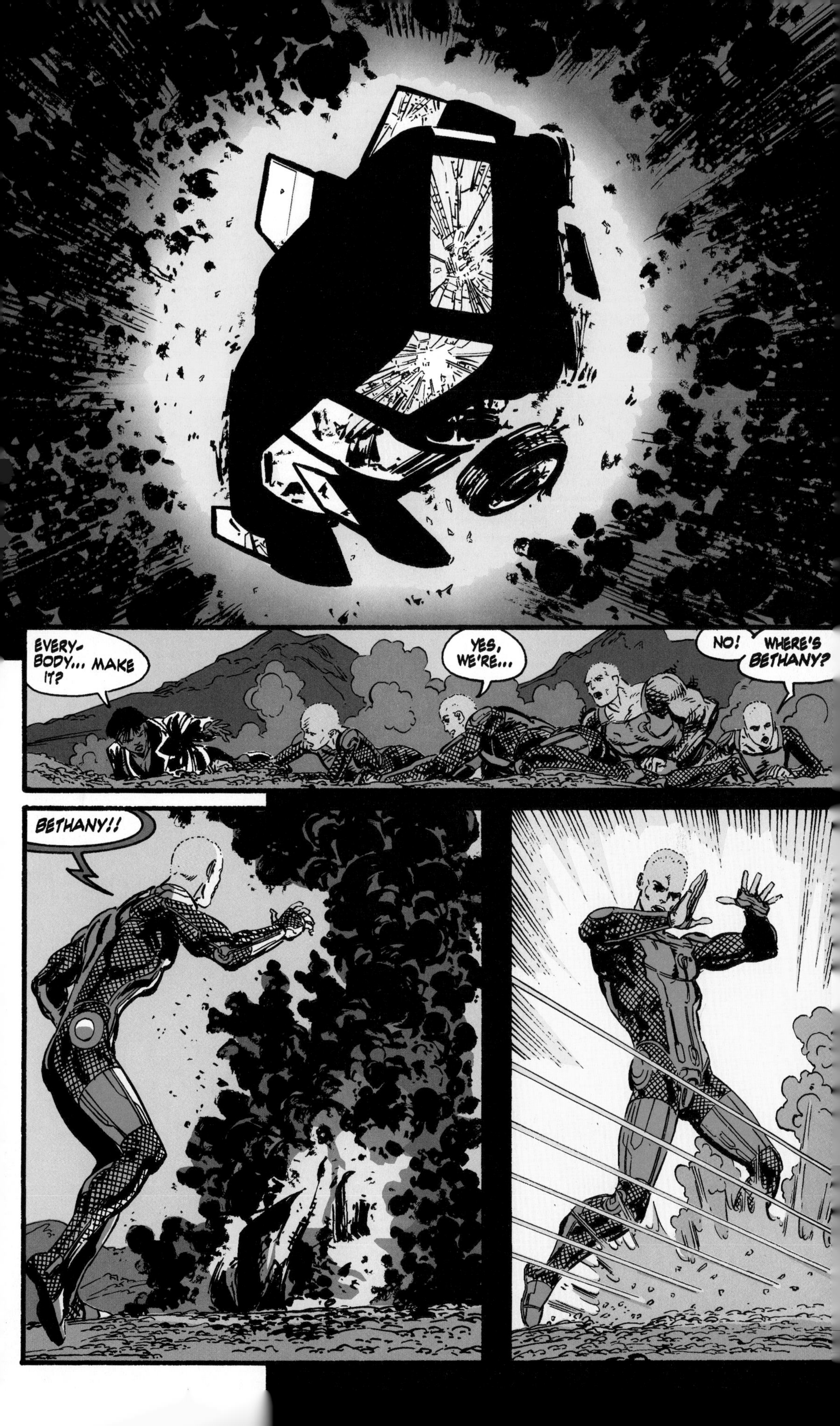
EVERY-BODY... MAKE IT?
YES, WE'RE...
NO! WHERE'S BETHANY?
BETHANY!!

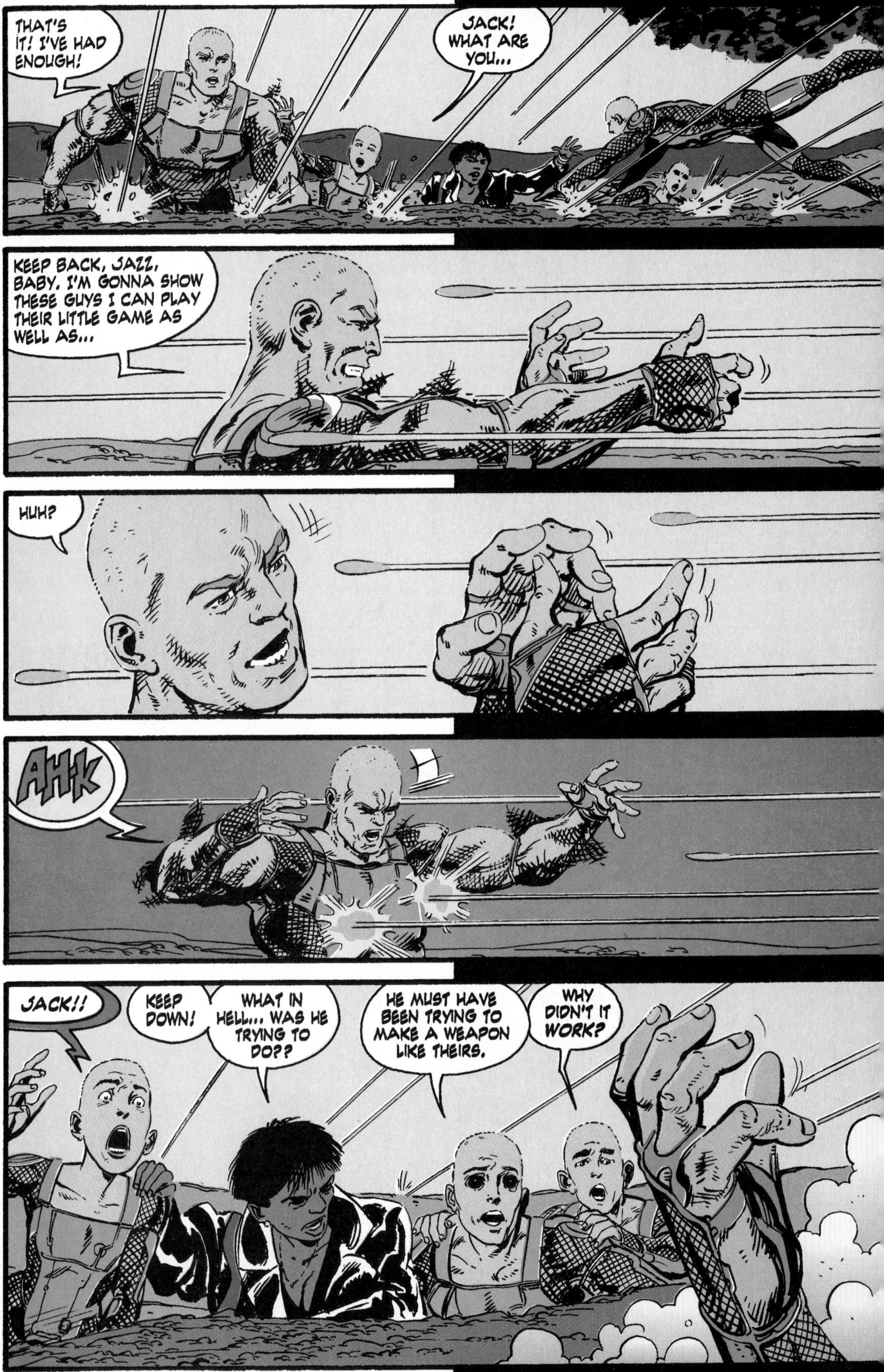
THAT'S IT! I'VE HAD ENOUGH!
JACK! WHAT ARE YOU...
KEEP BACK, JAZZ, BABY. I'M GONNA SHOW THESE GUYS I CAN PLAY THEIR LITTLE GAME AS WELL AS...
HUH?
AH-K
JACK!!
KEEP DOWN!
WHAT IN HELL... WAS HE TRYING TO DO??
HE MUST HAVE BEEN TRYING TO MAKE A WEAPON LIKE THEIRS.
WHY DIDN'T IT WORK?

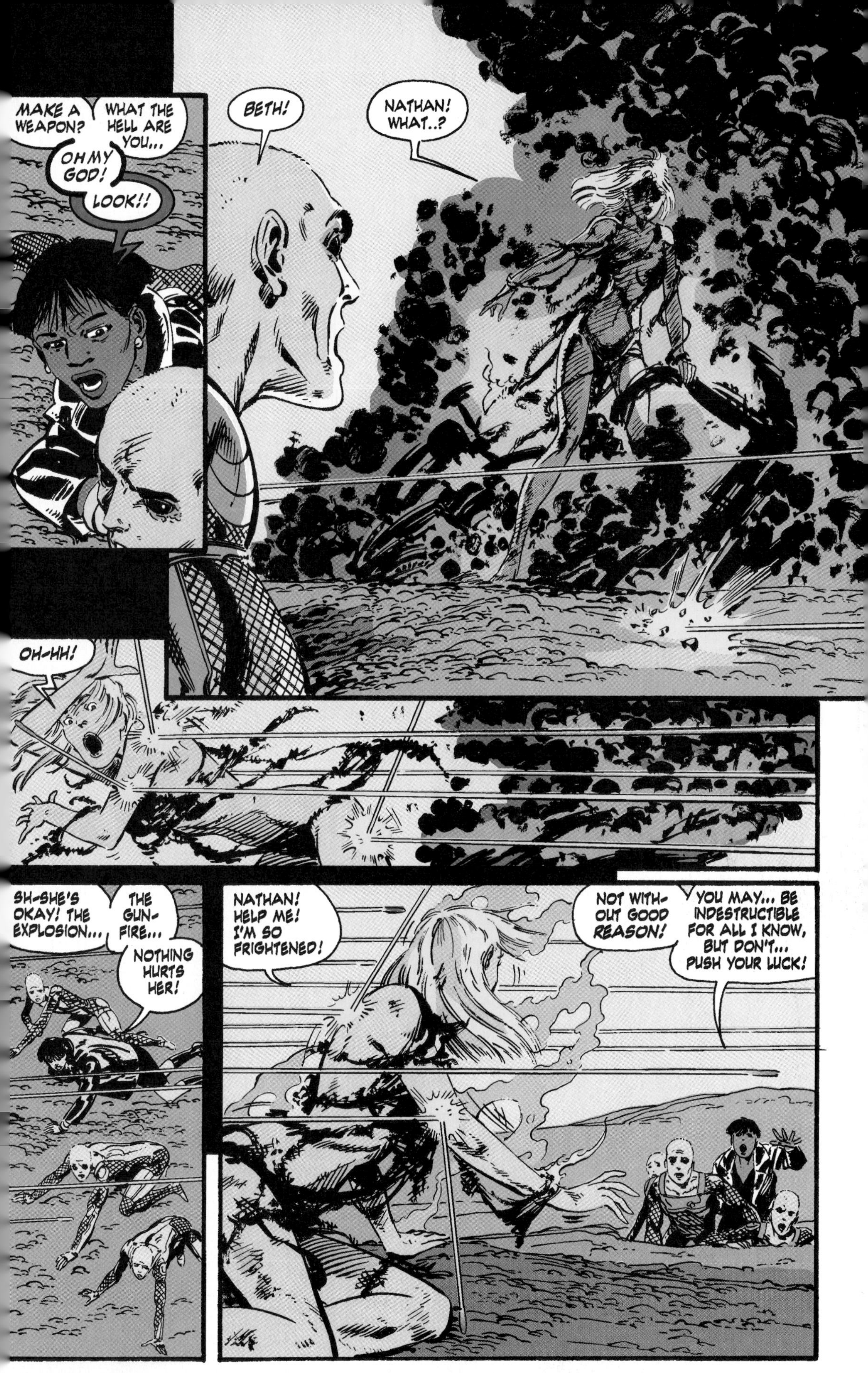
MAKE A WEAPON?
WHAT THE HELL ARE YOU...
OH MY GOD!
LOOK!!
BETH!
NATHAN! WHAT..?
OH-HH!
SH-SHE'S OKAY! THE EXPLOSION...
THE GUN-FIRE...
NOTHING HURTS HER!
NATHAN! HELP ME! I'M SO FRIGHTENED!
NOT WITH-OUT GOOD REASON!
YOU MAY... BE INDESTRUCTIBLE FOR ALL I KNOW, BUT DON'T... PUSH YOUR LUCK!

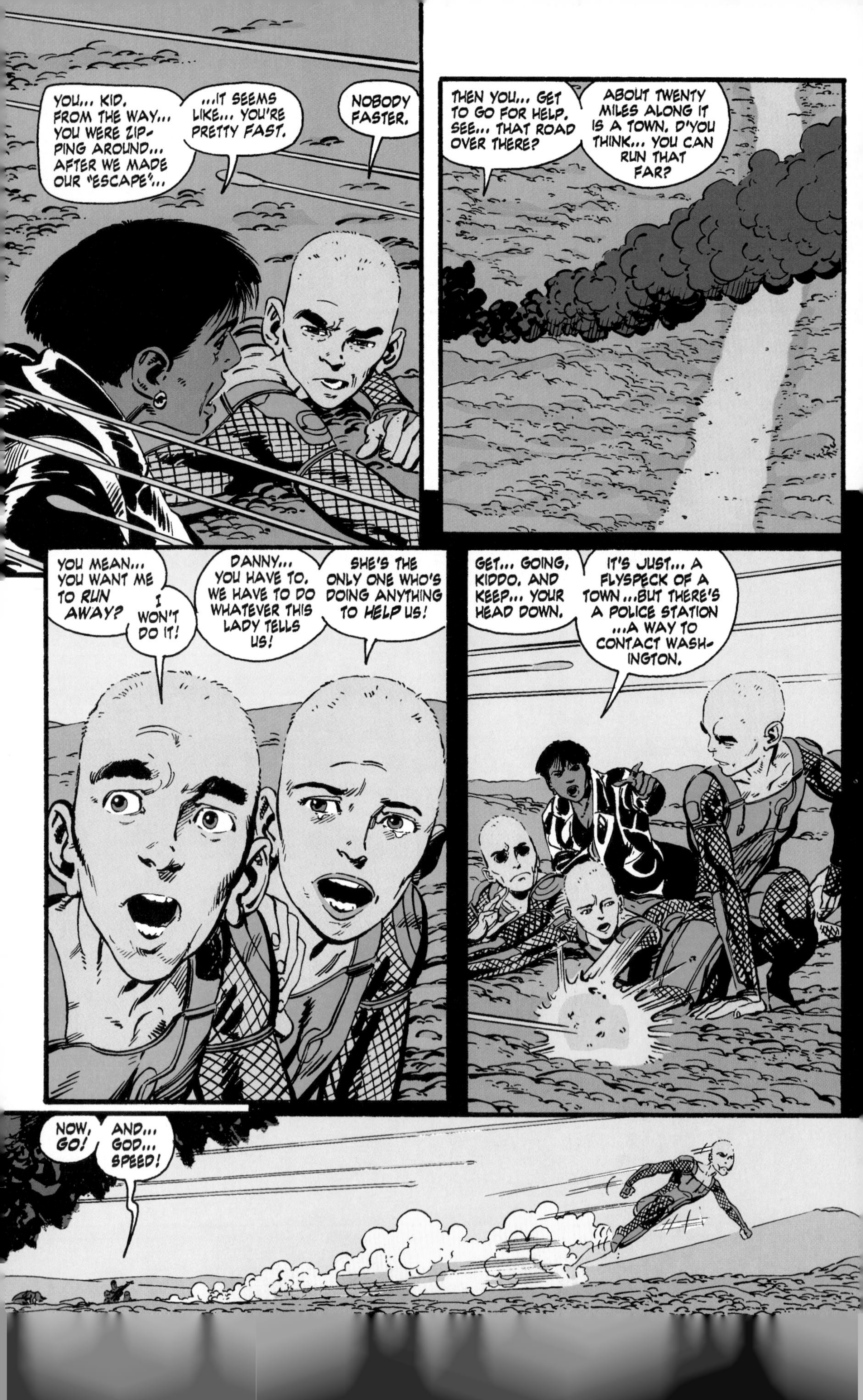
YOU... KID. FROM THE WAY... YOU WERE ZIP-PING AROUND... AFTER WE MADE OUR "ESCAPE"...
...IT SEEMS LIKE... YOU'RE PRETTY FAST.
NOBODY FASTER.
THEN YOU... GET TO GO FOR HELP. SEE... THAT ROAD OVER THERE?
ABOUT TWENTY MILES ALONG IT IS A TOWN. D'YOU THINK... YOU CAN RUN THAT FAR?
YOU MEAN... YOU WANT ME TO RUN AWAY?
I WON'T DO IT!
DANNY... YOU HAVE TO. WE HAVE TO DO WHATEVER THIS LADY TELLS US!
SHE'S THE ONLY ONE WHO'S DOING ANYTHING TO HELP US!
GET... GOING, KIDDO. AND KEEP... YOUR HEAD DOWN.
IT'S JUST... A FLYSPECK OF A TOWN ...BUT THERE'S A POLICE STATION ...A WAY TO CONTACT WASH-INGTON.
NOW, GO!
AND... GOD... SPEED!

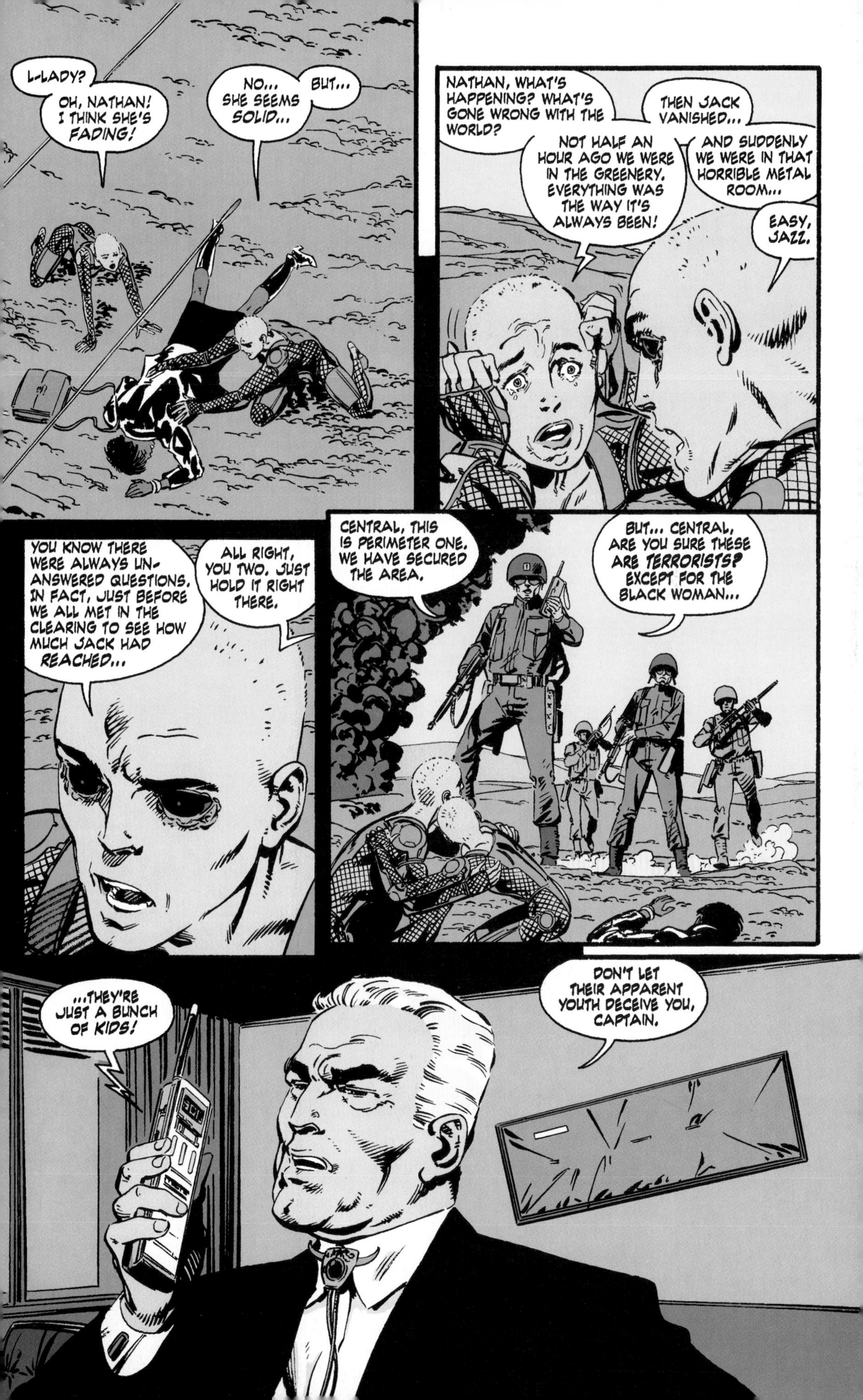
L-LADY?
OH, NATHAN! I THINK SHE'S FADING!
NO... SHE SEEMS SOLID...
BUT...
NATHAN, WHAT'S HAPPENING? WHAT'S GONE WRONG WITH THE WORLD?
NOT HALF AN HOUR AGO WE WERE IN THE GREENERY. EVERYTHING WAS THE WAY IT'S ALWAYS BEEN!
THEN JACK VANISHED...
AND SUDDENLY WE WERE IN THAT HORRIBLE METAL ROOM...
EASY, JAZZ.
YOU KNOW THERE WERE ALWAYS UN-ANSWERED QUESTIONS. IN FACT, JUST BEFORE WE ALL MET IN THE CLEARING TO SEE HOW MUCH JACK HAD REACHED...
ALL RIGHT, YOU TWO. JUST HOLD IT RIGHT THERE.
CENTRAL, THIS IS PERIMETER ONE. WE HAVE SECURED THE AREA.
BUT... CENTRAL, ARE YOU SURE THESE ARE TERRORISTS? EXCEPT FOR THE BLACK WOMAN...
...THEY'RE JUST A BUNCH OF KIDS!
DON'T LET THEIR APPARENT YOUTH DECEIVE YOU, CAPTAIN.

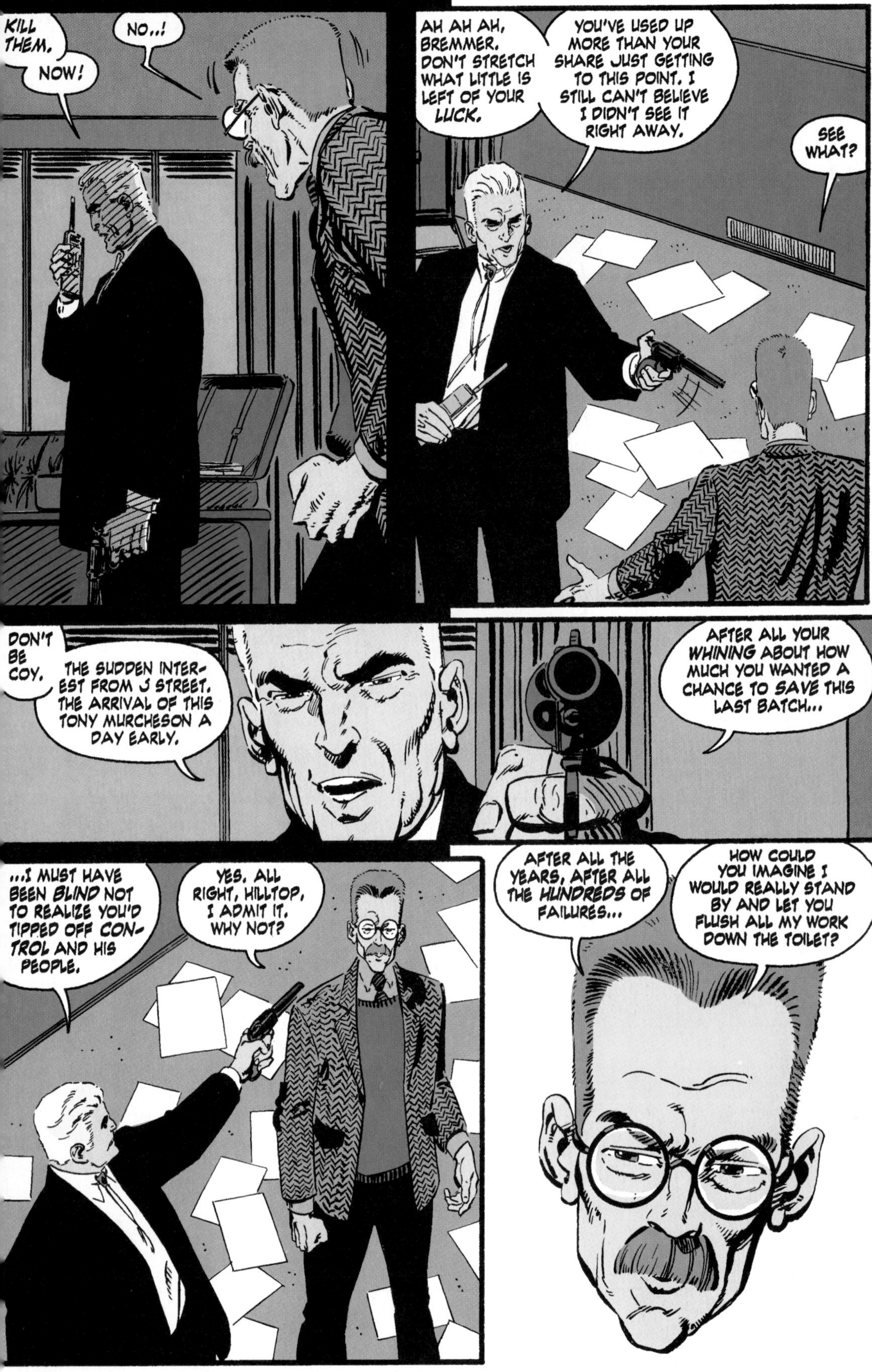
KILL THEM. NOW!
NO..!
AH AH AH, BREMMER. DON'T STRETCH WHAT LITTLE IS LEFT OF YOUR LUCK.
YOU'VE USED UP MORE THAN YOUR SHARE JUST GETTING TO THIS POINT. I STILL CAN'T BELIEVE I DIDN'T SEE IT RIGHT AWAY.
SEE WHAT?
DON'T BE COY.
THE SUDDEN INTEREST FROM J STREET. THE ARRIVAL OF THIS TONY MURCHESON A DAY EARLY.
AFTER ALL YOUR WHINING ABOUT HOW MUCH YOU WANTED A CHANCE TO SAVE THIS LAST BATCH...
...I MUST HAVE BEEN BLIND NOT TO REALIZE YOU'D TIPPED OFF CONTROL AND HIS PEOPLE.
YES. ALL RIGHT, HILLTOP, I ADMIT IT. WHY NOT?
AFTER ALL THE YEARS, AFTER ALL THE HUNDREDS OF FAILURES...
HOW COULD YOU IMAGINE I WOULD REALLY STAND BY AND LET YOU FLUSH ALL MY WORK DOWN THE TOILET?

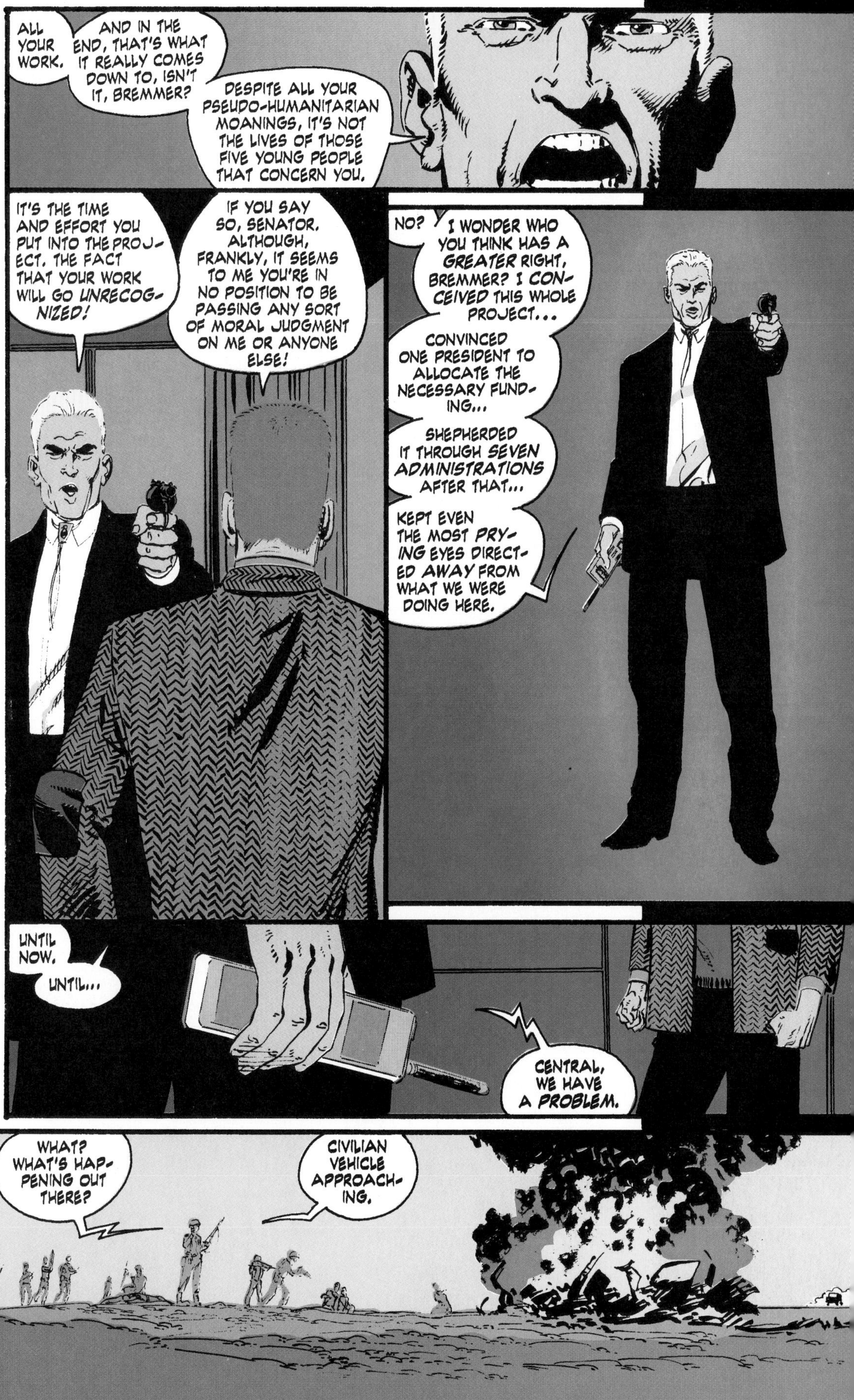
ALL YOUR WORK.
AND IN THE END, THAT'S WHAT IT REALLY COMES DOWN TO, ISN'T IT, BREMMER?
DESPITE ALL YOUR PSEUDO-HUMANITARIAN MOANINGS, IT'S NOT THE LIVES OF THOSE FIVE YOUNG PEOPLE THAT CONCERN YOU.
IT'S THE TIME AND EFFORT YOU PUT INTO THE PROJECT. THE FACT THAT YOUR WORK WILL GO UNRECOGNIZED!
IF YOU SAY SO, SENATOR. ALTHOUGH, FRANKLY, IT SEEMS TO ME YOU'RE IN NO POSITION TO BE PASSING ANY SORT OF MORAL JUDGMENT ON ME OR ANYONE ELSE!
NO?
I WONDER WHO YOU THINK HAS A GREATER RIGHT, BREMMER? I CONCEIVED THIS WHOLE PROJECT...
CONVINCED ONE PRESIDENT TO ALLOCATE THE NECESSARY FUNDING...
SHEPHERDED IT THROUGH SEVEN ADMINISTRATIONS AFTER THAT...
KEPT EVEN THE MOST PRYING EYES DIRECTED AWAY FROM WHAT WE WERE DOING HERE.
UNTIL NOW.
UNTIL...
CENTRAL, WE HAVE A PROBLEM.
WHAT? WHAT'S HAPPENING OUT THERE?
CIVILIAN VEHICLE APPROACHING.

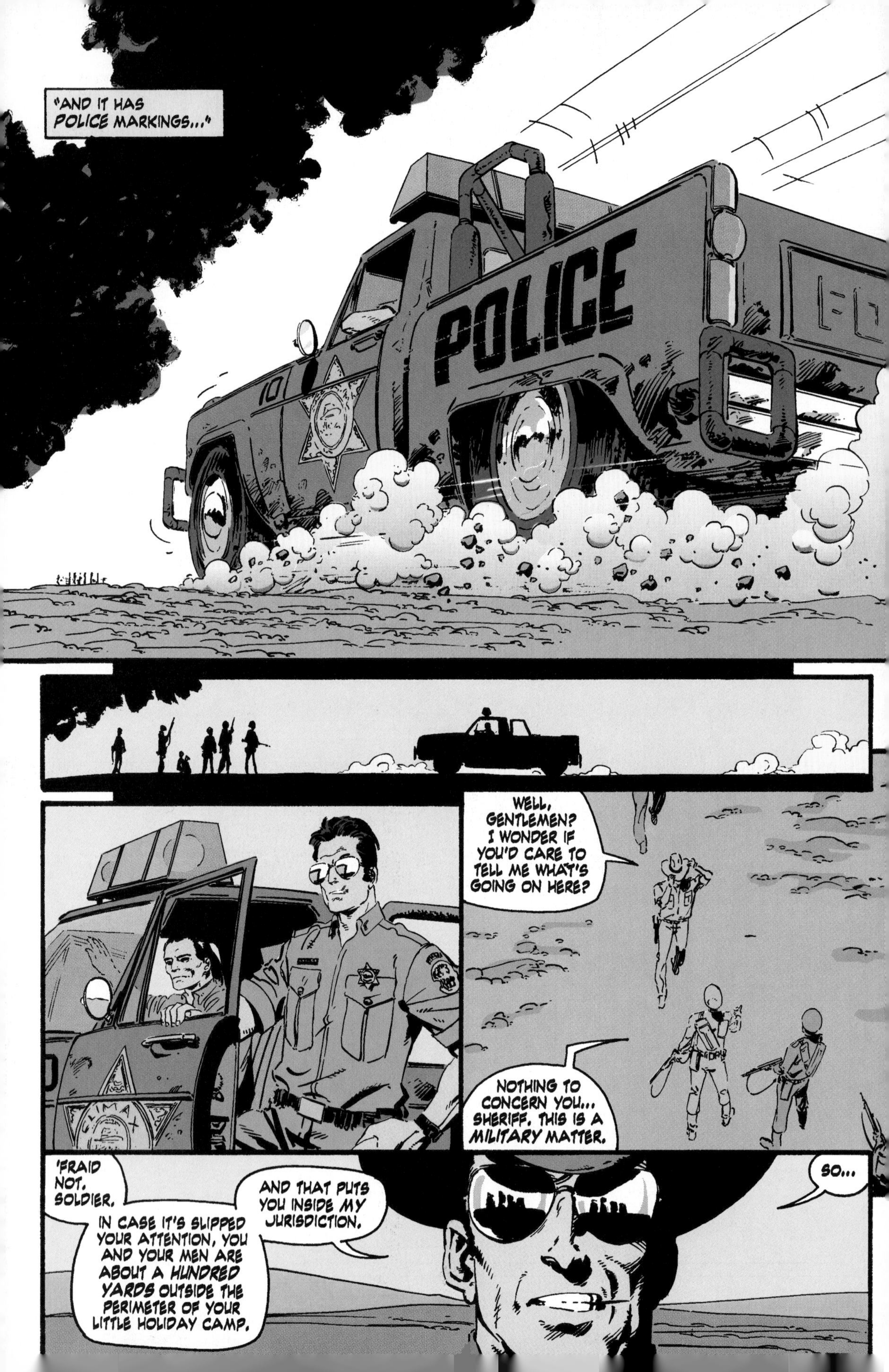
"AND IT HAS POLICE MARKINGS..."
POLICE
101
WELL, GENTLEMEN? I WONDER IF YOU'D CARE TO TELL ME WHAT'S GOING ON HERE?
NOTHING TO CONCERN YOU... SHERIFF. THIS IS A MILITARY MATTER.
'FRAID NOT, SOLDIER.
IN CASE IT'S SLIPPED YOUR ATTENTION, YOU AND YOUR MEN ARE ABOUT A HUNDRED YARDS OUTSIDE THE PERIMETER OF YOUR LITTLE HOLIDAY CAMP.
AND THAT PUTS YOU INSIDE MY JURISDICTION.
SO...

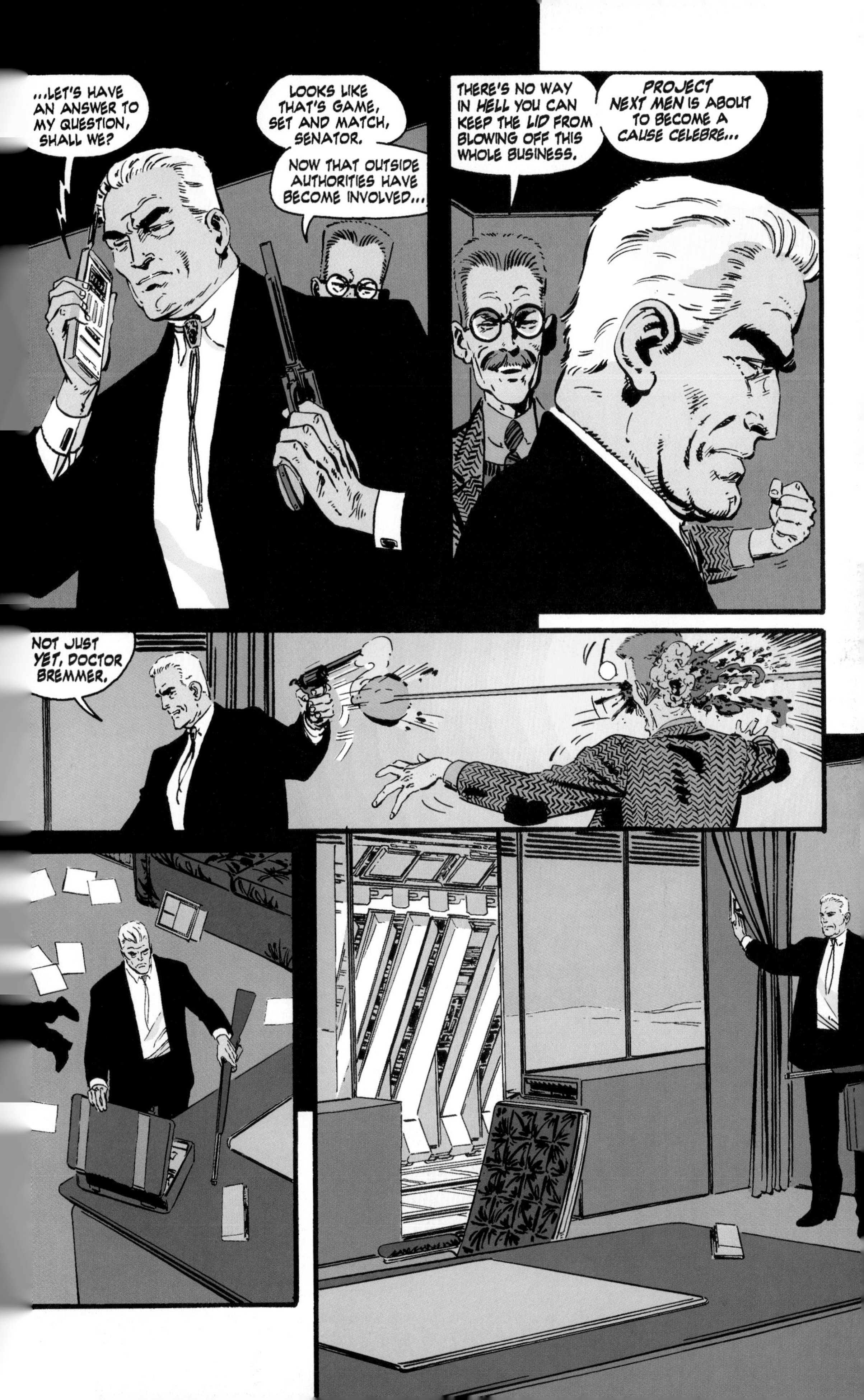
...LET'S HAVE AN ANSWER TO MY QUESTION, SHALL WE?
LOOKS LIKE THAT'S GAME, SET AND MATCH, SENATOR.
NOW THAT OUTSIDE AUTHORITIES HAVE BECOME INVOLVED...
THERE'S NO WAY IN HELL YOU CAN KEEP THE LID FROM BLOWING OFF THIS WHOLE BUSINESS.
PROJECT NEXT MEN IS ABOUT TO BECOME A CAUSE CELEBRE...
NOT JUST YET, DOCTOR BREMMER.

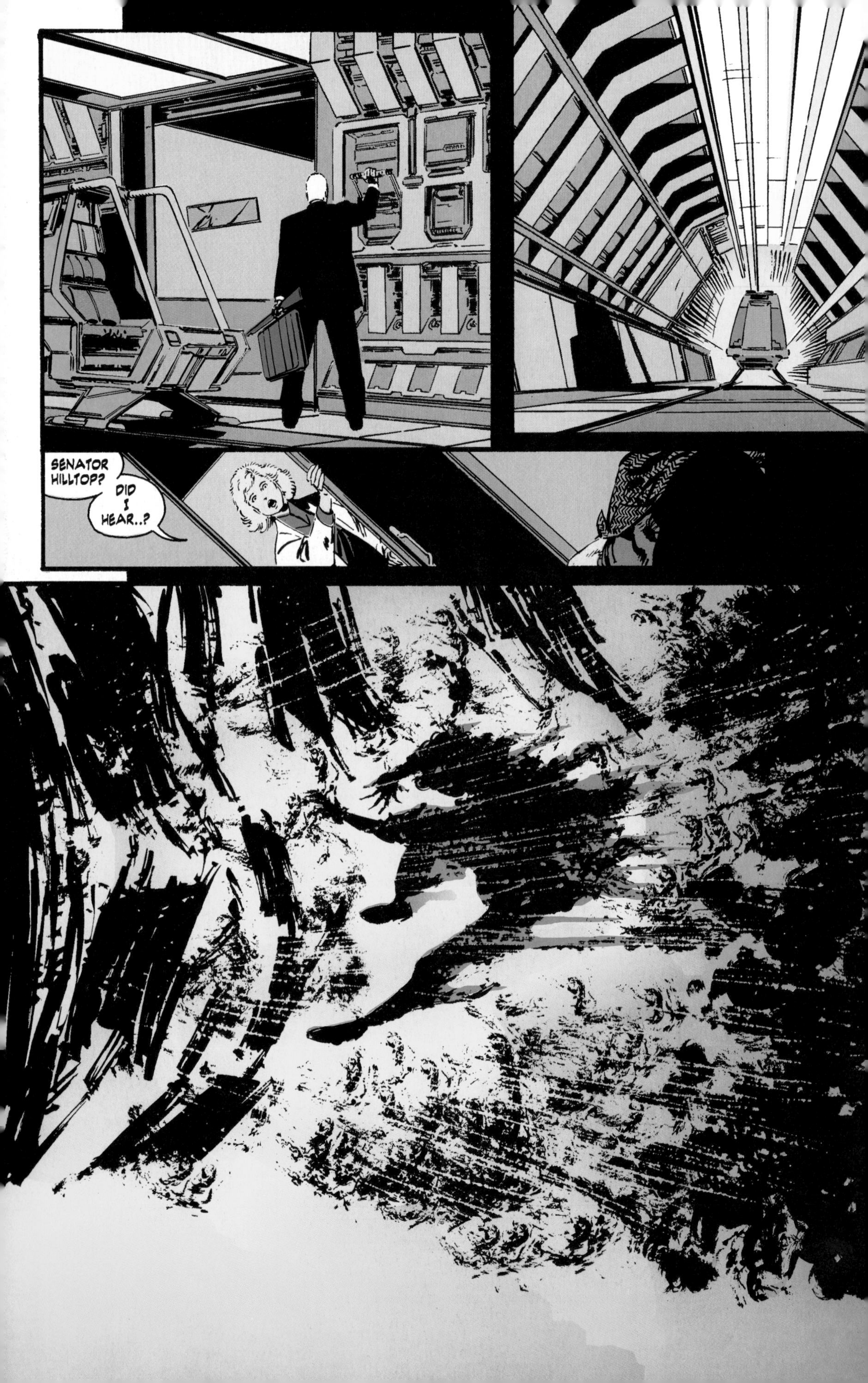
SENATOR HILLTOP?
DID I HEAR..?

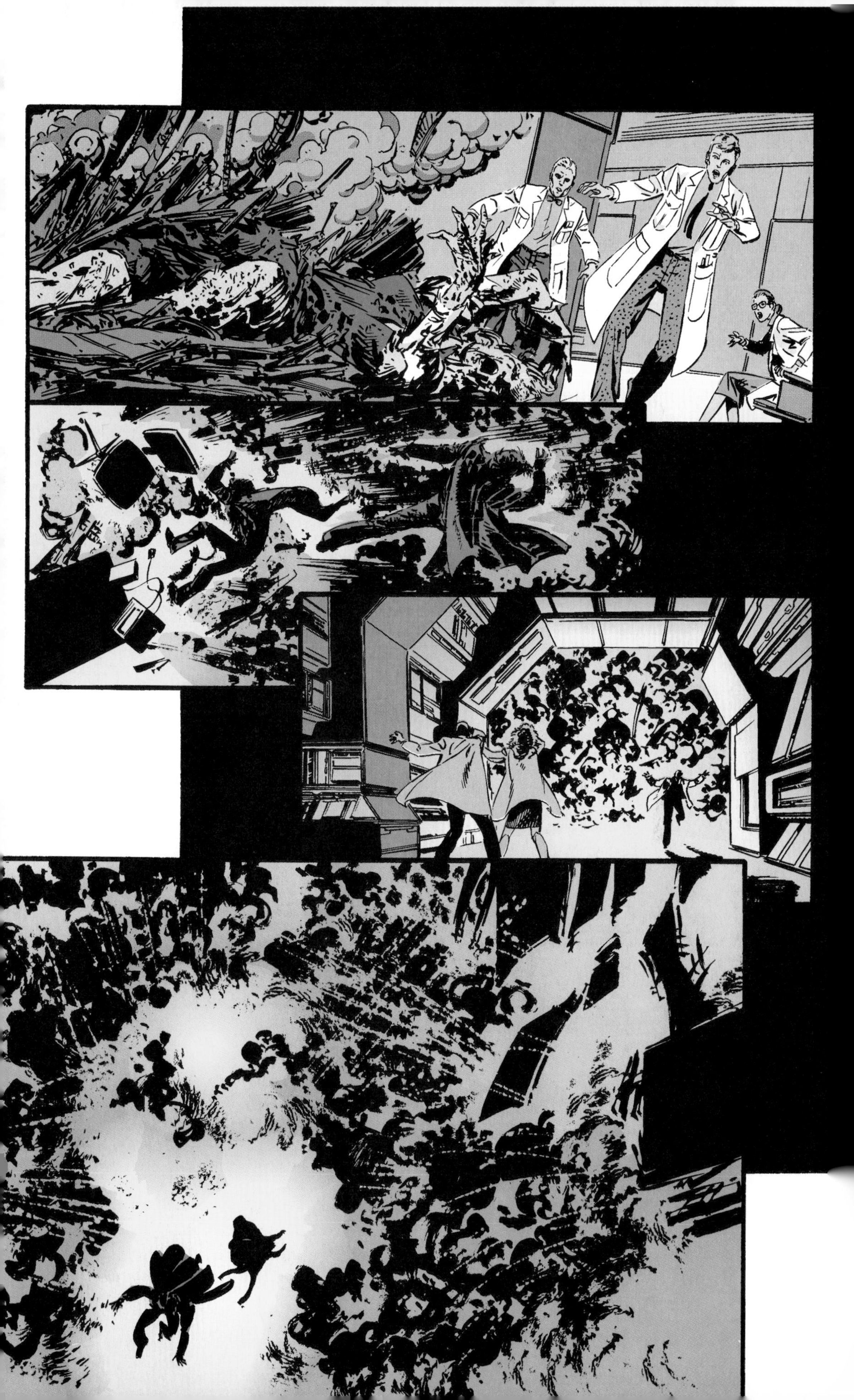

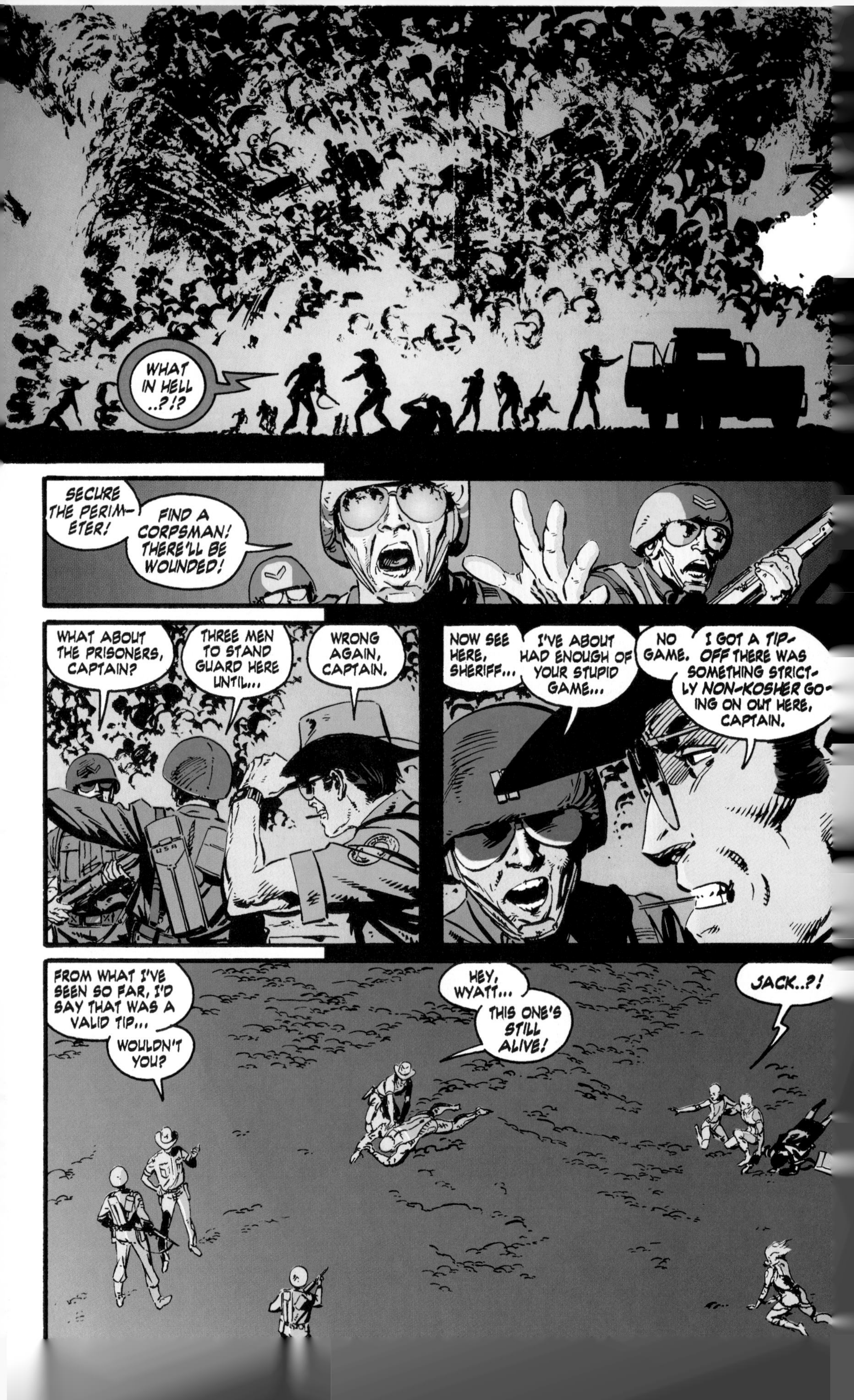
WHAT IN HELL ..?!?
SECURE THE PERIMETER!
FIND A CORPSMAN! THERE'LL BE WOUNDED!
WHAT ABOUT THE PRISONERS, CAPTAIN?
THREE MEN TO STAND GUARD HERE UNTIL...
WRONG AGAIN, CAPTAIN.
NOW SEE HERE, SHERIFF...
I'VE ABOUT HAD ENOUGH OF YOUR STUPID GAME...
NO GAME.
I GOT A TIP-OFF THERE WAS SOMETHING STRICTLY NON-KOSHER GOING ON OUT HERE, CAPTAIN.
FROM WHAT I'VE SEEN SO FAR, I'D SAY THAT WAS A VALID TIP...
WOULDN'T YOU?
HEY, WYATT...
THIS ONE'S STILL ALIVE!
JACK..?!

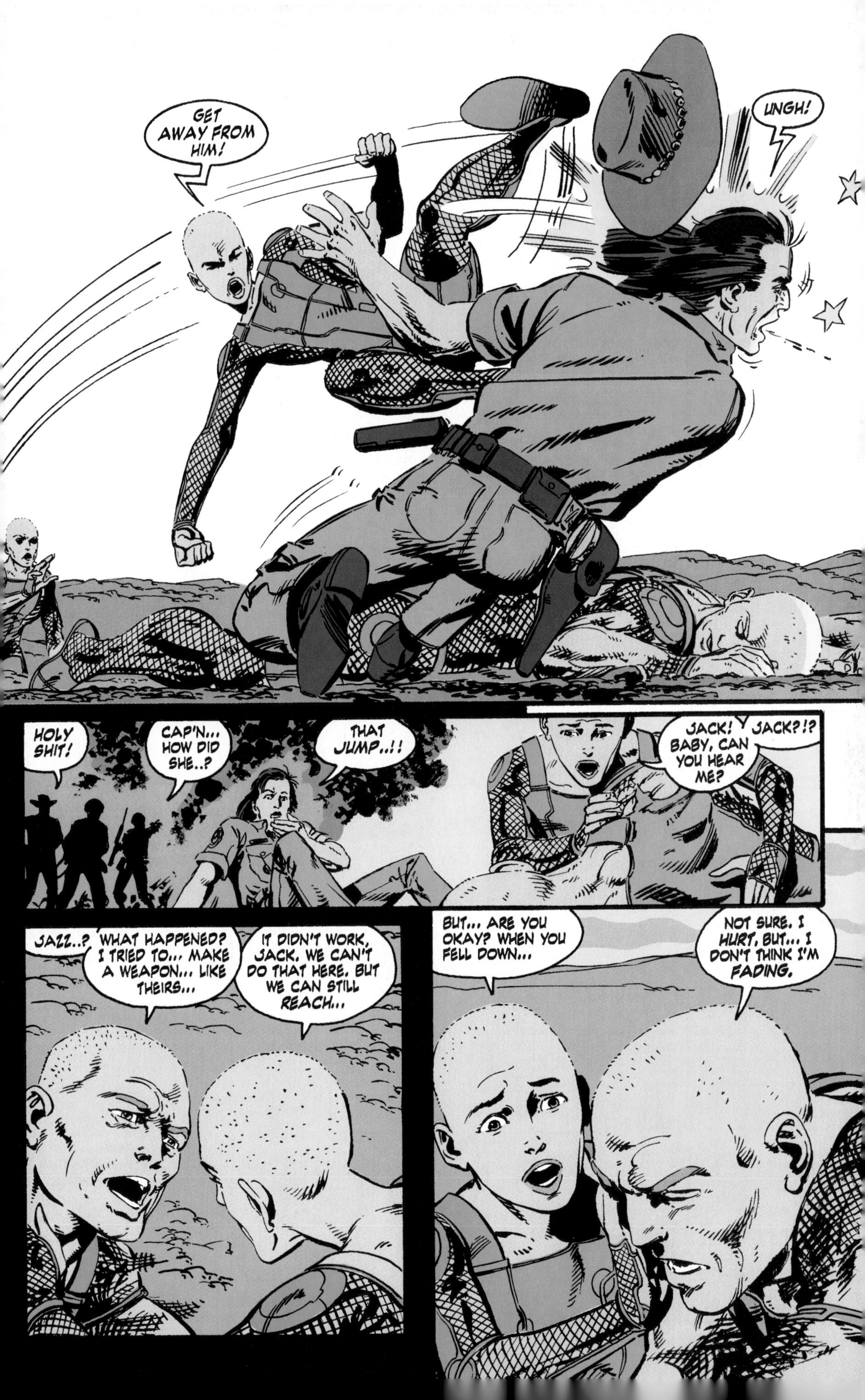
GET AWAY FROM HIM!
UNGH!
HOLY SHIT!
CAP'N... HOW DID SHE..?
THAT JUMP..!!
JACK! BABY, CAN YOU HEAR ME?
JACK?!?
JAZZ..?
WHAT HAPPENED? I TRIED TO... MAKE A WEAPON... LIKE THEIRS...
IT DIDN'T WORK, JACK. WE CAN'T DO THAT HERE. BUT WE CAN STILL REACH...
BUT... ARE YOU OKAY? WHEN YOU FELL DOWN...
NOT SURE. I HURT, BUT... I DON'T THINK I'M FADING.

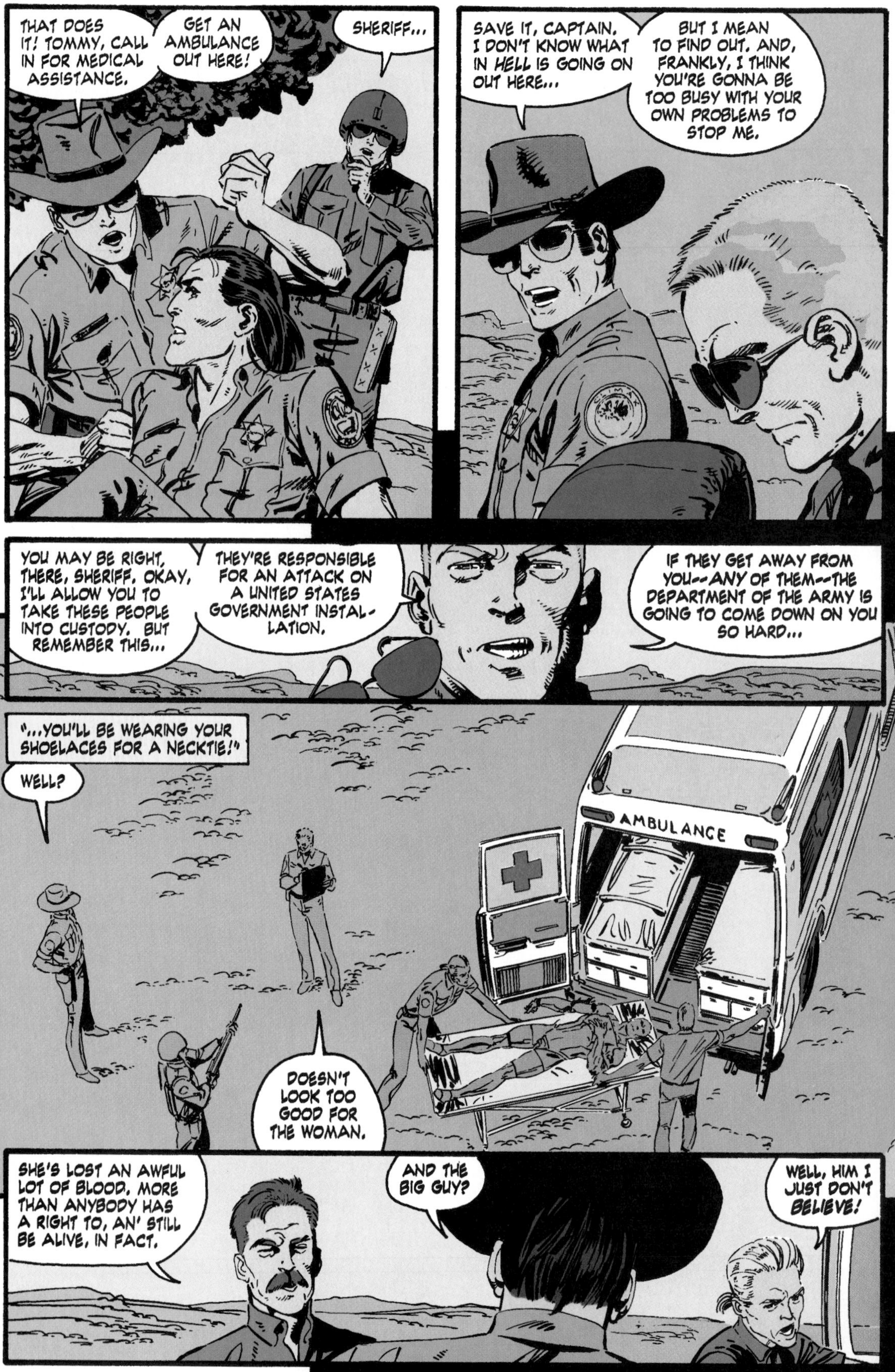
THAT DOES IT! TOMMY, CALL IN FOR MEDICAL ASSISTANCE.
GET AN AMBULANCE OUT HERE!
SHERIFF...
SAVE IT, CAPTAIN. I DON'T KNOW WHAT IN HELL IS GOING ON OUT HERE...
BUT I MEAN TO FIND OUT. AND, FRANKLY, I THINK YOU'RE GONNA BE TOO BUSY WITH YOUR OWN PROBLEMS TO STOP ME.
YOU MAY BE RIGHT, THERE, SHERIFF. OKAY, I'LL ALLOW YOU TO TAKE THESE PEOPLE INTO CUSTODY. BUT REMEMBER THIS...
THEY'RE RESPONSIBLE FOR AN ATTACK ON A UNITED STATES GOVERNMENT INSTAL-LATION.
IF THEY GET AWAY FROM YOU--ANY OF THEM--THE DEPARTMENT OF THE ARMY IS GOING TO COME DOWN ON YOU SO HARD...
"...YOU'LL BE WEARING YOUR SHOELACES FOR A NECKTIE!"
WELL?
AMBULANCE
DOESN'T LOOK TOO GOOD FOR THE WOMAN.
SHE'S LOST AN AWFUL LOT OF BLOOD, MORE THAN ANYBODY HAS A RIGHT TO, AN' STILL BE ALIVE, IN FACT.
AND THE BIG GUY?
WELL, HIM I JUST DON'T BELIEVE!

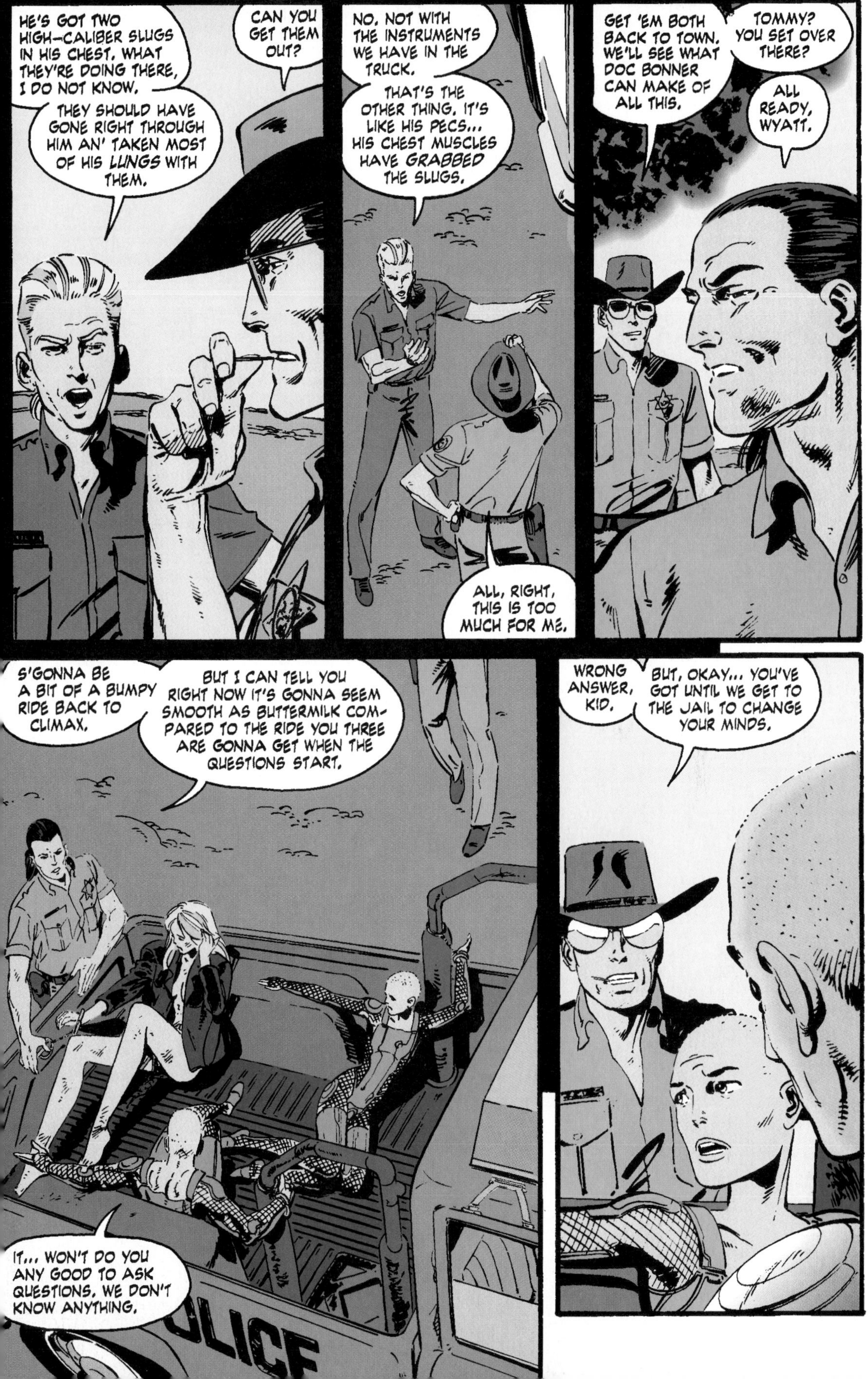
HE'S GOT TWO HIGH-CALIBER SLUGS IN HIS CHEST. WHAT THEY'RE DOING THERE, I DO NOT KNOW.
CAN YOU GET THEM OUT?
THEY SHOULD HAVE GONE RIGHT THROUGH HIM AN' TAKEN MOST OF HIS LUNGS WITH THEM.
NO. NOT WITH THE INSTRUMENTS WE HAVE IN THE TRUCK.
THAT'S THE OTHER THING. IT'S LIKE HIS PECS... HIS CHEST MUSCLES HAVE GRABBED THE SLUGS.
ALL, RIGHT, THIS IS TOO MUCH FOR ME.
GET 'EM BOTH BACK TO TOWN. WE'LL SEE WHAT DOC BONNER CAN MAKE OF ALL THIS.
TOMMY? YOU SET OVER THERE?
ALL READY, WYATT.
S'GONNA BE A BIT OF A BUMPY RIDE BACK TO CLIMAX.
BUT I CAN TELL YOU RIGHT NOW IT'S GONNA SEEM SMOOTH AS BUTTERMILK COMPARED TO THE RIDE YOU THREE ARE GONNA GET WHEN THE QUESTIONS START.
IT... WON'T DO YOU ANY GOOD TO ASK QUESTIONS. WE DON'T KNOW ANYTHING.
POLICE
WRONG ANSWER, KID.
BUT, OKAY... YOU'VE GOT UNTIL WE GET TO THE JAIL TO CHANGE YOUR MINDS.

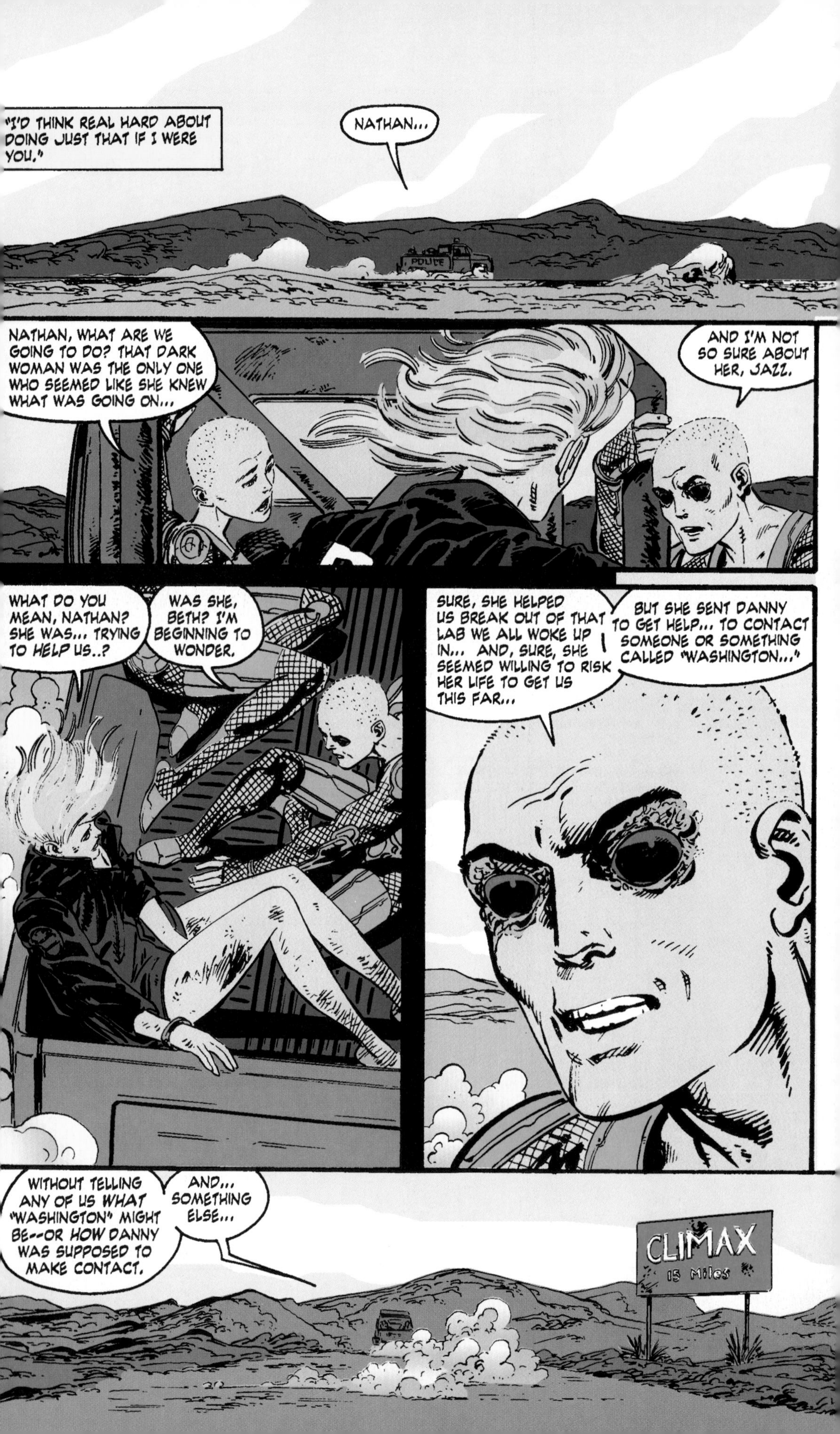
"I'D THINK REAL HARD ABOUT DOING JUST THAT IF I WERE YOU."
NATHAN...
POLICE
NATHAN, WHAT ARE WE GOING TO DO? THAT DARK WOMAN WAS THE ONLY ONE WHO SEEMED LIKE SHE KNEW WHAT WAS GOING ON...
AND I'M NOT SO SURE ABOUT HER, JAZZ.
WHAT DO YOU MEAN, NATHAN? SHE WAS... TRYING TO HELP US..?
WAS SHE, BETH? I'M BEGINNING TO WONDER.
SURE, SHE HELPED US BREAK OUT OF THAT LAB WE ALL WOKE UP IN... AND, SURE, SHE SEEMED WILLING TO RISK HER LIFE TO GET US THIS FAR...
BUT SHE SENT DANNY TO GET HELP... TO CONTACT SOMEONE OR SOMETHING CALLED "WASHINGTON..."
WITHOUT TELLING ANY OF US WHAT "WASHINGTON" MIGHT BE--OR HOW DANNY WAS SUPPOSED TO MAKE CONTACT.
AND... SOMETHING ELSE...
CLIMAX
15 Miles

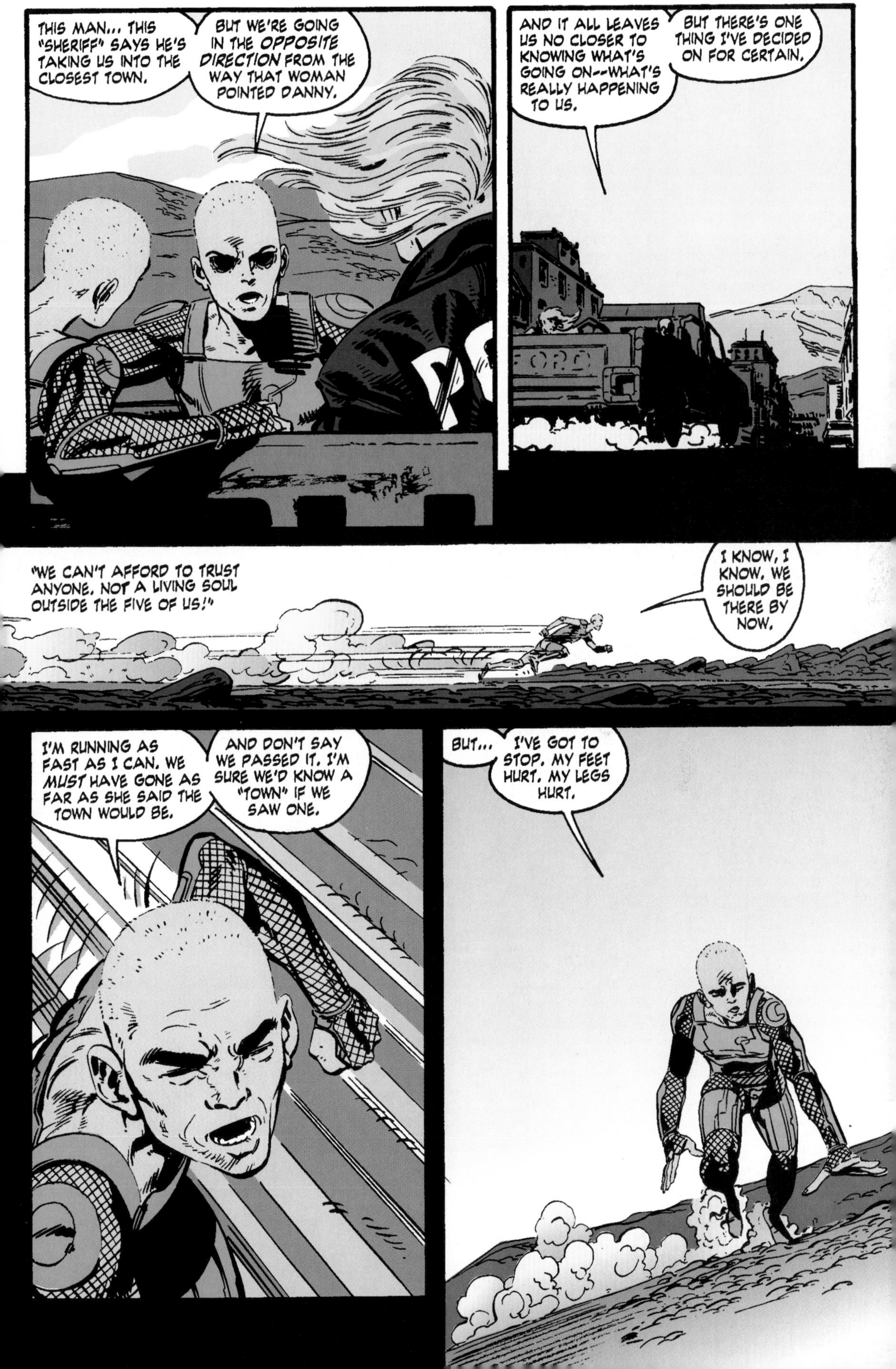
THIS MAN... THIS "SHERIFF" SAYS HE'S TAKING US INTO THE CLOSEST TOWN.
BUT WE'RE GOING IN THE *OPPOSITE DIRECTION* FROM THE WAY THAT WOMAN POINTED DANNY.
AND IT ALL LEAVES US NO CLOSER TO KNOWING WHAT'S GOING ON--WHAT'S REALLY HAPPENING TO US.
BUT THERE'S ONE THING I'VE DECIDED ON FOR CERTAIN.
"WE CAN'T AFFORD TO TRUST ANYONE. NOT A LIVING SOUL OUTSIDE THE FIVE OF US!"
I KNOW, I KNOW. WE SHOULD BE THERE BY NOW.
I'M RUNNING AS FAST AS I CAN. WE *MUST* HAVE GONE AS FAR AS SHE SAID THE TOWN WOULD BE.
AND DON'T SAY WE PASSED IT. I'M SURE WE'D KNOW A "TOWN" IF WE SAW ONE.
BUT...
I'VE GOT TO STOP. MY FEET HURT. MY LEGS HURT.

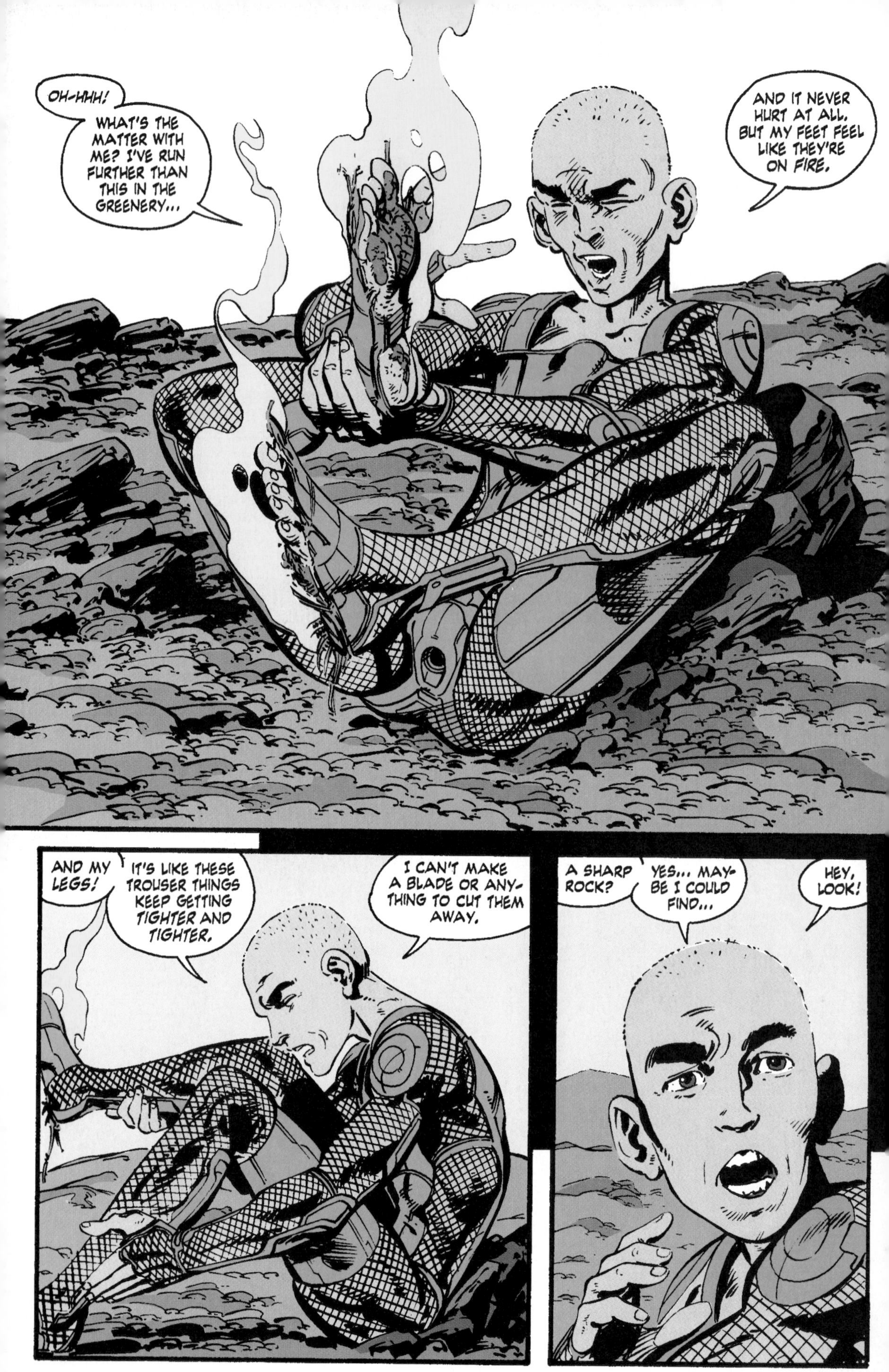
OH-HHH!
WHAT'S THE MATTER WITH ME? I'VE RUN FURTHER THAN THIS IN THE GREENERY...
AND IT NEVER HURT AT ALL. BUT MY FEET FEEL LIKE THEY'RE ON FIRE.
AND MY LEGS!
IT'S LIKE THESE TROUSER THINGS KEEP GETTING TIGHTER AND TIGHTER.
I CAN'T MAKE A BLADE OR ANY-THING TO CUT THEM AWAY.
A SHARP ROCK?
YES... MAY-BE I COULD FIND...
HEY, LOOK!

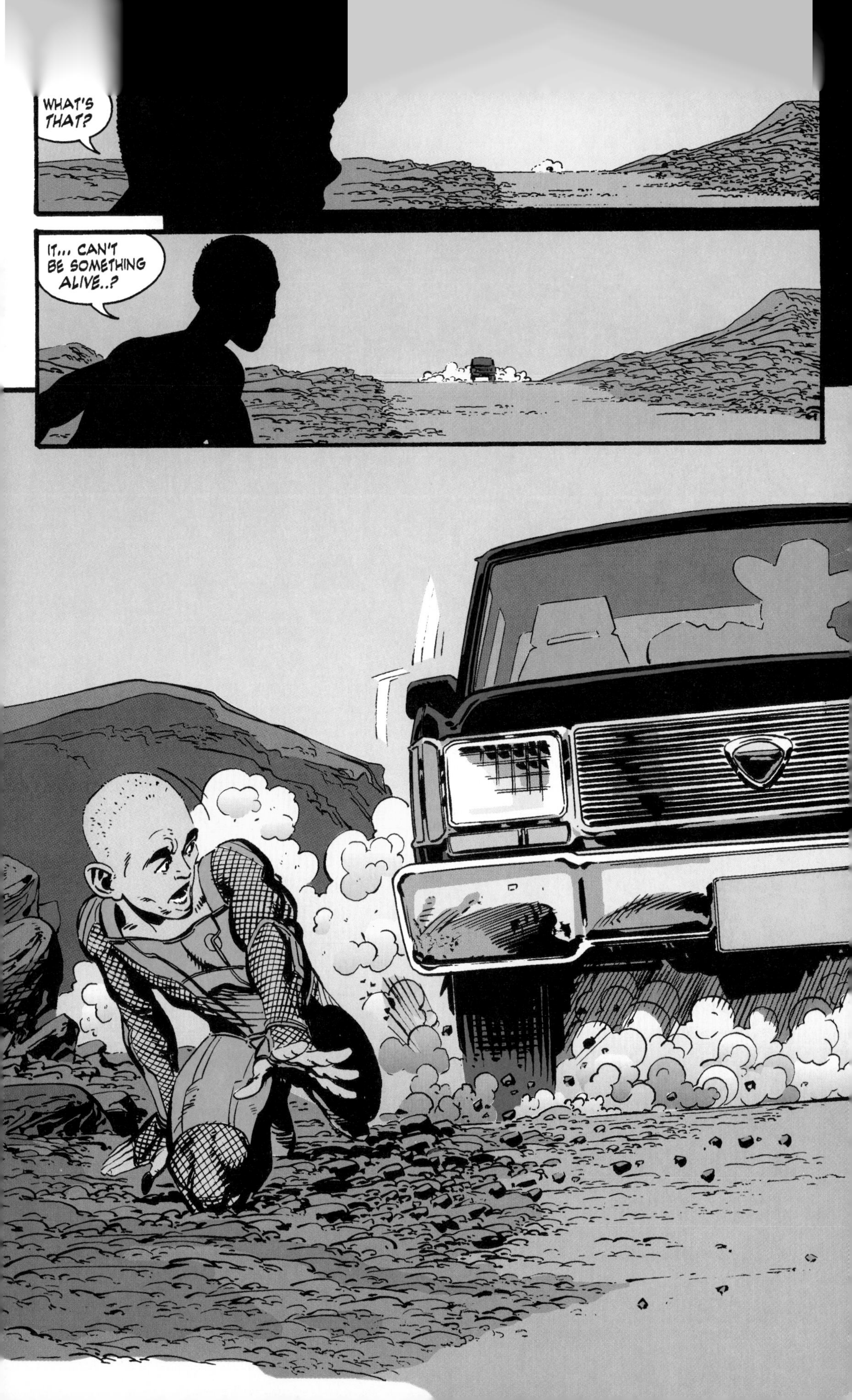
WHAT'S THAT?
IT... CAN'T BE SOMETHING ALIVE..?

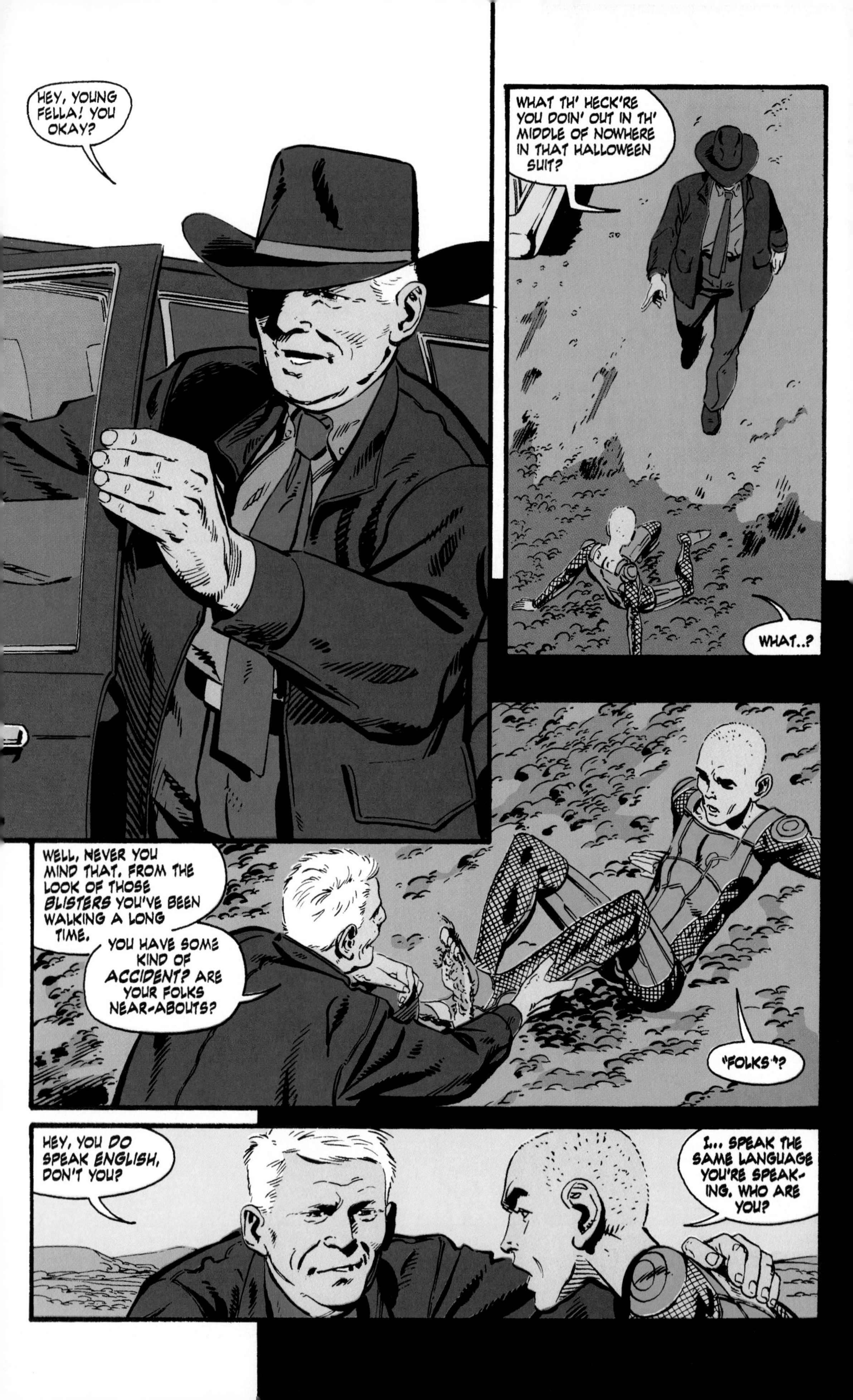
HEY, YOUNG FELLA! YOU OKAY?
WHAT TH' HECK'RE YOU DOIN' OUT IN TH' MIDDLE OF NOWHERE IN THAT HALLOWEEN SUIT?
WHAT..?
WELL, NEVER YOU MIND THAT. FROM THE LOOK OF THOSE BLISTERS YOU'VE BEEN WALKING A LONG TIME.
YOU HAVE SOME KIND OF ACCIDENT? ARE YOUR FOLKS NEAR-ABOUTS?
"FOLKS"?
HEY, YOU DO SPEAK ENGLISH, DON'T YOU?
I... SPEAK THE SAME LANGUAGE YOU'RE SPEAK-ING. WHO ARE YOU?

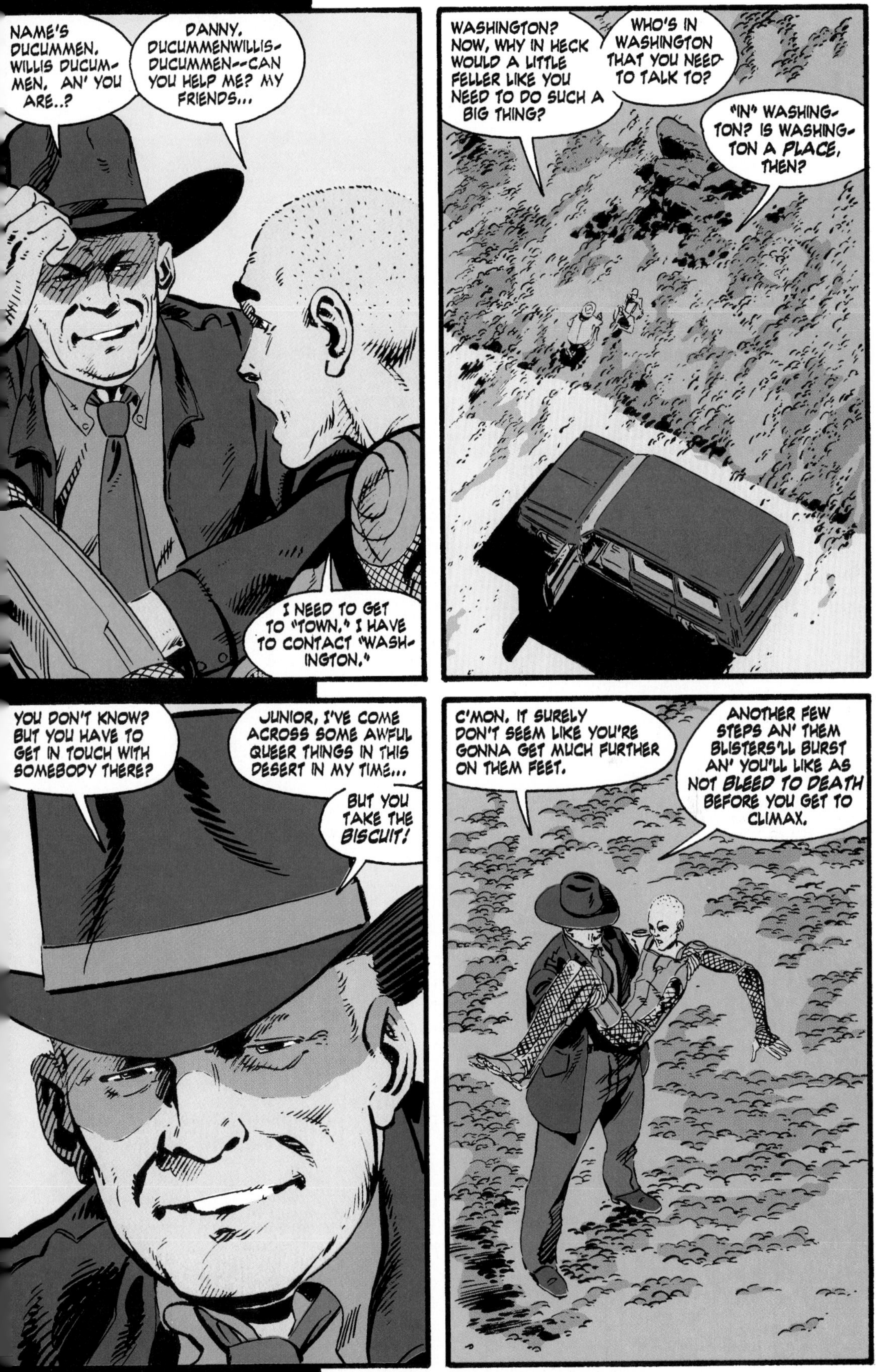
NAME'S DUCUMMEN. WILLIS DUCUMMEN. AN' YOU ARE..?
DANNY. DUCUMMENWILLIS-DUCUMMEN--CAN YOU HELP ME? MY FRIENDS...
I NEED TO GET TO "TOWN." I HAVE TO CONTACT "WASHINGTON."
WASHINGTON? NOW, WHY IN HECK WOULD A LITTLE FELLER LIKE YOU NEED TO DO SUCH A BIG THING?
WHO'S IN WASHINGTON THAT YOU NEED TO TALK TO?
"IN" WASHINGTON? IS WASHINGTON A PLACE, THEN?
YOU DON'T KNOW? BUT YOU HAVE TO GET IN TOUCH WITH SOMEBODY THERE?
JUNIOR, I'VE COME ACROSS SOME AWFUL QUEER THINGS IN THIS DESERT IN MY TIME...
BUT YOU TAKE THE BISCUIT!
C'MON. IT SURELY DON'T SEEM LIKE YOU'RE GONNA GET MUCH FURTHER ON THEM FEET.
ANOTHER FEW STEPS AN' THEM BLISTERS'LL BURST AN' YOU'LL LIKE AS NOT BLEED TO DEATH BEFORE YOU GET TO CLIMAX.

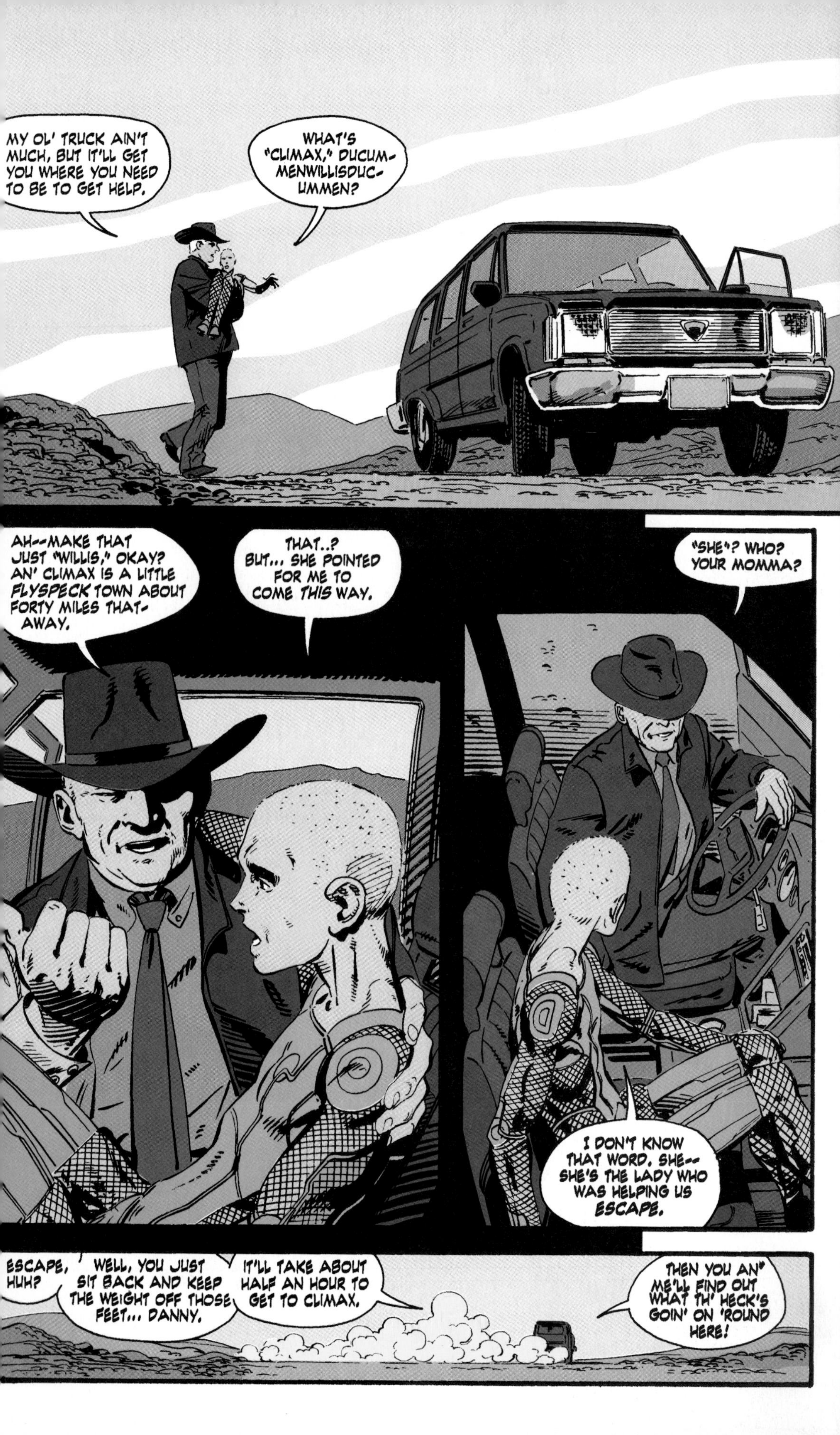
MY OL' TRUCK AIN'T MUCH, BUT IT'LL GET YOU WHERE YOU NEED TO BE TO GET HELP.
WHAT'S "CLIMAX," DUCUM-MENWILLISDUC-UMMEN?
AH--MAKE THAT JUST "WILLIS," OKAY? AN' CLIMAX IS A LITTLE *FLYSPECK* TOWN ABOUT FORTY MILES THAT-AWAY.
THAT..? BUT... SHE POINTED FOR ME TO COME *THIS* WAY.
"SHE"? WHO? YOUR MOMMA?
I DON'T KNOW THAT WORD. SHE--SHE'S THE LADY WHO WAS HELPING US *ESCAPE*.
ESCAPE, HUH?
WELL, YOU JUST SIT BACK AND KEEP THE WEIGHT OFF THOSE FEET... DANNY.
IT'LL TAKE ABOUT HALF AN HOUR TO GET TO CLIMAX.
THEN YOU AN' ME'LL FIND OUT WHAT TH' HECK'S GOIN' ON 'ROUND HERE!

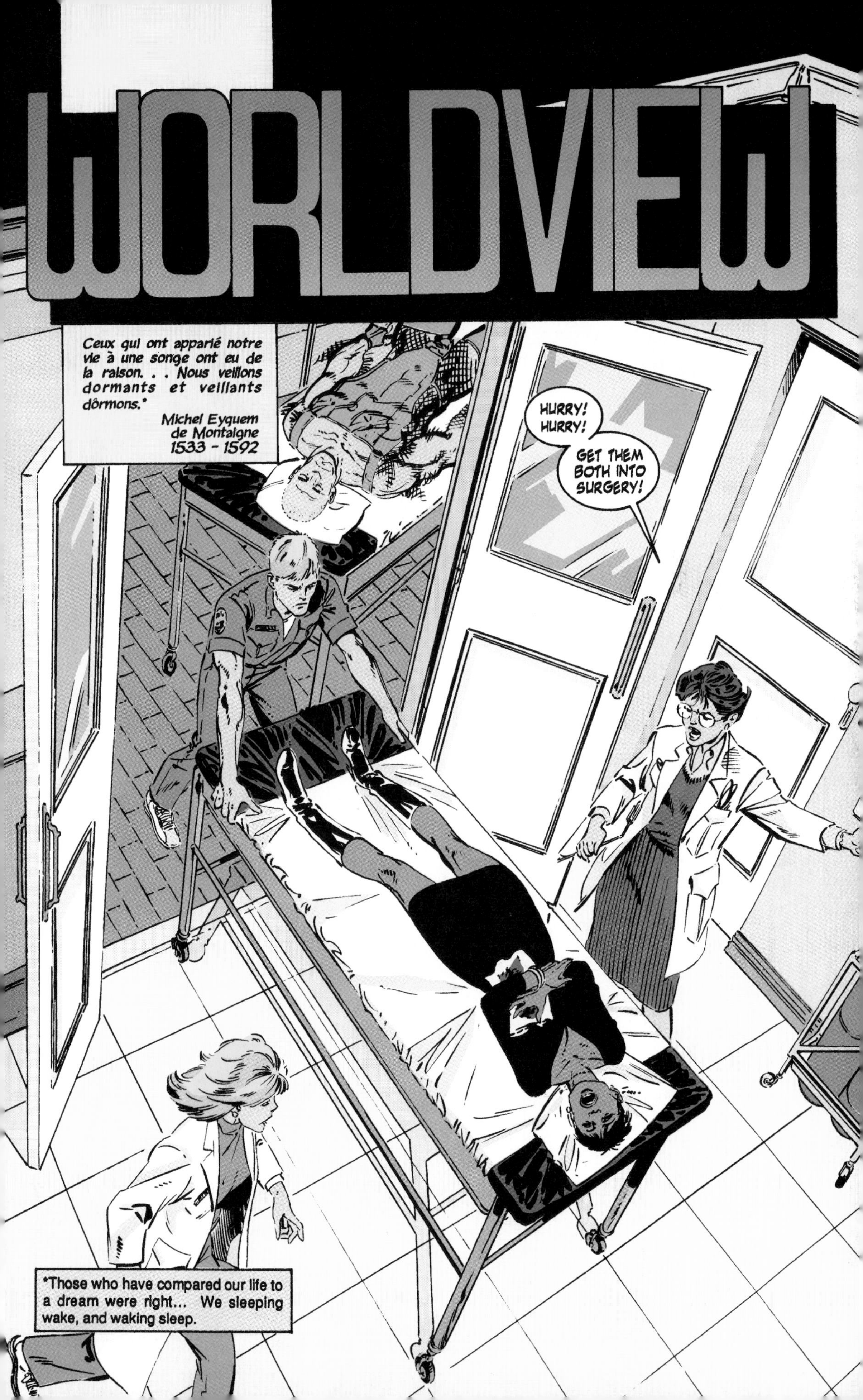
WORLDVIEW
Ceux qui ont apparié notre vie à une songe ont eu de la raison. . . Nous veillons dormants et veillants dôrmons.*
Michel Eyquem de Montaigne 1533 - 1592
HURRY! HURRY!
GET THEM BOTH INTO SURGERY!
*Those who have compared our life to a dream were right... We sleeping wake, and waking sleep.

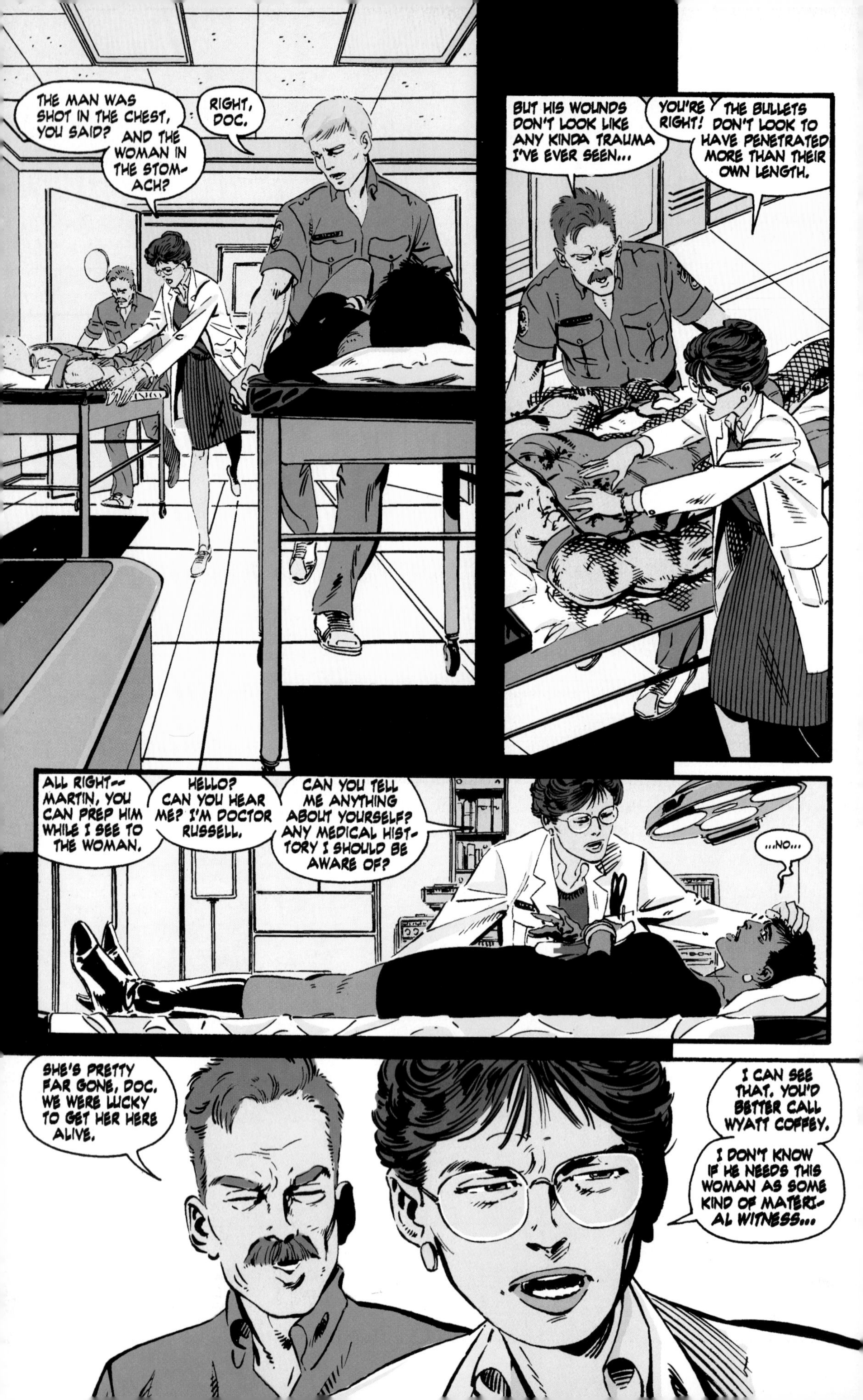
THE MAN WAS SHOT IN THE CHEST, YOU SAID?
AND THE WOMAN IN THE STOMACH?
RIGHT, DOC.
BUT HIS WOUNDS DON'T LOOK LIKE ANY KINDA TRAUMA I'VE EVER SEEN...
YOU'RE RIGHT!
THE BULLETS DON'T LOOK TO HAVE PENETRATED MORE THAN THEIR OWN LENGTH.
ALL RIGHT-- MARTIN, YOU CAN PREP HIM WHILE I SEE TO THE WOMAN.
HELLO? CAN YOU HEAR ME? I'M DOCTOR RUSSELL.
CAN YOU TELL ME ANYTHING ABOUT YOURSELF? ANY MEDICAL HISTORY I SHOULD BE AWARE OF?
...NO...
SHE'S PRETTY FAR GONE, DOC. WE WERE LUCKY TO GET HER HERE ALIVE.
I CAN SEE THAT. YOU'D BETTER CALL WYATT COFFEY.
I DON'T KNOW IF HE NEEDS THIS WOMAN AS SOME KIND OF MATERIAL WITNESS...

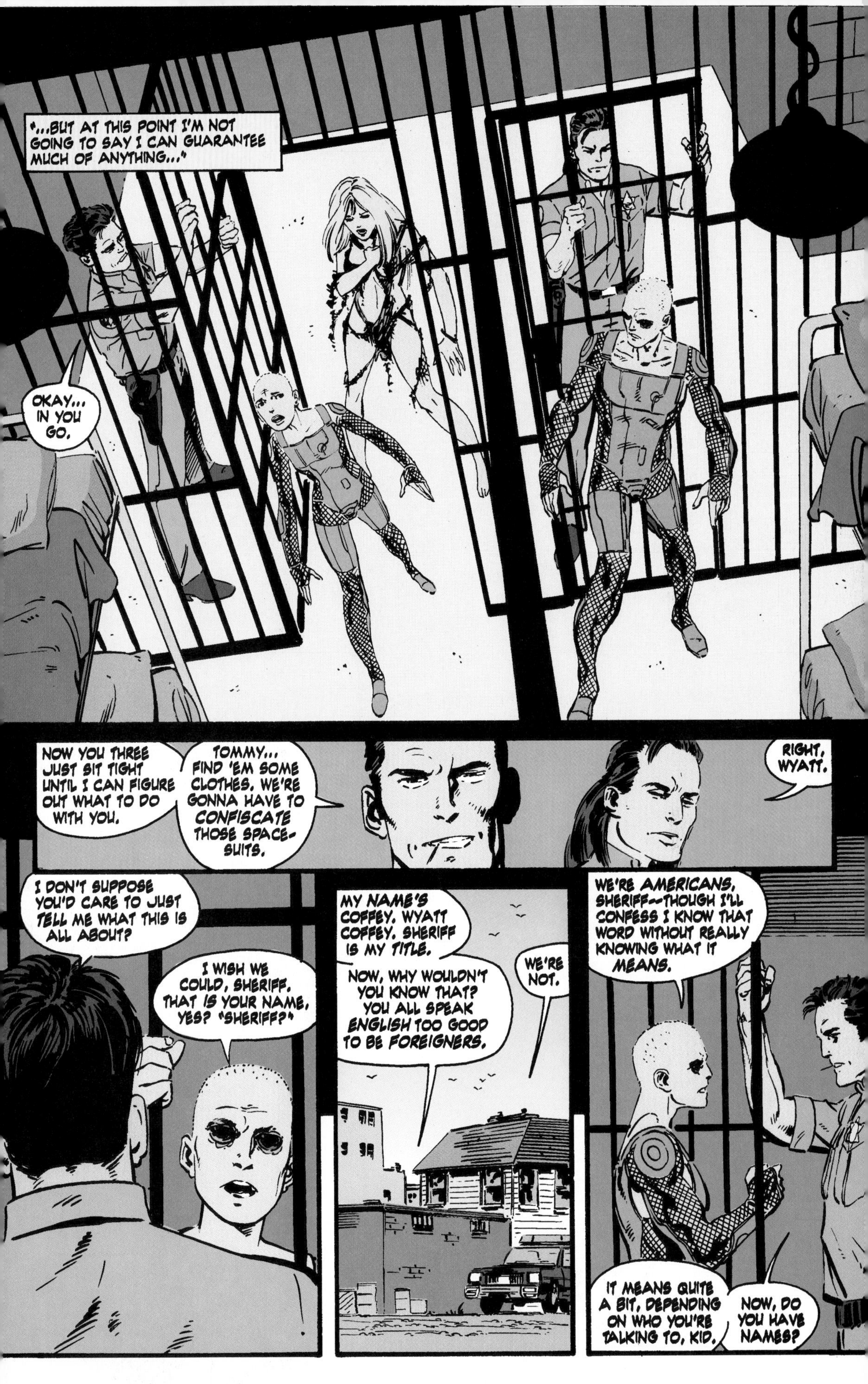
"...BUT AT THIS POINT I'M NOT GOING TO SAY I CAN GUARANTEE MUCH OF ANYTHING..."
OKAY... IN YOU GO.
NOW YOU THREE JUST SIT TIGHT UNTIL I CAN FIGURE OUT WHAT TO DO WITH YOU.
TOMMY... FIND 'EM SOME CLOTHES. WE'RE GONNA HAVE TO CONFISCATE THOSE SPACE-SUITS.
RIGHT, WYATT.
I DON'T SUPPOSE YOU'D CARE TO JUST TELL ME WHAT THIS IS ALL ABOUT?
I WISH WE COULD, SHERIFF. THAT IS YOUR NAME, YES? "SHERIFF?"
MY NAME'S COFFEY. WYATT COFFEY. SHERIFF IS MY TITLE.
NOW, WHY WOULDN'T YOU KNOW THAT? YOU ALL SPEAK ENGLISH TOO GOOD TO BE FOREIGNERS.
WE'RE NOT.
WE'RE AMERICANS, SHERIFF--THOUGH I'LL CONFESS I KNOW THAT WORD WITHOUT REALLY KNOWING WHAT IT MEANS.
IT MEANS QUITE A BIT, DEPENDING ON WHO YOU'RE TALKING TO, KID.
NOW, DO YOU HAVE NAMES?

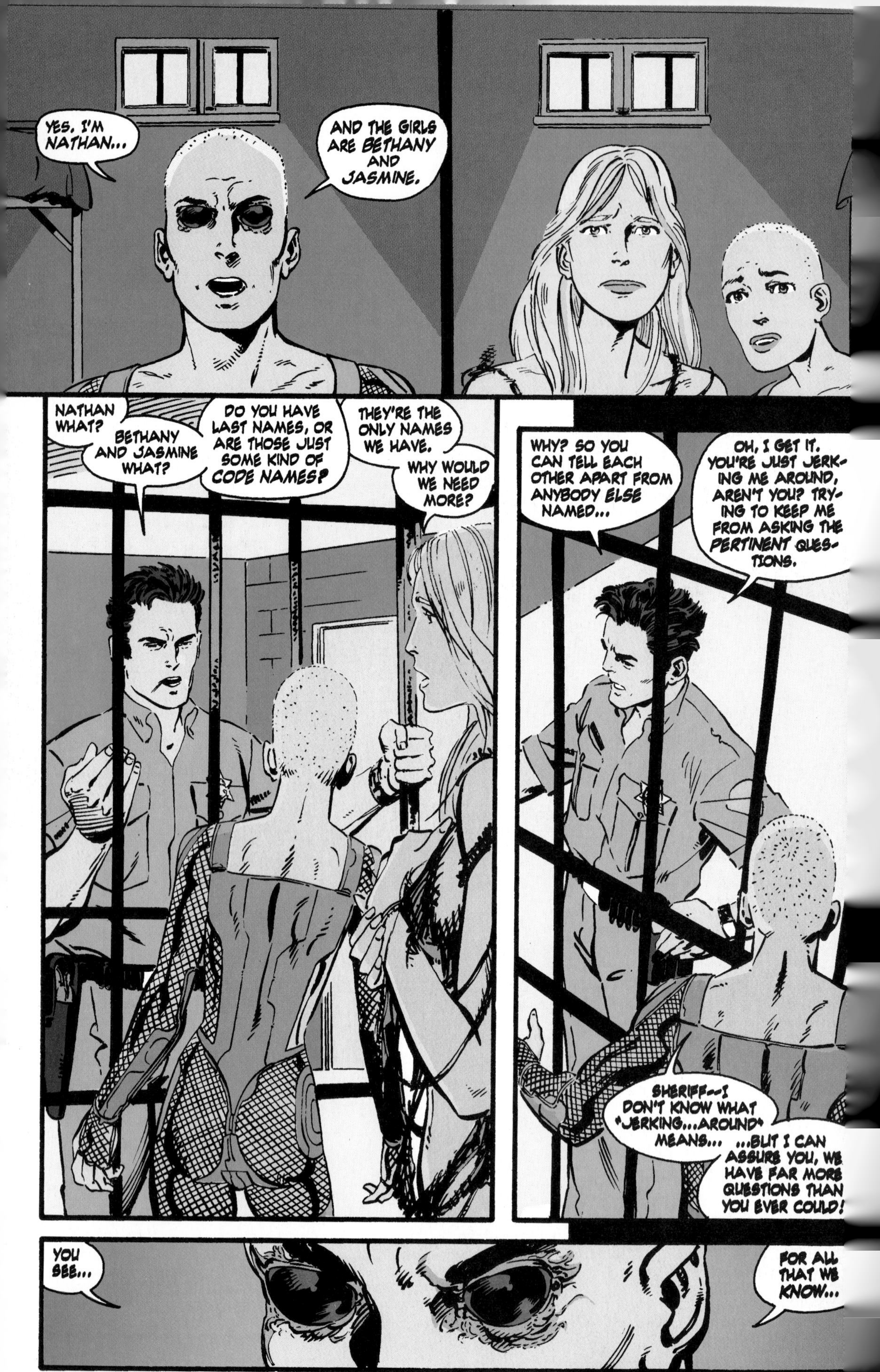
YES, I'M NATHAN...
AND THE GIRLS ARE BETHANY AND JASMINE.
NATHAN WHAT?
BETHANY AND JASMINE WHAT?
DO YOU HAVE LAST NAMES, OR ARE THOSE JUST SOME KIND OF CODE NAMES?
THEY'RE THE ONLY NAMES WE HAVE.
WHY WOULD WE NEED MORE?
WHY? SO YOU CAN TELL EACH OTHER APART FROM ANYBODY ELSE NAMED...
OH, I GET IT. YOU'RE JUST JERKING ME AROUND, AREN'T YOU? TRYING TO KEEP ME FROM ASKING THE PERTINENT QUESTIONS.
SHERIFF--I DON'T KNOW WHAT "JERKING...AROUND" MEANS...
...BUT I CAN ASSURE YOU, WE HAVE FAR MORE QUESTIONS THAN YOU EVER COULD!
YOU SEE...
FOR ALL THAT WE KNOW...

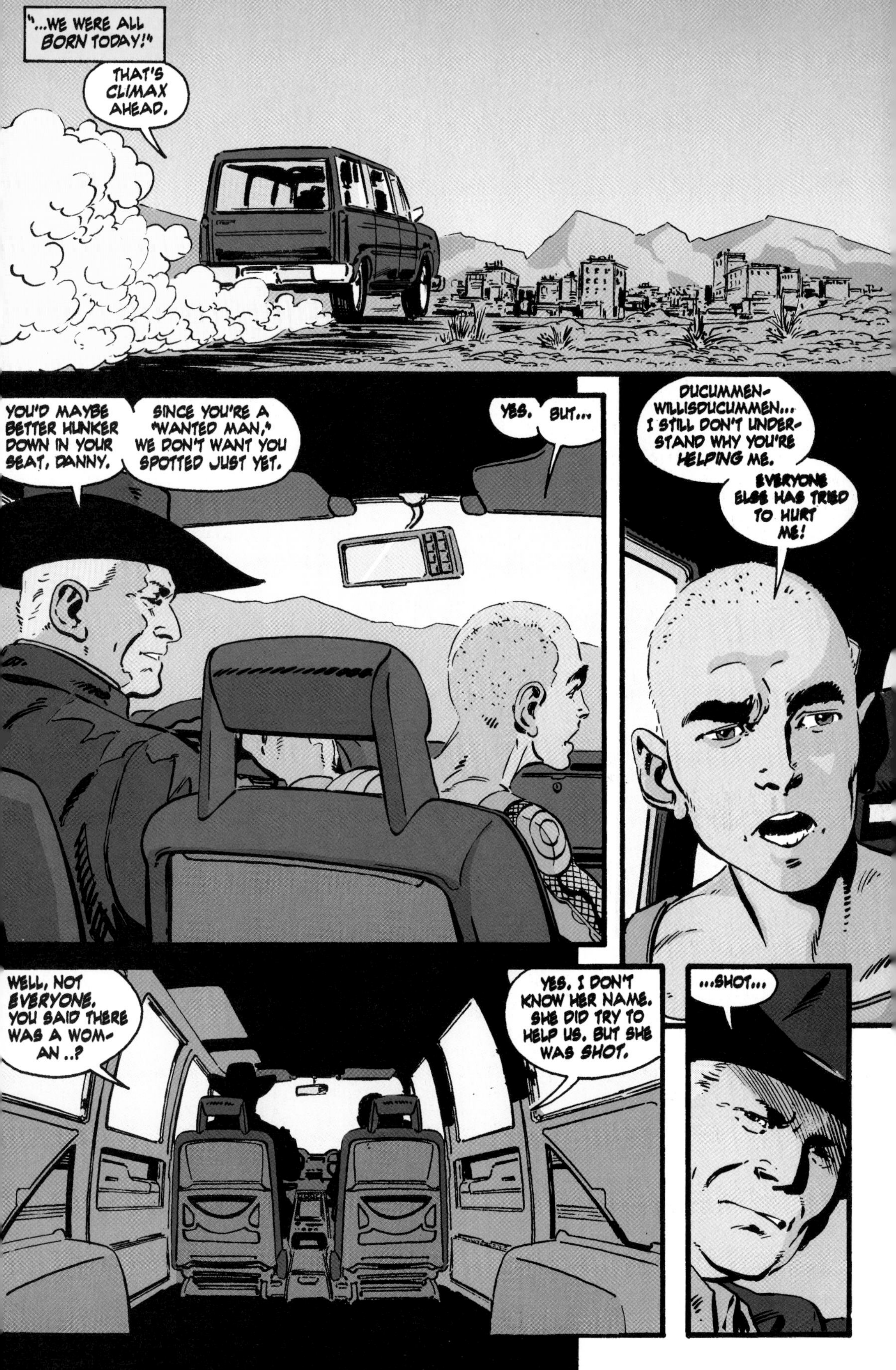
"...WE WERE ALL BORN TODAY!"
THAT'S CLIMAX AHEAD.
YOU'D MAYBE BETTER HUNKER DOWN IN YOUR SEAT, DANNY.
SINCE YOU'RE A "WANTED MAN," WE DON'T WANT YOU SPOTTED JUST YET.
YES.
BUT...
DUCUMMEN-WILLISDUCUMMEN... I STILL DON'T UNDER-STAND WHY YOU'RE HELPING ME.
EVERYONE ELSE HAS TRIED TO HURT ME!
WELL, NOT EVERYONE. YOU SAID THERE WAS A WOM-AN ..?
YES. I DON'T KNOW HER NAME. SHE DID TRY TO HELP US. BUT SHE WAS SHOT.
...SHOT...

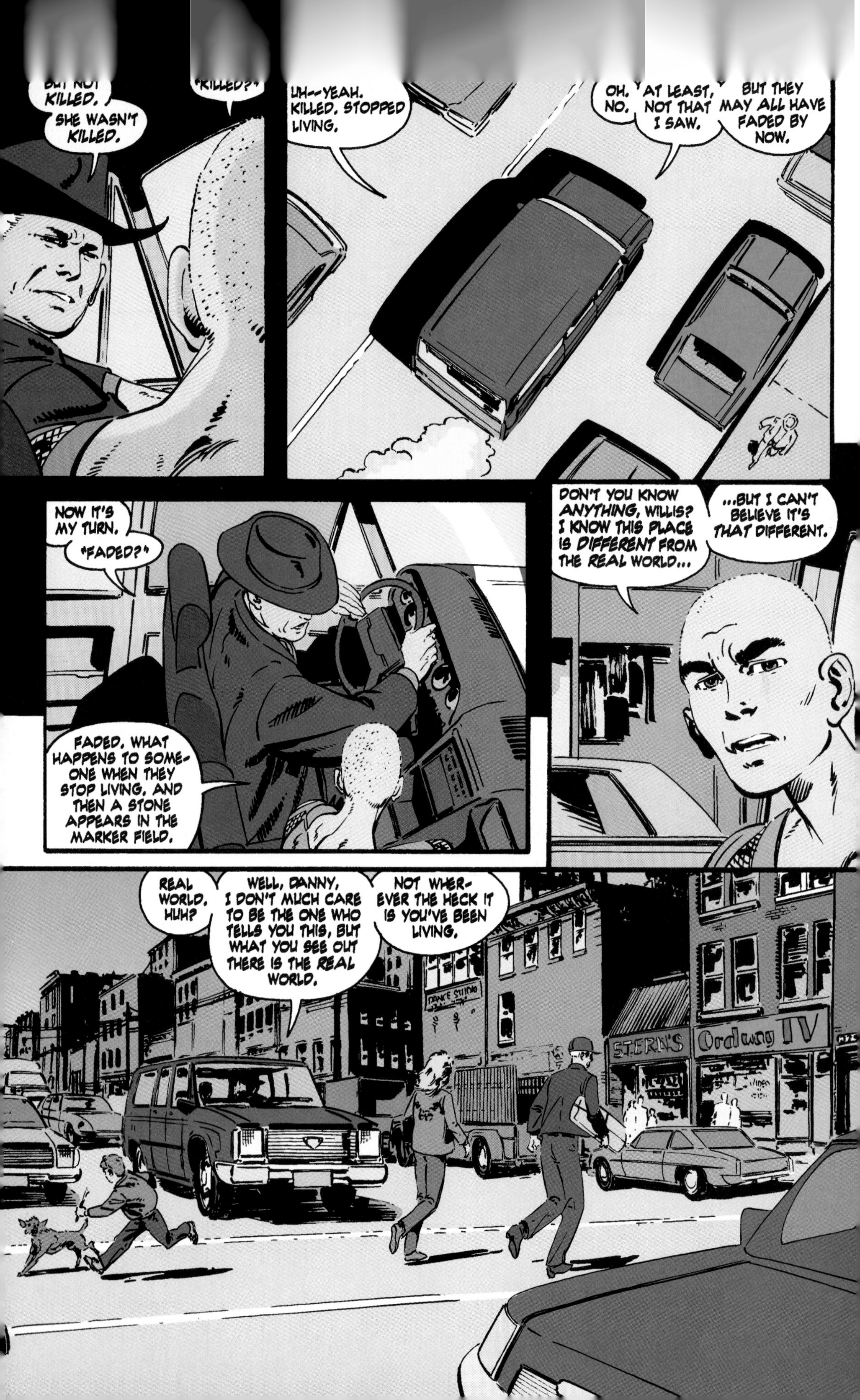
BUT NOT KILLED.
SHE WASN'T KILLED.
"KILLED?"
UH--YEAH. KILLED. STOPPED LIVING.
OH. NO.
AT LEAST, NOT THAT I SAW.
BUT THEY MAY ALL HAVE FADED BY NOW.
NOW IT'S MY TURN.
"FADED?"
FADED. WHAT HAPPENS TO SOME-ONE WHEN THEY STOP LIVING, AND THEN A STONE APPEARS IN THE MARKER FIELD.
DON'T YOU KNOW ANYTHING, WILLIS? I KNOW THIS PLACE IS DIFFERENT FROM THE REAL WORLD...
...BUT I CAN'T BELIEVE IT'S THAT DIFFERENT.
REAL WORLD. HUH?
WELL, DANNY, I DON'T MUCH CARE TO BE THE ONE WHO TELLS YOU THIS, BUT WHAT YOU SEE OUT THERE IS THE REAL WORLD.
NOT WHER-EVER THE HECK IT IS YOU'VE BEEN LIVING.
DANCE STUDIO
STERN'S
Ordway TV

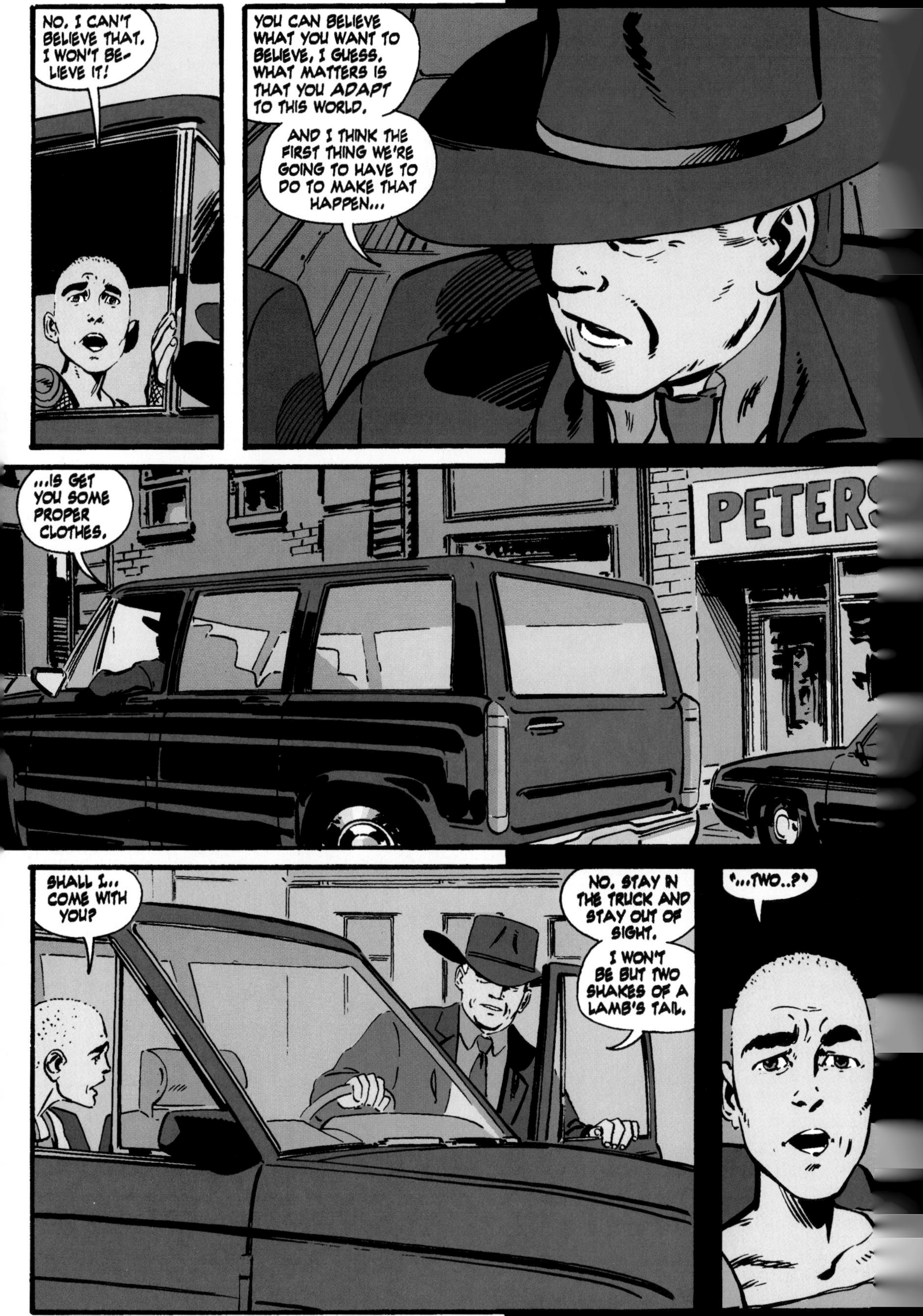
NO. I CAN'T BELIEVE THAT. I WON'T BE-LIEVE IT!
YOU CAN BELIEVE WHAT YOU WANT TO BELIEVE, I GUESS. WHAT MATTERS IS THAT YOU ADAPT TO THIS WORLD.
AND I THINK THE FIRST THING WE'RE GOING TO HAVE TO DO TO MAKE THAT HAPPEN...
...IS GET YOU SOME PROPER CLOTHES.
PETERS
SHALL I... COME WITH YOU?
NO. STAY IN THE TRUCK AND STAY OUT OF SIGHT.
I WON'T BE BUT TWO SHAKES OF A LAMB'S TAIL.
"...TWO...?"

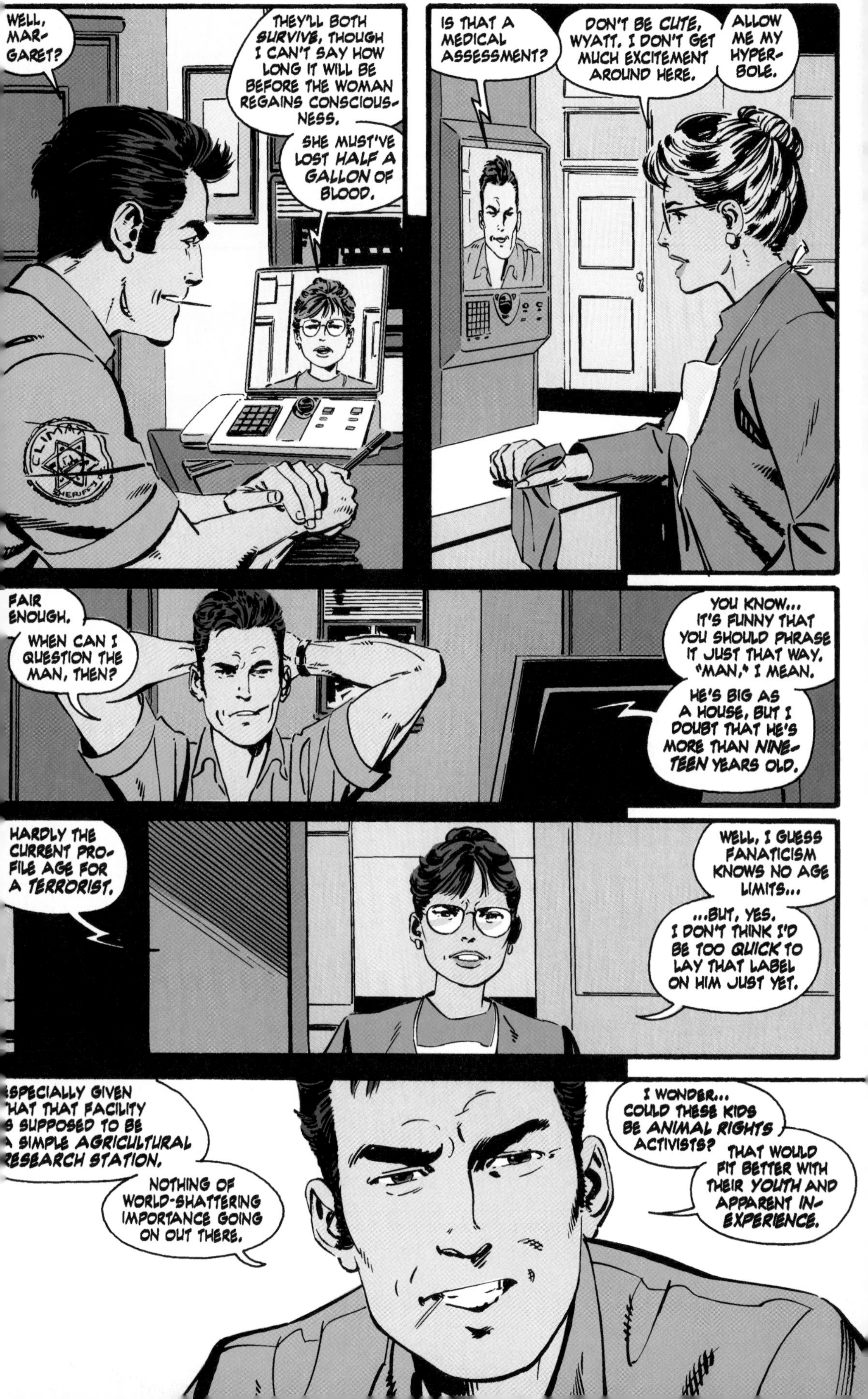
WELL, MARGARET?
THEY'LL BOTH SURVIVE, THOUGH I CAN'T SAY HOW LONG IT WILL BE BEFORE THE WOMAN REGAINS CONSCIOUSNESS.
SHE MUST'VE LOST HALF A GALLON OF BLOOD.
IS THAT A MEDICAL ASSESSMENT?
DON'T BE CUTE, WYATT. I DON'T GET MUCH EXCITEMENT AROUND HERE.
ALLOW ME MY HYPERBOLE.
FAIR ENOUGH.
WHEN CAN I QUESTION THE MAN, THEN?
YOU KNOW... IT'S FUNNY THAT YOU SHOULD PHRASE IT JUST THAT WAY. "MAN," I MEAN.
HE'S BIG AS A HOUSE, BUT I DOUBT THAT HE'S MORE THAN NINETEEN YEARS OLD.
HARDLY THE CURRENT PROFILE AGE FOR A TERRORIST.
WELL, I GUESS FANATICISM KNOWS NO AGE LIMITS...
...BUT, YES. I DON'T THINK I'D BE TOO QUICK TO LAY THAT LABEL ON HIM JUST YET.
ESPECIALLY GIVEN THAT THAT FACILITY IS SUPPOSED TO BE A SIMPLE AGRICULTURAL RESEARCH STATION.
NOTHING OF WORLD-SHATTERING IMPORTANCE GOING ON OUT THERE.
I WONDER... COULD THESE KIDS BE ANIMAL RIGHTS ACTIVISTS?
THAT WOULD FIT BETTER WITH THEIR YOUTH AND APPARENT INEXPERIENCE.

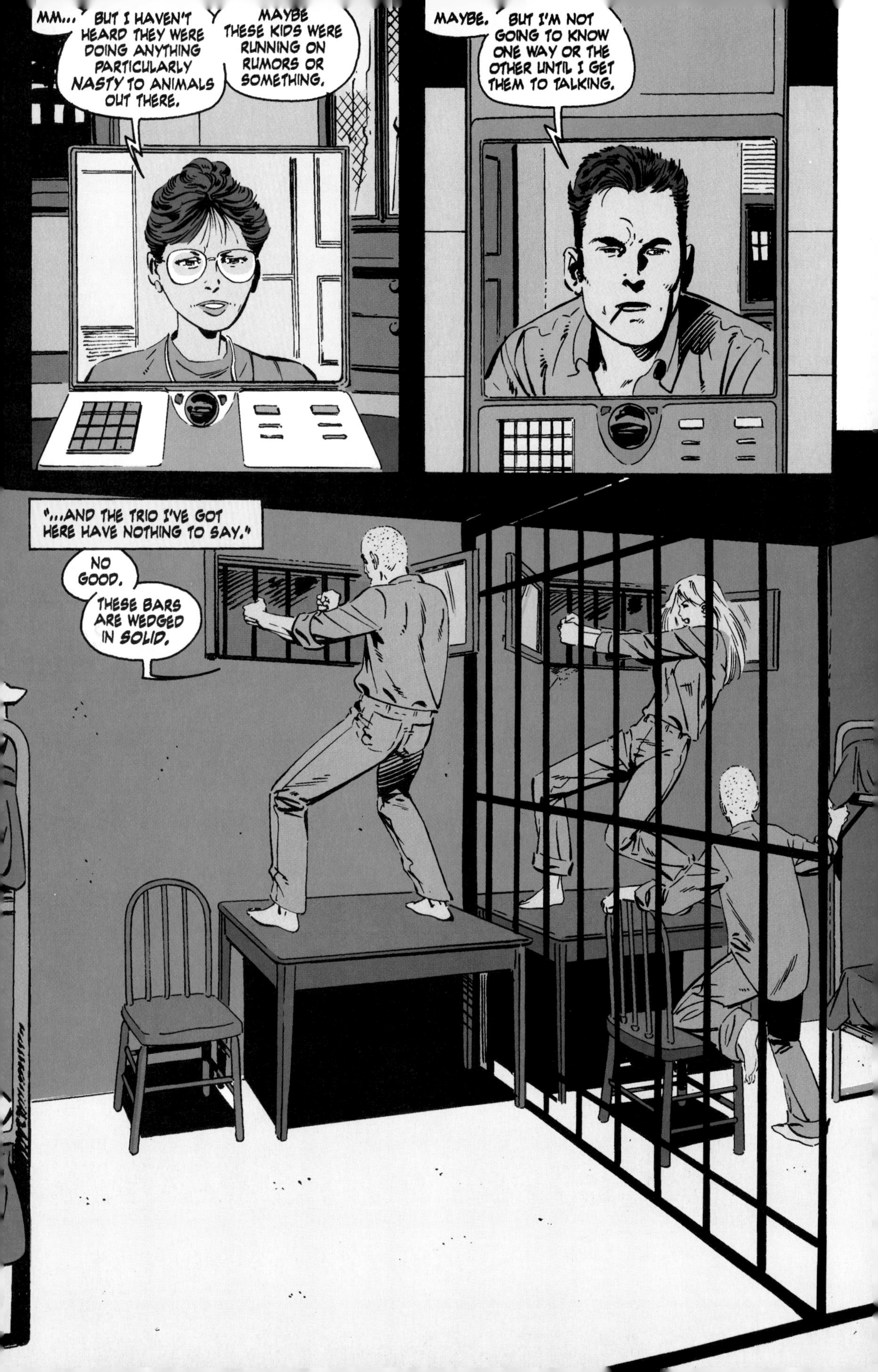
MM...
BUT I HAVEN'T HEARD THEY WERE DOING ANYTHING PARTICULARLY NASTY TO ANIMALS OUT THERE.
MAYBE THESE KIDS WERE RUNNING ON RUMORS OR SOMETHING.
MAYBE.
BUT I'M NOT GOING TO KNOW ONE WAY OR THE OTHER UNTIL I GET THEM TO TALKING.
"...AND THE TRIO I'VE GOT HERE HAVE NOTHING TO SAY."
NO GOOD.
THESE BARS ARE WEDGED IN SOLID.

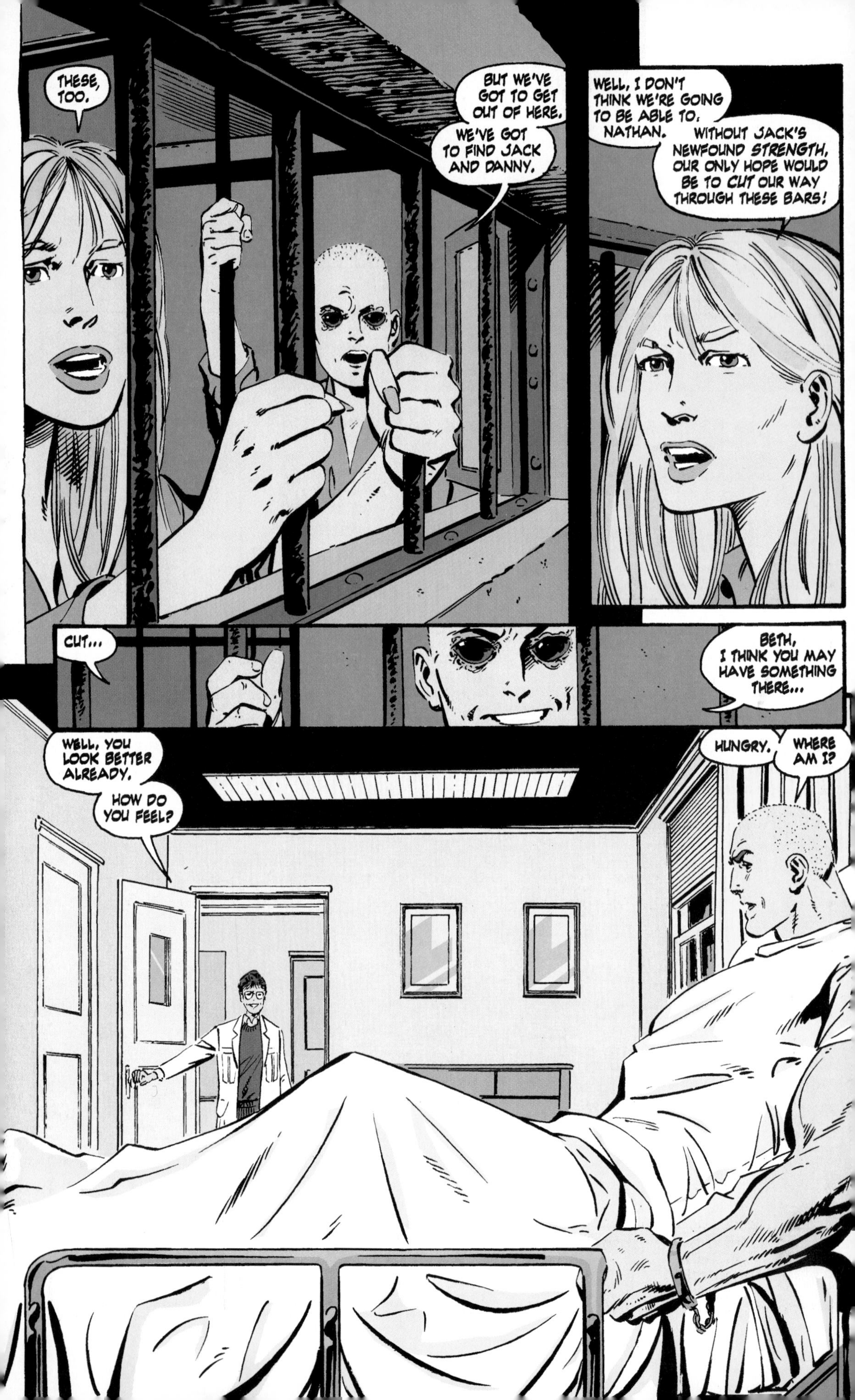
THESE, TOO.
BUT WE'VE GOT TO GET OUT OF HERE.
WE'VE GOT TO FIND JACK AND DANNY.
WELL, I DON'T THINK WE'RE GOING TO BE ABLE TO, NATHAN.
WITHOUT JACK'S NEWFOUND STRENGTH, OUR ONLY HOPE WOULD BE TO CUT OUR WAY THROUGH THESE BARS!
CUT...
BETH, I THINK YOU MAY HAVE SOMETHING THERE...
WELL, YOU LOOK BETTER ALREADY.
HOW DO YOU FEEL?
HUNGRY.
WHERE AM I?

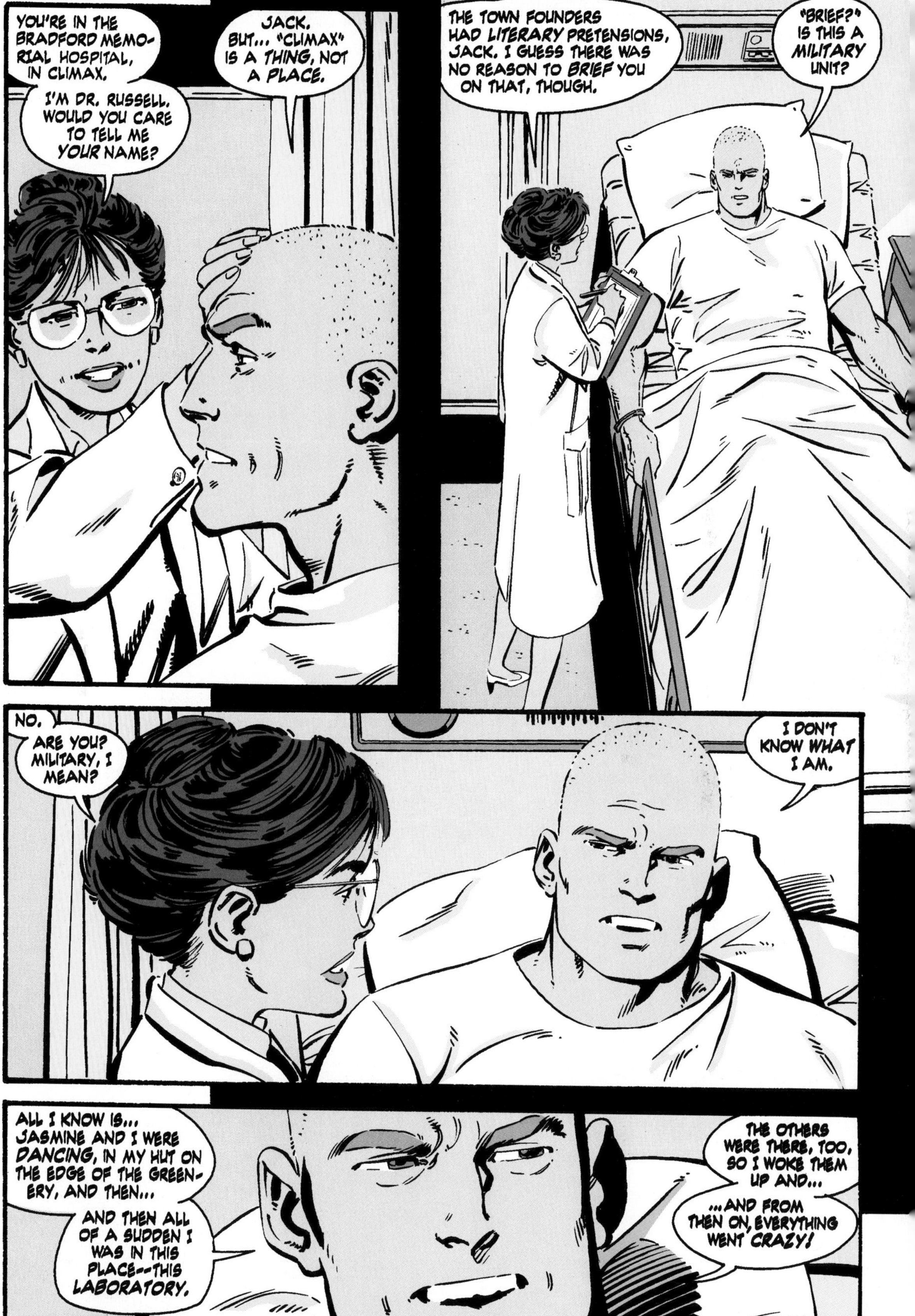
YOU'RE IN THE BRADFORD MEMORIAL HOSPITAL, IN CLIMAX.
I'M DR. RUSSELL. WOULD YOU CARE TO TELL ME *YOUR* NAME?
JACK. BUT... "CLIMAX" IS A *THING*, NOT A *PLACE*.
THE TOWN FOUNDERS HAD *LITERARY* PRETENSIONS, JACK. I GUESS THERE WAS NO REASON TO *BRIEF* YOU ON THAT, THOUGH.
"BRIEF?" IS THIS A *MILITARY* UNIT?
NO.
ARE YOU? MILITARY, I MEAN?
I DON'T KNOW *WHAT* I AM.
ALL I KNOW IS... JASMINE AND I WERE *DANCING*, IN MY HUT ON THE EDGE OF THE GREENERY, AND THEN...
AND THEN ALL OF A SUDDEN I WAS IN THIS PLACE--THIS *LABORATORY*.
THE OTHERS WERE THERE, TOO, SO I WOKE THEM UP AND...
...AND FROM THEN ON, EVERYTHING WENT *CRAZY*!

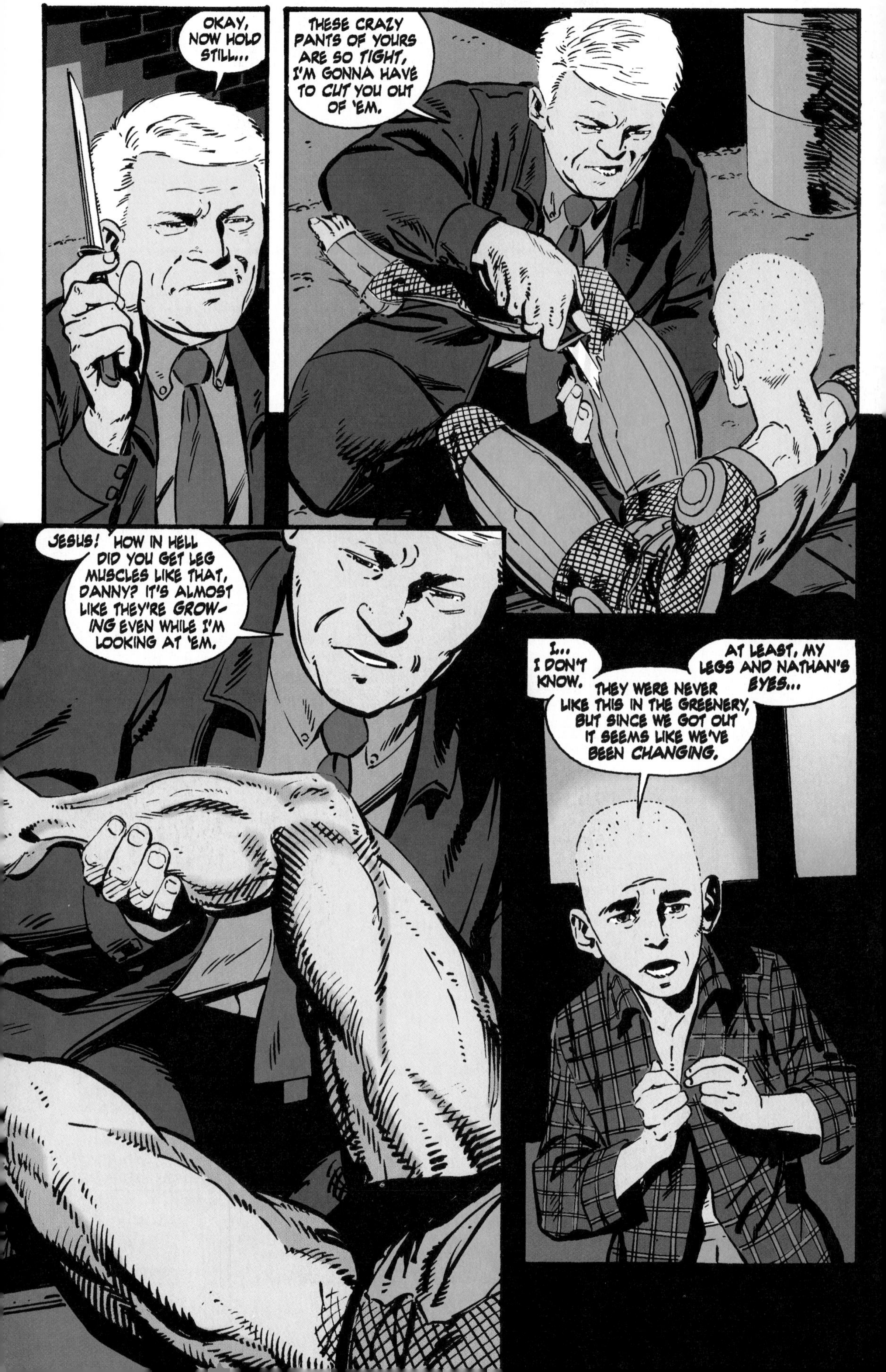
OKAY, NOW HOLD STILL...
THESE CRAZY PANTS OF YOURS ARE SO TIGHT, I'M GONNA HAVE TO CUT YOU OUT OF 'EM.
JESUS! HOW IN HELL DID YOU GET LEG MUSCLES LIKE THAT, DANNY? IT'S ALMOST LIKE THEY'RE GROWING EVEN WHILE I'M LOOKING AT 'EM.
I... I DON'T KNOW.
AT LEAST, MY LEGS AND NATHAN'S EYES...
THEY WERE NEVER LIKE THIS IN THE GREENERY, BUT SINCE WE GOT OUT IT SEEMS LIKE WE'VE BEEN CHANGING.

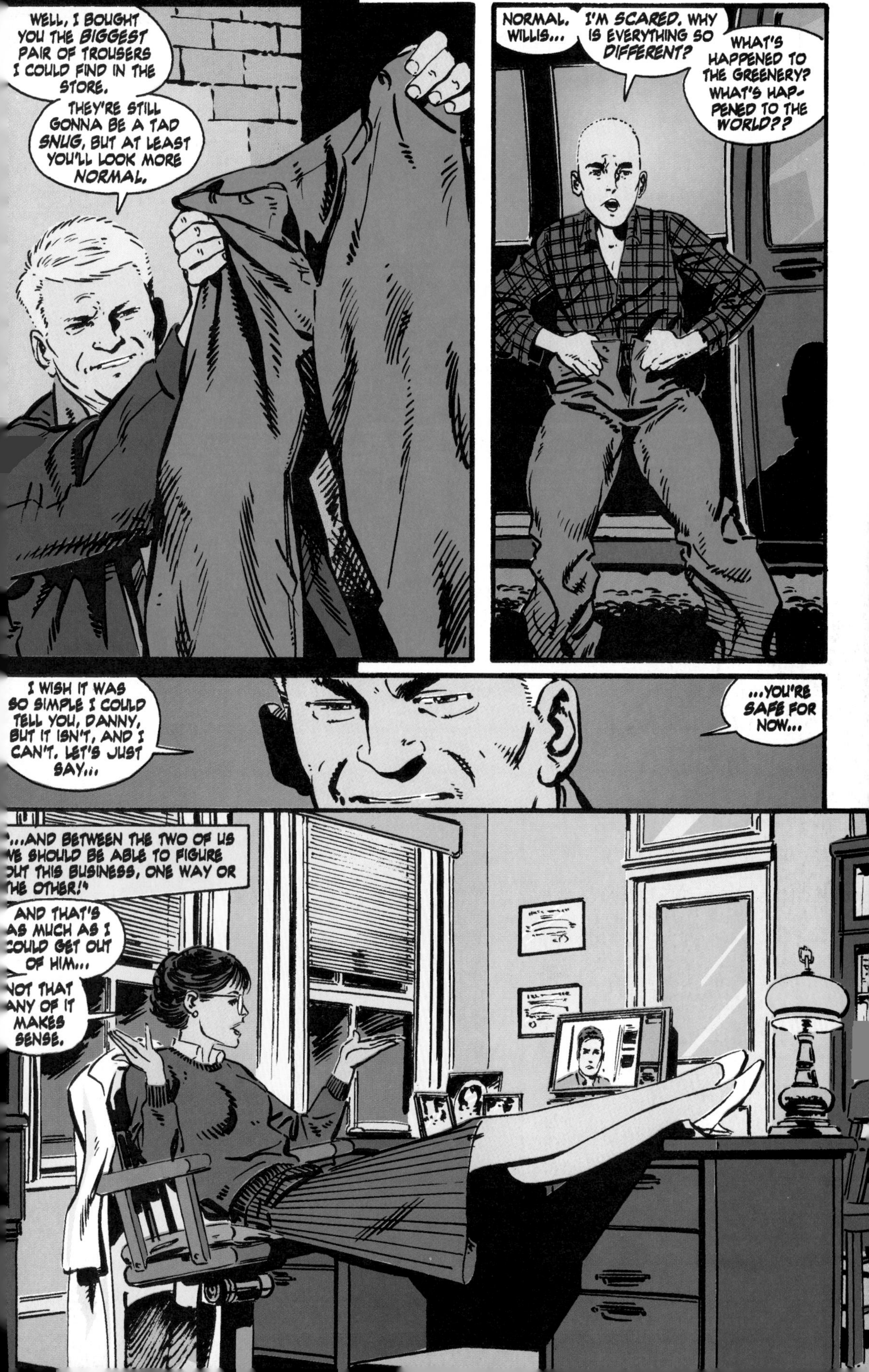
WELL, I BOUGHT YOU THE BIGGEST PAIR OF TROUSERS I COULD FIND IN THE STORE.
THEY'RE STILL GONNA BE A TAD SNUG, BUT AT LEAST YOU'LL LOOK MORE NORMAL.
NORMAL. WILLIS...
I'M SCARED. WHY IS EVERYTHING SO DIFFERENT?
WHAT'S HAPPENED TO THE GREENERY? WHAT'S HAP-PENED TO THE WORLD??
I WISH IT WAS SO SIMPLE I COULD TELL YOU, DANNY, BUT IT ISN'T, AND I CAN'T. LET'S JUST SAY...
...YOU'RE SAFE FOR NOW...
"...AND BETWEEN THE TWO OF US WE SHOULD BE ABLE TO FIGURE OUT THIS BUSINESS, ONE WAY OR THE OTHER!"
AND THAT'S AS MUCH AS I COULD GET OUT OF HIM...
NOT THAT ANY OF IT MAKES SENSE.

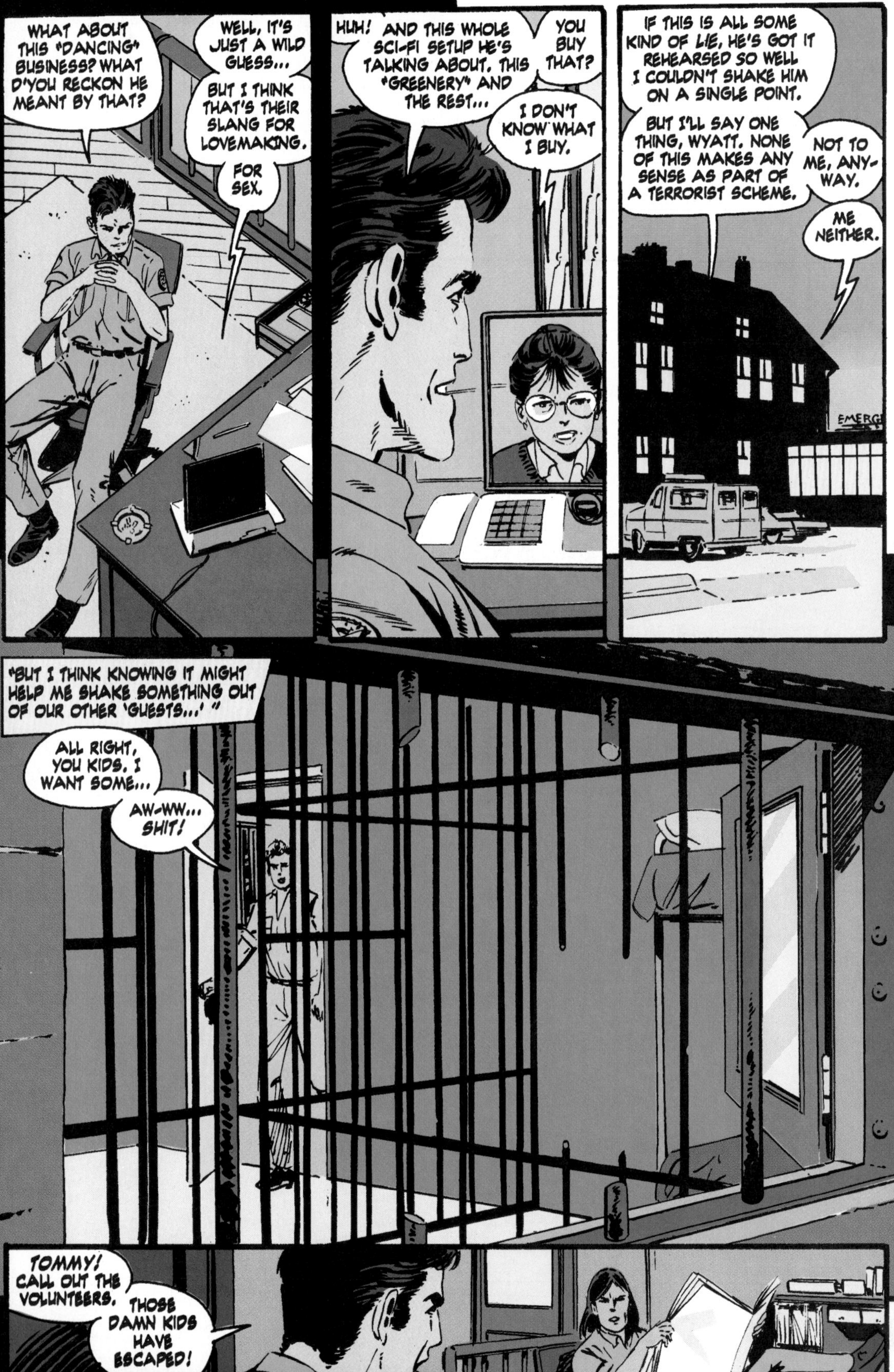
WHAT ABOUT THIS "DANCING" BUSINESS? WHAT D'YOU RECKON HE MEANT BY THAT?
WELL, IT'S JUST A WILD GUESS...
BUT I THINK THAT'S THEIR SLANG FOR LOVEMAKING.
FOR SEX.
HUH! AND THIS WHOLE SCI-FI SETUP HE'S TALKING ABOUT. THIS "GREENERY" AND THE REST...
YOU BUY THAT?
I DON'T KNOW WHAT I BUY.
IF THIS IS ALL SOME KIND OF LIE, HE'S GOT IT REHEARSED SO WELL I COULDN'T SHAKE HIM ON A SINGLE POINT.
BUT I'LL SAY ONE THING, WYATT. NONE OF THIS MAKES ANY SENSE AS PART OF A TERRORIST SCHEME.
NOT TO ME, ANYWAY.
ME NEITHER.
EMERG
"BUT I THINK KNOWING IT MIGHT HELP ME SHAKE SOMETHING OUT OF OUR OTHER 'GUESTS...'"
ALL RIGHT, YOU KIDS. I WANT SOME...
AW-WW... SHIT!
TOMMY! CALL OUT THE VOLUNTEERS.
THOSE DAMN KIDS HAVE ESCAPED!

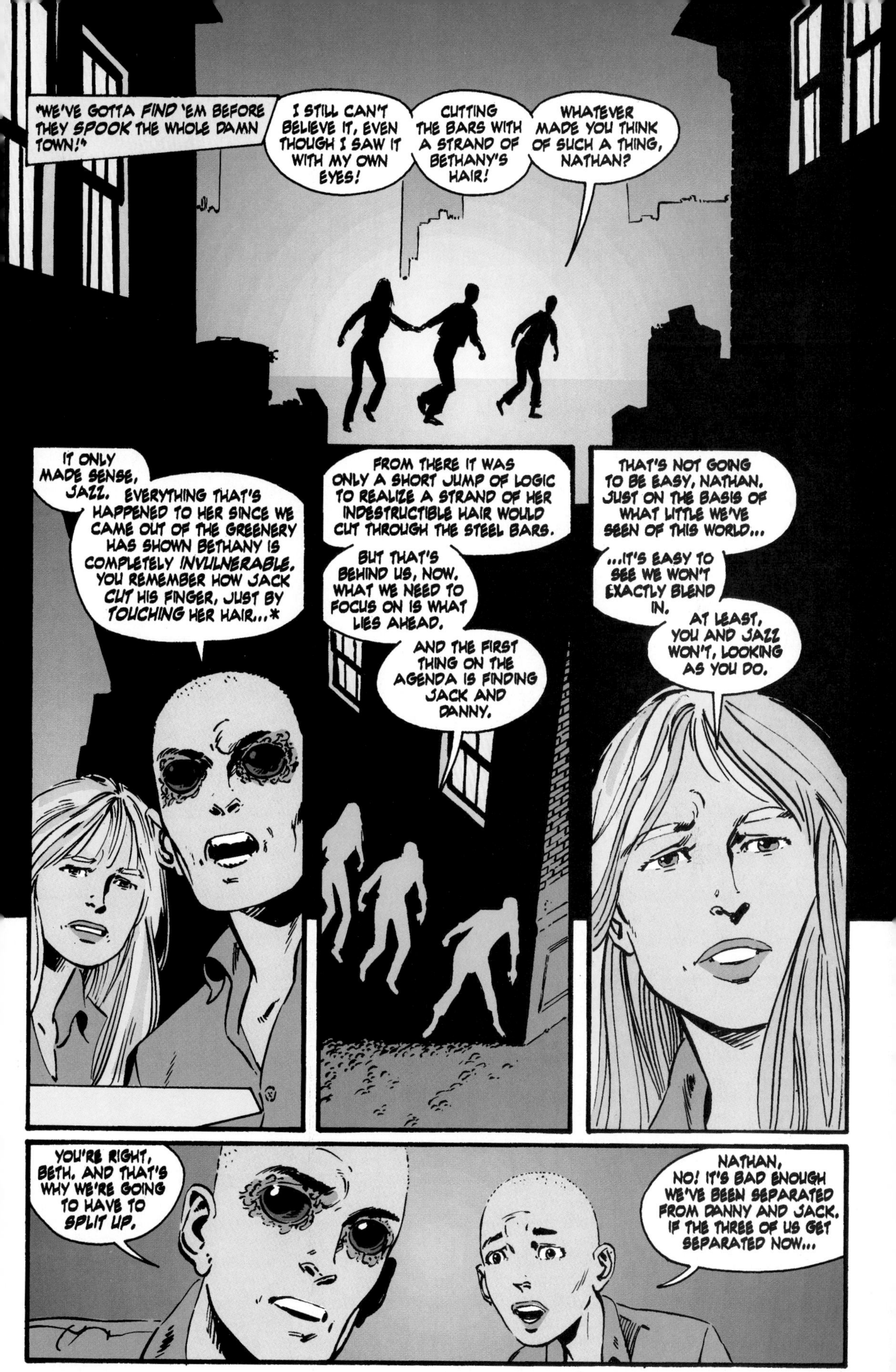

"WE'VE GOTTA FIND 'EM BEFORE THEY SPOOK THE WHOLE DAMN TOWN!"
I STILL CAN'T BELIEVE IT, EVEN THOUGH I SAW IT WITH MY OWN EYES!
CUTTING THE BARS WITH A STRAND OF BETHANY'S HAIR!
WHATEVER MADE YOU THINK OF SUCH A THING, NATHAN?
IT ONLY MADE SENSE, JAZZ.
EVERYTHING THAT'S HAPPENED TO HER SINCE WE CAME OUT OF THE GREENERY HAS SHOWN BETHANY IS COMPLETELY INVULNERABLE. YOU REMEMBER HOW JACK CUT HIS FINGER, JUST BY TOUCHING HER HAIR...*
FROM THERE IT WAS ONLY A SHORT JUMP OF LOGIC TO REALIZE A STRAND OF HER INDESTRUCTIBLE HAIR WOULD CUT THROUGH THE STEEL BARS.
BUT THAT'S BEHIND US, NOW. WHAT WE NEED TO FOCUS ON IS WHAT LIES AHEAD.
AND THE FIRST THING ON THE AGENDA IS FINDING JACK AND DANNY.
THAT'S NOT GOING TO BE EASY, NATHAN. JUST ON THE BASIS OF WHAT LITTLE WE'VE SEEN OF THIS WORLD...
...IT'S EASY TO SEE WE WON'T EXACTLY BLEND IN.
AT LEAST, YOU AND JAZZ WON'T, LOOKING AS YOU DO.
YOU'RE RIGHT, BETH. AND THAT'S WHY WE'RE GOING TO HAVE TO SPLIT UP.
NATHAN, NO! IT'S BAD ENOUGH WE'VE BEEN SEPARATED FROM DANNY AND JACK. IF THE THREE OF US GET SEPARATED NOW...

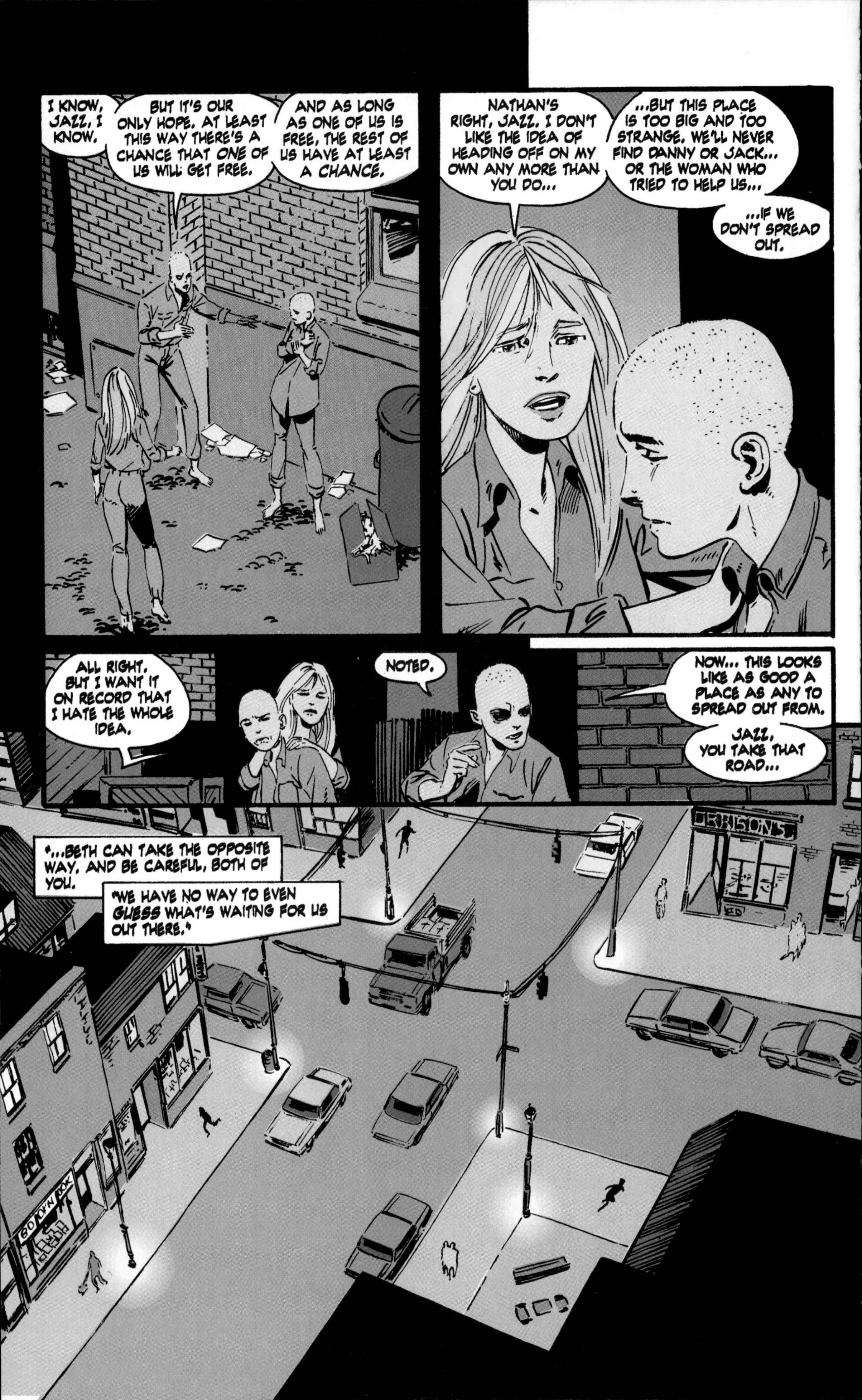

I KNOW, JAZZ, I KNOW.
BUT IT'S OUR ONLY HOPE. AT LEAST THIS WAY THERE'S A CHANCE THAT ONE OF US WILL GET FREE.
AND AS LONG AS ONE OF US IS FREE, THE REST OF US HAVE AT LEAST A CHANCE.
NATHAN'S RIGHT, JAZZ. I DON'T LIKE THE IDEA OF HEADING OFF ON MY OWN ANY MORE THAN YOU DO...
...BUT THIS PLACE IS TOO BIG AND TOO STRANGE. WE'LL NEVER FIND DANNY OR JACK... OR THE WOMAN WHO TRIED TO HELP US...
...IF WE DON'T SPREAD OUT.
ALL RIGHT, BUT I WANT IT ON RECORD THAT I HATE THE WHOLE IDEA.
NOTED.
NOW... THIS LOOKS LIKE AS GOOD A PLACE AS ANY TO SPREAD OUT FROM.
JAZZ, YOU TAKE THAT ROAD...
"...BETH CAN TAKE THE OPPOSITE WAY. AND BE CAREFUL, BOTH OF YOU.
"WE HAVE NO WAY TO EVEN GUESS WHAT'S WAITING FOR US OUT THERE."

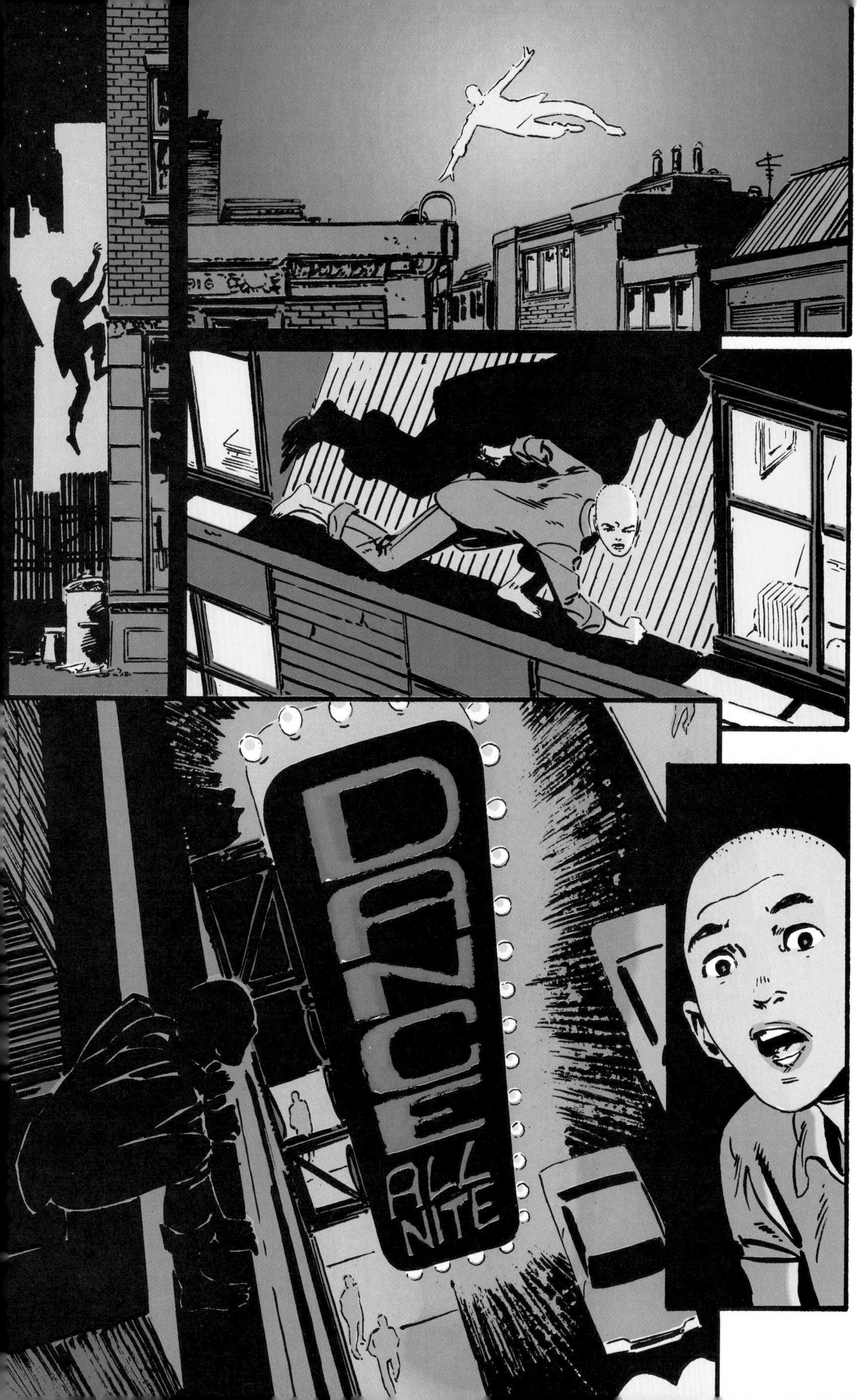
DANCE
ALL NITE

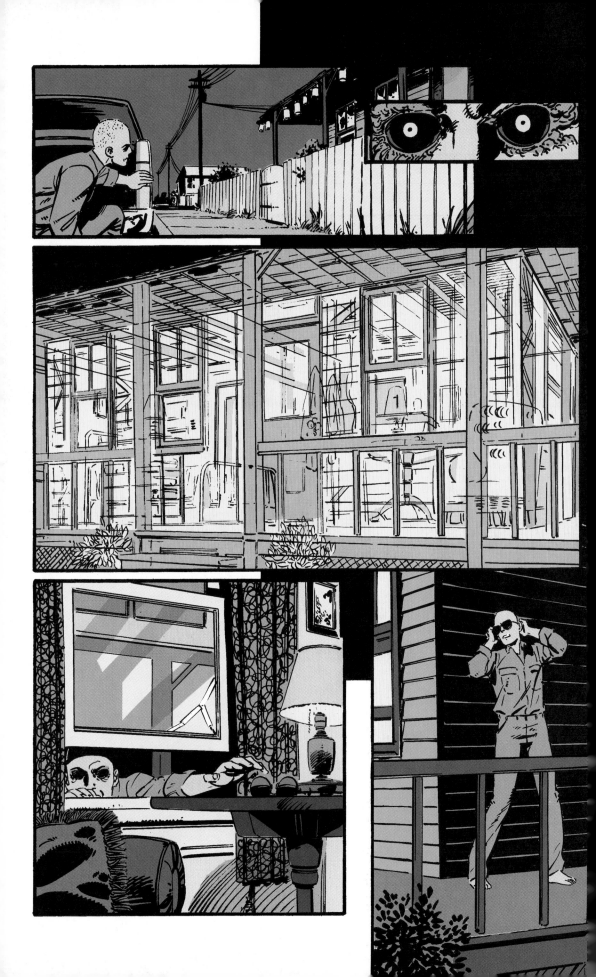

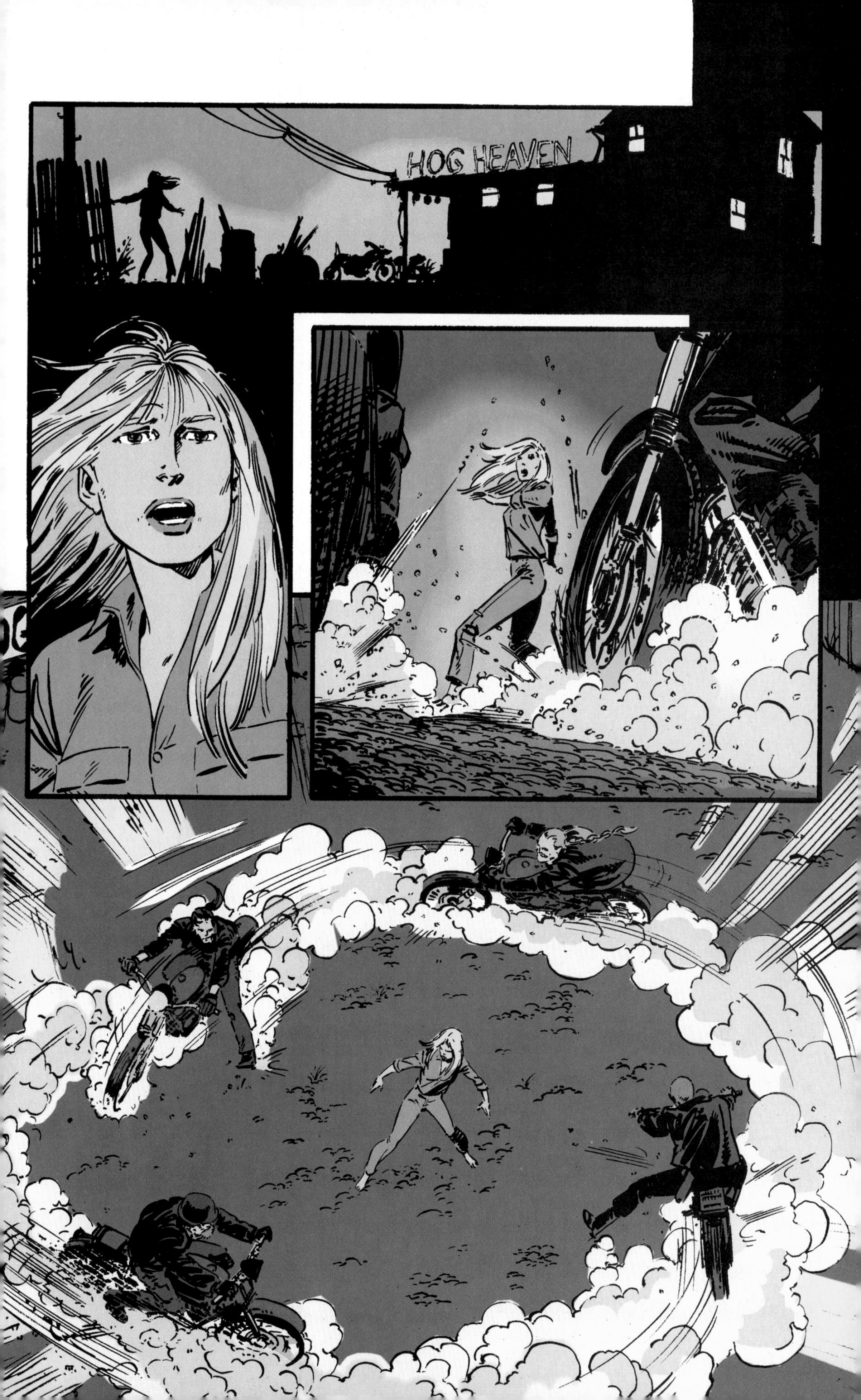
HOG HEAVEN

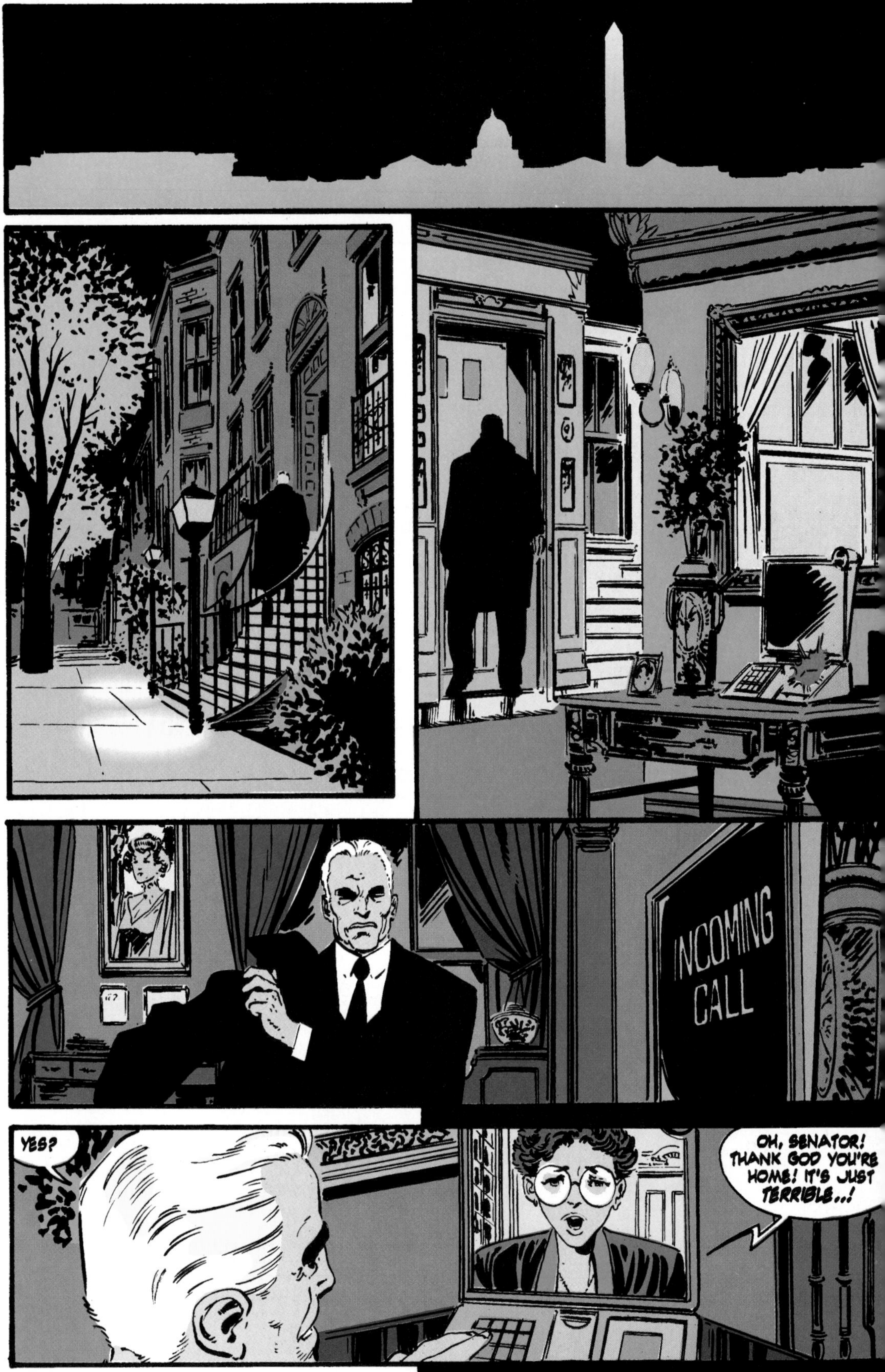
INCOMING CALL
YES?
OH, SENATOR! THANK GOD YOU'RE HOME! IT'S JUST TERRIBLE...!

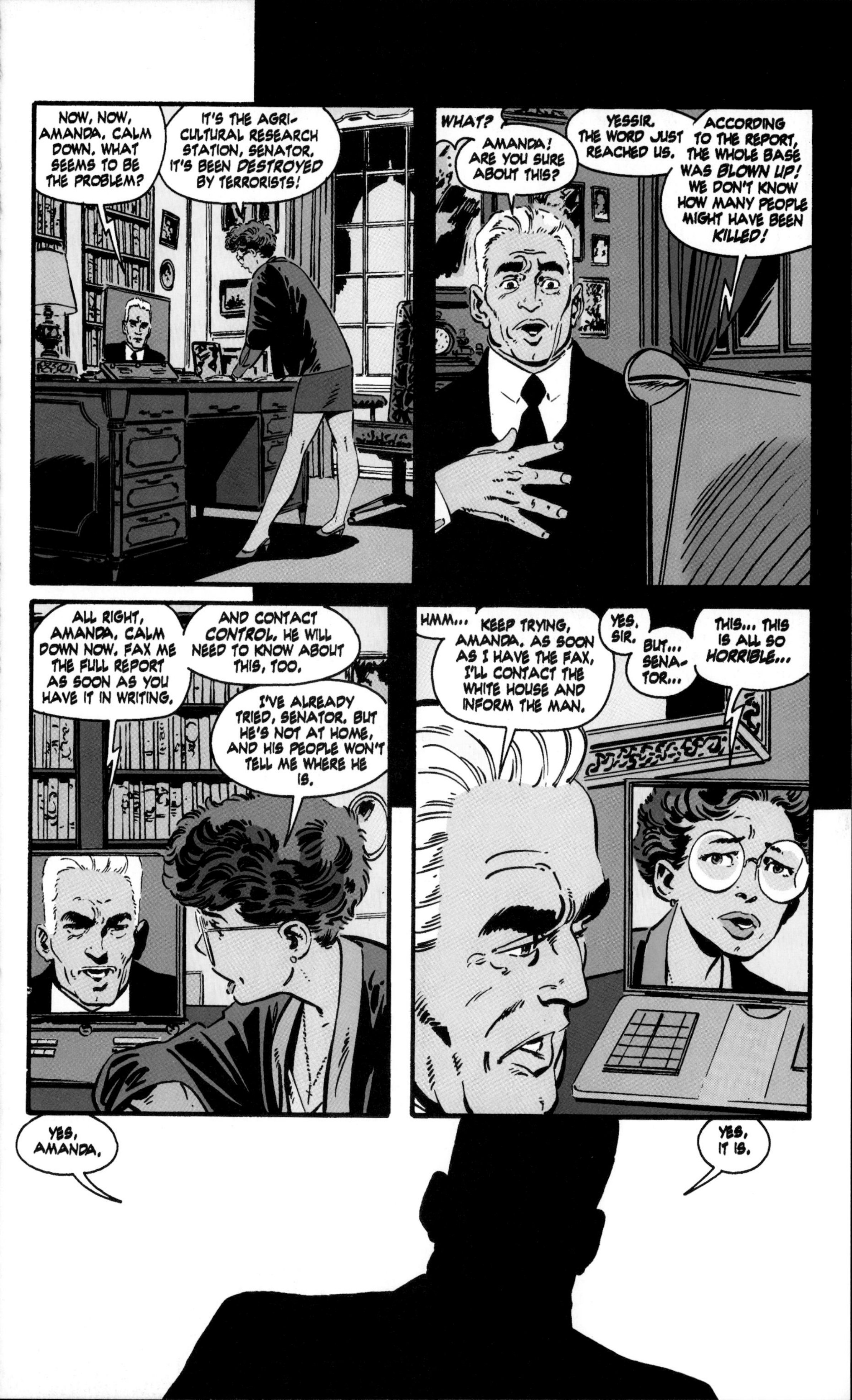
NOW, NOW, AMANDA. CALM DOWN. WHAT SEEMS TO BE THE PROBLEM?
IT'S THE AGRICULTURAL RESEARCH STATION, SENATOR. IT'S BEEN DESTROYED BY TERRORISTS!
WHAT?
AMANDA! ARE YOU SURE ABOUT THIS?
YESSIR. THE WORD JUST REACHED US.
ACCORDING TO THE REPORT, THE WHOLE BASE WAS BLOWN UP! WE DON'T KNOW HOW MANY PEOPLE MIGHT HAVE BEEN KILLED!
ALL RIGHT, AMANDA. CALM DOWN NOW. FAX ME THE FULL REPORT AS SOON AS YOU HAVE IT IN WRITING.
AND CONTACT CONTROL. HE WILL NEED TO KNOW ABOUT THIS, TOO.
I'VE ALREADY TRIED, SENATOR. BUT HE'S NOT AT HOME, AND HIS PEOPLE WON'T TELL ME WHERE HE IS.
HMM...
KEEP TRYING, AMANDA. AS SOON AS I HAVE THE FAX, I'LL CONTACT THE WHITE HOUSE AND INFORM THE MAN.
YES, SIR.
BUT... SENATOR...
THIS... THIS IS ALL SO HORRIBLE...
YES, AMANDA.
YES, IT IS.

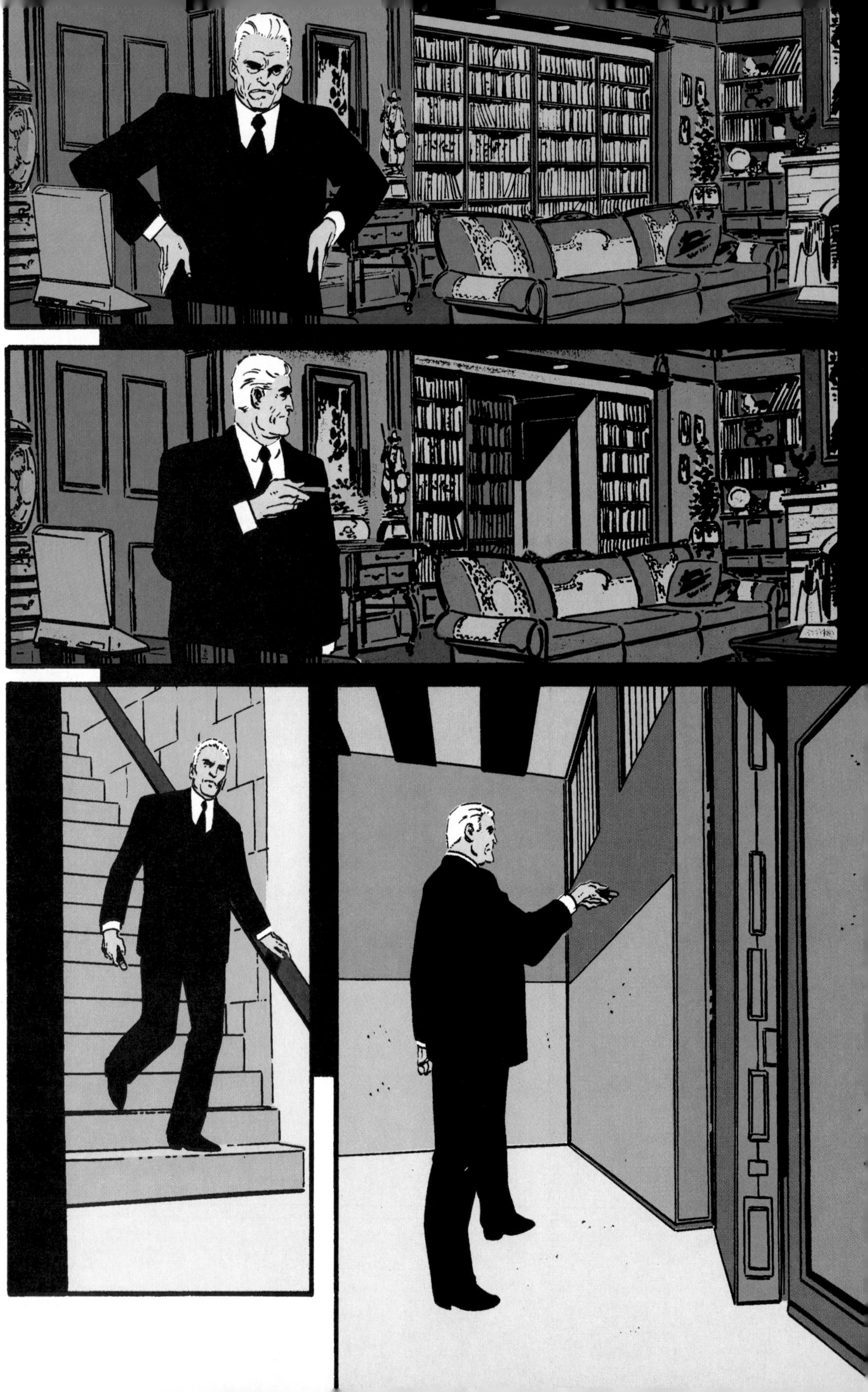

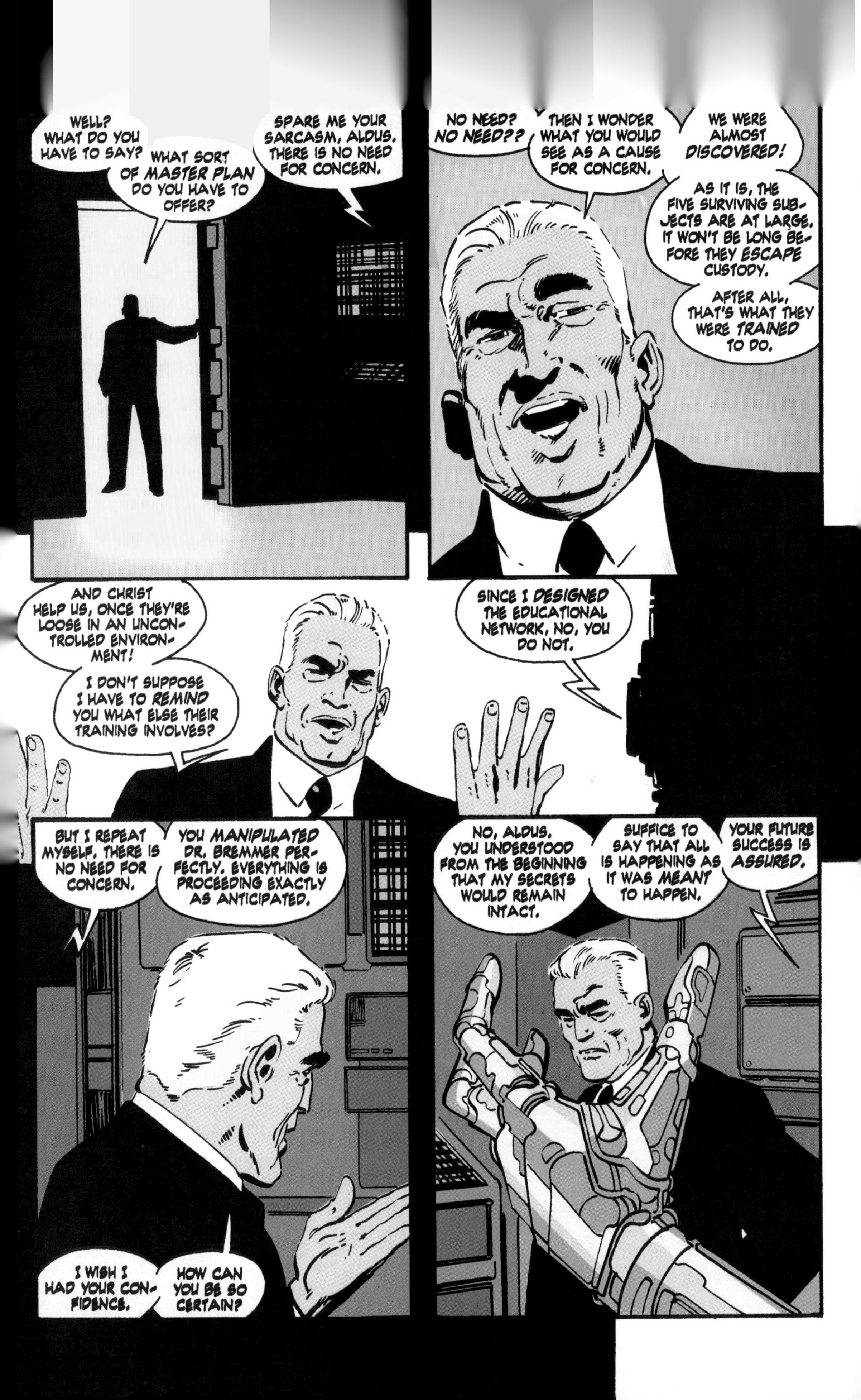
WELL? WHAT DO YOU HAVE TO SAY?
WHAT SORT OF MASTER PLAN DO YOU HAVE TO OFFER?
SPARE ME YOUR SARCASM, ALDUS. THERE IS NO NEED FOR CONCERN.
NO NEED? NO NEED??
THEN I WONDER WHAT YOU WOULD SEE AS A CAUSE FOR CONCERN.
WE WERE ALMOST DISCOVERED!
AS IT IS, THE FIVE SURVIVING SUBJECTS ARE AT LARGE. IT WON'T BE LONG BEFORE THEY ESCAPE CUSTODY.
AFTER ALL, THAT'S WHAT THEY WERE TRAINED TO DO.
AND CHRIST HELP US, ONCE THEY'RE LOOSE IN AN UNCONTROLLED ENVIRONMENT!
I DON'T SUPPOSE I HAVE TO REMIND YOU WHAT ELSE THEIR TRAINING INVOLVES?
SINCE I DESIGNED THE EDUCATIONAL NETWORK, NO, YOU DO NOT.
BUT I REPEAT MYSELF. THERE IS NO NEED FOR CONCERN.
YOU MANIPULATED DR. BREMMER PERFECTLY. EVERYTHING IS PROCEEDING EXACTLY AS ANTICIPATED.
I WISH I HAD YOUR CONFIDENCE.
HOW CAN YOU BE SO CERTAIN?
NO, ALDUS. YOU UNDERSTOOD FROM THE BEGINNING THAT MY SECRETS WOULD REMAIN INTACT.
SUFFICE TO SAY THAT ALL IS HAPPENING AS IT WAS MEANT TO HAPPEN.
YOUR FUTURE SUCCESS IS ASSURED.

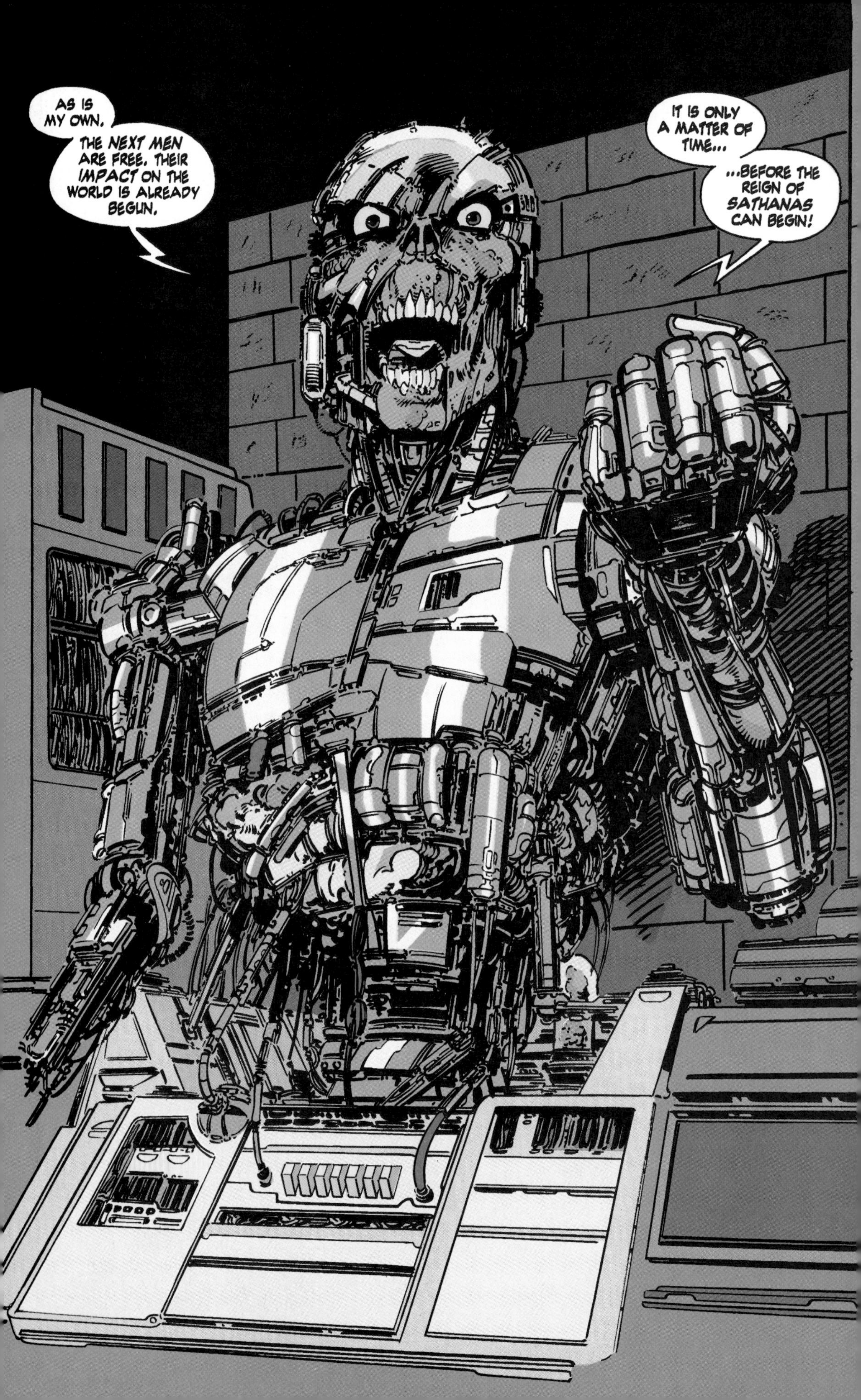
AS IS MY OWN.
THE NEXT MEN ARE FREE. THEIR IMPACT ON THE WORLD IS ALREADY BEGUN.
IT IS ONLY A MATTER OF TIME...
...BEFORE THE REIGN OF SATHANAS CAN BEGIN!

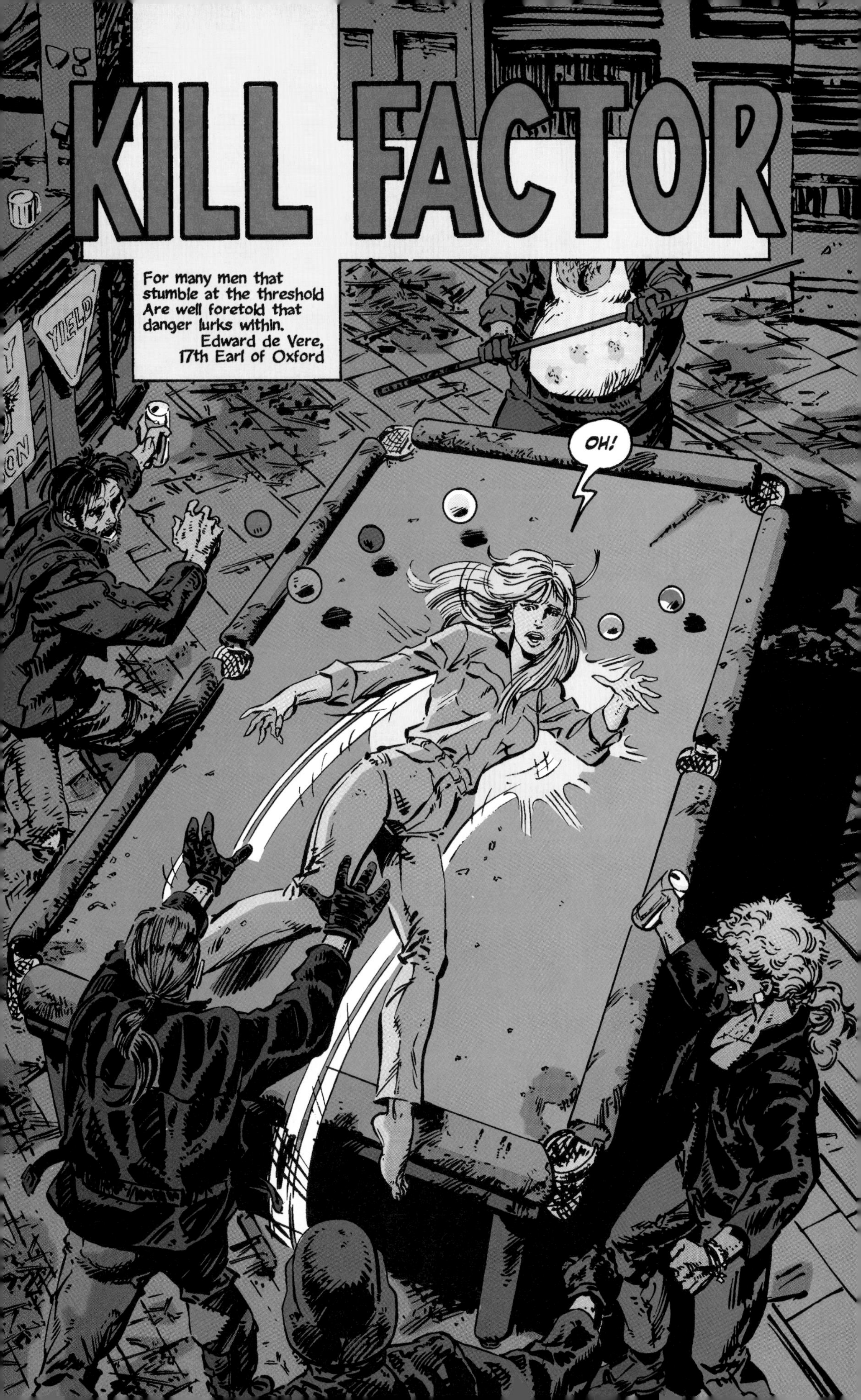
KILL FACTOR
For many men that stumble at the threshold Are well foretold that danger lurks within.
Edward de Vere, 17th Earl of Oxford
YIELD
OH!

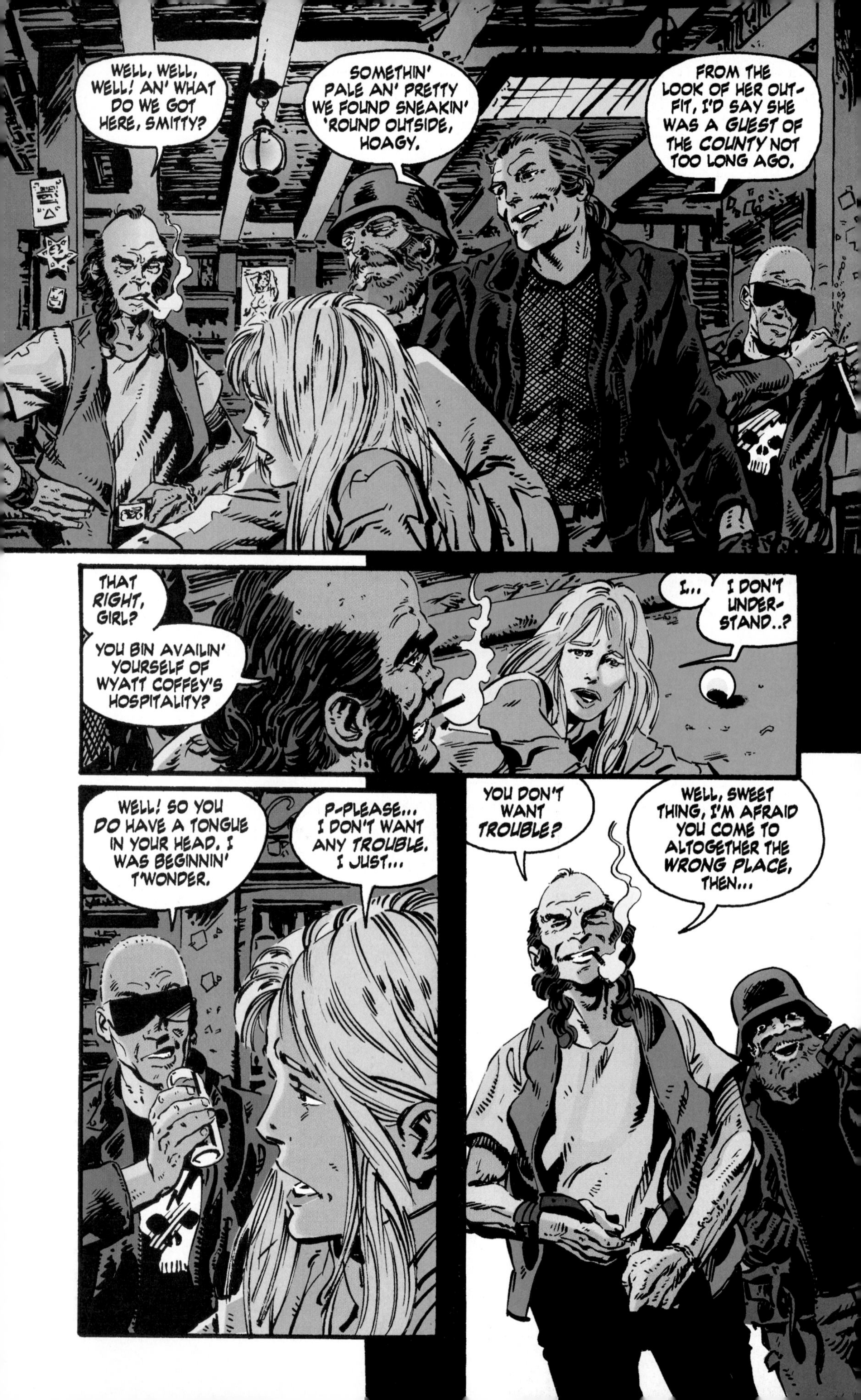
WELL, WELL, WELL! AN' WHAT DO WE GOT HERE, SMITTY?
SOMETHIN' PALE AN' PRETTY WE FOUND SNEAKIN' 'ROUND OUTSIDE, HOAGY.
FROM THE LOOK OF HER OUT-FIT, I'D SAY SHE WAS A GUEST OF THE COUNTY NOT TOO LONG AGO.
THAT RIGHT, GIRL?
YOU BIN AVAILIN' YOURSELF OF WYATT COFFEY'S HOSPITALITY?
I...
I DON'T UNDER-STAND..?
WELL! SO YOU DO HAVE A TONGUE IN YOUR HEAD. I WAS BEGINNIN' T'WONDER.
P-PLEASE... I DON'T WANT ANY TROUBLE. I JUST...
YOU DON'T WANT TROUBLE?
WELL, SWEET THING, I'M AFRAID YOU COME TO ALTOGETHER THE WRONG PLACE, THEN...

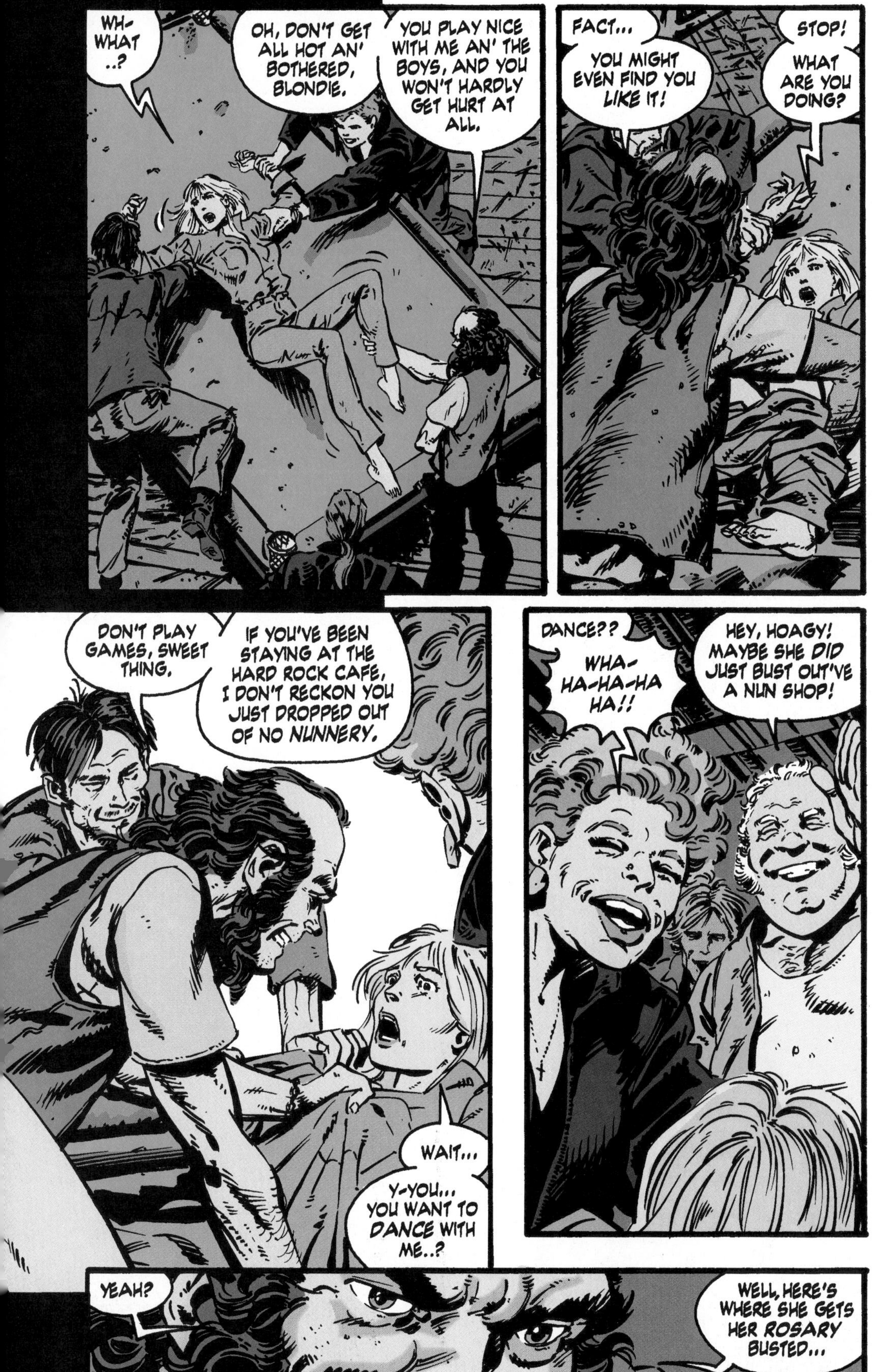

WH-WHAT ..?
OH, DON'T GET ALL HOT AN' BOTHERED, BLONDIE.
YOU PLAY NICE WITH ME AN' THE BOYS, AND YOU WON'T HARDLY GET HURT AT ALL.
FACT...
YOU MIGHT EVEN FIND YOU LIKE IT!
STOP!
WHAT ARE YOU DOING?
DON'T PLAY GAMES, SWEET THING.
IF YOU'VE BEEN STAYING AT THE HARD ROCK CAFE, I DON'T RECKON YOU JUST DROPPED OUT OF NO NUNNERY.
WAIT...
Y-YOU... YOU WANT TO DANCE WITH ME..?
DANCE??
WHA-HA-HA-HA HA!!
HEY, HOAGY! MAYBE SHE DID JUST BUST OUT'VE A NUN SHOP!
YEAH?
WELL, HERE'S WHERE SHE GETS HER ROSARY BUSTED...

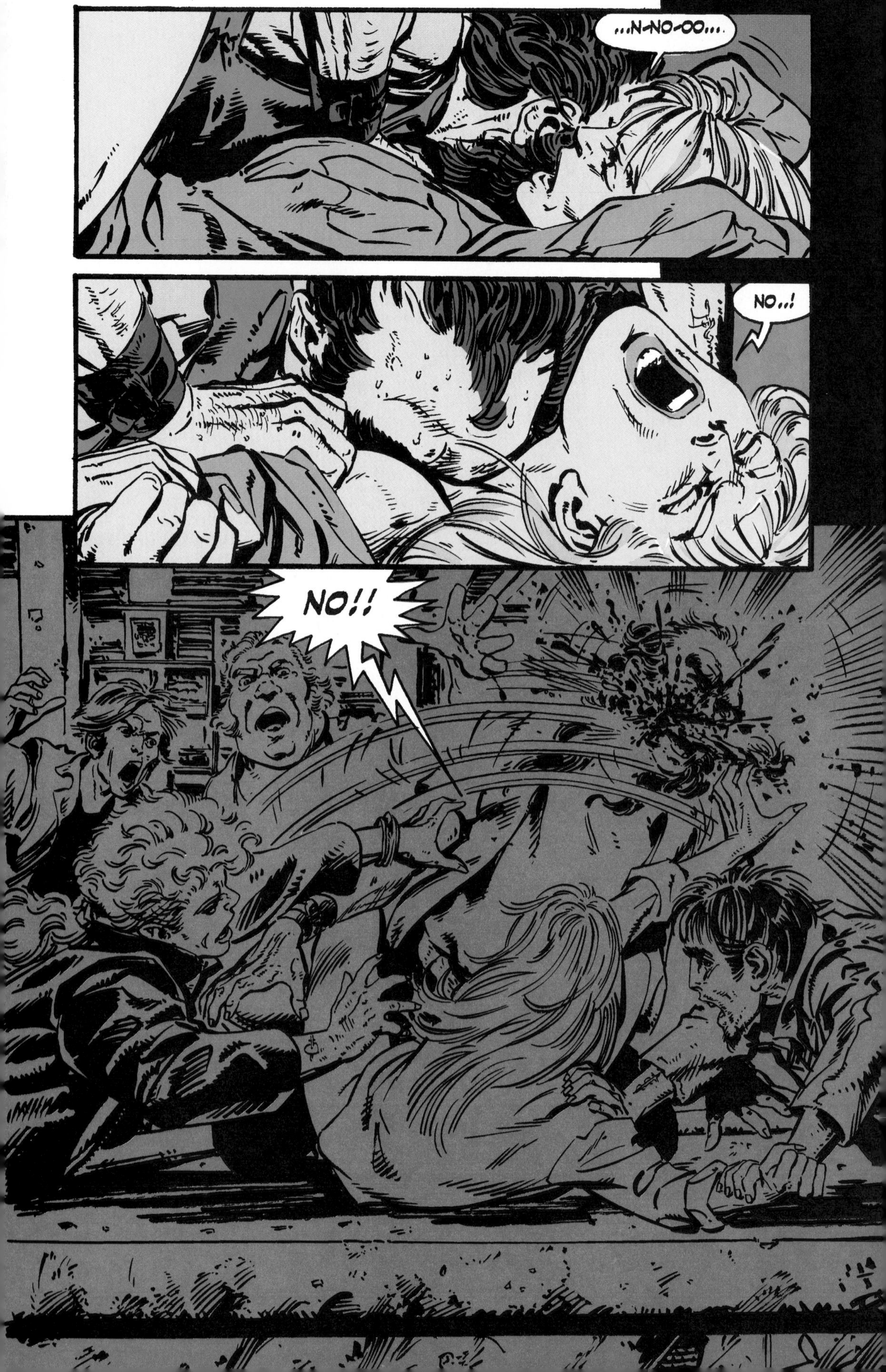
...N-NO-OO....
NO..!
NO!!

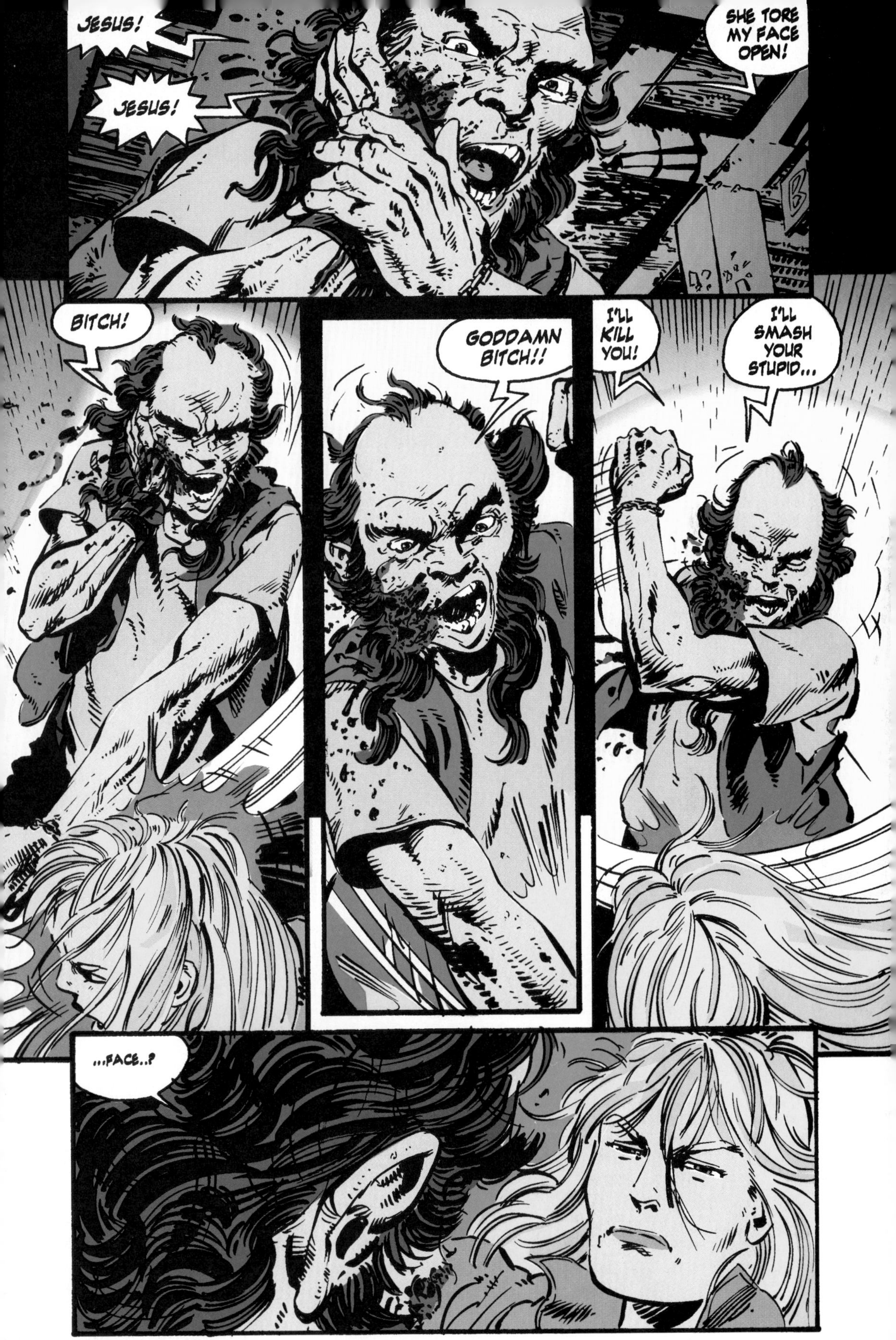
JESUS!
JESUS!
SHE TORE MY FACE OPEN!
BITCH!
GODDAMN BITCH!!
I'LL KILL YOU!
I'LL SMASH YOUR STUPID...
...FACE..?

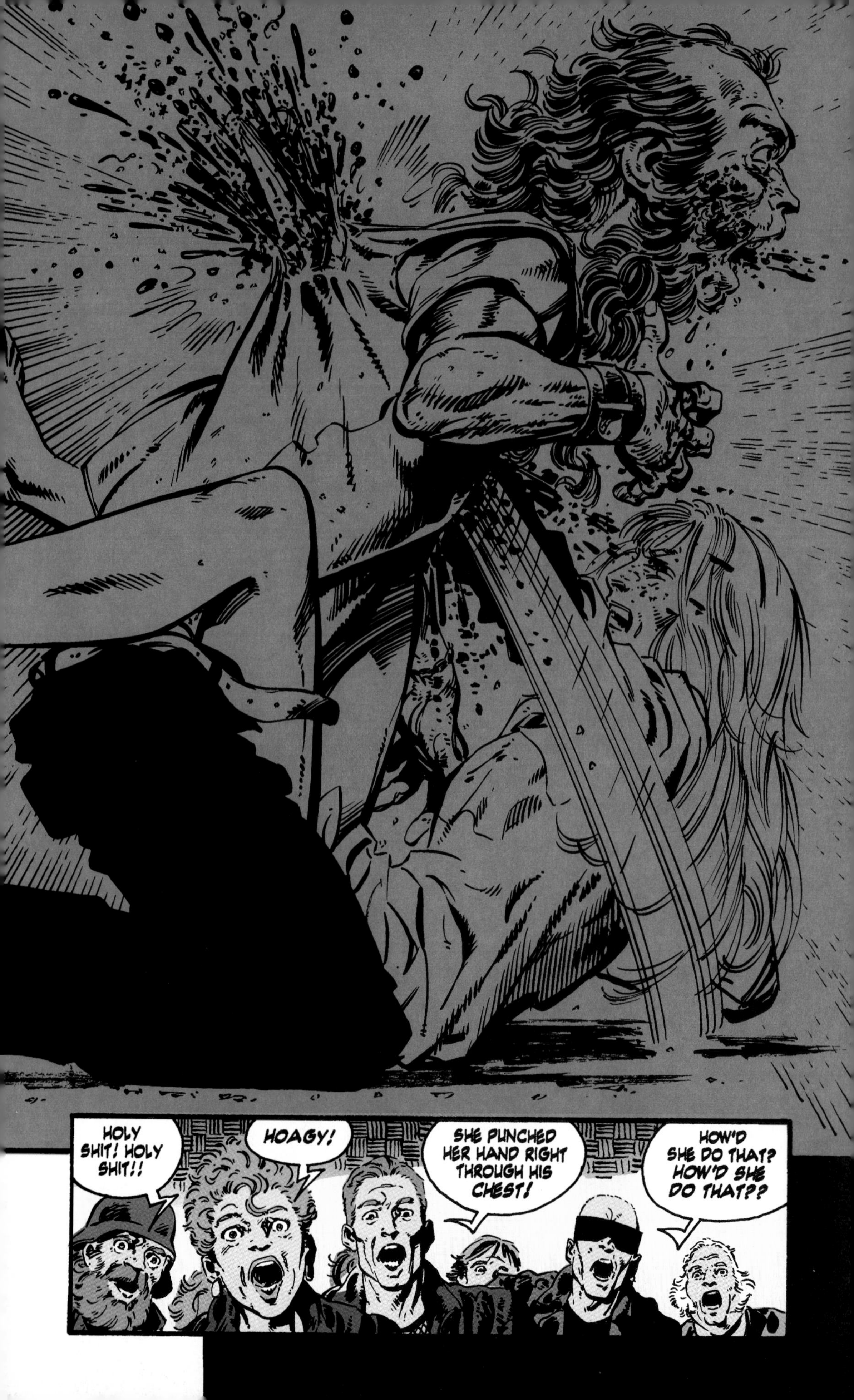

HOLY SHIT! HOLY SHIT!!
HOAGY!
SHE PUNCHED HER HAND RIGHT THROUGH HIS CHEST!
HOW'D SHE DO THAT? HOW'D SHE DO THAT??

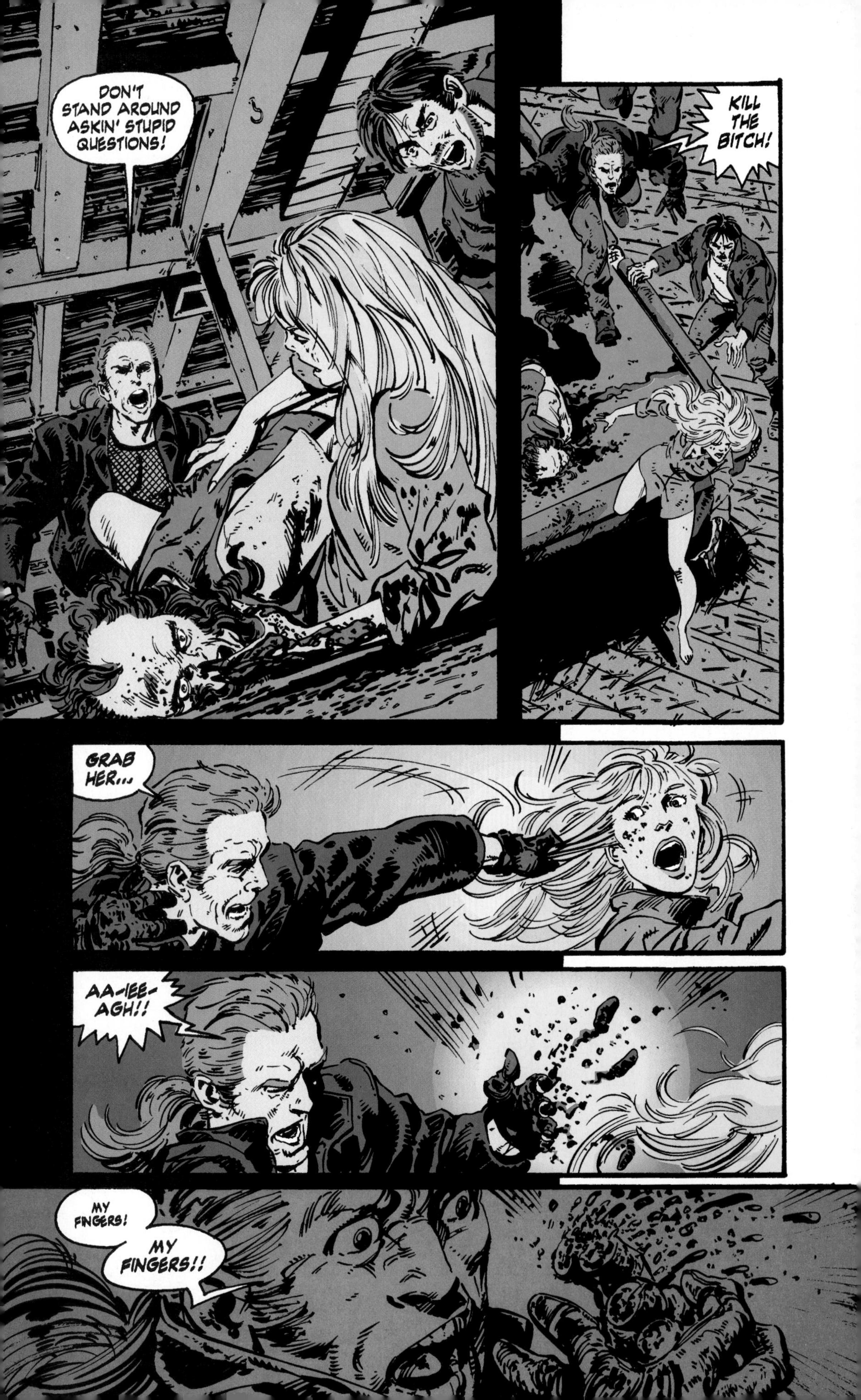
DON'T STAND AROUND ASKIN' STUPID QUESTIONS!
KILL THE BITCH!
GRAB HER...
AA-IEE-AGH!!
MY FINGERS!
MY FINGERS!!

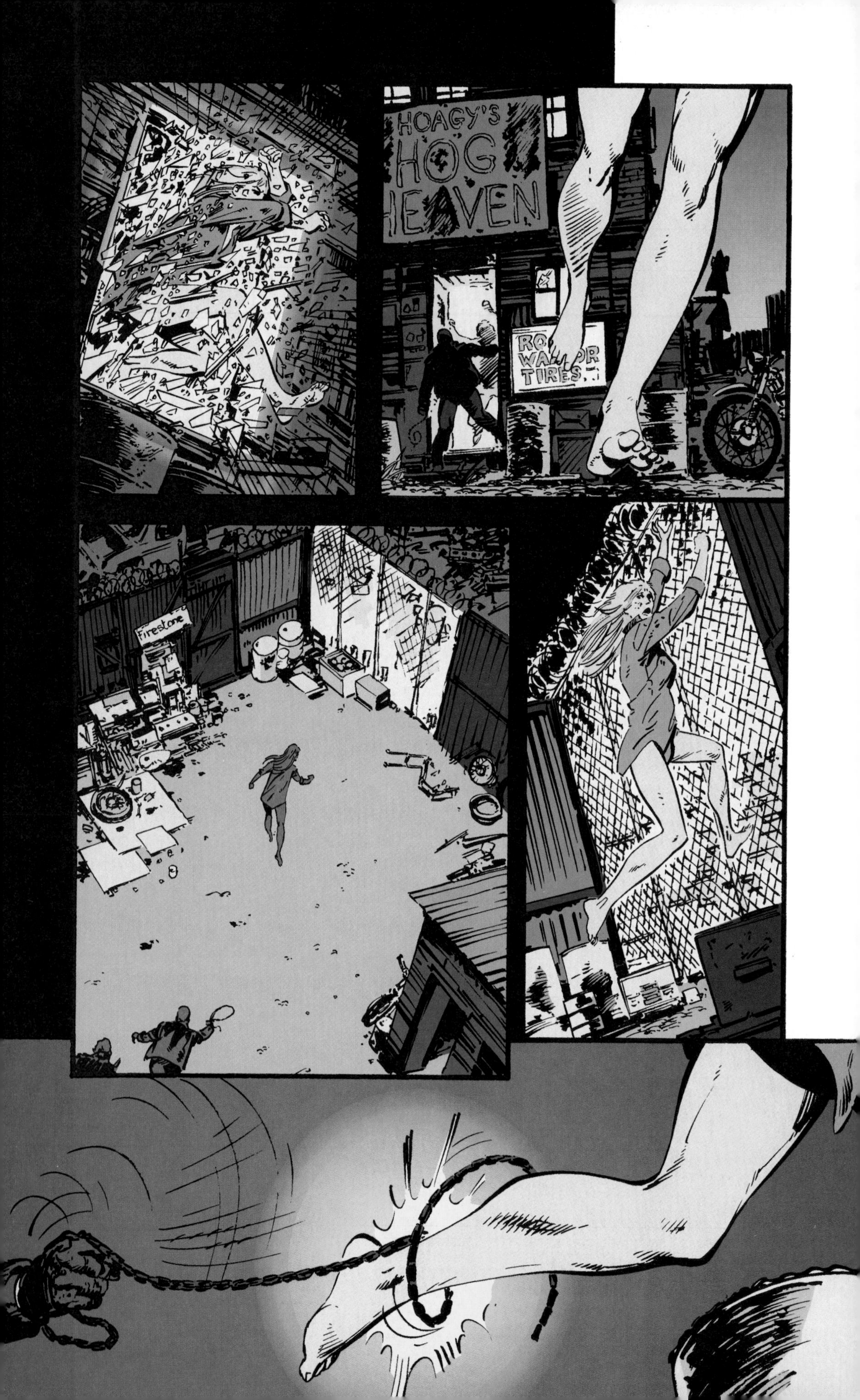
HOAGY'S
HOG
TIRES
Firestone

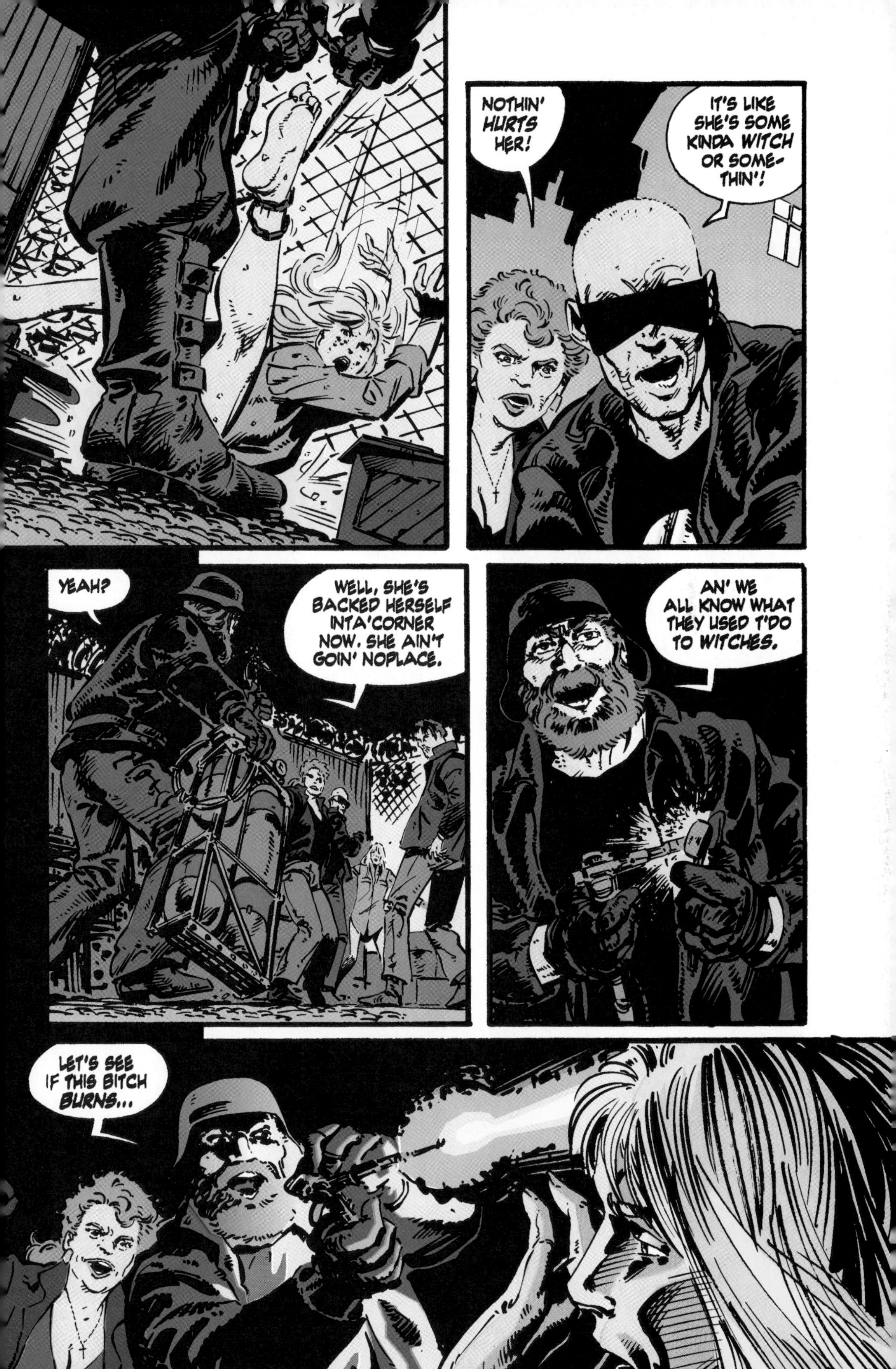
NOTHIN' HURTS HER!
IT'S LIKE SHE'S SOME KINDA WITCH OR SOME-THIN'!
YEAH?
WELL, SHE'S BACKED HERSELF INTA'CORNER NOW. SHE AIN'T GOIN' NOPLACE.
AN' WE ALL KNOW WHAT THEY USED T'DO TO WITCHES.
LET'S SEE IF THIS BITCH BURNS...

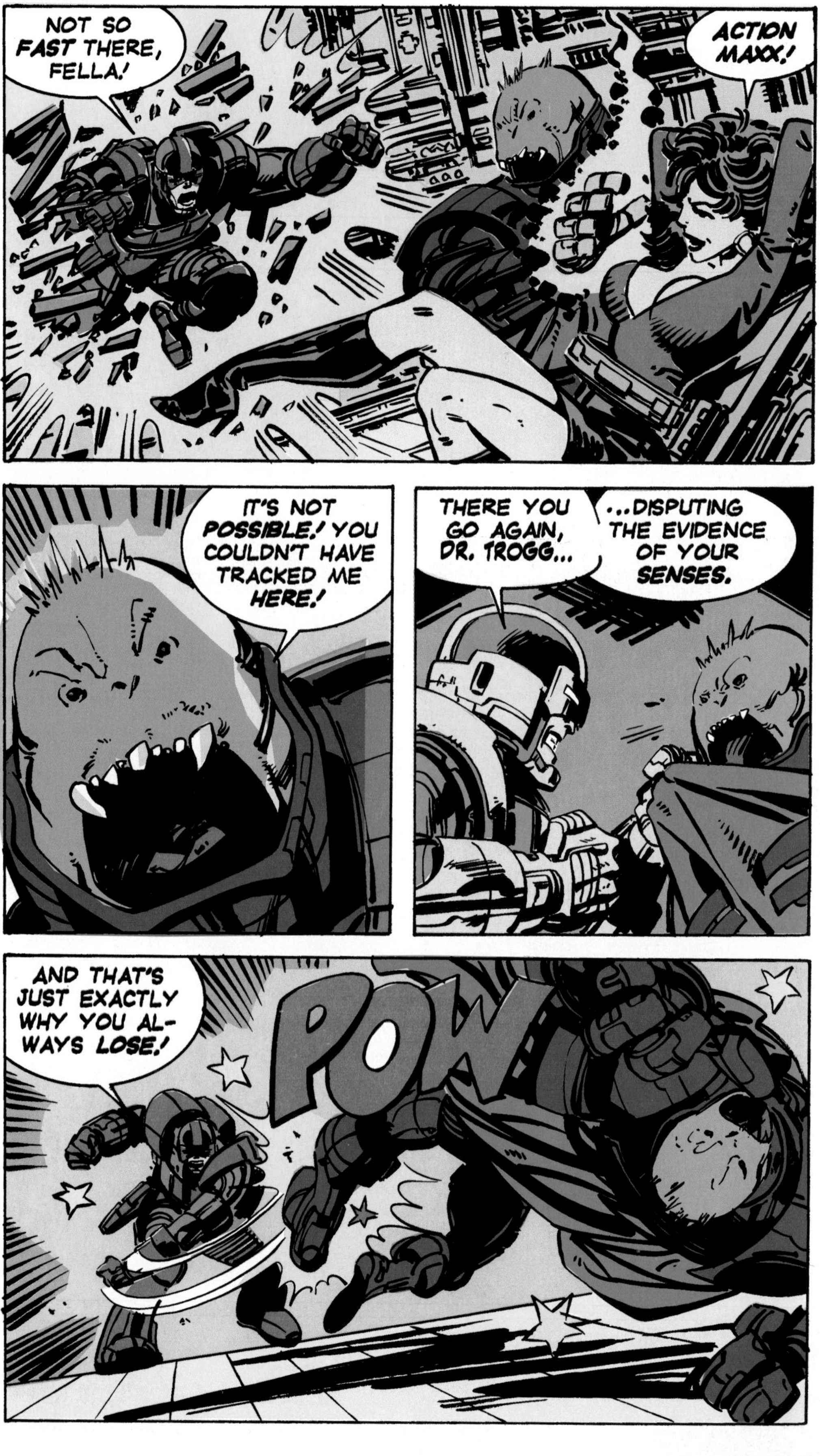
NOT SO FAST THERE, FELLA!
ACTION MAXX!
IT'S NOT POSSIBLE! YOU COULDN'T HAVE TRACKED ME HERE!
THERE YOU GO AGAIN, DR. TROGG...
...DISPUTING THE EVIDENCE OF YOUR SENSES.
AND THAT'S JUST EXACTLY WHY YOU AL-WAYS LOSE!
POW

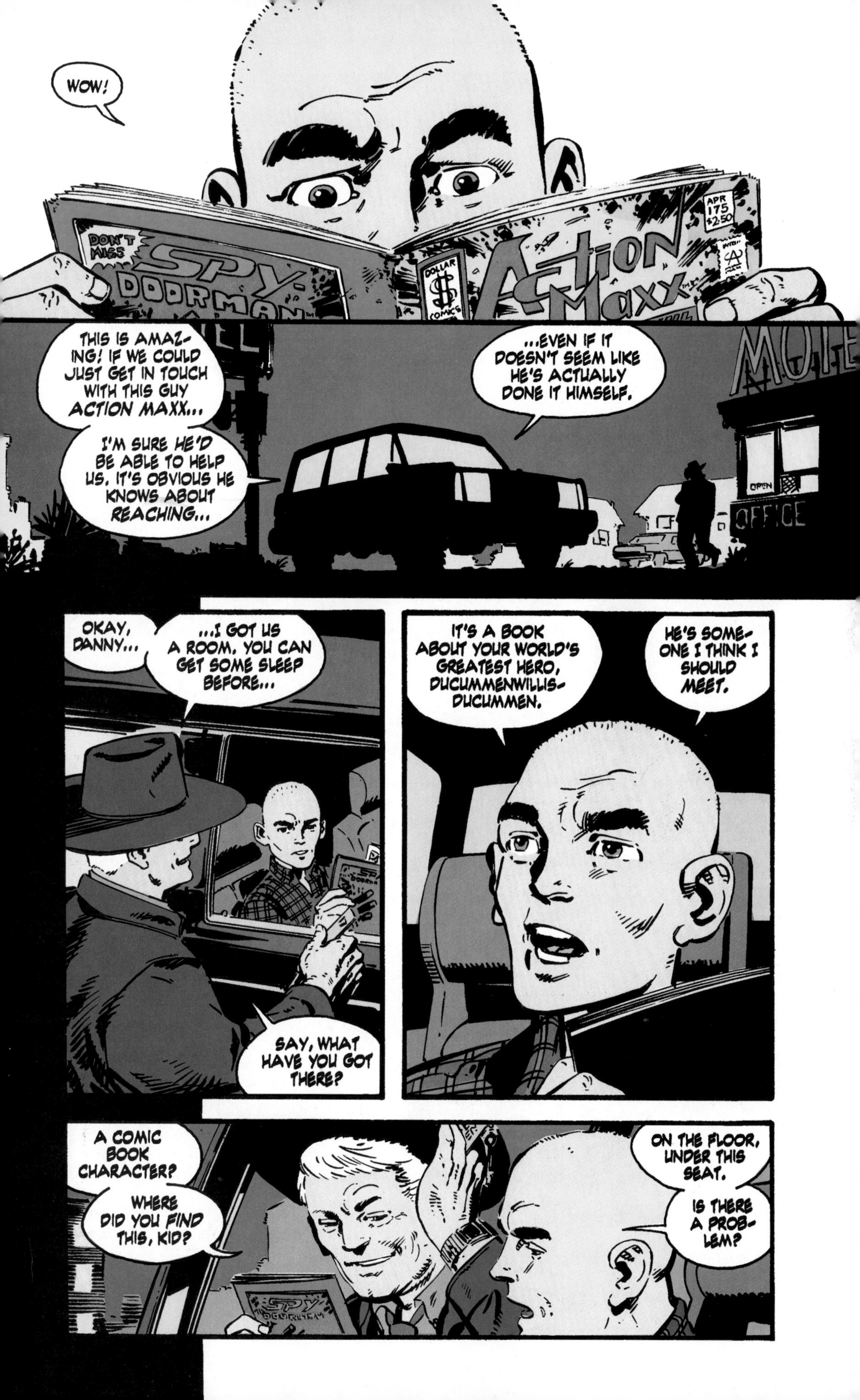
WOW!
DON'T MISS
SPY-DOORMAN
DOLLAR $ COMICS
APR 175 $2.50
Action Maxx
THIS IS AMAZING! IF WE COULD JUST GET IN TOUCH WITH THIS GUY ACTION MAXX...
I'M SURE HE'D BE ABLE TO HELP US. IT'S OBVIOUS HE KNOWS ABOUT REACHING...
...EVEN IF IT DOESN'T SEEM LIKE HE'S ACTUALLY DONE IT HIMSELF.
MOTEL
OPEN
OFFICE
OKAY, DANNY...
...I GOT US A ROOM. YOU CAN GET SOME SLEEP BEFORE...
SAY, WHAT HAVE YOU GOT THERE?
IT'S A BOOK ABOUT YOUR WORLD'S GREATEST HERO, DUCUMMENWILLIS-DUCUMMEN.
HE'S SOMEONE I THINK I SHOULD MEET.
A COMIC BOOK CHARACTER?
WHERE DID YOU FIND THIS, KID?
ON THE FLOOR, UNDER THIS SEAT.
IS THERE A PROBLEM?

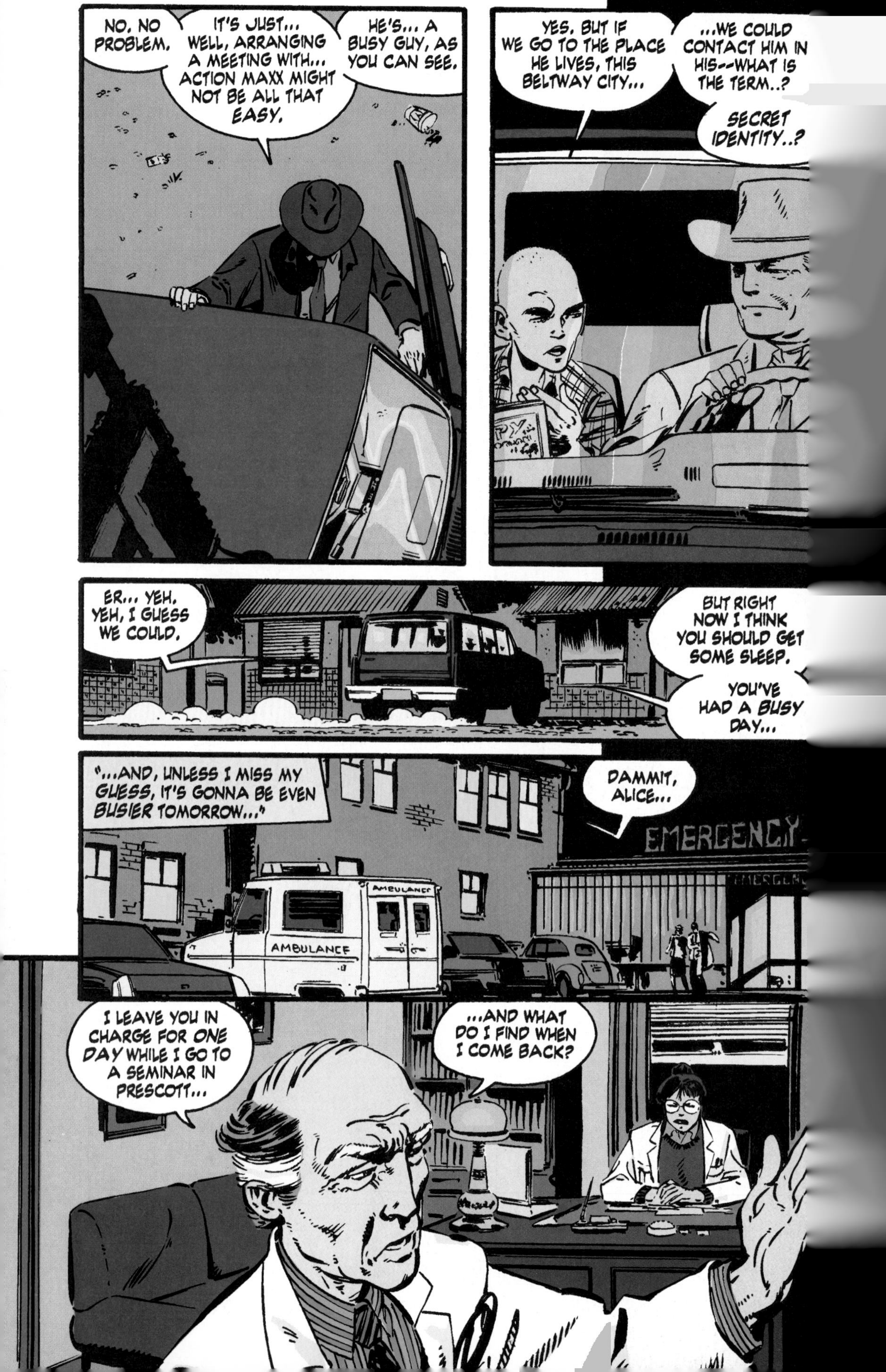
NO. NO PROBLEM.
IT'S JUST... WELL, ARRANGING A MEETING WITH... ACTION MAXX MIGHT NOT BE ALL THAT EASY.
HE'S... A BUSY GUY, AS YOU CAN SEE.
YES. BUT IF WE GO TO THE PLACE HE LIVES, THIS BELTWAY CITY...
...WE COULD CONTACT HIM IN HIS--WHAT IS THE TERM..?
SECRET IDENTITY..?
ER... YEH. YEH, I GUESS WE COULD.
BUT RIGHT NOW I THINK YOU SHOULD GET SOME SLEEP.
YOU'VE HAD A BUSY DAY...
"...AND, UNLESS I MISS MY GUESS, IT'S GONNA BE EVEN BUSIER TOMORROW..."
DAMMIT, ALICE...
EMERGENCY
AMBULANCE
AMBULANCE
I LEAVE YOU IN CHARGE FOR ONE DAY WHILE I GO TO A SEMINAR IN PRESCOTT...
...AND WHAT DO I FIND WHEN I COME BACK?

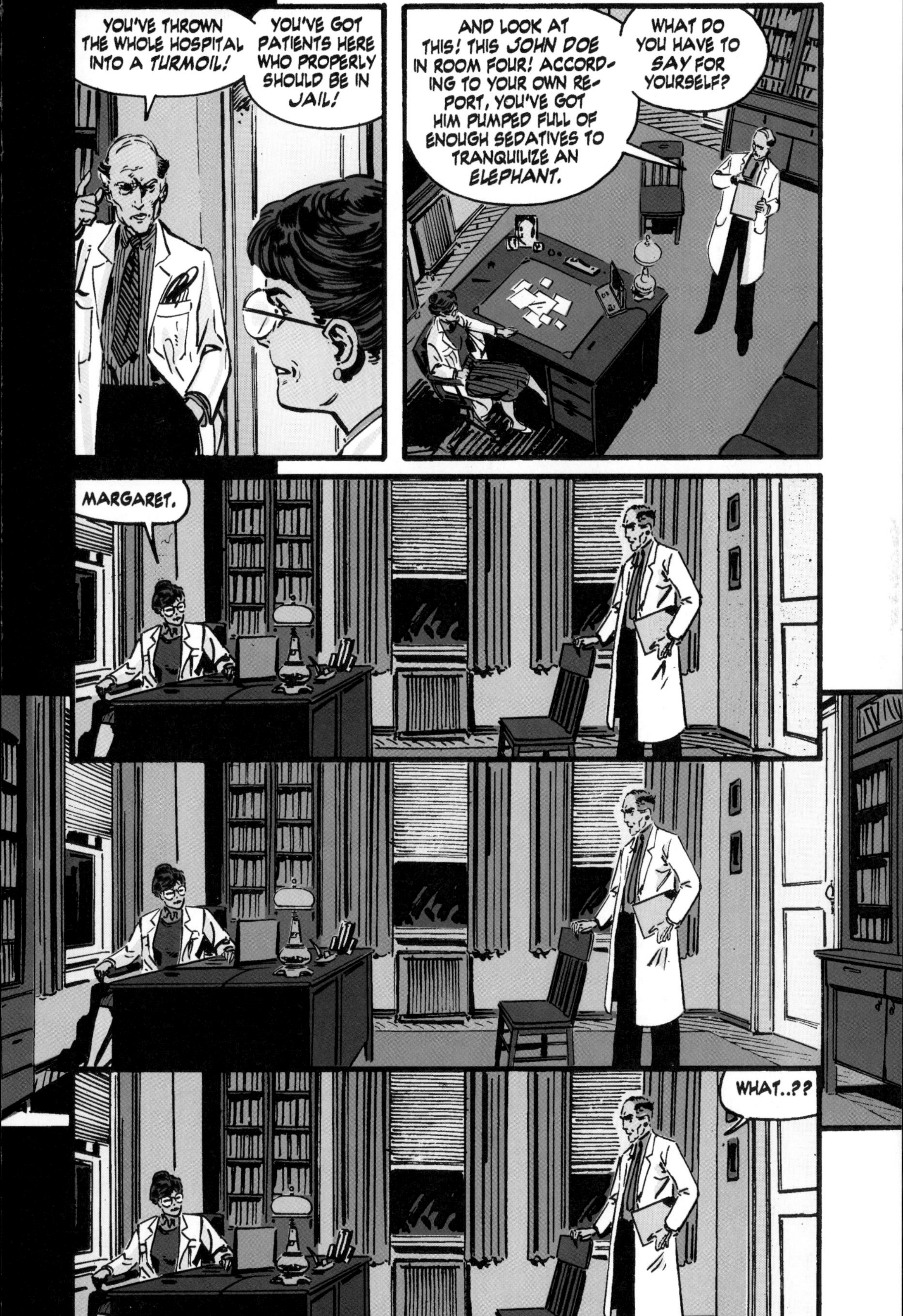
YOU'VE THROWN THE WHOLE HOSPITAL INTO A TURMOIL!
YOU'VE GOT PATIENTS HERE WHO PROPERLY SHOULD BE IN JAIL!
AND LOOK AT THIS! THIS JOHN DOE IN ROOM FOUR! ACCORDING TO YOUR OWN REPORT, YOU'VE GOT HIM PUMPED FULL OF ENOUGH SEDATIVES TO TRANQUILIZE AN ELEPHANT.
WHAT DO YOU HAVE TO SAY FOR YOURSELF?
MARGARET.
WHAT..??

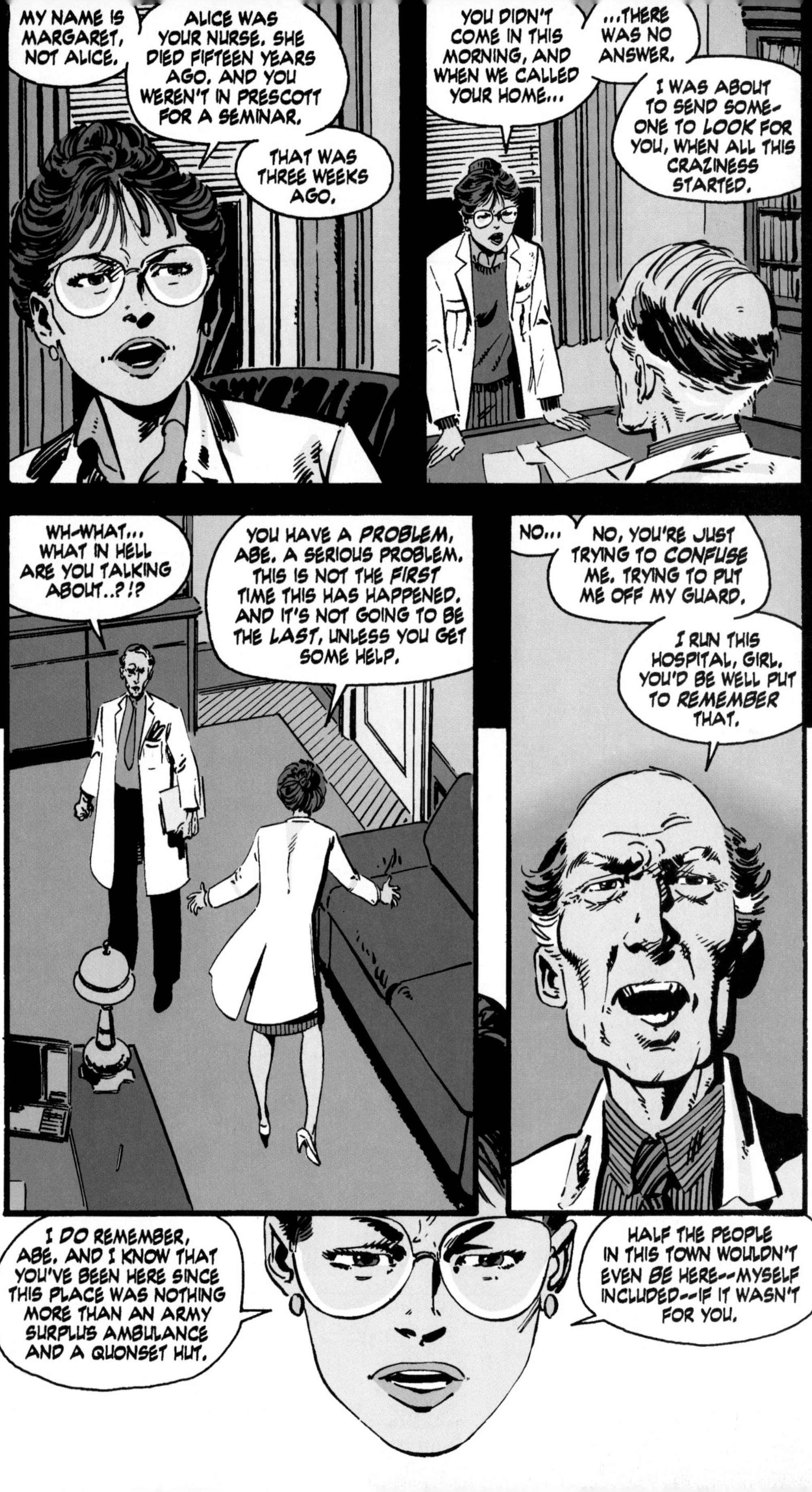
MY NAME IS MARGARET, NOT ALICE.
ALICE WAS YOUR NURSE. SHE DIED FIFTEEN YEARS AGO. AND YOU WEREN'T IN PRESCOTT FOR A SEMINAR.
THAT WAS THREE WEEKS AGO.
YOU DIDN'T COME IN THIS MORNING, AND WHEN WE CALLED YOUR HOME...
...THERE WAS NO ANSWER.
I WAS ABOUT TO SEND SOME-ONE TO LOOK FOR YOU, WHEN ALL THIS CRAZINESS STARTED.
WH-WHAT... WHAT IN HELL ARE YOU TALKING ABOUT..?!?
YOU HAVE A PROBLEM, ABE. A SERIOUS PROBLEM. THIS IS NOT THE FIRST TIME THIS HAS HAPPENED. AND IT'S NOT GOING TO BE THE LAST, UNLESS YOU GET SOME HELP.
NO...
NO, YOU'RE JUST TRYING TO CONFUSE ME. TRYING TO PUT ME OFF MY GUARD.
I RUN THIS HOSPITAL, GIRL. YOU'D BE WELL PUT TO REMEMBER THAT.
I DO REMEMBER, ABE. AND I KNOW THAT YOU'VE BEEN HERE SINCE THIS PLACE WAS NOTHING MORE THAN AN ARMY SURPLUS AMBULANCE AND A QUONSET HUT.
HALF THE PEOPLE IN THIS TOWN WOULDN'T EVEN BE HERE--MYSELF INCLUDED--IF IT WASN'T FOR YOU.

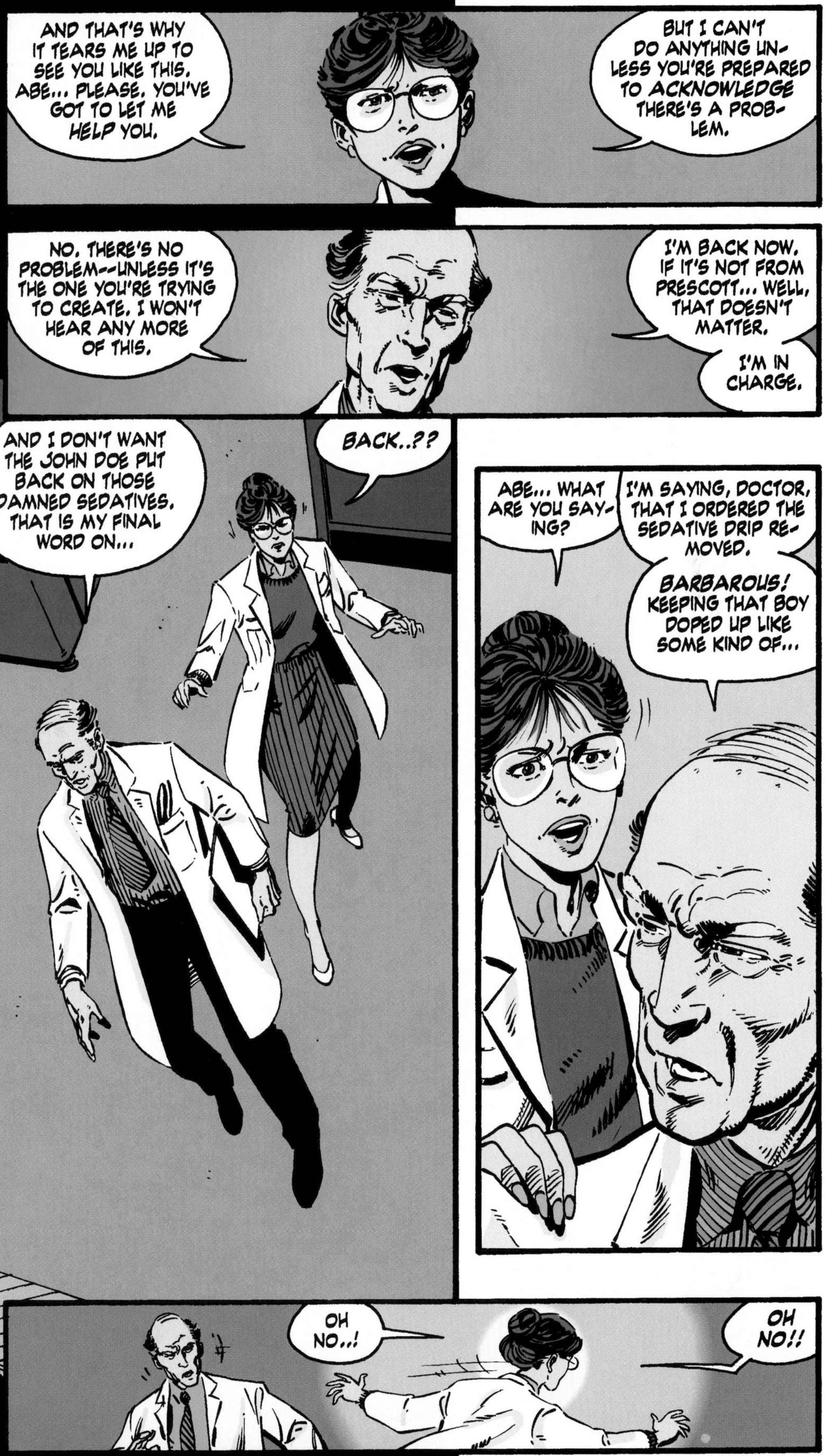
AND THAT'S WHY IT TEARS ME UP TO SEE YOU LIKE THIS. ABE... PLEASE. YOU'VE GOT TO LET ME HELP YOU.
BUT I CAN'T DO ANYTHING UNLESS YOU'RE PREPARED TO ACKNOWLEDGE THERE'S A PROBLEM.
NO. THERE'S NO PROBLEM--UNLESS IT'S THE ONE YOU'RE TRYING TO CREATE. I WON'T HEAR ANY MORE OF THIS.
I'M BACK NOW. IF IT'S NOT FROM PRESCOTT... WELL, THAT DOESN'T MATTER.
I'M IN CHARGE.
AND I DON'T WANT THE JOHN DOE PUT BACK ON THOSE DAMNED SEDATIVES. THAT IS MY FINAL WORD ON...
BACK..??
ABE... WHAT ARE YOU SAYING?
I'M SAYING, DOCTOR, THAT I ORDERED THE SEDATIVE DRIP REMOVED.
BARBAROUS! KEEPING THAT BOY DOPED UP LIKE SOME KIND OF...
OH NO..!
OH NO!!

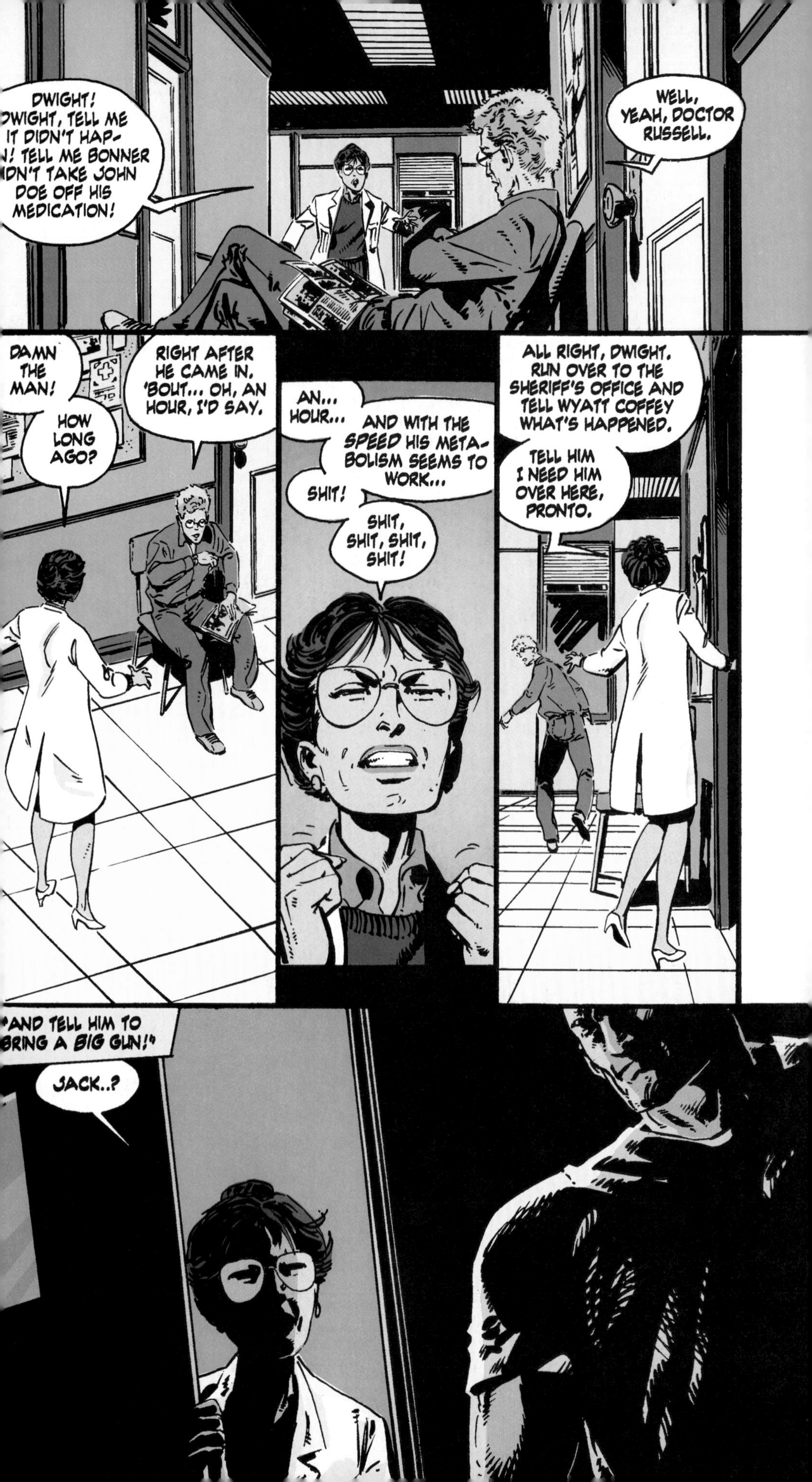
DWIGHT! DWIGHT, TELL ME IT DIDN'T HAP- N! TELL ME BONNER DN'T TAKE JOHN DOE OFF HIS MEDICATION!
WELL, YEAH, DOCTOR RUSSELL.
DAMN THE MAN!
HOW LONG AGO?
RIGHT AFTER HE CAME IN. 'BOUT... OH, AN HOUR, I'D SAY.
AN... HOUR...
AND WITH THE SPEED HIS META- BOLISM SEEMS TO WORK...
SHIT!
SHIT, SHIT, SHIT, SHIT!
ALL RIGHT, DWIGHT. RUN OVER TO THE SHERIFF'S OFFICE AND TELL WYATT COFFEY WHAT'S HAPPENED.
TELL HIM I NEED HIM OVER HERE, PRONTO.
"AND TELL HIM TO BRING A BIG GUN!"
JACK..?

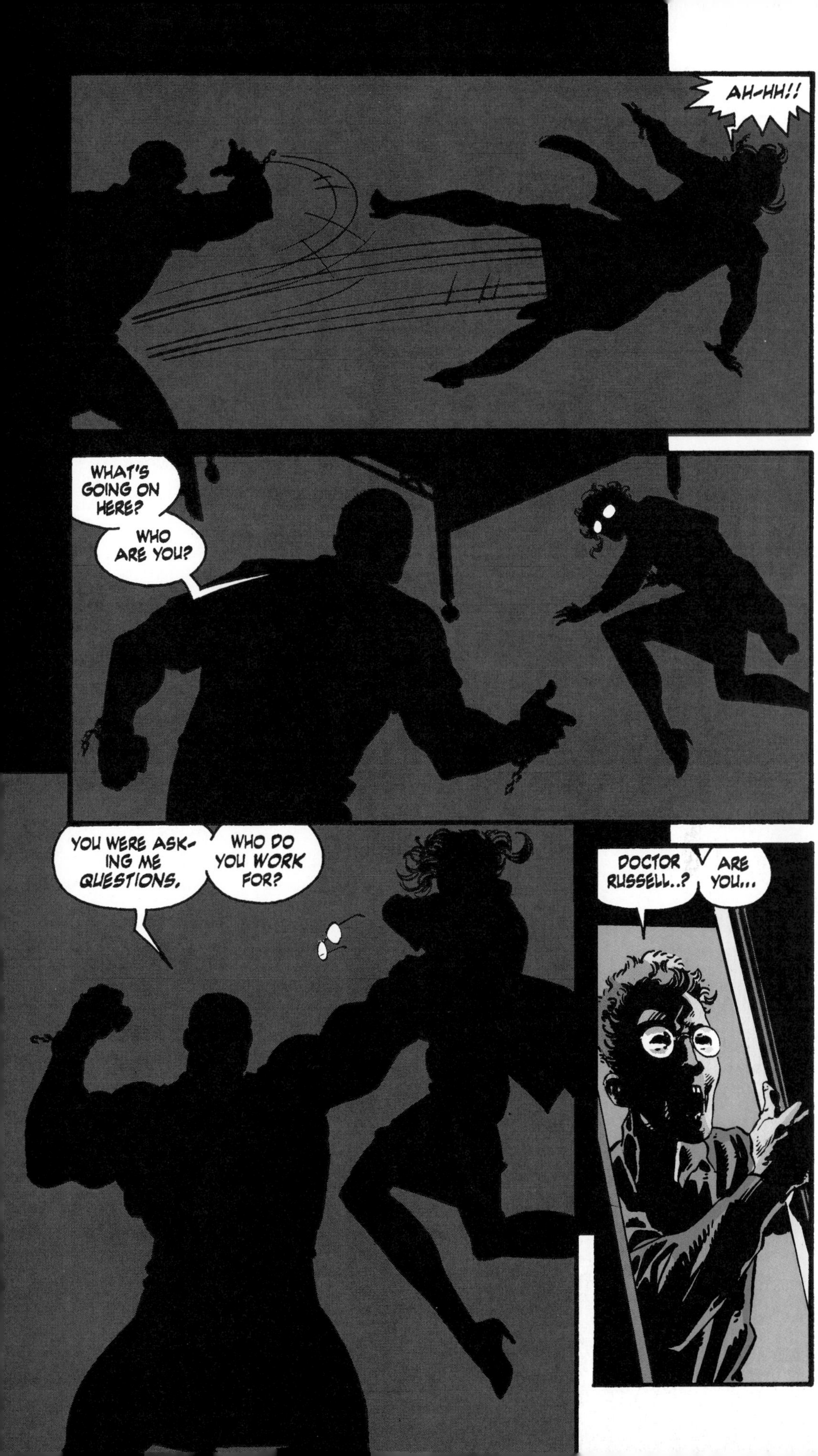
AH-HH!!
WHAT'S GOING ON HERE?
WHO ARE YOU?
YOU WERE ASKING ME QUESTIONS.
WHO DO YOU WORK FOR?
DOCTOR RUSSELL..?
ARE YOU...

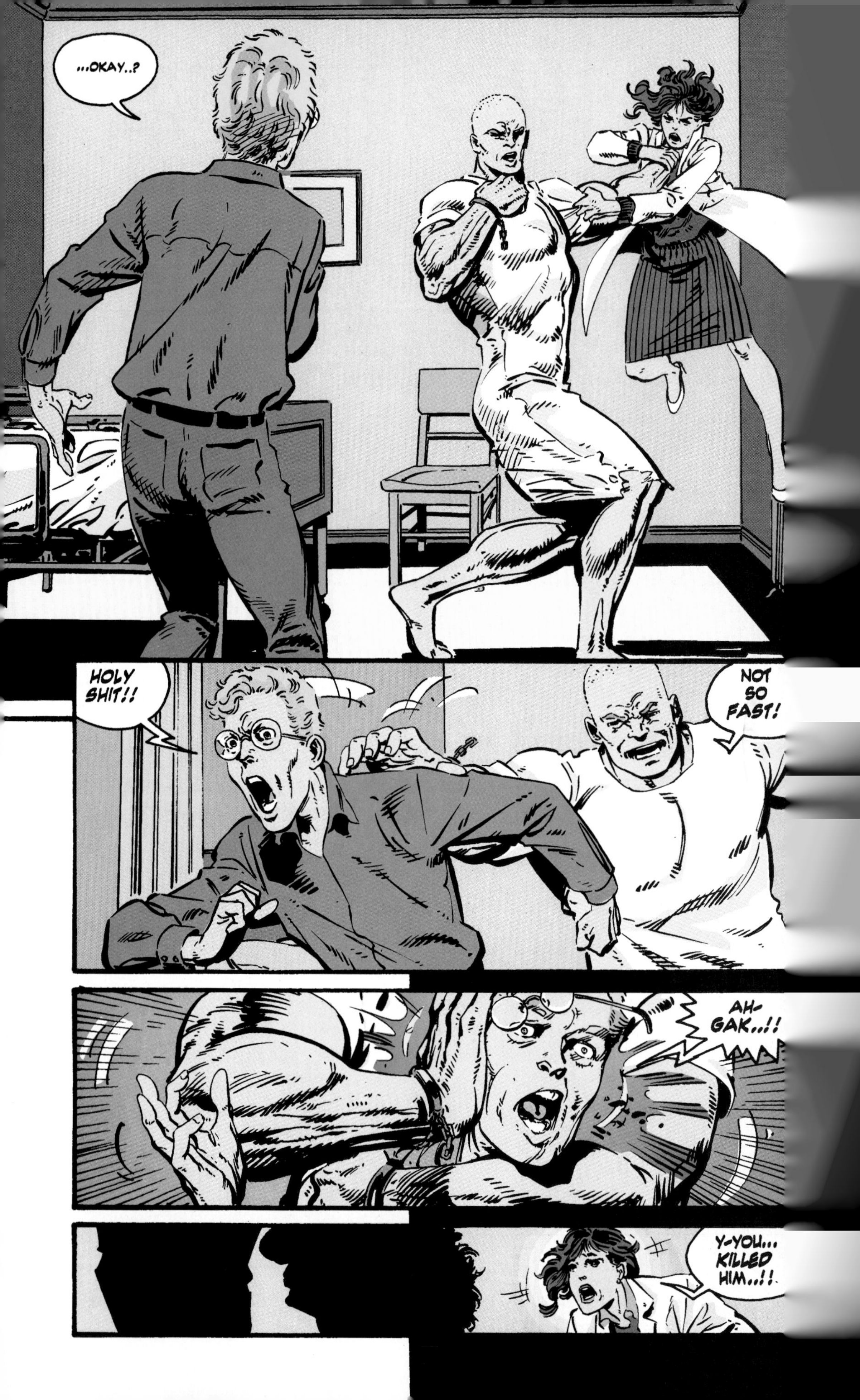
...OKAY..?
HOLY SHIT!!
NOT SO FAST!
AH-GAK..!!
Y-YOU... KILLED HIM..!!

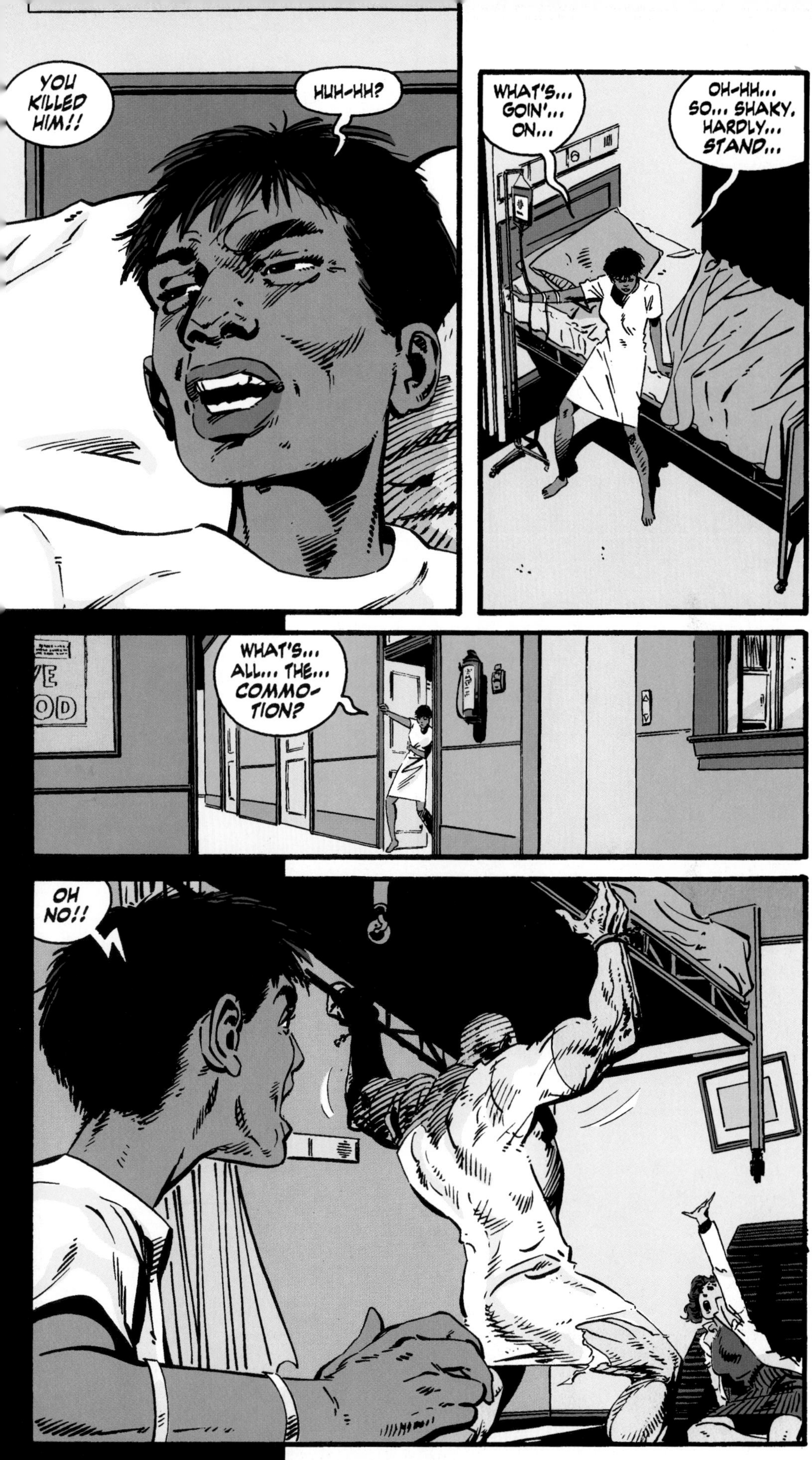
YOU KILLED HIM!!
HUH-HH?
WHAT'S... GOIN'... ON...
OH-HH... SO... SHAKY. HARDLY... STAND...
WHAT'S... ALL... THE... COMMOTION?
OH NO!!

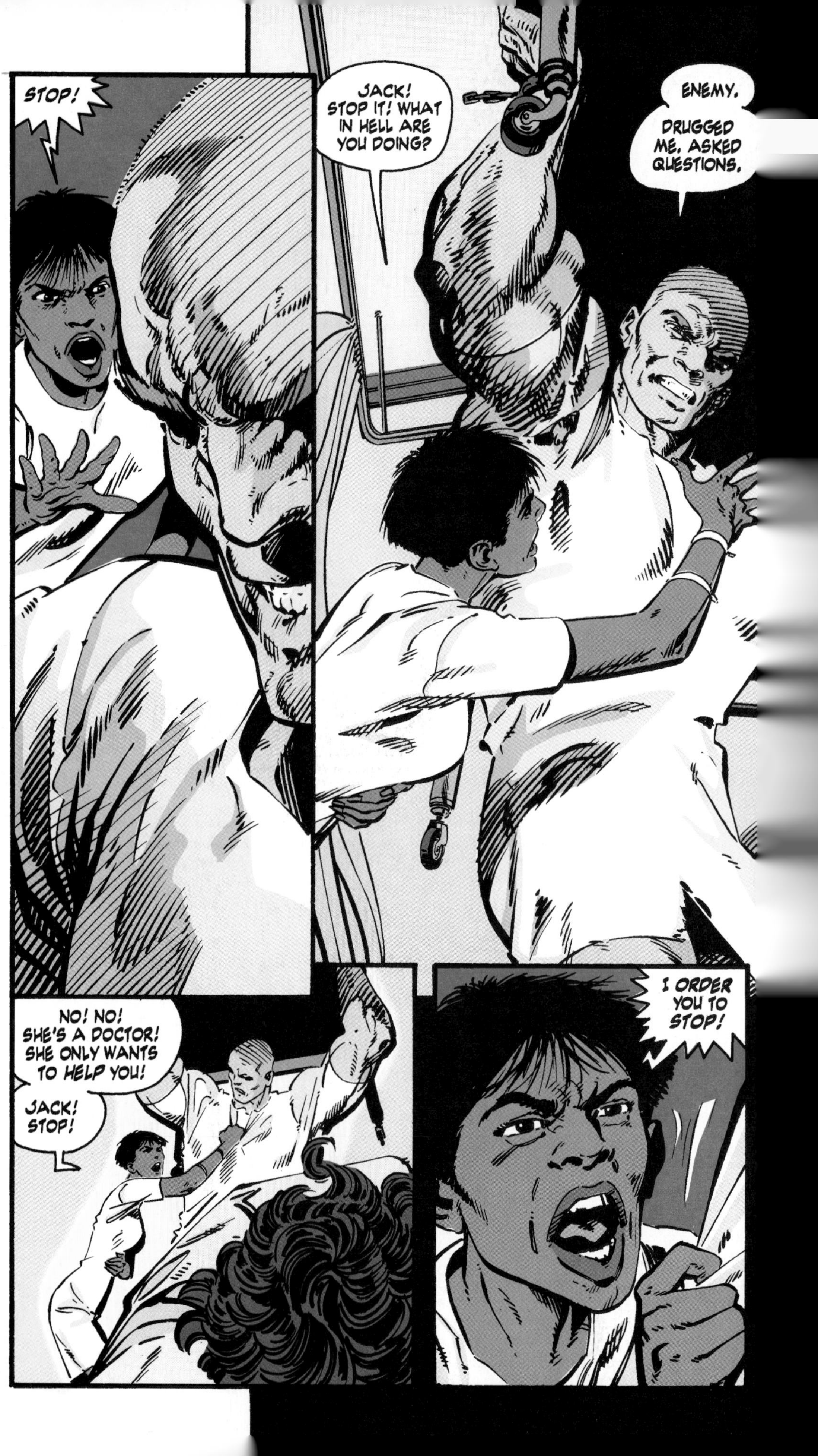
STOP!
JACK! STOP IT! WHAT IN HELL ARE YOU DOING?
ENEMY.
DRUGGED ME. ASKED QUESTIONS.
NO! NO! SHE'S A DOCTOR! SHE ONLY WANTS TO HELP YOU!
JACK! STOP!
I ORDER YOU TO STOP!

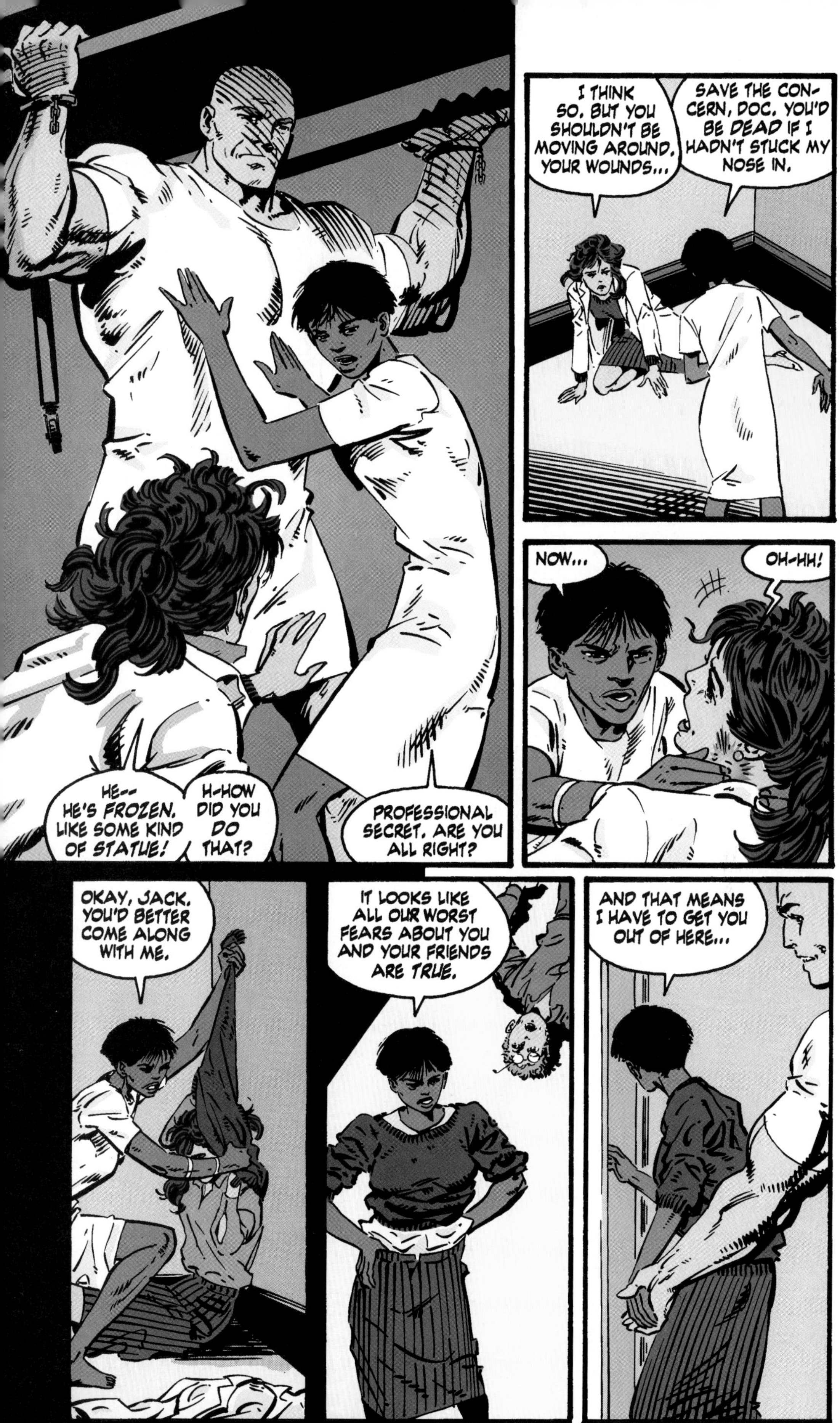
HE-- HE'S FROZEN. LIKE SOME KIND OF STATUE!
H-HOW DID YOU DO THAT?
PROFESSIONAL SECRET. ARE YOU ALL RIGHT?
I THINK SO. BUT YOU SHOULDN'T BE MOVING AROUND. YOUR WOUNDS...
SAVE THE CON-CERN, DOC. YOU'D BE DEAD IF I HADN'T STUCK MY NOSE IN.
NOW...
OH-HH!
OKAY, JACK. YOU'D BETTER COME ALONG WITH ME.
IT LOOKS LIKE ALL OUR WORST FEARS ABOUT YOU AND YOUR FRIENDS ARE TRUE.
AND THAT MEANS I HAVE TO GET YOU OUT OF HERE...

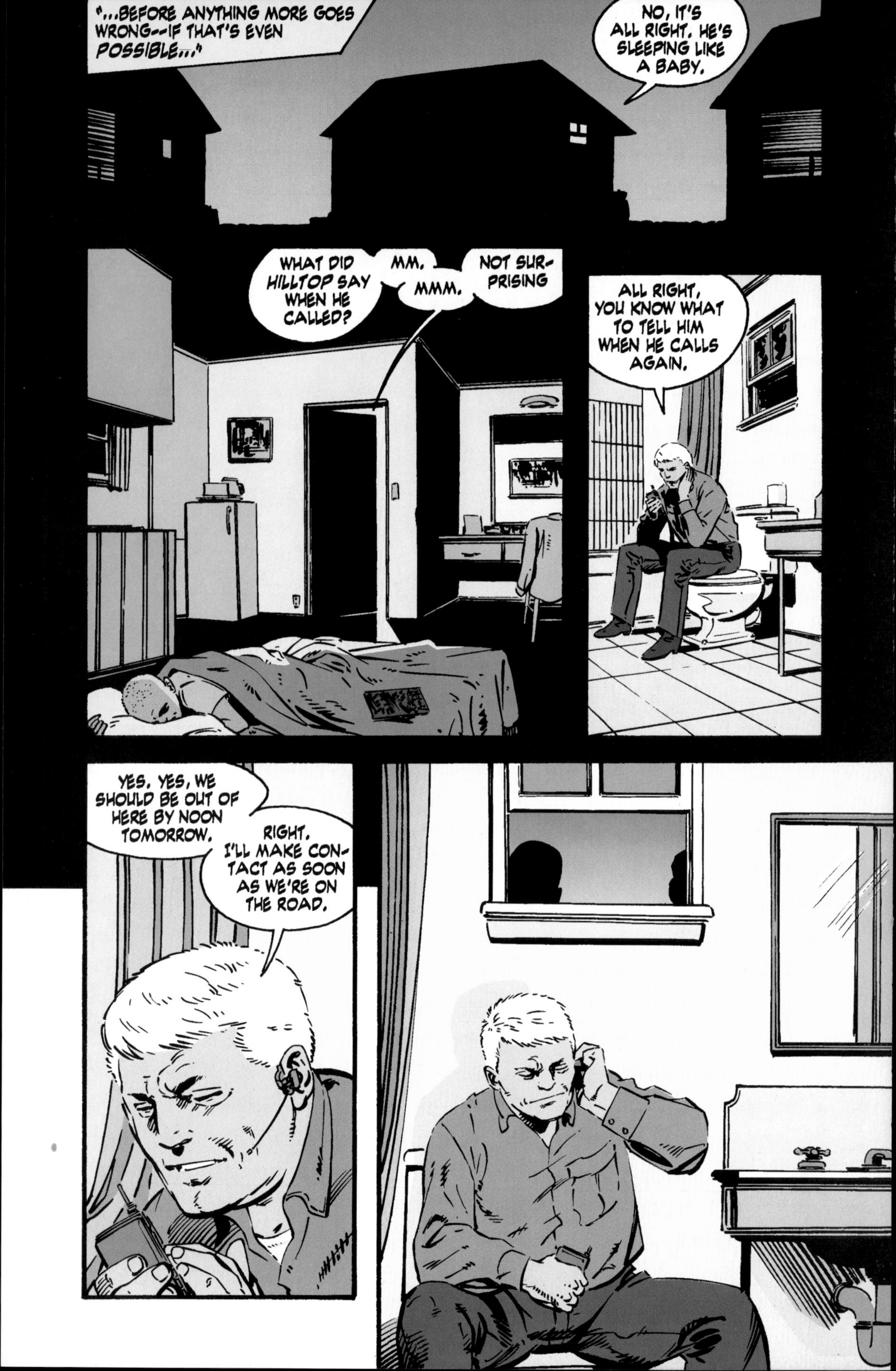
"...BEFORE ANYTHING MORE GOES WRONG--IF THAT'S EVEN POSSIBLE..."
NO, IT'S ALL RIGHT. HE'S SLEEPING LIKE A BABY.
WHAT DID HILLTOP SAY WHEN HE CALLED?
MM.
MMM.
NOT SURPRISING
ALL RIGHT, YOU KNOW WHAT TO TELL HIM WHEN HE CALLS AGAIN.
YES. YES, WE SHOULD BE OUT OF HERE BY NOON TOMORROW.
RIGHT. I'LL MAKE CONTACT AS SOON AS WE'RE ON THE ROAD.

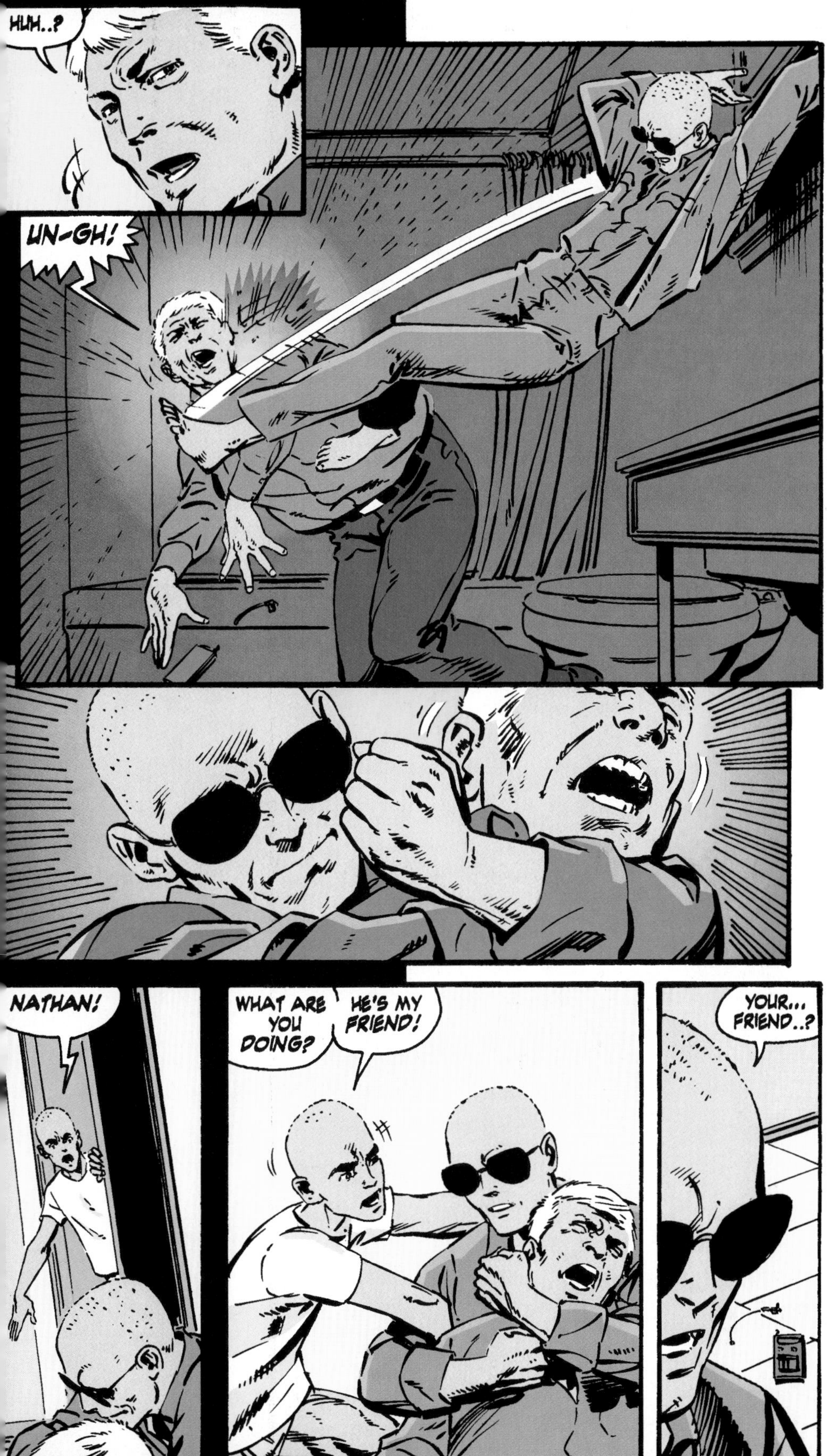
HUH..?
UN-GH!
NATHAN!
WHAT ARE YOU DOING?
HE'S MY FRIEND!
YOUR... FRIEND..?

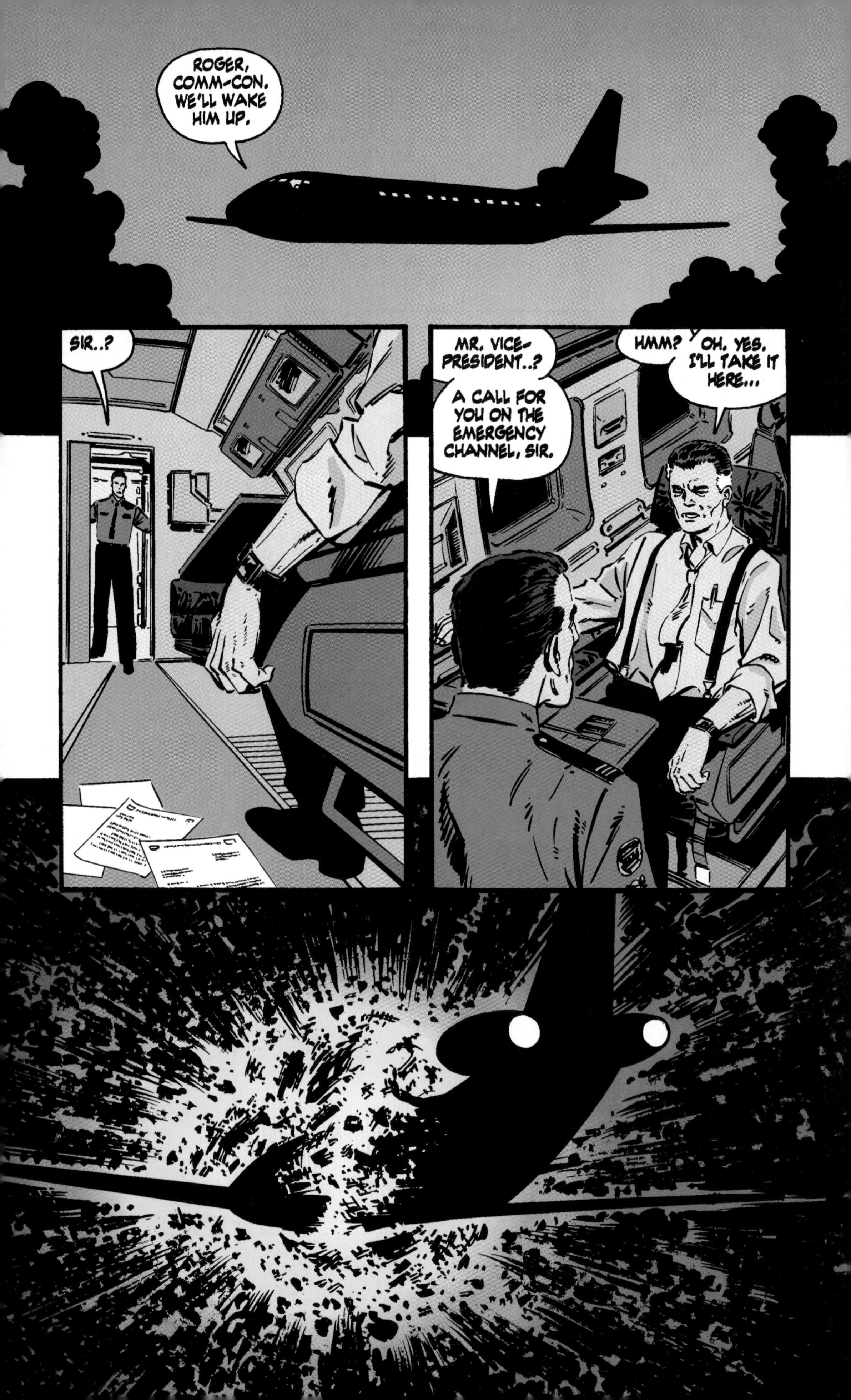
ROGER, COMM-CON. WE'LL WAKE HIM UP.
SIR..?
MR. VICE-PRESIDENT..?
A CALL FOR YOU ON THE EMERGENCY CHANNEL, SIR.
HMM?
OH. YES. I'LL TAKE IT HERE...

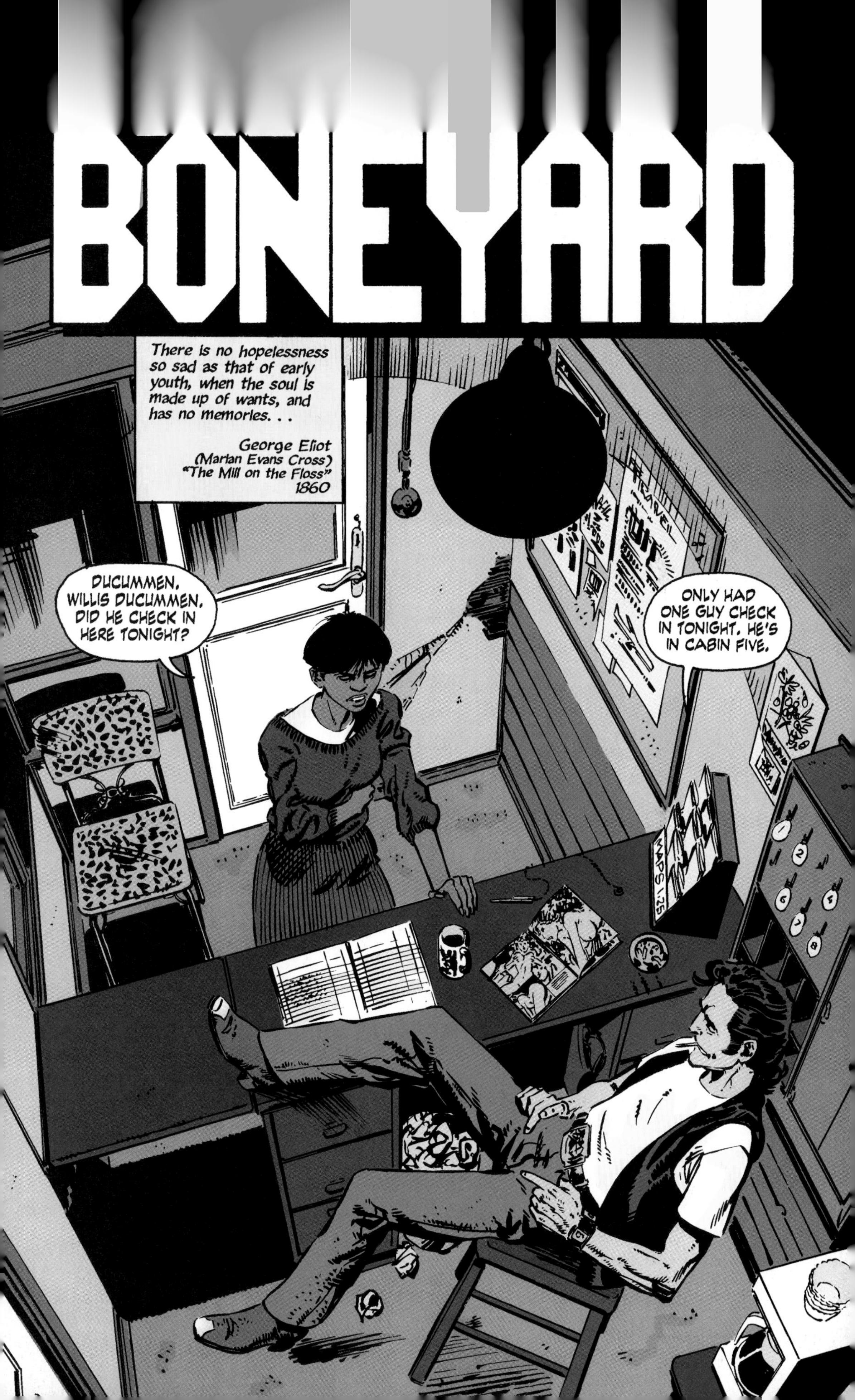
BONEYARD
There is no hopelessness so sad as that of early youth, when the soul is made up of wants, and has no memories. . .
George Eliot
(Marian Evans Cross)
"The Mill on the Floss"
1860
DUCUMMEN. WILLIS DUCUMMEN. DID HE CHECK IN HERE TONIGHT?
ONLY HAD ONE GUY CHECK IN TONIGHT. HE'S IN CABIN FIVE.
MAPS 1.25

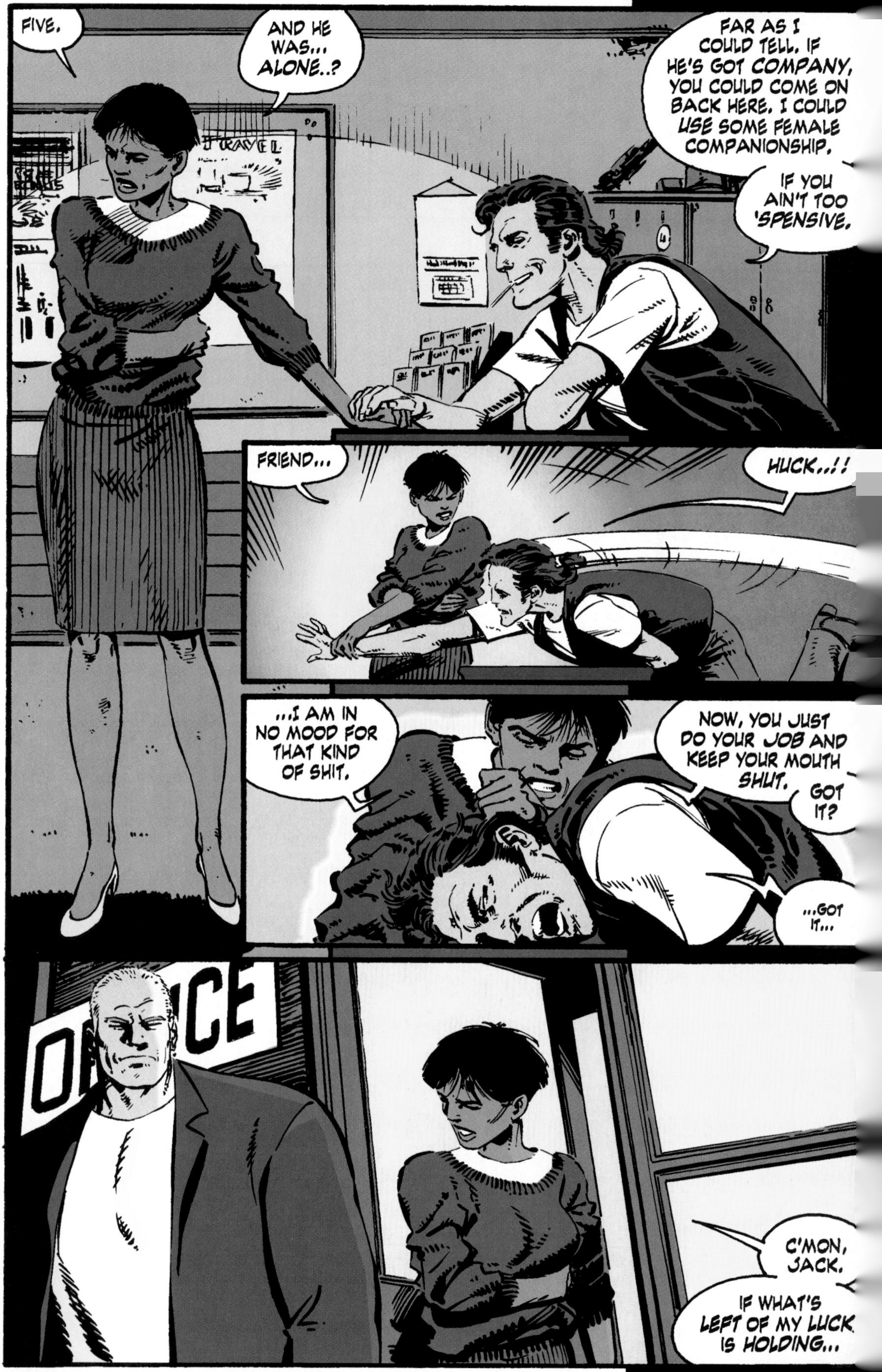
FIVE.
AND HE WAS... ALONE..?
FAR AS I COULD TELL. IF HE'S GOT COMPANY, YOU COULD COME ON BACK HERE. I COULD USE SOME FEMALE COMPANIONSHIP.
IF YOU AIN'T TOO 'SPENSIVE.
FRIEND...
HUCK..!!
...I AM IN NO MOOD FOR THAT KIND OF SHIT.
NOW, YOU JUST DO YOUR JOB AND KEEP YOUR MOUTH SHUT.
GOT IT?
...GOT IT...
OFFICE
C'MON, JACK.
IF WHAT'S LEFT OF MY LUCK IS HOLDING...

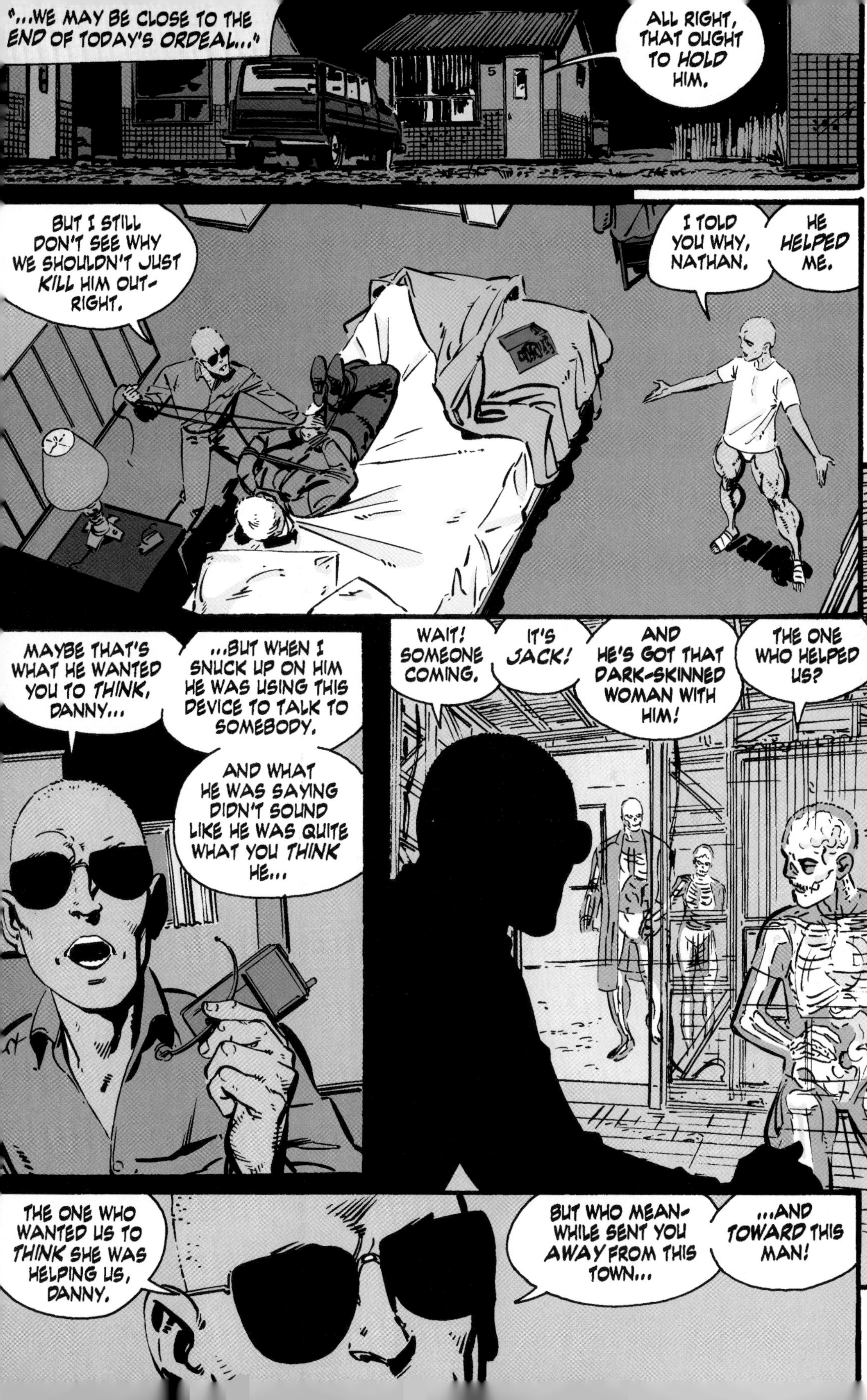
"...WE MAY BE CLOSE TO THE END OF TODAY'S ORDEAL..."
ALL RIGHT, THAT OUGHT TO HOLD HIM.
BUT I STILL DON'T SEE WHY WE SHOULDN'T JUST KILL HIM OUT-RIGHT.
I TOLD YOU WHY, NATHAN.
HE HELPED ME.
MAYBE THAT'S WHAT HE WANTED YOU TO THINK, DANNY...
...BUT WHEN I SNUCK UP ON HIM HE WAS USING THIS DEVICE TO TALK TO SOMEBODY.
AND WHAT HE WAS SAYING DIDN'T SOUND LIKE HE WAS QUITE WHAT YOU THINK HE...
WAIT! SOMEONE COMING.
IT'S JACK!
AND HE'S GOT THAT DARK-SKINNED WOMAN WITH HIM!
THE ONE WHO HELPED US?
THE ONE WHO WANTED US TO THINK SHE WAS HELPING US, DANNY.
BUT WHO MEAN-WHILE SENT YOU AWAY FROM THIS TOWN...
...AND TOWARD THIS MAN!

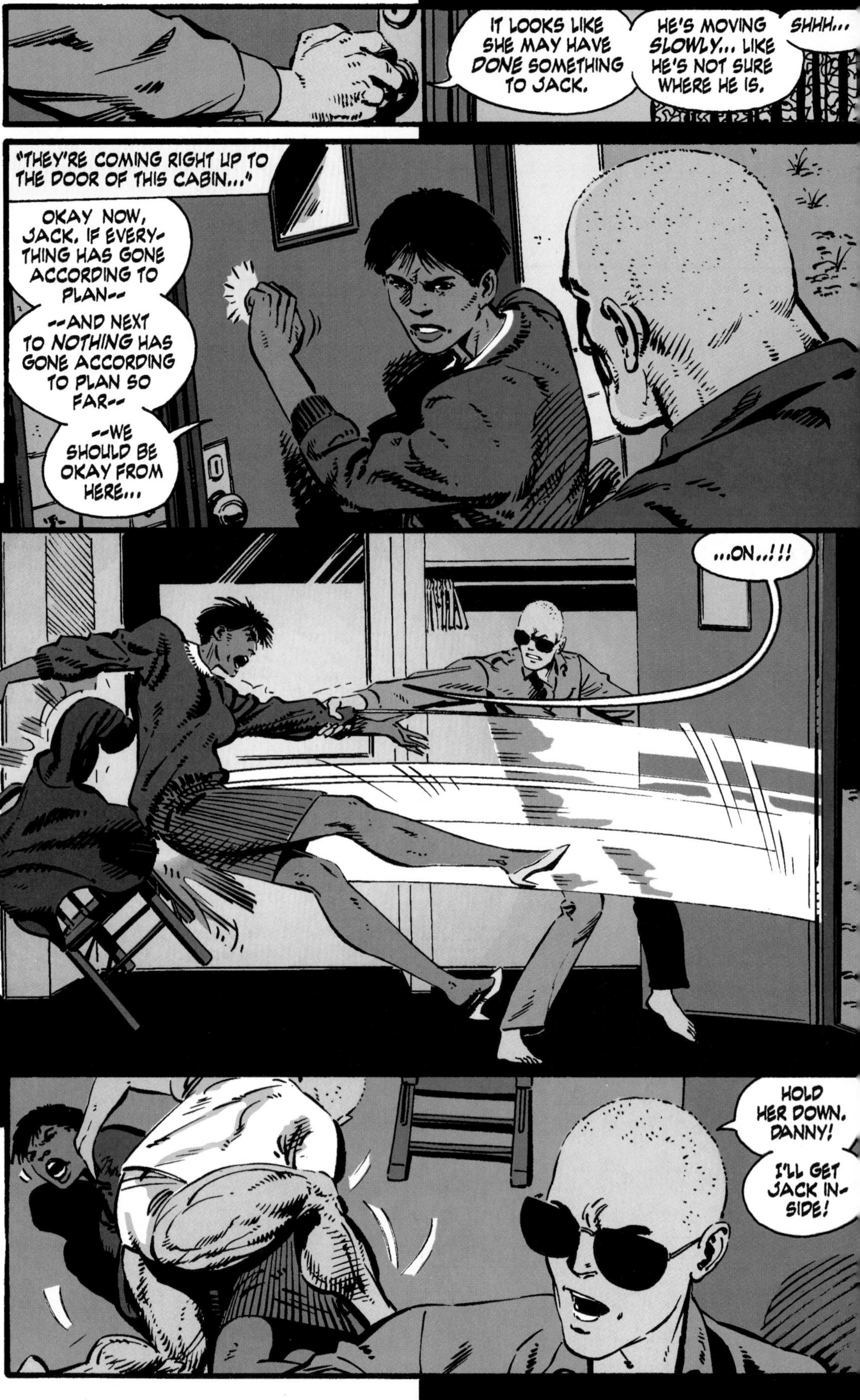

IT LOOKS LIKE SHE MAY HAVE DONE SOMETHING TO JACK.
HE'S MOVING SLOWLY... LIKE HE'S NOT SURE WHERE HE IS.
SHHH...
"THEY'RE COMING RIGHT UP TO THE DOOR OF THIS CABIN..."
OKAY NOW, JACK. IF EVERYTHING HAS GONE ACCORDING TO PLAN--
--AND NEXT TO NOTHING HAS GONE ACCORDING TO PLAN SO FAR--
--WE SHOULD BE OKAY FROM HERE...
...ON..!!!
HOLD HER DOWN, DANNY!
I'LL GET JACK INSIDE!

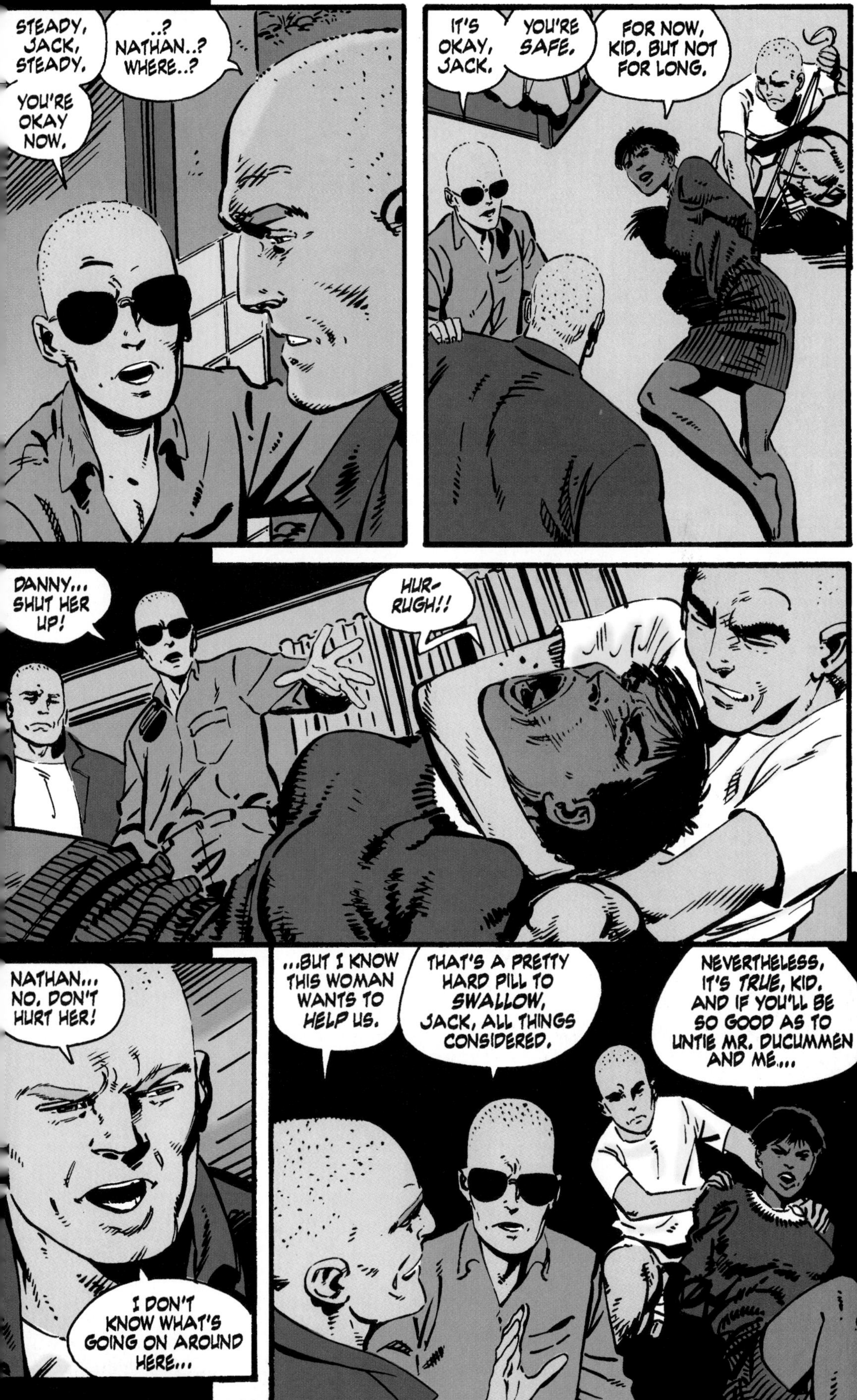
STEADY, JACK, STEADY.
..? NATHAN..? WHERE..?
YOU'RE OKAY NOW.
IT'S OKAY, JACK.
YOU'RE SAFE.
FOR NOW, KID, BUT NOT FOR LONG.
DANNY... SHUT HER UP!
HUR-RUGH!!
NATHAN... NO, DON'T HURT HER!
I DON'T KNOW WHAT'S GOING ON AROUND HERE...
...BUT I KNOW THIS WOMAN WANTS TO HELP US.
THAT'S A PRETTY HARD PILL TO SWALLOW, JACK, ALL THINGS CONSIDERED.
NEVERTHELESS, IT'S TRUE, KID, AND IF YOU'LL BE SO GOOD AS TO UNTIE MR. DUCUMMEN AND ME....

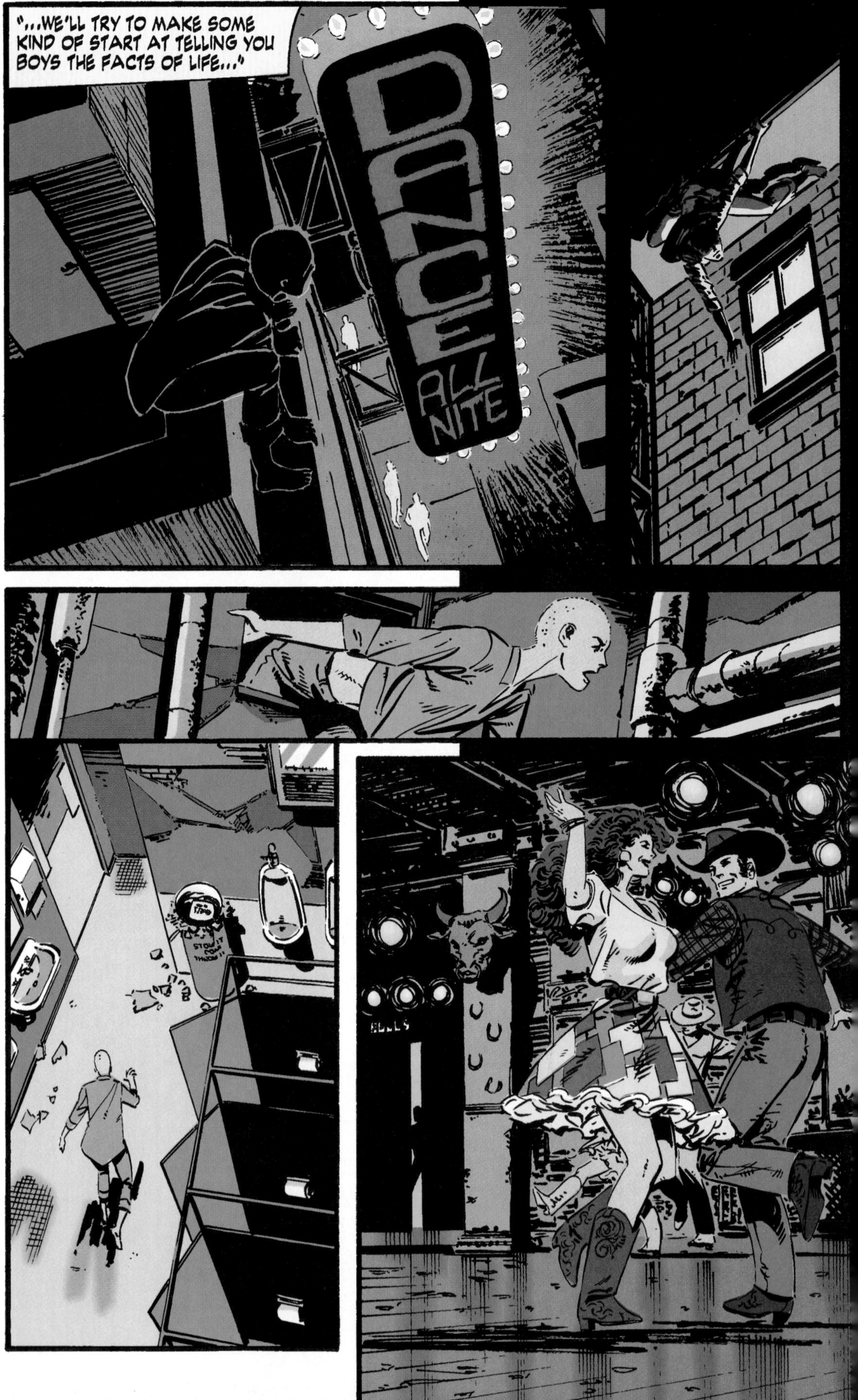
"...WE'LL TRY TO MAKE SOME KIND OF START AT TELLING YOU BOYS THE FACTS OF LIFE..."
DANCE
ALL NITE

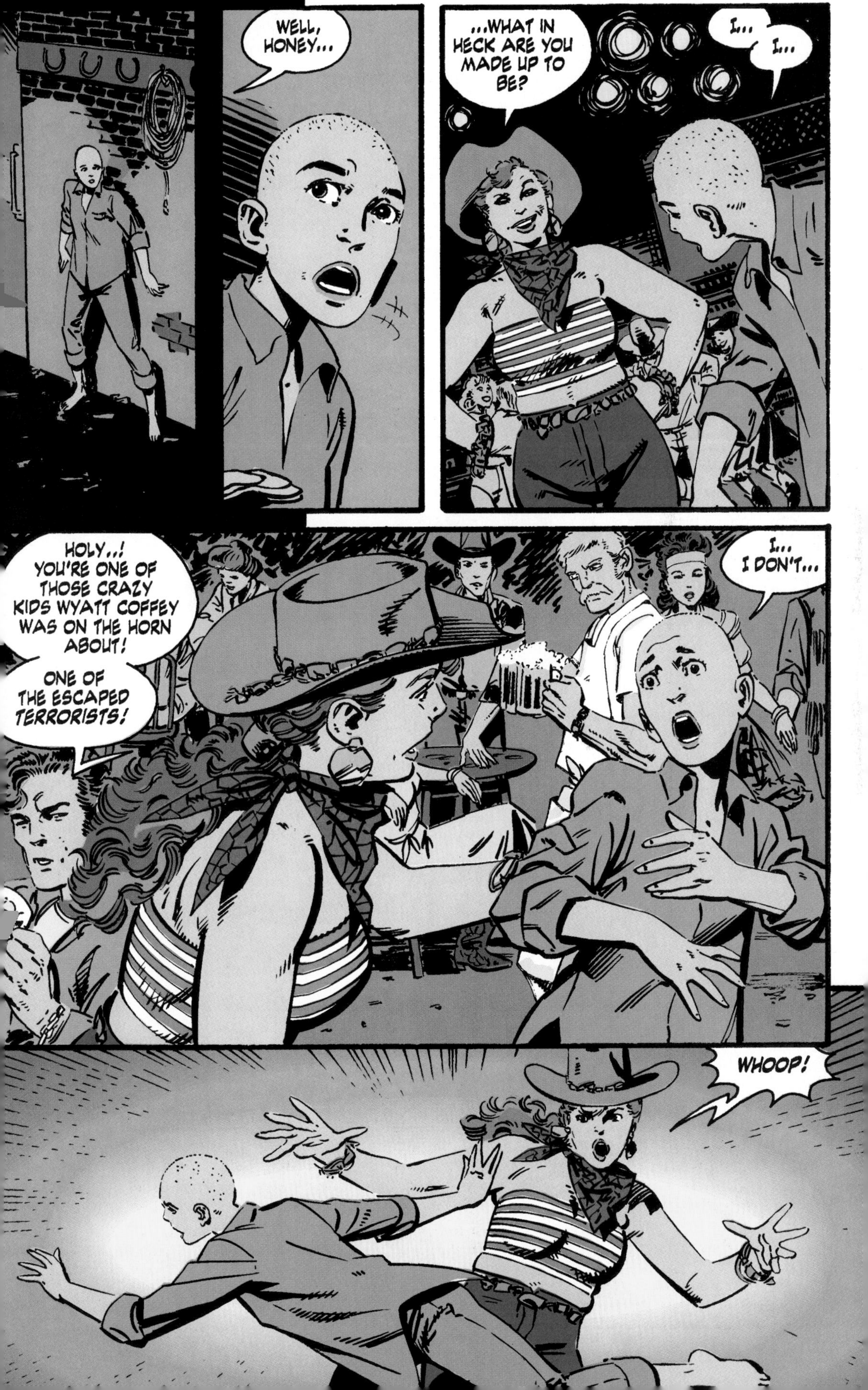
WELL, HONEY...
...WHAT IN HECK ARE YOU MADE UP TO BE?
I...
I...
HOLY..! YOU'RE ONE OF THOSE CRAZY KIDS WYATT COFFEY WAS ON THE HORN ABOUT!
ONE OF THE ESCAPED TERRORISTS!
I... I DON'T...
WHOOP!

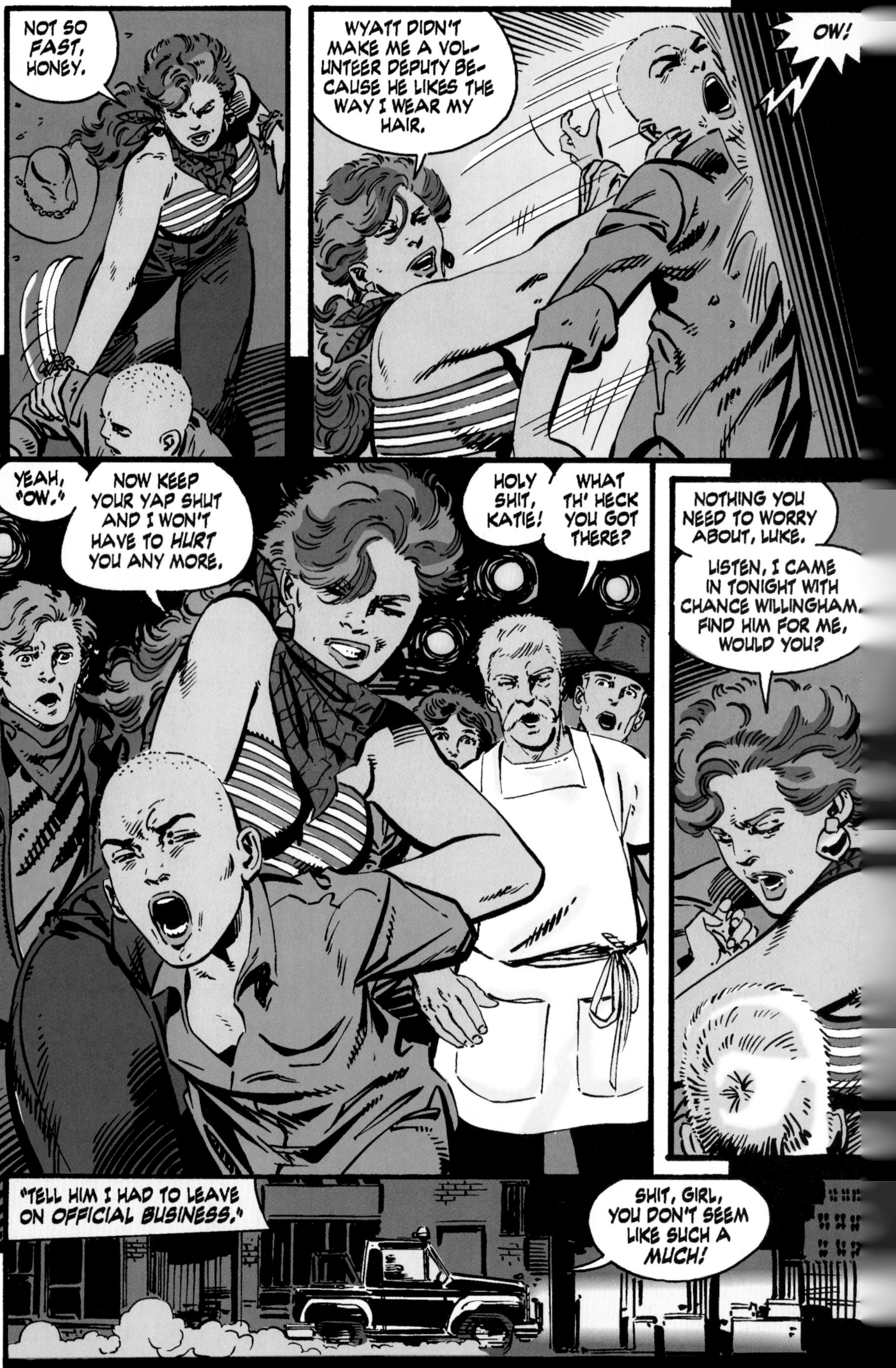

NOT SO FAST, HONEY.
WYATT DIDN'T MAKE ME A VOLUNTEER DEPUTY BECAUSE HE LIKES THE WAY I WEAR MY HAIR.
OW!
YEAH, "OW."
NOW KEEP YOUR YAP SHUT AND I WON'T HAVE TO HURT YOU ANY MORE.
HOLY SHIT, KATIE!
WHAT TH' HECK YOU GOT THERE?
NOTHING YOU NEED TO WORRY ABOUT, LUKE.
LISTEN, I CAME IN TONIGHT WITH CHANCE WILLINGHAM. FIND HIM FOR ME, WOULD YOU?
"TELL HIM I HAD TO LEAVE ON OFFICIAL BUSINESS."
SHIT, GIRL, YOU DON'T SEEM LIKE SUCH A MUCH!

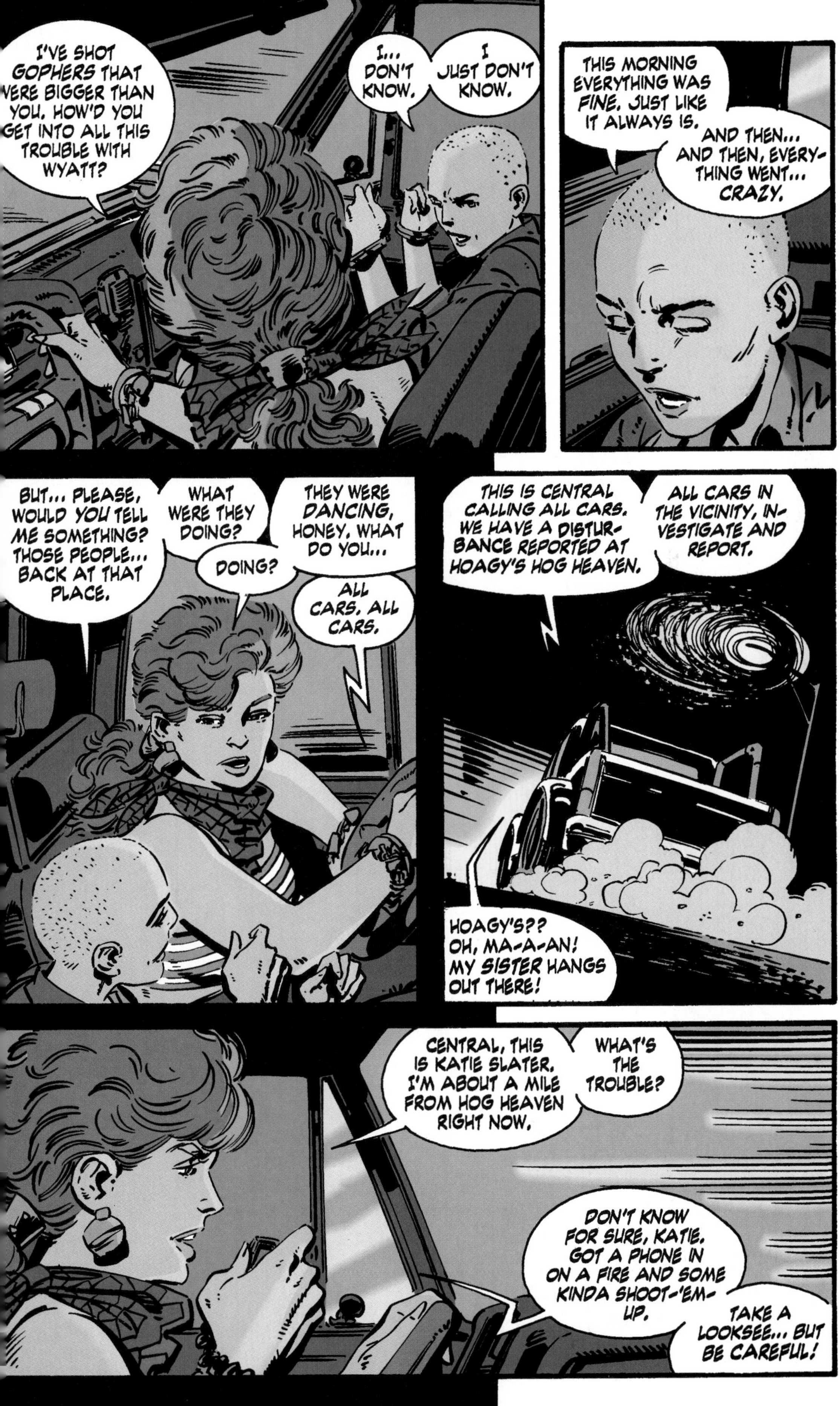

I'VE SHOT GOPHERS THAT WERE BIGGER THAN YOU. HOW'D YOU GET INTO ALL THIS TROUBLE WITH WYATT?
I... DON'T KNOW.
I JUST DON'T KNOW.
THIS MORNING EVERYTHING WAS FINE. JUST LIKE IT ALWAYS IS.
AND THEN... AND THEN, EVERYTHING WENT... CRAZY.
BUT... PLEASE, WOULD YOU TELL ME SOMETHING? THOSE PEOPLE... BACK AT THAT PLACE.
WHAT WERE THEY DOING?
DOING?
THEY WERE DANCING, HONEY. WHAT DO YOU...
ALL CARS. ALL CARS.
THIS IS CENTRAL CALLING ALL CARS. WE HAVE A DISTURBANCE REPORTED AT HOAGY'S HOG HEAVEN.
ALL CARS IN THE VICINITY, INVESTIGATE AND REPORT.
HOAGY'S?? OH, MA-A-AN! MY SISTER HANGS OUT THERE!
CENTRAL, THIS IS KATIE SLATER. I'M ABOUT A MILE FROM HOG HEAVEN RIGHT NOW.
WHAT'S THE TROUBLE?
DON'T KNOW FOR SURE, KATIE. GOT A PHONE IN ON A FIRE AND SOME KINDA SHOOT-'EM-UP.
TAKE A LOOKSEE... BUT BE CAREFUL!

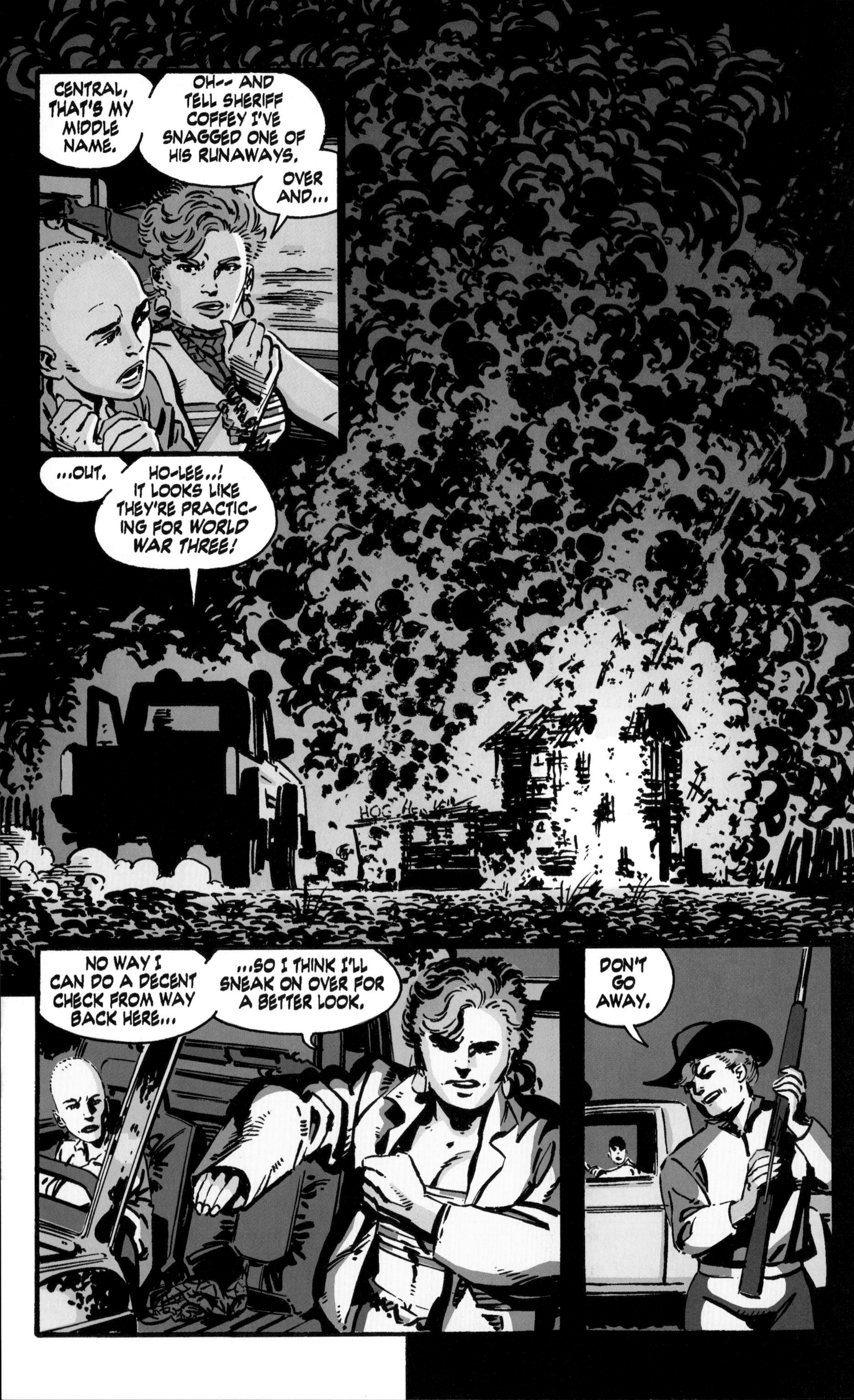
CENTRAL, THAT'S MY MIDDLE NAME.
OH-- AND TELL SHERIFF COFFEY I'VE SNAGGED ONE OF HIS RUNAWAYS.
OVER AND...
...OUT.
HO-LEE..! IT LOOKS LIKE THEY'RE PRACTIC-ING FOR WORLD WAR THREE!
NO WAY I CAN DO A DECENT CHECK FROM WAY BACK HERE...
...SO I THINK I'LL SNEAK ON OVER FOR A BETTER LOOK.
DON'T GO AWAY.

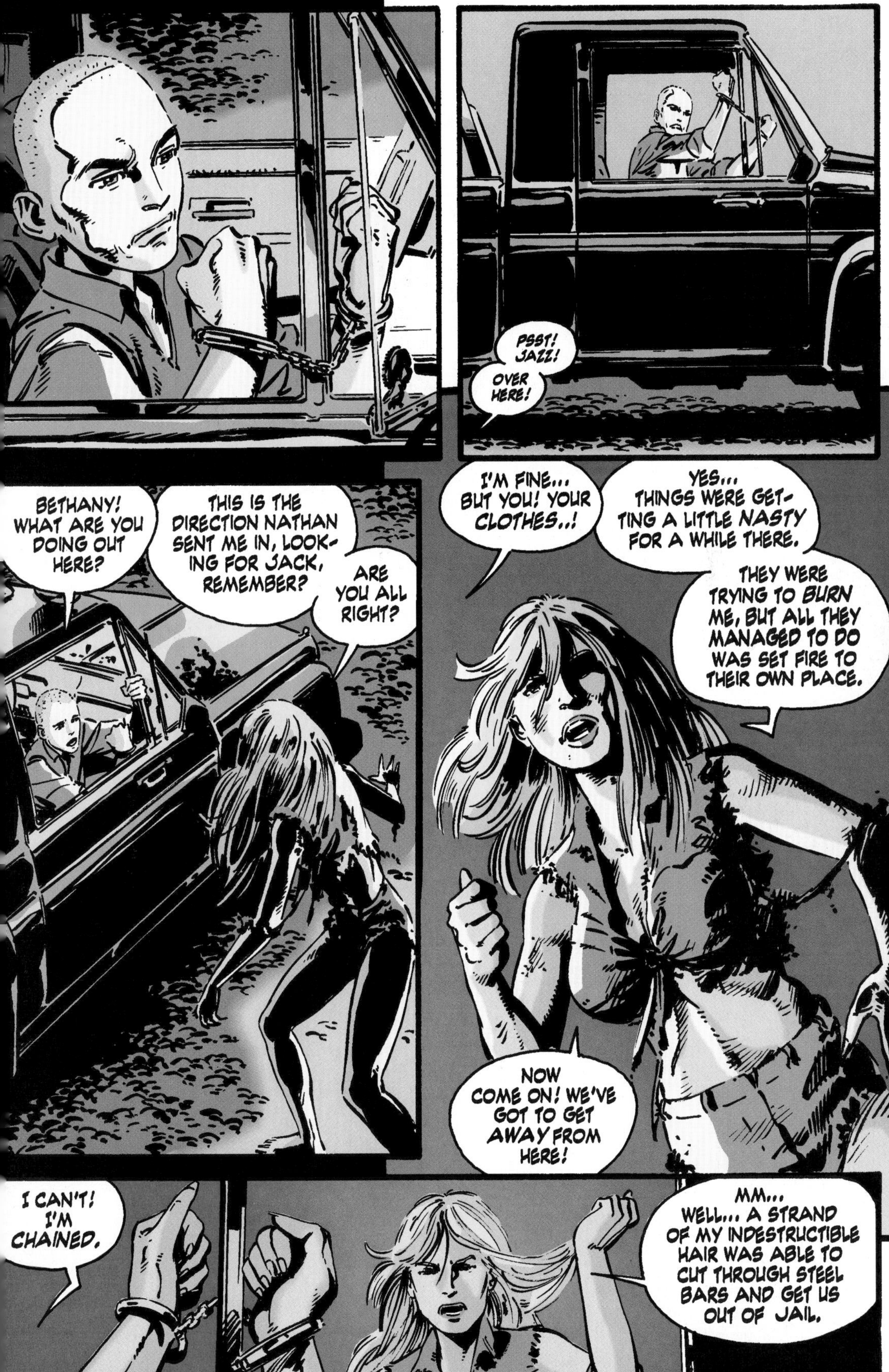

PSST! JAZZ!
OVER HERE!
BETHANY! WHAT ARE YOU DOING OUT HERE?
THIS IS THE DIRECTION NATHAN SENT ME IN, LOOKING FOR JACK, REMEMBER?
ARE YOU ALL RIGHT?
I'M FINE... BUT YOU! YOUR CLOTHES..!
YES... THINGS WERE GETTING A LITTLE NASTY FOR A WHILE THERE.
THEY WERE TRYING TO BURN ME, BUT ALL THEY MANAGED TO DO WAS SET FIRE TO THEIR OWN PLACE.
NOW COME ON! WE'VE GOT TO GET AWAY FROM HERE!
I CAN'T! I'M CHAINED.
MM... WELL... A STRAND OF MY INDESTRUCTIBLE HAIR WAS ABLE TO CUT THROUGH STEEL BARS AND GET US OUT OF JAIL.

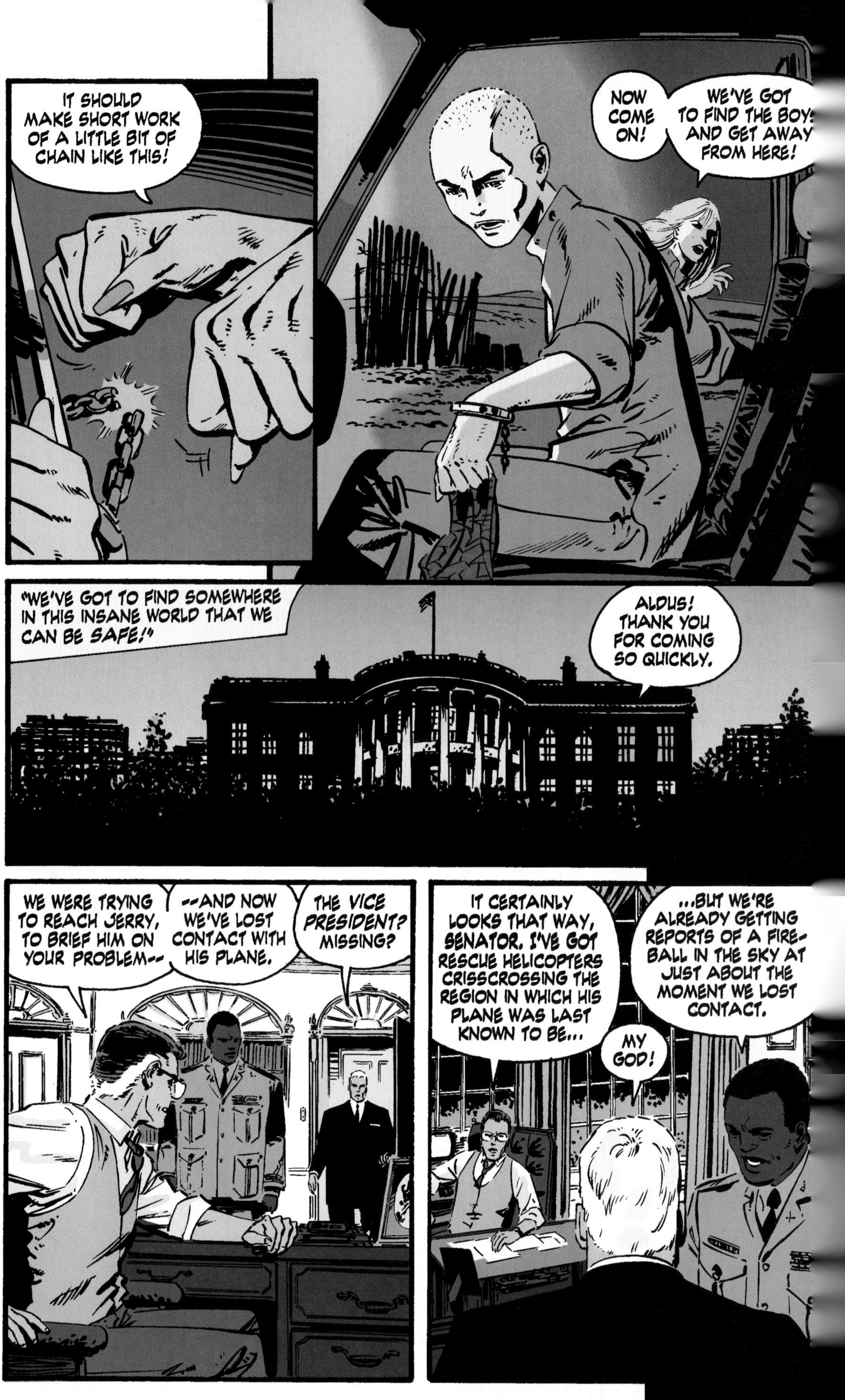
IT SHOULD MAKE SHORT WORK OF A LITTLE BIT OF CHAIN LIKE THIS!
NOW COME ON!
WE'VE GOT TO FIND THE BOYS AND GET AWAY FROM HERE!
"WE'VE GOT TO FIND SOMEWHERE IN THIS INSANE WORLD THAT WE CAN BE SAFE!"
ALDUS! THANK YOU FOR COMING SO QUICKLY.
WE WERE TRYING TO REACH JERRY, TO BRIEF HIM ON YOUR PROBLEM--
--AND NOW WE'VE LOST CONTACT WITH HIS PLANE.
THE VICE PRESIDENT? MISSING?
IT CERTAINLY LOOKS THAT WAY, SENATOR. I'VE GOT RESCUE HELICOPTERS CRISSCROSSING THE REGION IN WHICH HIS PLANE WAS LAST KNOWN TO BE...
MY GOD!
...BUT WE'RE ALREADY GETTING REPORTS OF A FIRE-BALL IN THE SKY AT JUST ABOUT THE MOMENT WE LOST CONTACT.

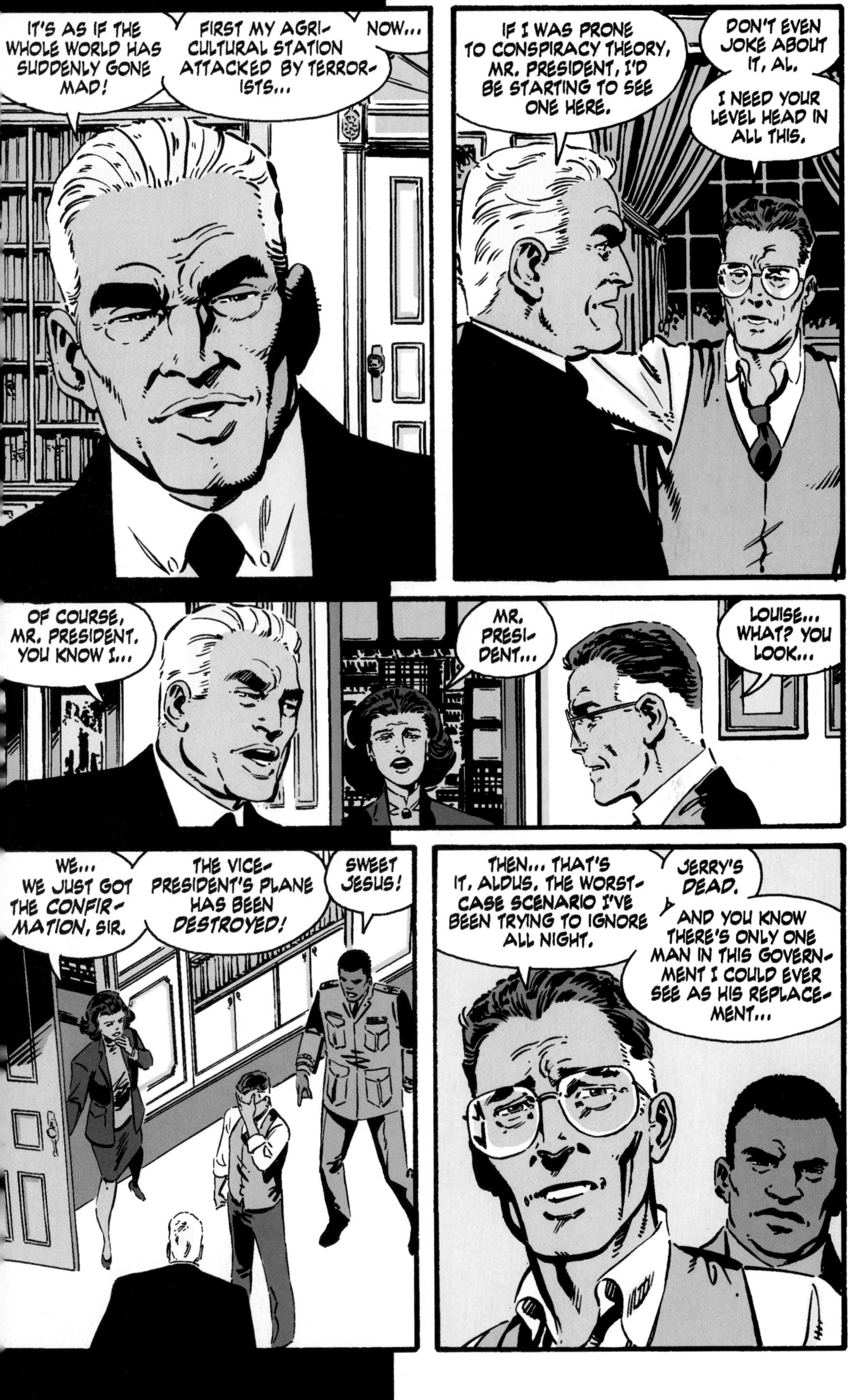
IT'S AS IF THE WHOLE WORLD HAS SUDDENLY GONE MAD!
FIRST MY AGRI-CULTURAL STATION ATTACKED BY TERROR-ISTS...
NOW...
IF I WAS PRONE TO CONSPIRACY THEORY, MR. PRESIDENT, I'D BE STARTING TO SEE ONE HERE.
DON'T EVEN JOKE ABOUT IT, AL.
I NEED YOUR LEVEL HEAD IN ALL THIS.
OF COURSE, MR. PRESIDENT. YOU KNOW I...
MR. PRESI-DENT...
LOUISE... WHAT? YOU LOOK...
WE... WE JUST GOT THE CONFIR-MATION, SIR.
THE VICE-PRESIDENT'S PLANE HAS BEEN DESTROYED!
SWEET JESUS!
THEN... THAT'S IT, ALDUS. THE WORST-CASE SCENARIO I'VE BEEN TRYING TO IGNORE ALL NIGHT.
JERRY'S DEAD.
AND YOU KNOW THERE'S ONLY ONE MAN IN THIS GOVERNMENT I COULD EVER SEE AS HIS REPLACE-MENT...

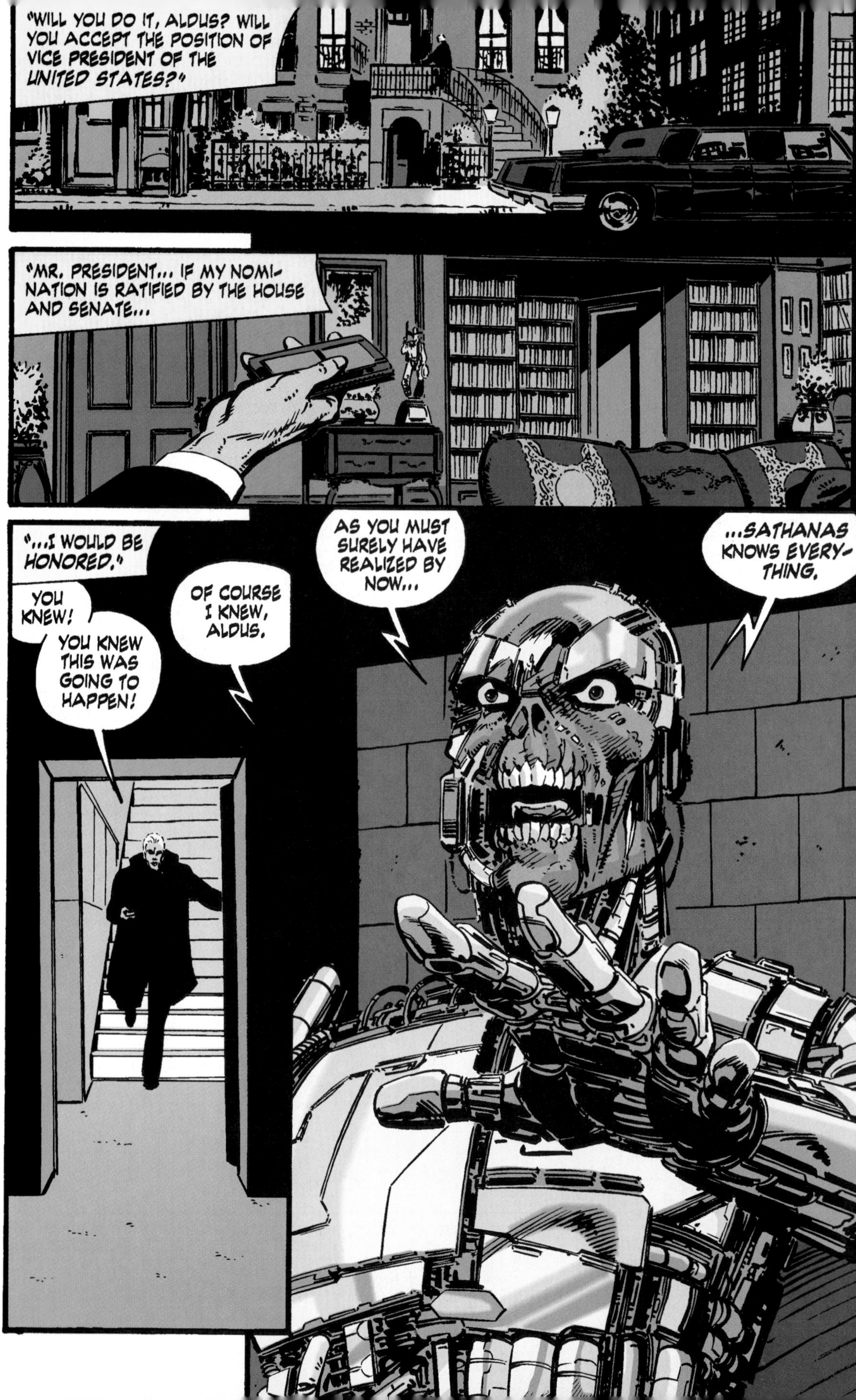
"WILL YOU DO IT, ALDUS? WILL YOU ACCEPT THE POSITION OF VICE PRESIDENT OF THE UNITED STATES?"
"MR. PRESIDENT... IF MY NOMINATION IS RATIFIED BY THE HOUSE AND SENATE...
"...I WOULD BE HONORED."
YOU KNEW!
YOU KNEW THIS WAS GOING TO HAPPEN!
OF COURSE I KNEW, ALDUS.
AS YOU MUST SURELY HAVE REALIZED BY NOW...
...SATHANAS KNOWS EVERYTHING.

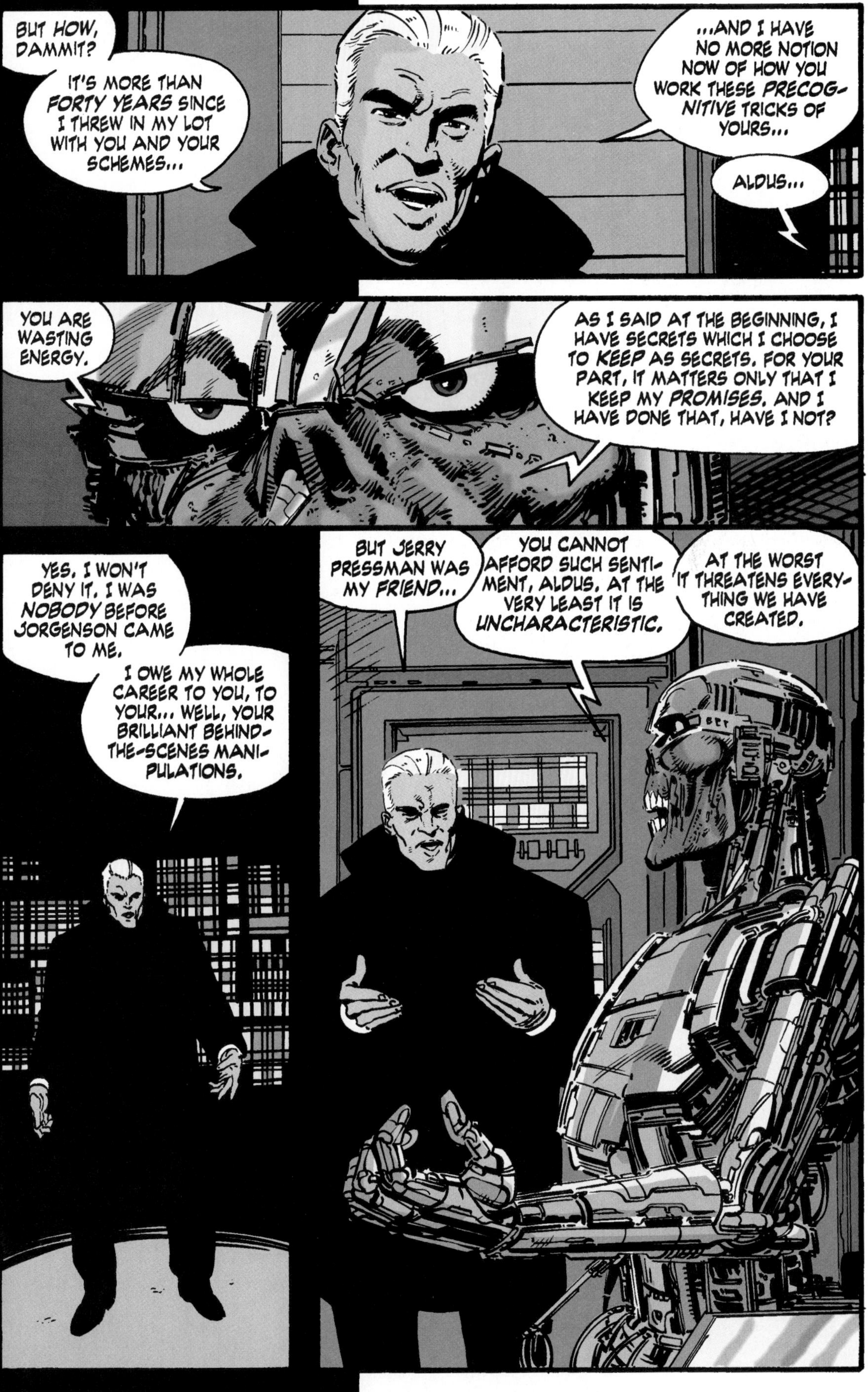
BUT HOW, DAMMIT?
IT'S MORE THAN FORTY YEARS SINCE I THREW IN MY LOT WITH YOU AND YOUR SCHEMES...
...AND I HAVE NO MORE NOTION NOW OF HOW YOU WORK THESE PRECOGNITIVE TRICKS OF YOURS...
ALDUS...
YOU ARE WASTING ENERGY.
AS I SAID AT THE BEGINNING, I HAVE SECRETS WHICH I CHOOSE TO KEEP AS SECRETS. FOR YOUR PART, IT MATTERS ONLY THAT I KEEP MY PROMISES. AND I HAVE DONE THAT, HAVE I NOT?
YES. I WON'T DENY IT. I WAS NOBODY BEFORE JORGENSON CAME TO ME.
I OWE MY WHOLE CAREER TO YOU, TO YOUR... WELL, YOUR BRILLIANT BEHIND-THE-SCENES MANIPULATIONS.
BUT JERRY PRESSMAN WAS MY FRIEND...
YOU CANNOT AFFORD SUCH SENTIMENT, ALDUS. AT THE VERY LEAST IT IS UNCHARACTERISTIC.
AT THE WORST IT THREATENS EVERYTHING WE HAVE CREATED.

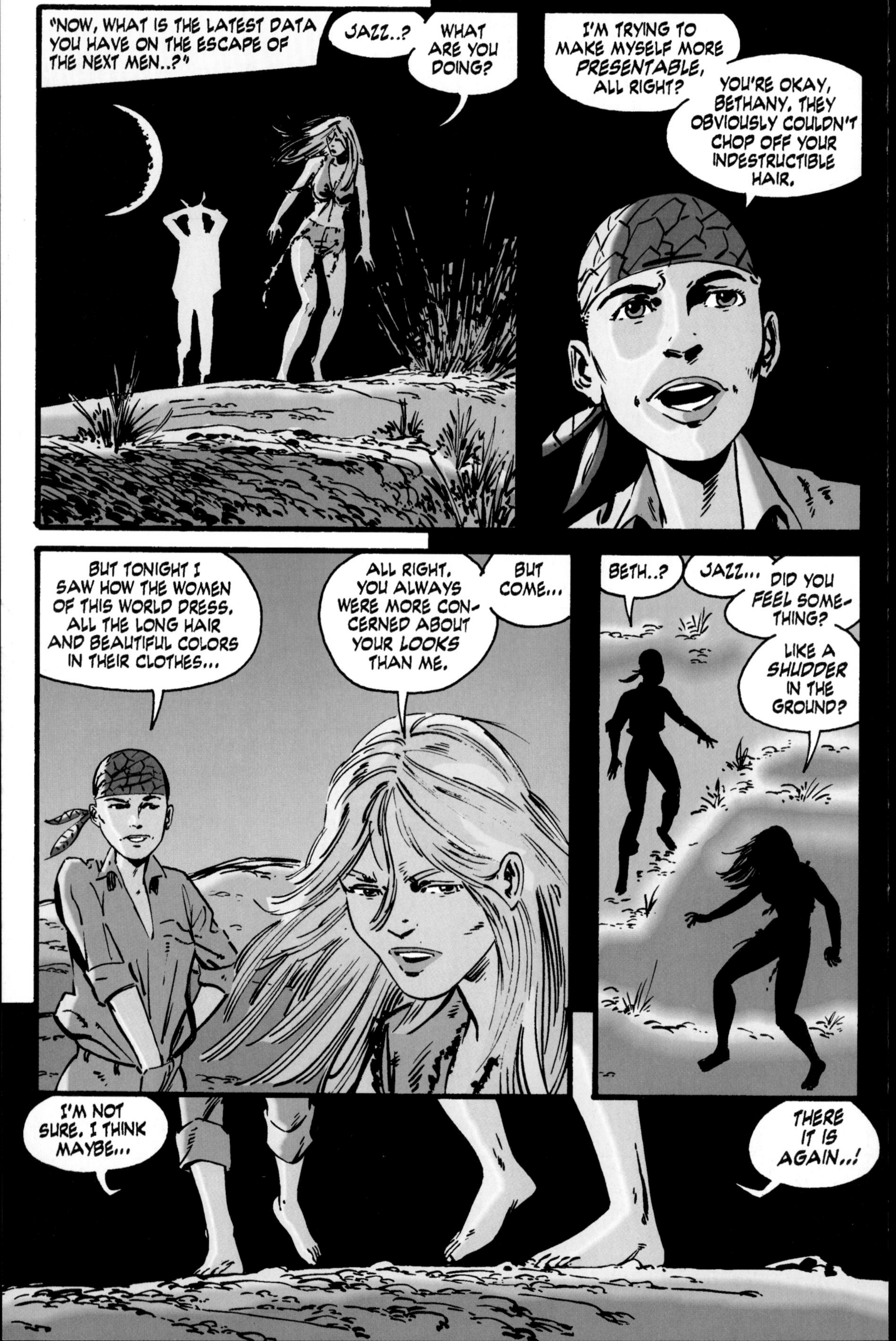
"NOW, WHAT IS THE LATEST DATA YOU HAVE ON THE ESCAPE OF THE NEXT MEN..?"
JAZZ..?
WHAT ARE YOU DOING?
I'M TRYING TO MAKE MYSELF MORE PRESENTABLE, ALL RIGHT?
YOU'RE OKAY, BETHANY. THEY OBVIOUSLY COULDN'T CHOP OFF YOUR INDESTRUCTIBLE HAIR.
BUT TONIGHT I SAW HOW THE WOMEN OF THIS WORLD DRESS. ALL THE LONG HAIR AND BEAUTIFUL COLORS IN THEIR CLOTHES...
ALL RIGHT. YOU ALWAYS WERE MORE CON-CERNED ABOUT YOUR LOOKS THAN ME.
BUT COME...
BETH..?
JAZZ...
DID YOU FEEL SOME-THING?
LIKE A SHUDDER IN THE GROUND?
I'M NOT SURE. I THINK MAYBE...
THERE IT IS AGAIN..!

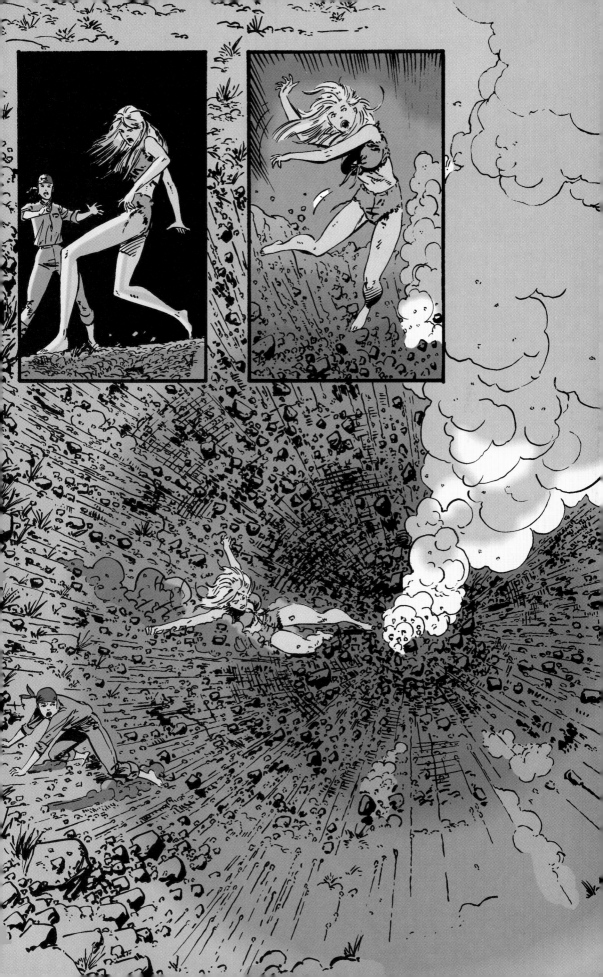

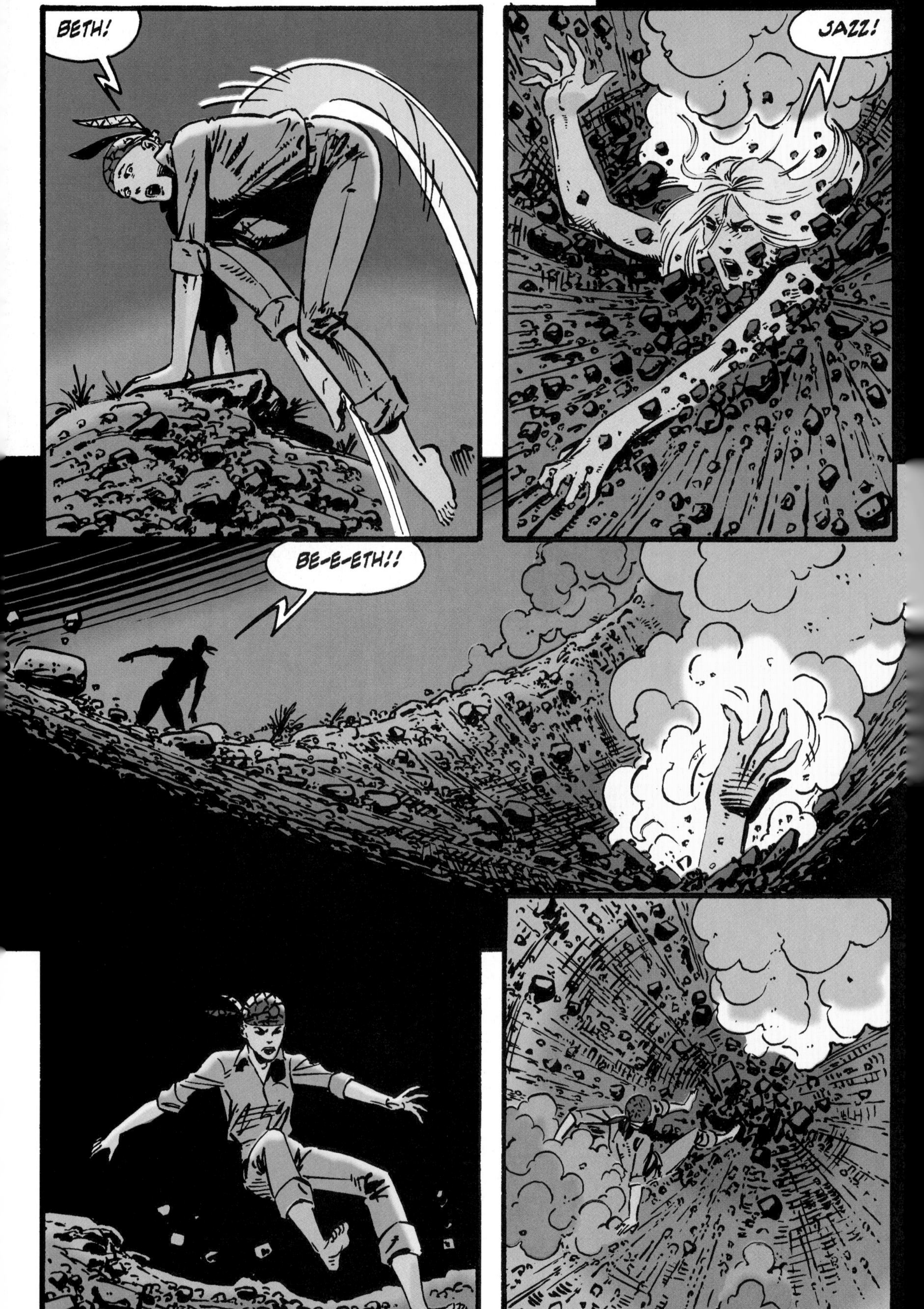
BETH!
JAZZ!
BE-E-ETH!!

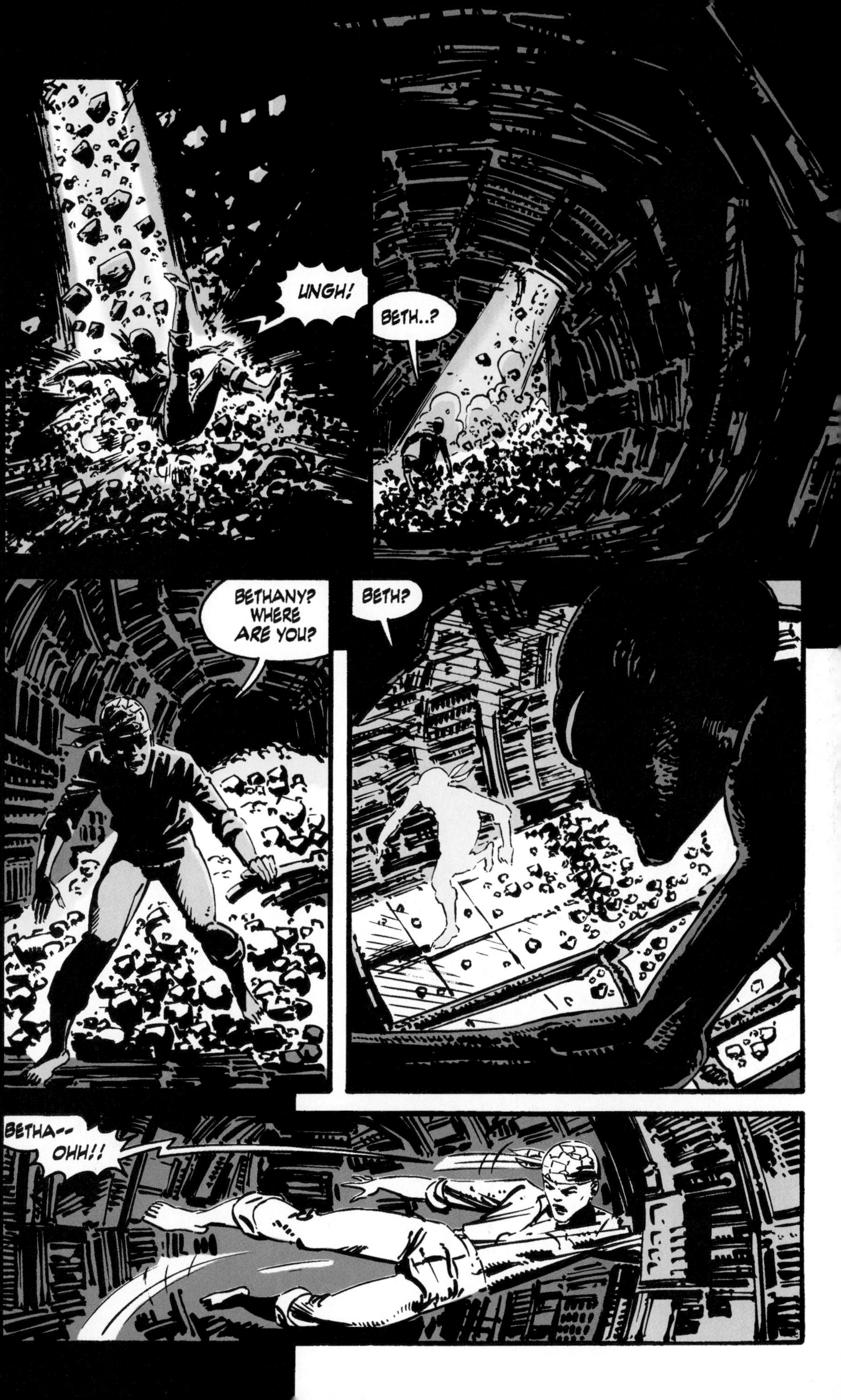
UNGH!
BETH..?
BETHANY? WHERE ARE YOU?
BETH?
BETHA-- OHH!!

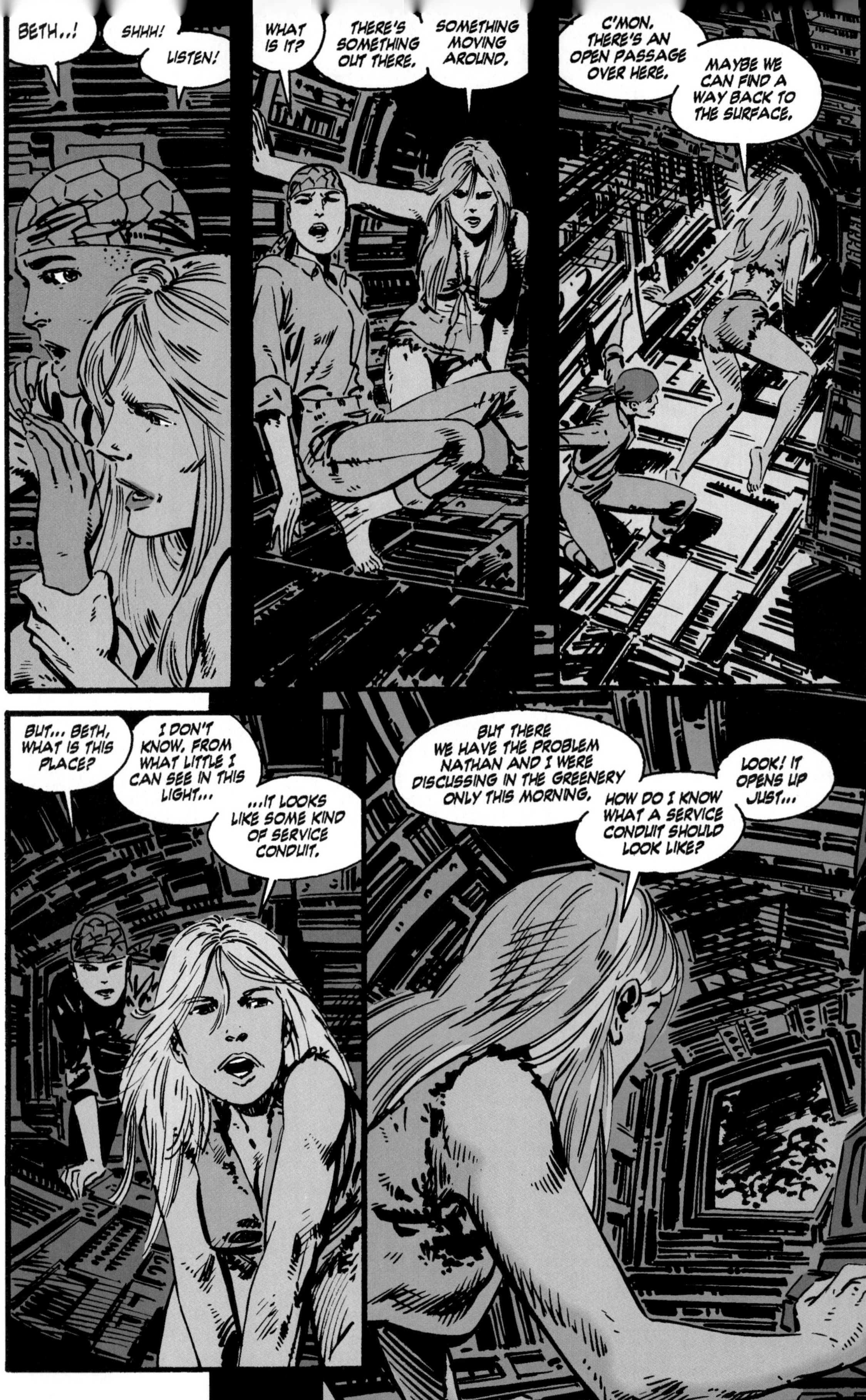

BETH..!
SHHH!
LISTEN!
WHAT IS IT?
THERE'S SOMETHING OUT THERE.
SOMETHING MOVING AROUND.
C'MON, THERE'S AN OPEN PASSAGE OVER HERE.
MAYBE WE CAN FIND A WAY BACK TO THE SURFACE.
BUT... BETH, WHAT IS THIS PLACE?
I DON'T KNOW. FROM WHAT LITTLE I CAN SEE IN THIS LIGHT...
...IT LOOKS LIKE SOME KIND OF SERVICE CONDUIT.
BUT THERE WE HAVE THE PROBLEM NATHAN AND I WERE DISCUSSING IN THE GREENERY ONLY THIS MORNING.
HOW DO I KNOW WHAT A SERVICE CONDUIT SHOULD LOOK LIKE?
LOOK! IT OPENS UP JUST...

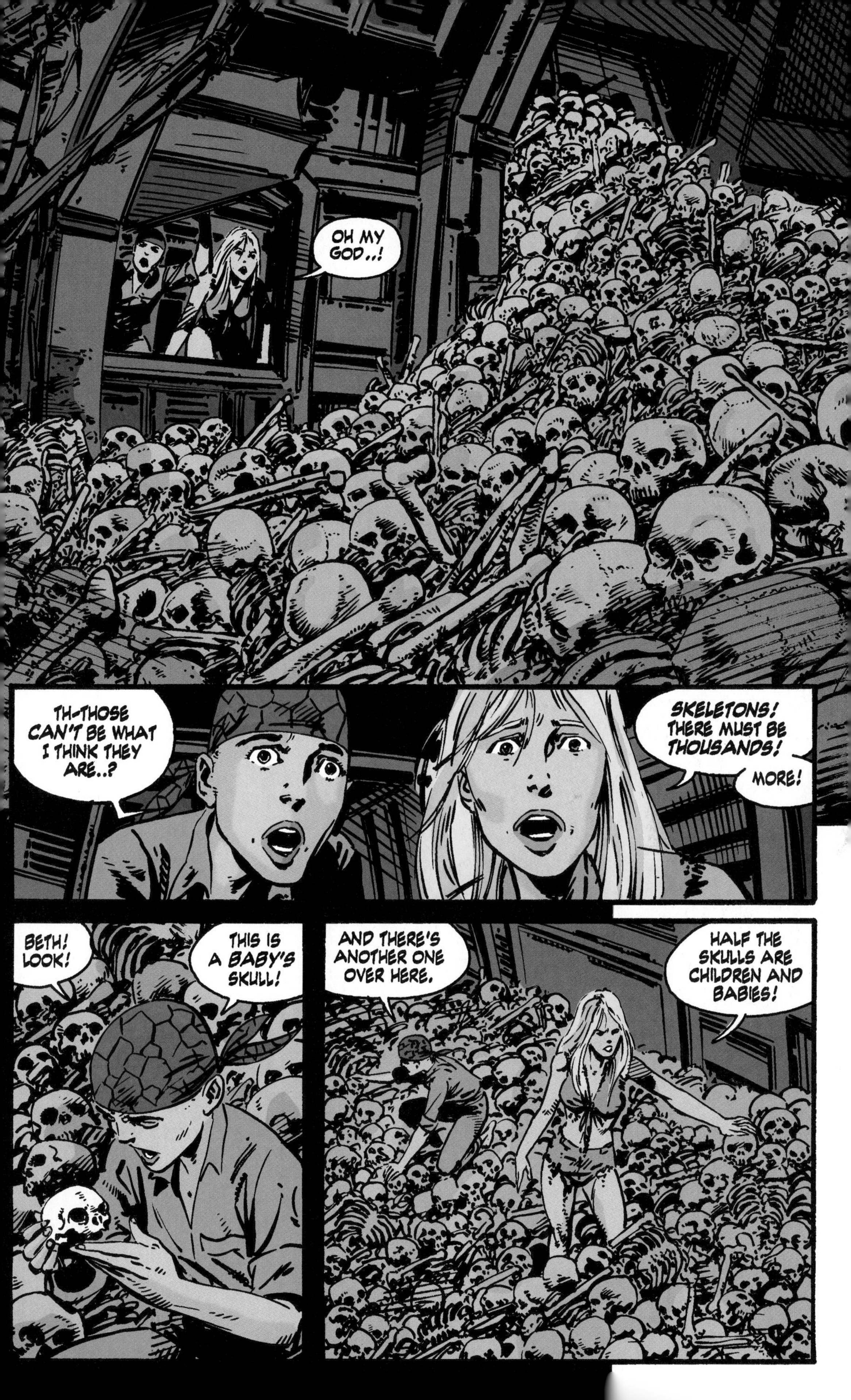
OH MY GOD..!
TH-THOSE CAN'T BE WHAT I THINK THEY ARE..?
SKELETONS! THERE MUST BE THOUSANDS!
MORE!
BETH! LOOK!
THIS IS A BABY'S SKULL!
AND THERE'S ANOTHER ONE OVER HERE.
HALF THE SKULLS ARE CHILDREN AND BABIES!

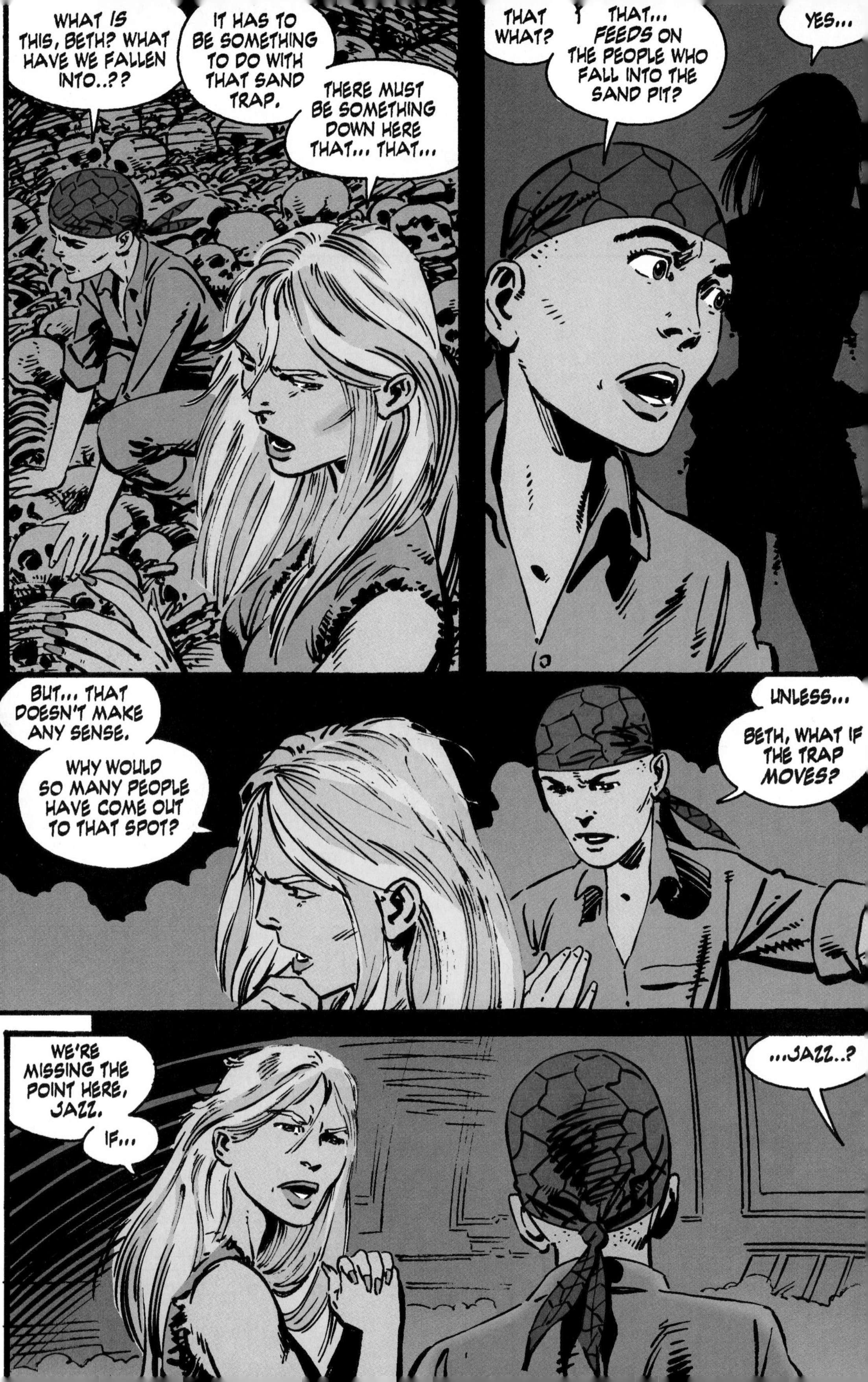
WHAT IS THIS, BETH? WHAT HAVE WE FALLEN INTO..??
IT HAS TO BE SOMETHING TO DO WITH THAT SAND TRAP.
THERE MUST BE SOMETHING DOWN HERE THAT... THAT...
THAT WHAT?
THAT... FEEDS ON THE PEOPLE WHO FALL INTO THE SAND PIT?
YES...
BUT... THAT DOESN'T MAKE ANY SENSE.
WHY WOULD SO MANY PEOPLE HAVE COME OUT TO THAT SPOT?
UNLESS...
BETH, WHAT IF THE TRAP MOVES?
WE'RE MISSING THE POINT HERE, JAZZ.
IF...
...JAZZ..?

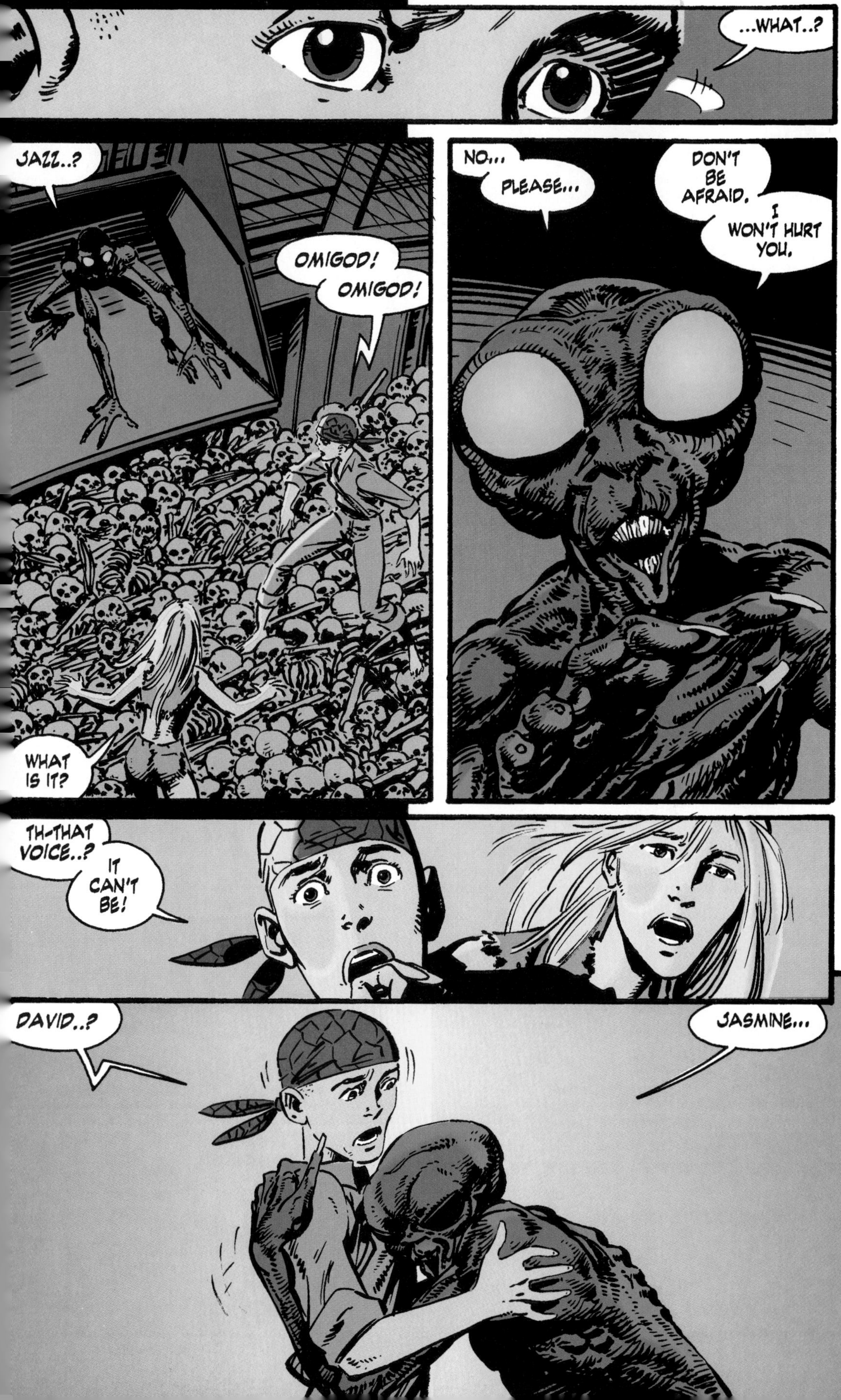
...WHAT..?
JAZZ..?
OMIGOD!
OMIGOD!
WHAT IS IT?
NO...
PLEASE...
DON'T BE AFRAID.
I WON'T HURT YOU.
TH-THAT VOICE..?
IT CAN'T BE!
DAVID..?
JASMINE...

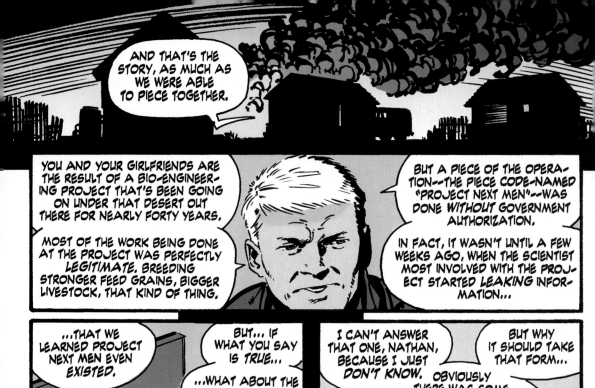

AND THAT'S THE STORY, AS MUCH AS WE WERE ABLE TO PIECE TOGETHER.

YOU AND YOUR GIRLFRIENDS ARE THE RESULT OF A BIO-ENGINEERING PROJECT THAT'S BEEN GOING ON UNDER THAT DESERT OUT THERE FOR NEARLY FORTY YEARS.

MOST OF THE WORK BEING DONE AT THE PROJECT WAS PERFECTLY *LEGITIMATE.* BREEDING STRONGER FEED GRAINS, BIGGER LIVESTOCK, THAT KIND OF THING.

BUT A PIECE OF THE OPERATION--THE PIECE CODE-NAMED *"PROJECT NEXT MEN"*--WAS DONE *WITHOUT* GOVERNMENT AUTHORIZATION.

IN FACT, IT WASN'T UNTIL A FEW WEEKS AGO, WHEN THE SCIENTIST MOST INVOLVED WITH THE PROJECT STARTED *LEAKING* INFORMATION...

...THAT WE LEARNED PROJECT NEXT MEN EVEN EXISTED.

BUT... IF WHAT YOU SAY IS *TRUE...*

...WHAT ABOUT THE WORLD WE GREW UP IN? WHAT ABOUT THE GREENERY?

I CAN'T ANSWER THAT ONE, NATHAN, BECAUSE I JUST *DON'T KNOW.*

BUT WHY IT SHOULD TAKE THAT FORM...

OBVIOUSLY THERE WAS SOME KIND OF EDUCATIONAL SYSTEM INVOLVED, TEACHING YOU ENGLISH AND GIVING YOU A BASIC COMPREHENSION OF THE WORLD.

HOLD IT!

WE HAVE A *PROBLEM.*

THERE'S A SMALL ARMY OF POLICE VEHICLES HEADED RIGHT THIS WAY.

DAMMIT! I SHOULD HAVE KNOWN BETTER THAN TO THINK THIS WAS OVER YET!

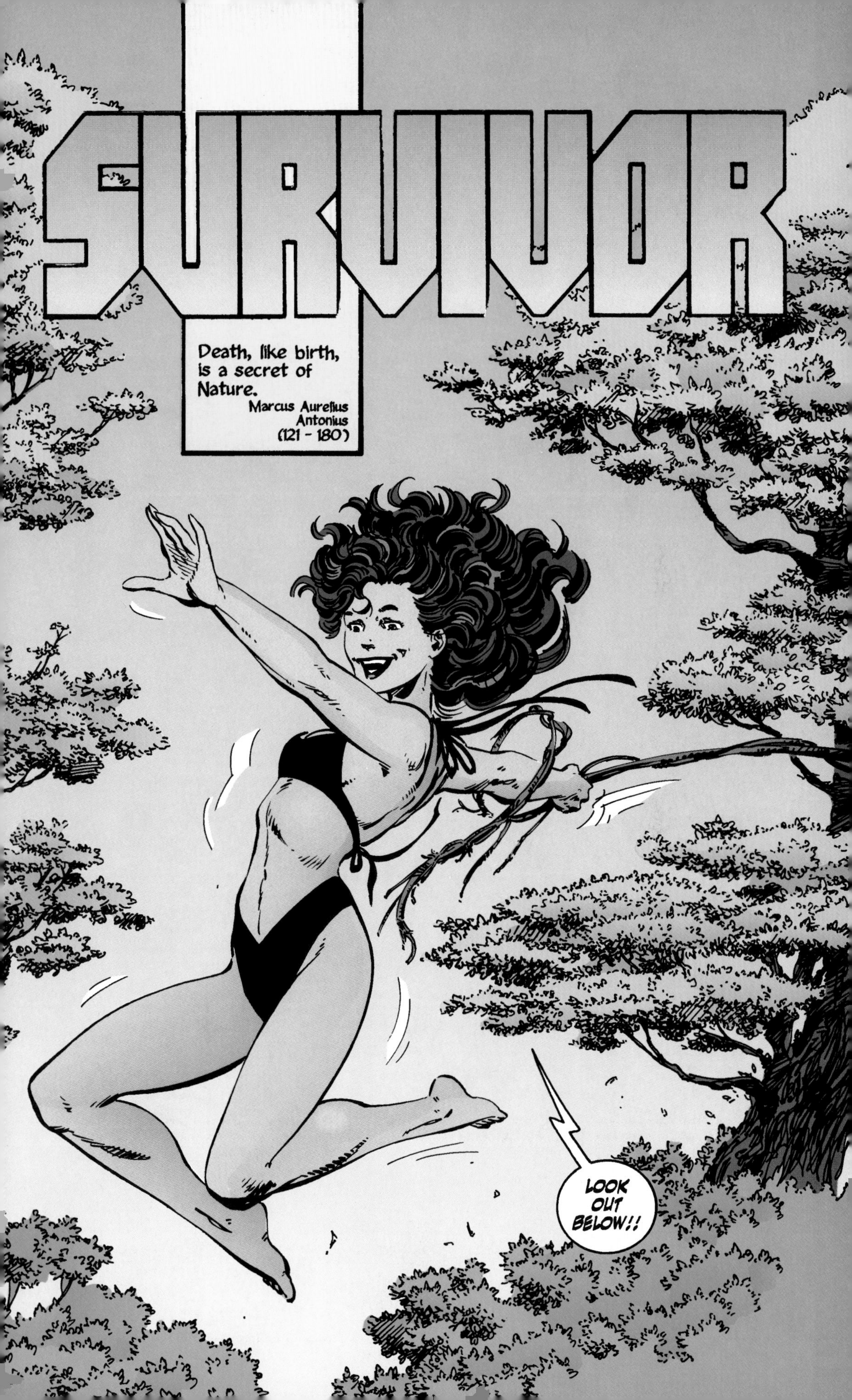
SURVIVOR
Death, like birth, is a secret of Nature.
Marcus Aurelius Antonius (121 - 180)
LOOK OUT BELOW!!

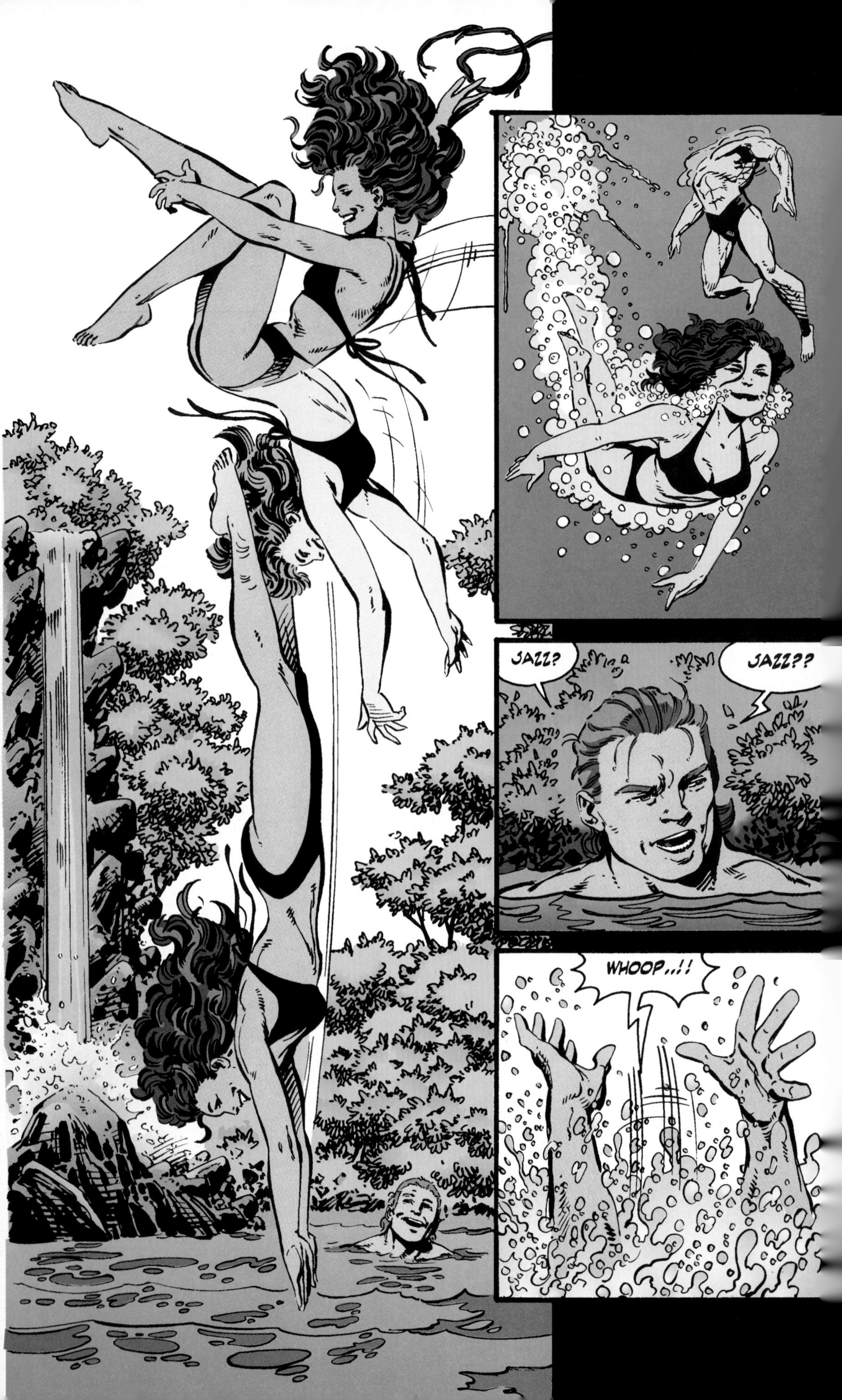
JAZZ?
JAZZ??
WHOOP..!!

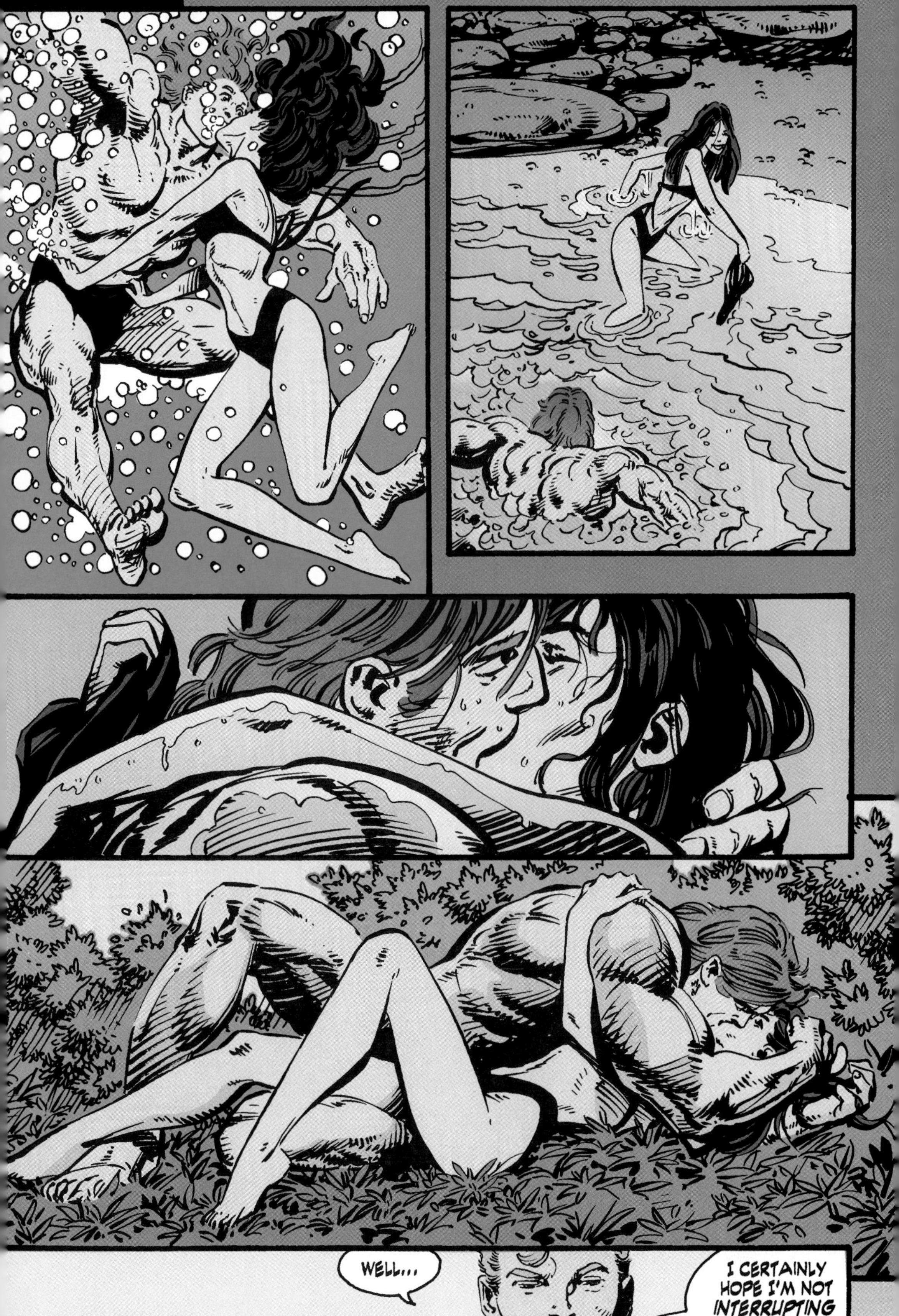
WELL...
I CERTAINLY HOPE I'M NOT INTERRUPTING ANYTHING..?

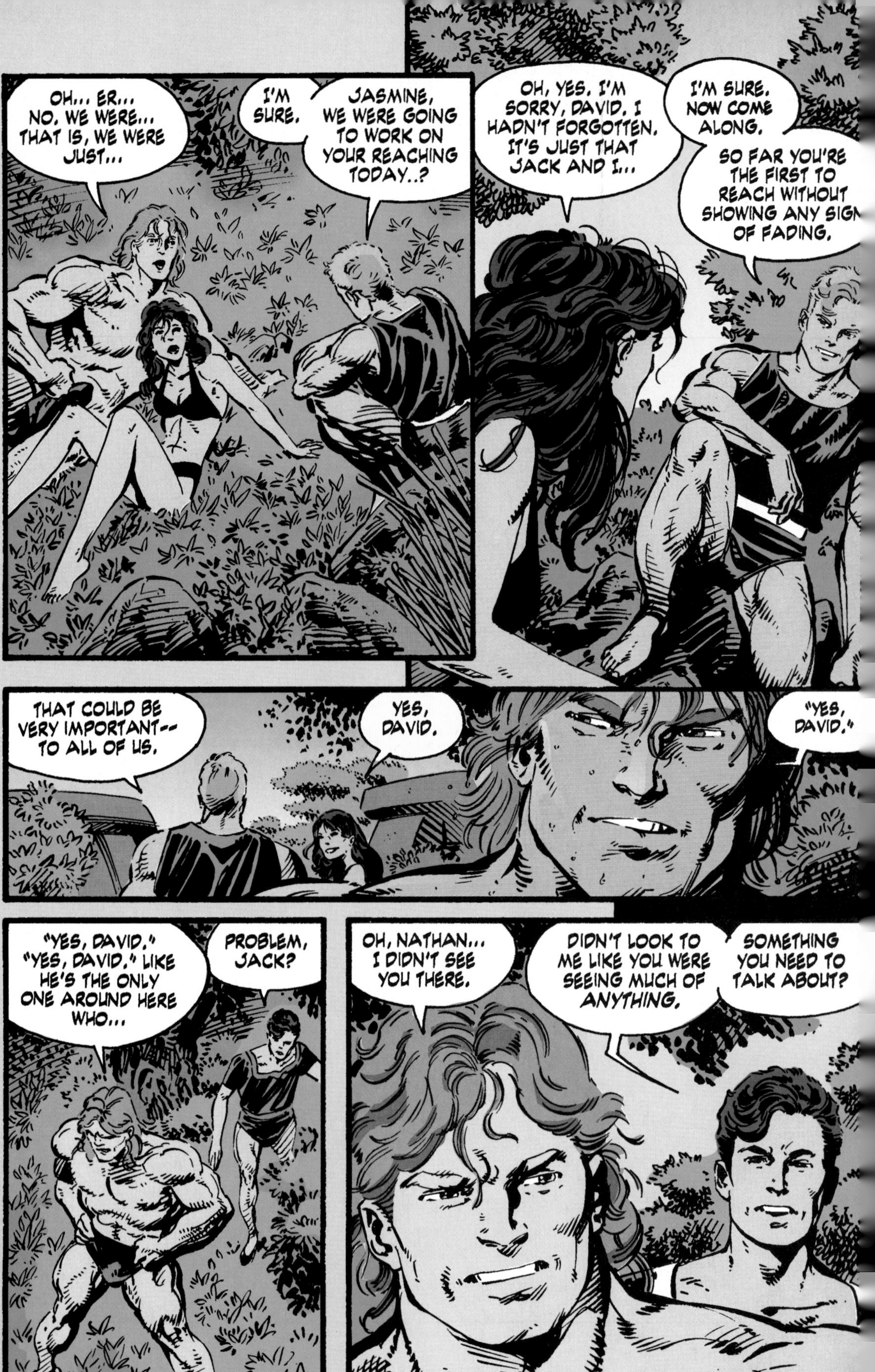
OH... ER... NO. WE WERE... THAT IS, WE WERE JUST...
I'M SURE.
JASMINE, WE WERE GOING TO WORK ON YOUR REACHING TODAY..?
OH, YES. I'M SORRY, DAVID. I HADN'T FORGOTTEN. IT'S JUST THAT JACK AND I...
I'M SURE. NOW COME ALONG.
SO FAR YOU'RE THE FIRST TO REACH WITHOUT SHOWING ANY SIGN OF FADING.
THAT COULD BE VERY IMPORTANT-- TO ALL OF US.
YES, DAVID.
"YES, DAVID."
"YES, DAVID." "YES, DAVID." LIKE HE'S THE ONLY ONE AROUND HERE WHO...
PROBLEM, JACK?
OH, NATHAN... I DIDN'T SEE YOU THERE.
DIDN'T LOOK TO ME LIKE YOU WERE SEEING MUCH OF ANYTHING.
SOMETHING YOU NEED TO TALK ABOUT?

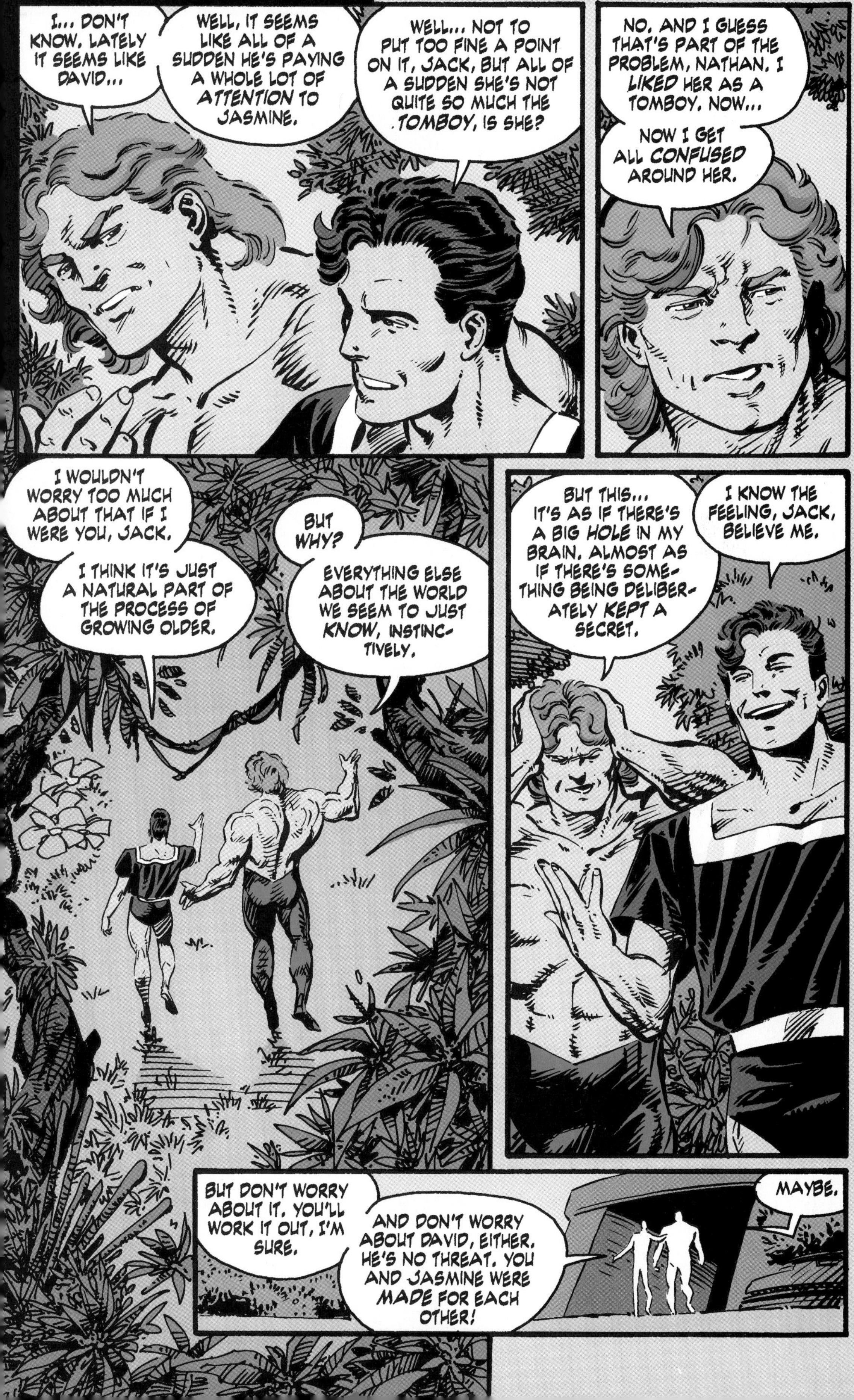

I... DON'T KNOW. LATELY IT SEEMS LIKE DAVID...
WELL, IT SEEMS LIKE ALL OF A SUDDEN HE'S PAYING A WHOLE LOT OF *ATTENTION* TO JASMINE.
WELL... NOT TO PUT TOO FINE A POINT ON IT, JACK, BUT ALL OF A SUDDEN SHE'S NOT QUITE SO MUCH THE *TOMBOY*, IS SHE?
NO, AND I GUESS THAT'S PART OF THE PROBLEM, NATHAN. I *LIKED* HER AS A TOMBOY. NOW...
NOW I GET ALL *CONFUSED* AROUND HER.
I WOULDN'T WORRY TOO MUCH ABOUT THAT IF I WERE YOU, JACK.
I THINK IT'S JUST A NATURAL PART OF THE PROCESS OF GROWING OLDER.
BUT *WHY*?
EVERYTHING ELSE ABOUT THE WORLD WE SEEM TO JUST *KNOW*, INSTINCTIVELY.
BUT THIS... IT'S AS IF THERE'S A BIG *HOLE* IN MY BRAIN. ALMOST AS IF THERE'S SOMETHING BEING DELIBERATELY *KEPT* A SECRET.
I KNOW THE FEELING, JACK, BELIEVE ME.
BUT DON'T WORRY ABOUT IT. YOU'LL WORK IT OUT, I'M SURE.
AND DON'T WORRY ABOUT DAVID, EITHER. HE'S NO THREAT. YOU AND JASMINE WERE *MADE* FOR EACH OTHER!
MAYBE.

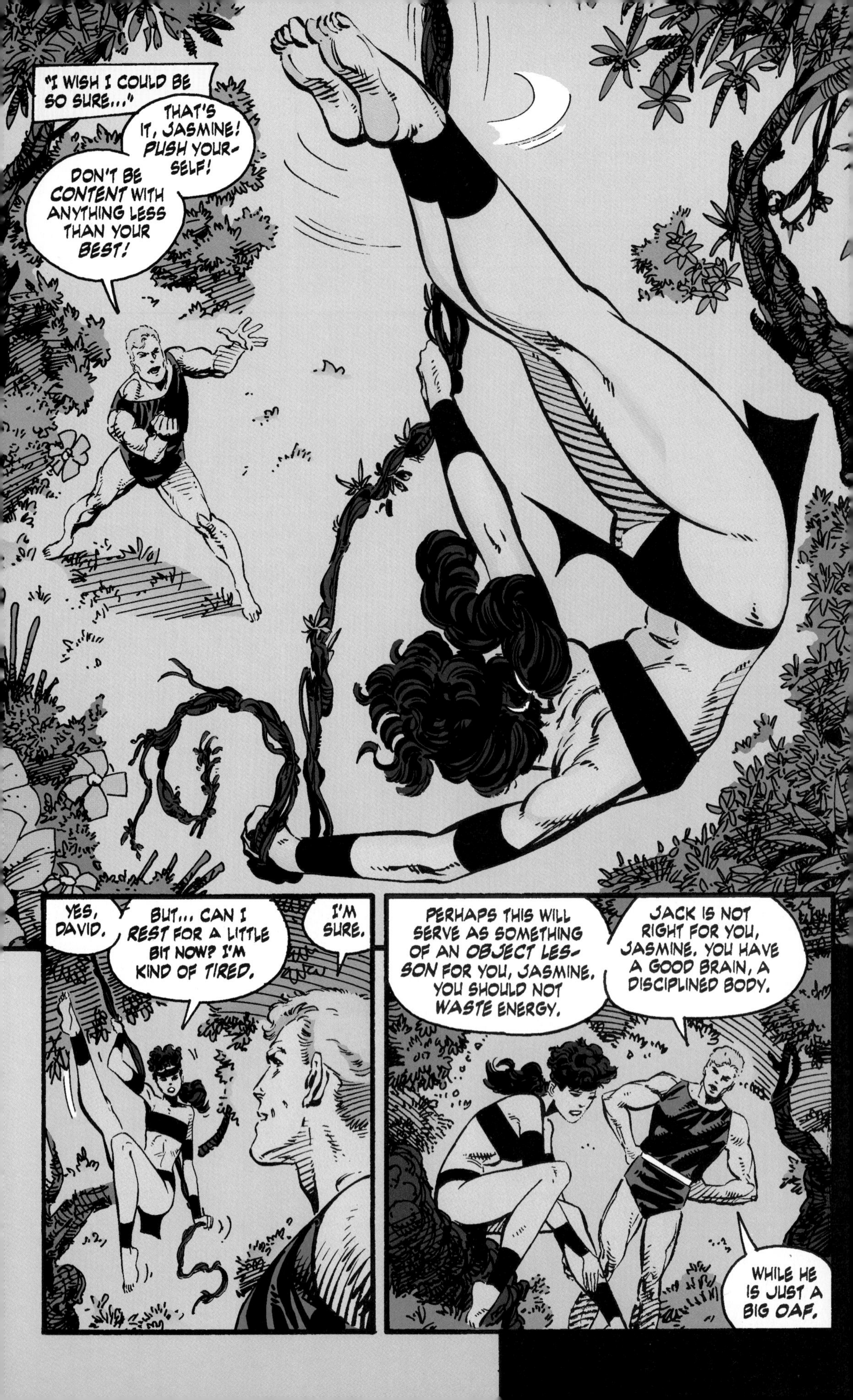
"I WISH I COULD BE SO SURE..."
THAT'S IT, JASMINE! PUSH YOURSELF!
DON'T BE CONTENT WITH ANYTHING LESS THAN YOUR BEST!
YES, DAVID.
BUT... CAN I REST FOR A LITTLE BIT NOW? I'M KIND OF TIRED.
I'M SURE.
PERHAPS THIS WILL SERVE AS SOMETHING OF AN OBJECT LESSON FOR YOU, JASMINE. YOU SHOULD NOT WASTE ENERGY.
JACK IS NOT RIGHT FOR YOU, JASMINE. YOU HAVE A GOOD BRAIN, A DISCIPLINED BODY.
WHILE HE IS JUST A BIG OAF.

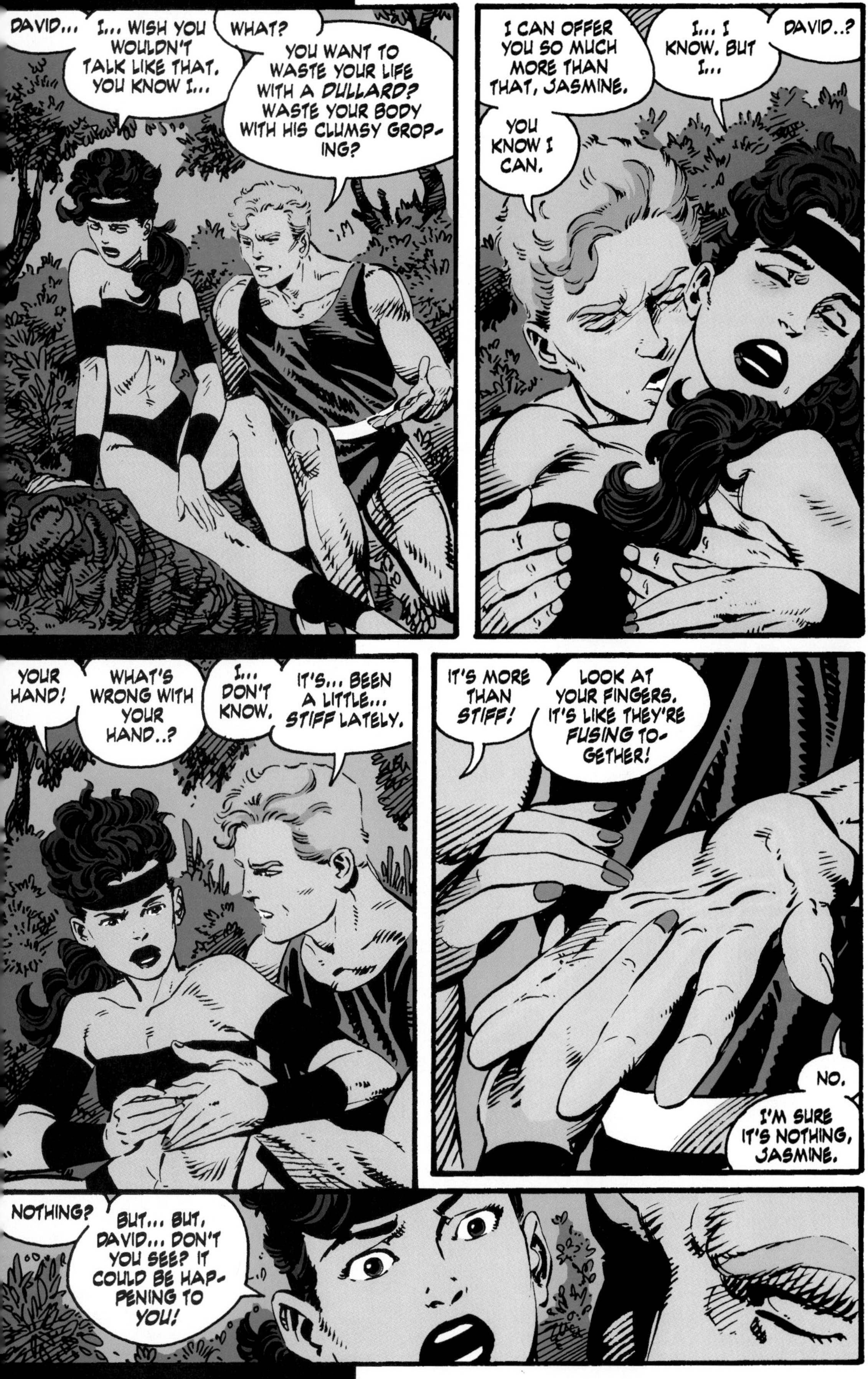
DAVID...
I... WISH YOU WOULDN'T TALK LIKE THAT. YOU KNOW I...
WHAT?
YOU WANT TO WASTE YOUR LIFE WITH A DULLARD? WASTE YOUR BODY WITH HIS CLUMSY GROP-ING?
I CAN OFFER YOU SO MUCH MORE THAN THAT, JASMINE.
YOU KNOW I CAN.
I... I KNOW. BUT I...
DAVID..?
YOUR HAND!
WHAT'S WRONG WITH YOUR HAND..?
I... DON'T KNOW.
IT'S... BEEN A LITTLE... STIFF LATELY.
IT'S MORE THAN STIFF!
LOOK AT YOUR FINGERS. IT'S LIKE THEY'RE FUSING TO-GETHER!
NO.
I'M SURE IT'S NOTHING, JASMINE.
NOTHING?
BUT... BUT, DAVID... DON'T YOU SEE? IT COULD BE HAP-PENING TO YOU!

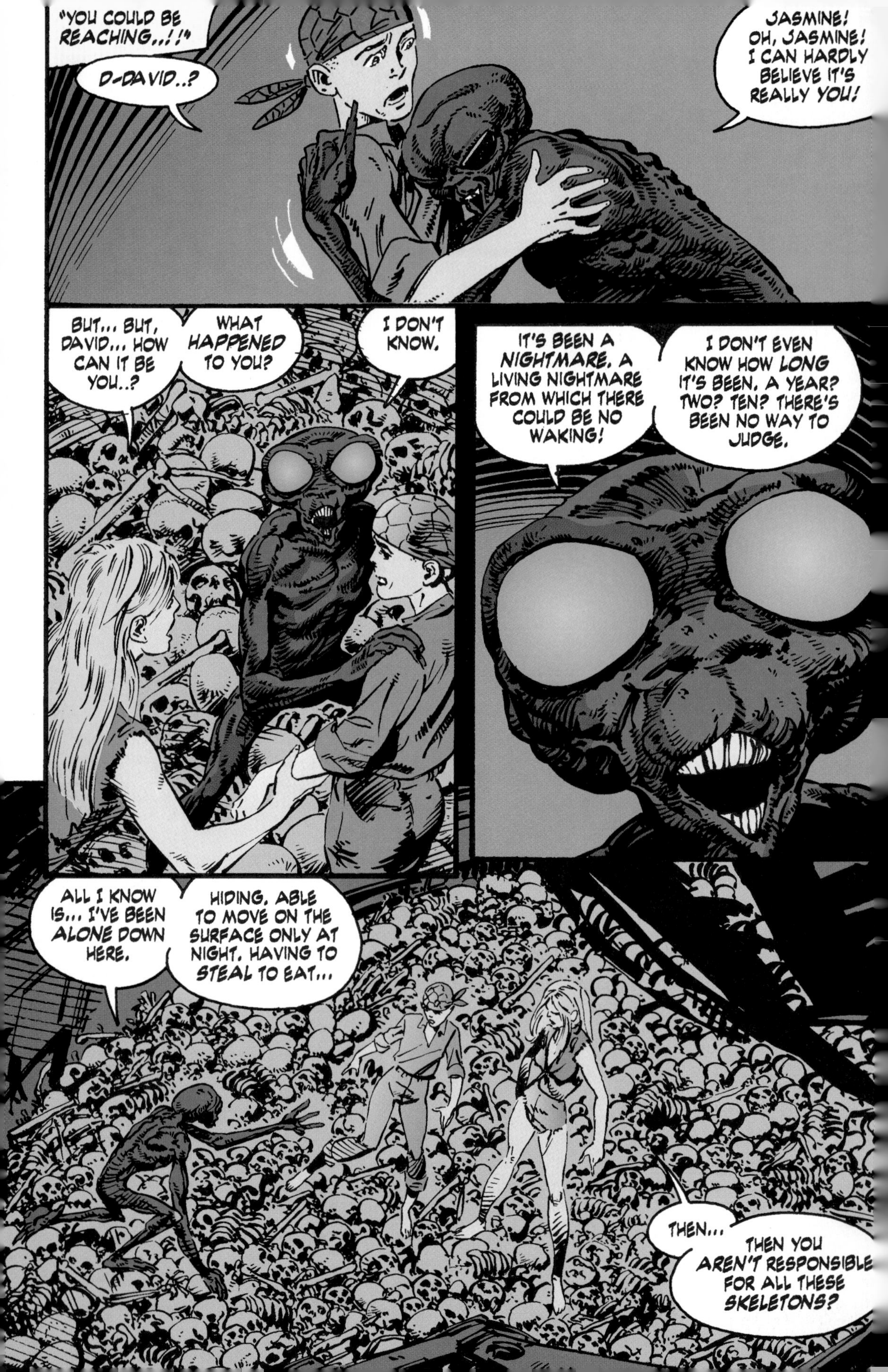
"YOU COULD BE REACHING..!!"
D-DAVID..?
JASMINE! OH, JASMINE! I CAN HARDLY BELIEVE IT'S REALLY YOU!
BUT... BUT, DAVID... HOW CAN IT BE YOU..?
WHAT HAPPENED TO YOU?
I DON'T KNOW.
IT'S BEEN A NIGHTMARE. A LIVING NIGHTMARE FROM WHICH THERE COULD BE NO WAKING!
I DON'T EVEN KNOW HOW LONG IT'S BEEN. A YEAR? TWO? TEN? THERE'S BEEN NO WAY TO JUDGE.
ALL I KNOW IS... I'VE BEEN ALONE DOWN HERE.
HIDING. ABLE TO MOVE ON THE SURFACE ONLY AT NIGHT. HAVING TO STEAL TO EAT...
THEN...
THEN YOU AREN'T RESPONSIBLE FOR ALL THESE SKELETONS?

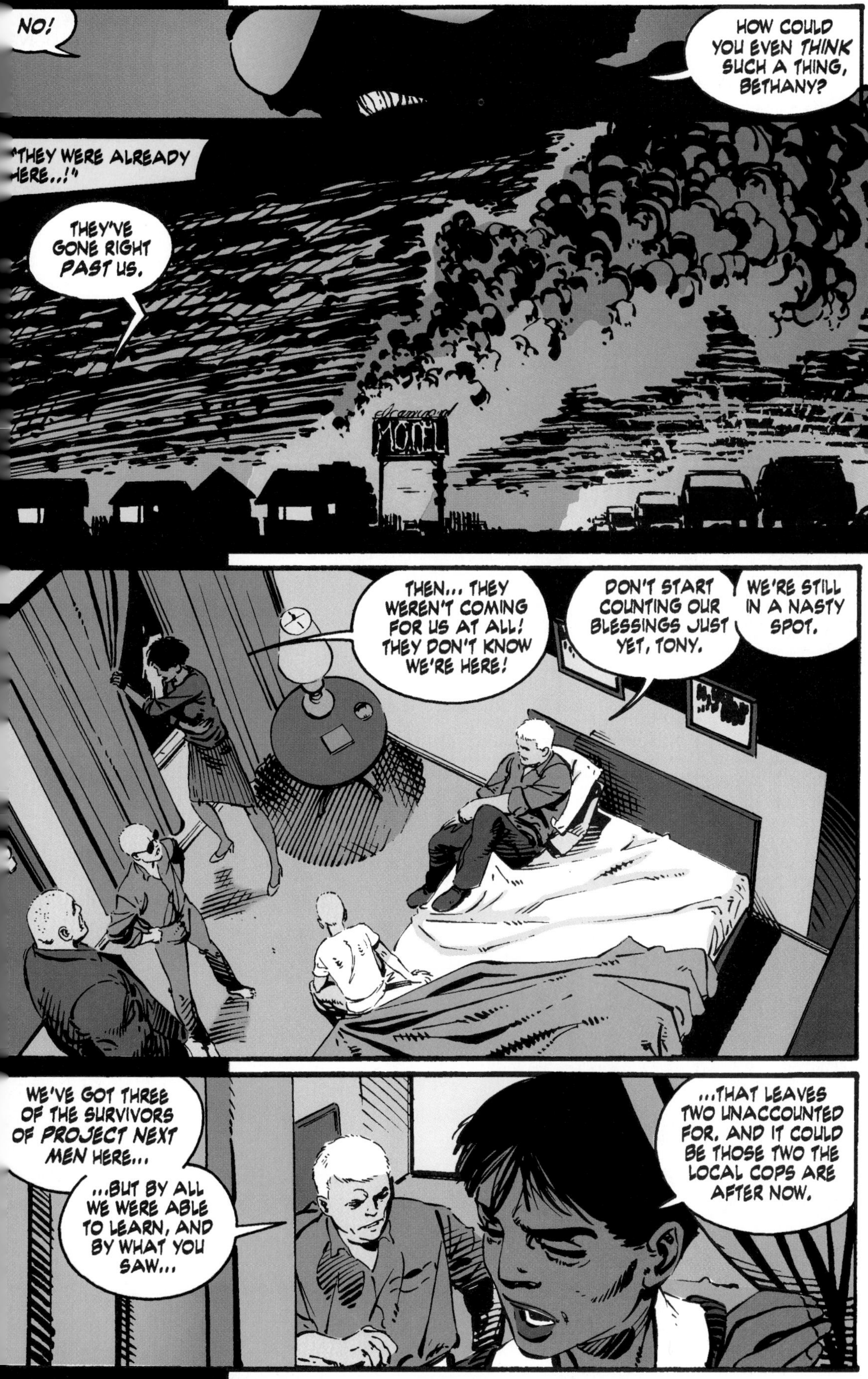
NO!
HOW COULD YOU EVEN THINK SUCH A THING, BETHANY?
"THEY WERE ALREADY HERE..!"
THEY'VE GONE RIGHT PAST US.
MOTEL
THEN... THEY WEREN'T COMING FOR US AT ALL! THEY DON'T KNOW WE'RE HERE!
DON'T START COUNTING OUR BLESSINGS JUST YET, TONY.
WE'RE STILL IN A NASTY SPOT.
WE'VE GOT THREE OF THE SURVIVORS OF PROJECT NEXT MEN HERE...
...BUT BY ALL WE WERE ABLE TO LEARN, AND BY WHAT YOU SAW...
...THAT LEAVES TWO UNACCOUNTED FOR. AND IT COULD BE THOSE TWO THE LOCAL COPS ARE AFTER NOW.

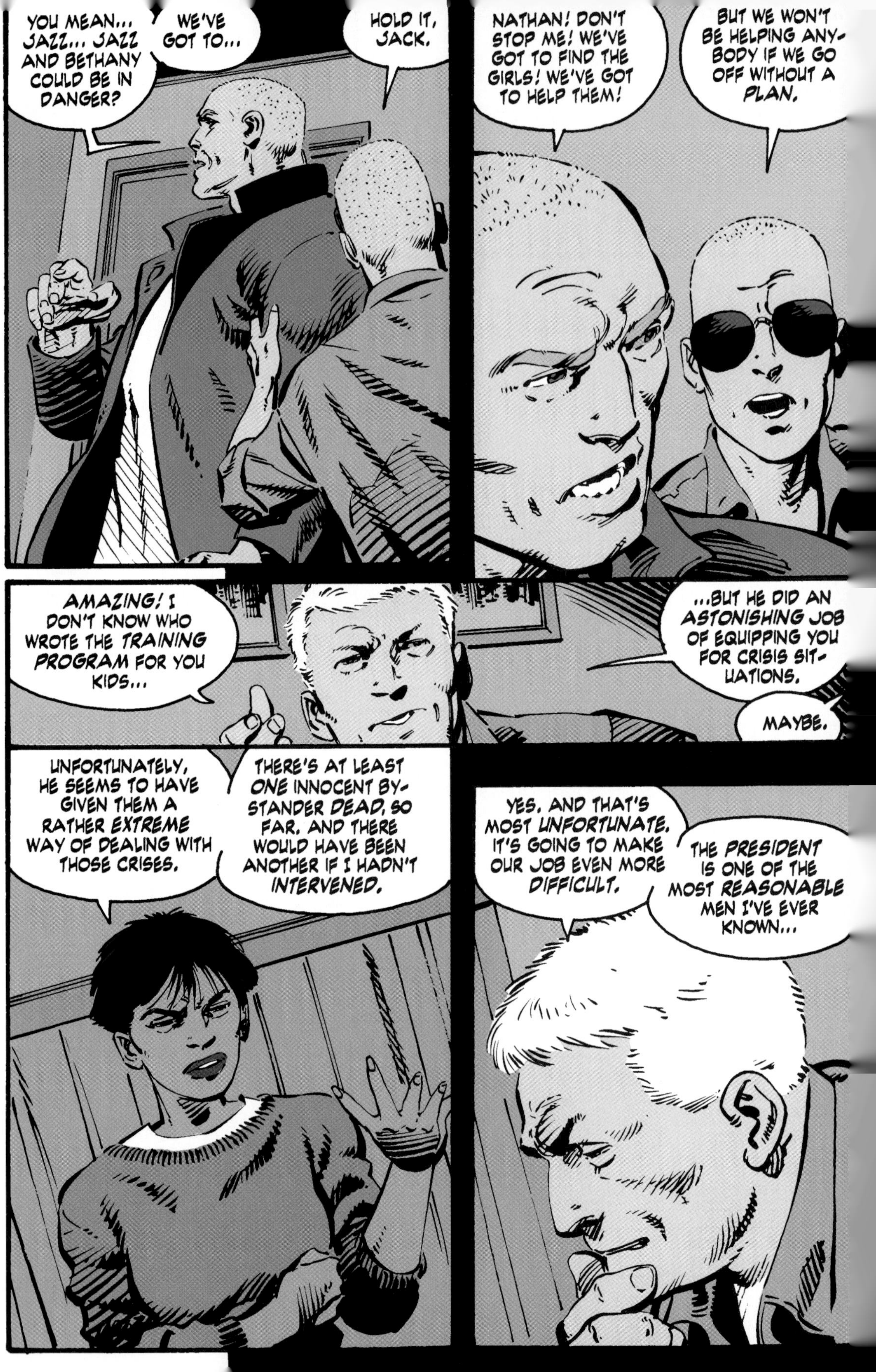
YOU MEAN... JAZZ... JAZZ AND BETHANY COULD BE IN DANGER?
WE'VE GOT TO...
HOLD IT, JACK.
NATHAN! DON'T STOP ME! WE'VE GOT TO FIND THE GIRLS! WE'VE GOT TO HELP THEM!
BUT WE WON'T BE HELPING ANY-BODY IF WE GO OFF WITHOUT A PLAN.
AMAZING! I DON'T KNOW WHO WROTE THE TRAINING PROGRAM FOR YOU KIDS...
...BUT HE DID AN ASTONISHING JOB OF EQUIPPING YOU FOR CRISIS SIT-UATIONS.
MAYBE.
UNFORTUNATELY, HE SEEMS TO HAVE GIVEN THEM A RATHER EXTREME WAY OF DEALING WITH THOSE CRISES.
THERE'S AT LEAST ONE INNOCENT BY-STANDER DEAD, SO FAR, AND THERE WOULD HAVE BEEN ANOTHER IF I HADN'T INTERVENED.
YES. AND THAT'S MOST UNFORTUNATE. IT'S GOING TO MAKE OUR JOB EVEN MORE DIFFICULT.
THE PRESIDENT IS ONE OF THE MOST REASONABLE MEN I'VE EVER KNOWN...

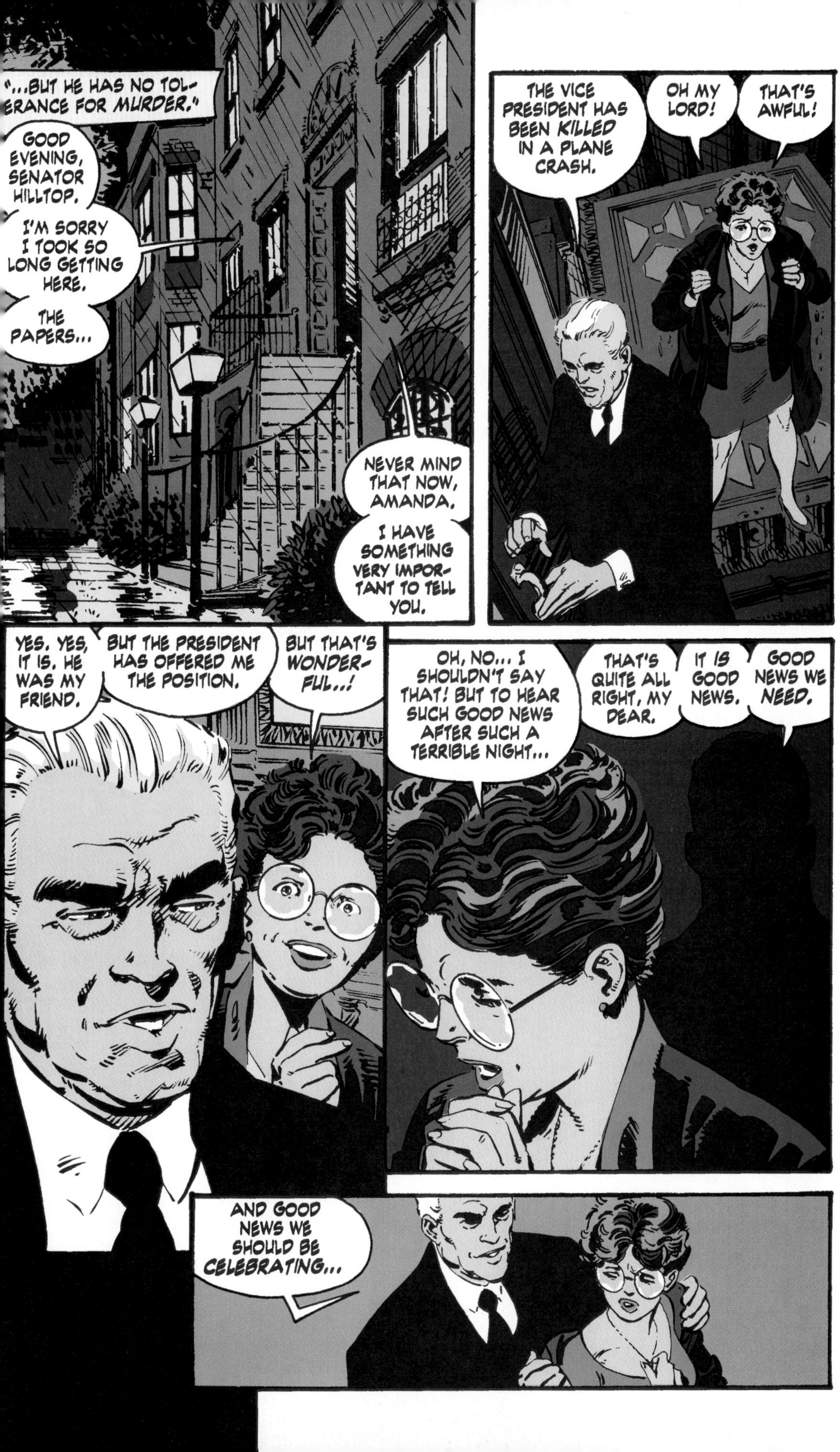
"...BUT HE HAS NO TOL-
ERANCE FOR MURDER."
GOOD EVENING, SENATOR HILLTOP.
I'M SORRY I TOOK SO LONG GETTING HERE.
THE PAPERS...
NEVER MIND THAT NOW, AMANDA.
I HAVE SOMETHING VERY IMPOR-TANT TO TELL YOU.
THE VICE PRESIDENT HAS BEEN KILLED IN A PLANE CRASH.
OH MY LORD!
THAT'S AWFUL!
YES. YES, IT IS. HE WAS MY FRIEND.
BUT THE PRESIDENT HAS OFFERED ME THE POSITION.
BUT THAT'S WONDER-FUL..!
OH, NO... I SHOULDN'T SAY THAT! BUT TO HEAR SUCH GOOD NEWS AFTER SUCH A TERRIBLE NIGHT...
THAT'S QUITE ALL RIGHT, MY DEAR.
IT IS GOOD NEWS.
GOOD NEWS WE NEED.
AND GOOD NEWS WE SHOULD BE CELEBRATING...

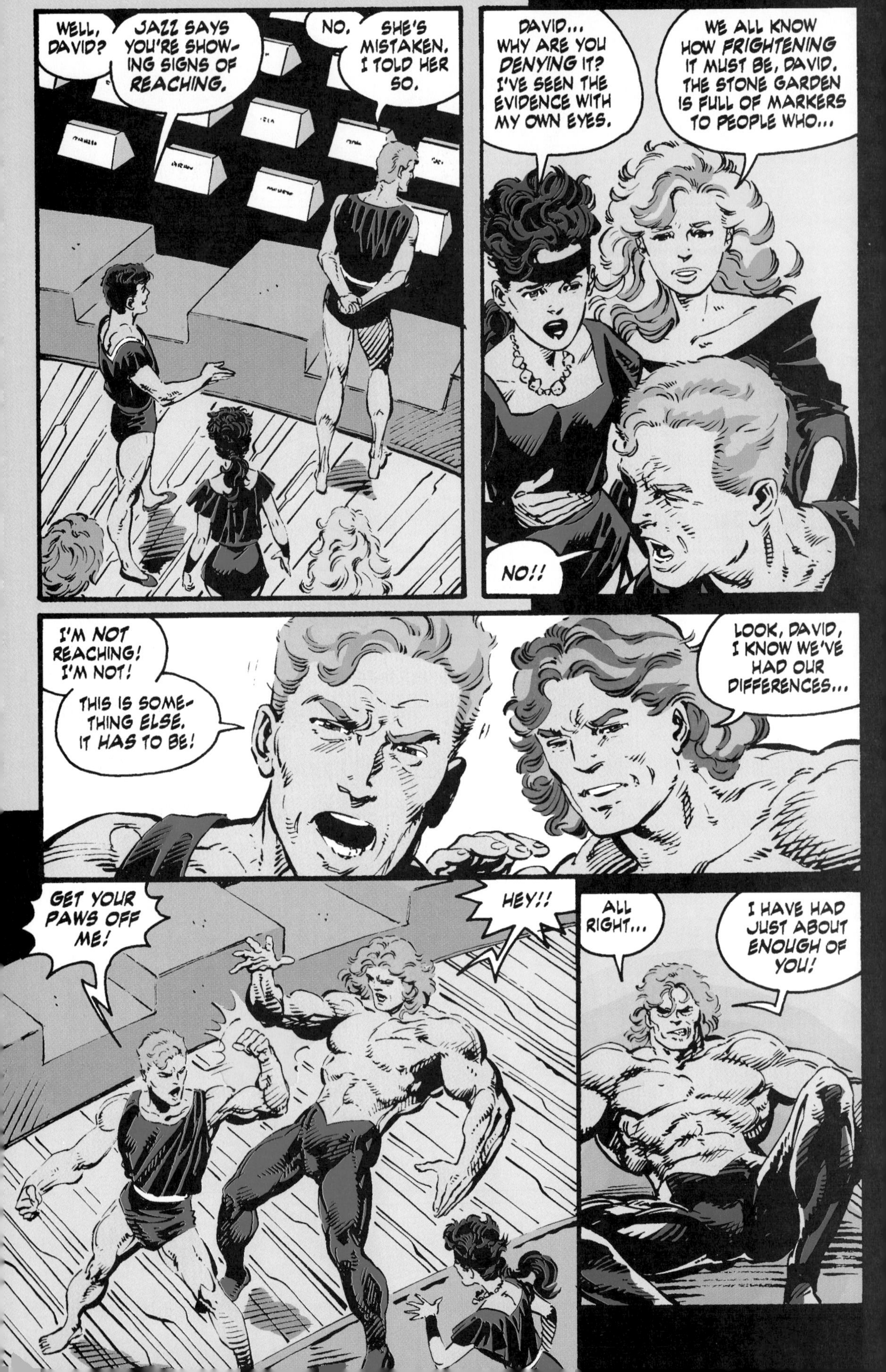
WELL, DAVID?
JAZZ SAYS YOU'RE SHOWING SIGNS OF REACHING.
NO.
SHE'S MISTAKEN. I TOLD HER SO.
DAVID... WHY ARE YOU DENYING IT? I'VE SEEN THE EVIDENCE WITH MY OWN EYES.
WE ALL KNOW HOW FRIGHTENING IT MUST BE, DAVID. THE STONE GARDEN IS FULL OF MARKERS TO PEOPLE WHO...
NO!!
I'M NOT REACHING! I'M NOT!
THIS IS SOMETHING ELSE. IT HAS TO BE!
LOOK, DAVID, I KNOW WE'VE HAD OUR DIFFERENCES...
GET YOUR PAWS OFF ME!
HEY!!
ALL RIGHT...
I HAVE HAD JUST ABOUT ENOUGH OF YOU!

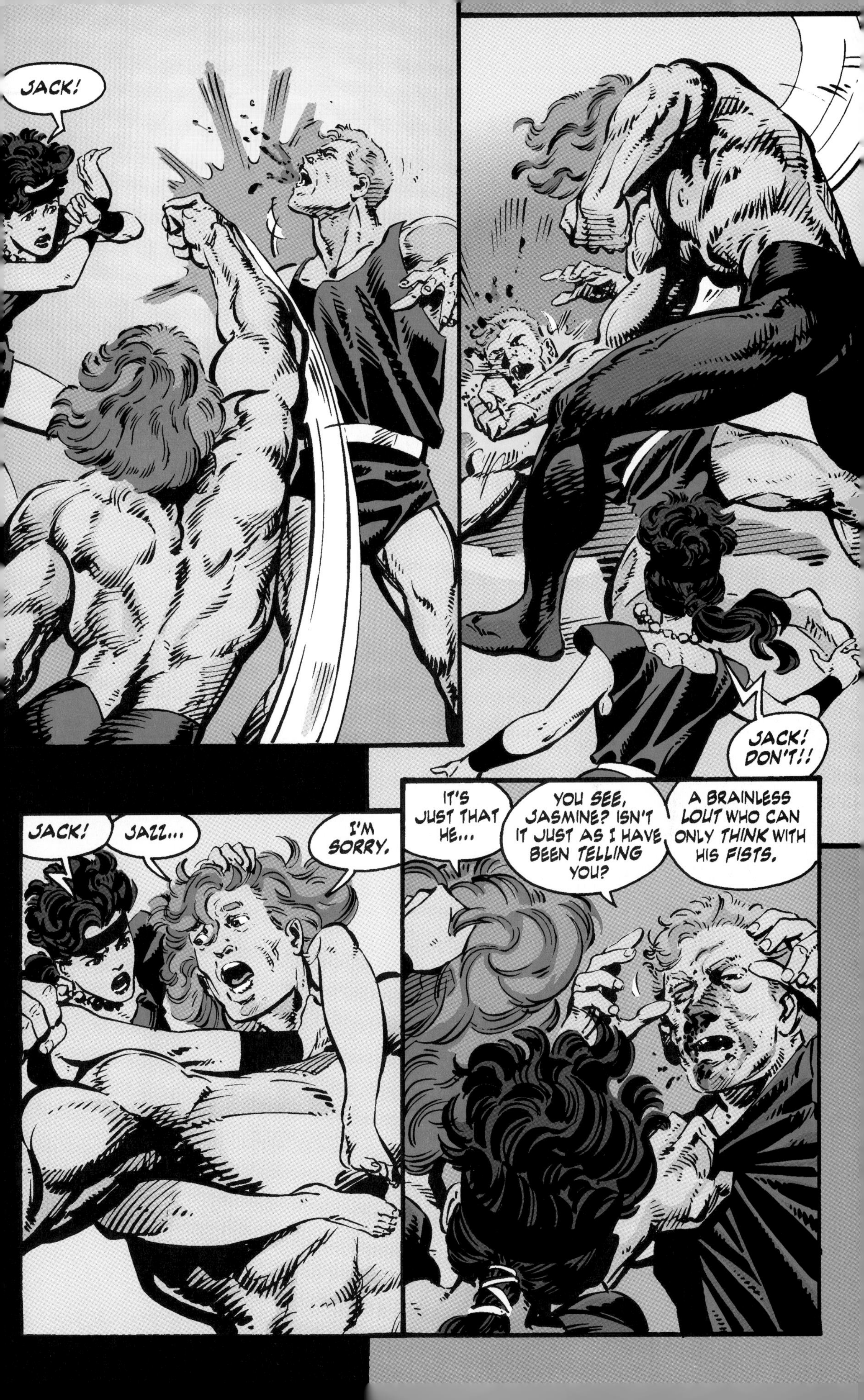
JACK!
JACK! DON'T!!
JACK!
JAZZ...
I'M SORRY.
IT'S JUST THAT HE...
YOU SEE, JASMINE? ISN'T IT JUST AS I HAVE BEEN TELLING YOU?
A BRAINLESS LOUT WHO CAN ONLY THINK WITH HIS FISTS.

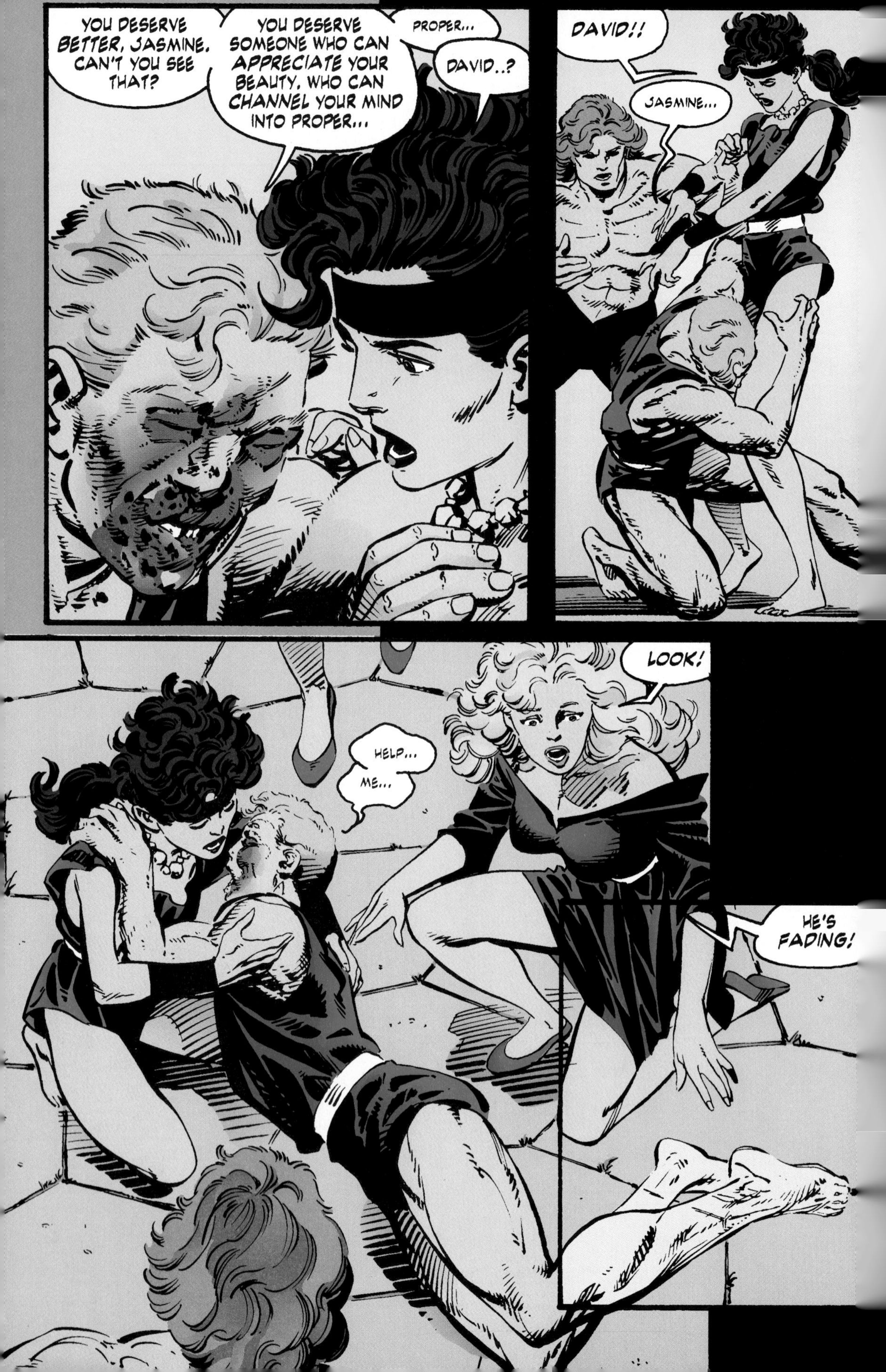
YOU DESERVE BETTER, JASMINE. CAN'T YOU SEE THAT?
YOU DESERVE SOMEONE WHO CAN APPRECIATE YOUR BEAUTY, WHO CAN CHANNEL YOUR MIND INTO PROPER...
PROPER...
DAVID..?
DAVID!!
JASMINE...
LOOK!
HELP...
ME...
HE'S FADING!

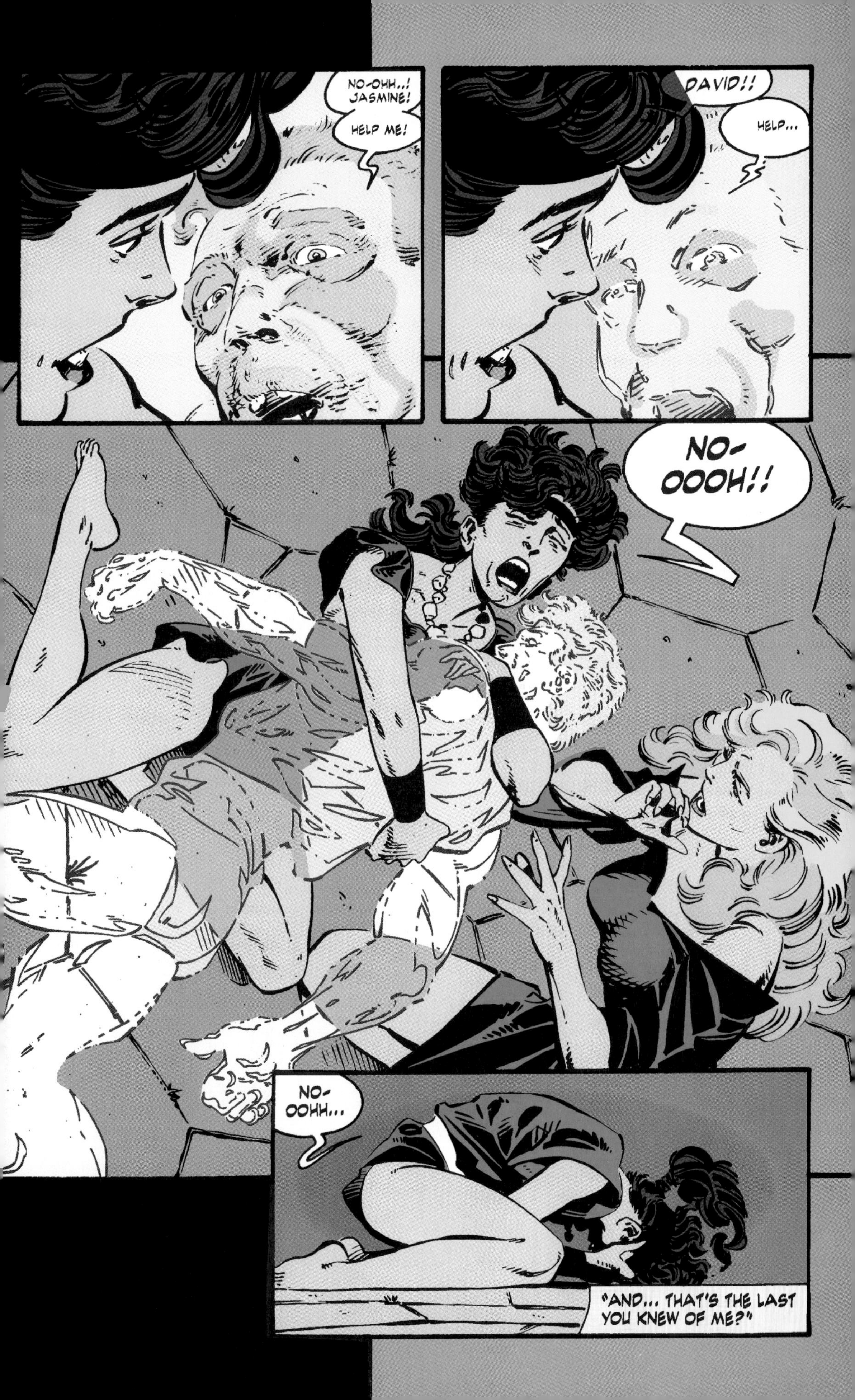
NO-OHH..! JASMINE!
HELP ME!
DAVID!!
HELP...
NO-OOOH!!
NO-OOHH...
"AND... THAT'S THE LAST YOU KNEW OF ME?"

YES, WE WENT TO THE STONE FIELD, LATER THAT DAY...

...AND THERE WAS A NEW MARKER WITH YOUR NAME ON IT.

AFTER A WHILE WE JUST STOPPED TALKING ABOUT YOU, TRIED TO STOP THINKING ABOUT YOU.

LIKE WE'D DONE WITH ALL THE OTHERS.

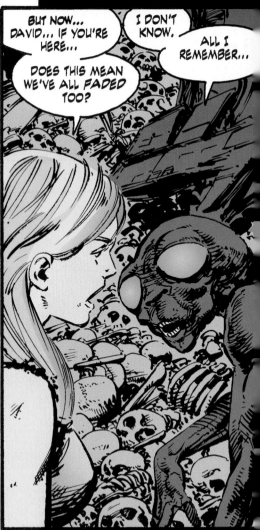

BUT NOW... DAVID... IF YOU'RE HERE...

DOES THIS MEAN WE'VE ALL FADED TOO?

I DON'T KNOW.

ALL I REMEMBER...

"THERE WAS DARK-NESS. ABSOLUTE DARK-NESS.

"I COULDN'T SEE OR MOVE, BUT I COULD HEAR."

OKAY, CALL IT.

WHAT'S THE TIME?

OH-FIVE THIRTY-ONE.

"THERE WAS A SENSA-TION OF MOVEMENT. OF BEING ROUGHLY HAN-DLED.

"AND... PAIN. THERE WAS A LOT OF PAIN."

DRAW THE USUAL BLOOD AND FLUID SAMPLES.

AND GET SOME OF THAT TISSUE. BREMMER WILL WANT TO RUN THE FULL TESTS.

"AFTER A WHILE THE PAIN STOPPED, THEN IT WAS QUIET FOR A LONG TIME.

"THEN THERE WAS MOVE-MENT AGAIN. AND A SENSATION OF FALLING.

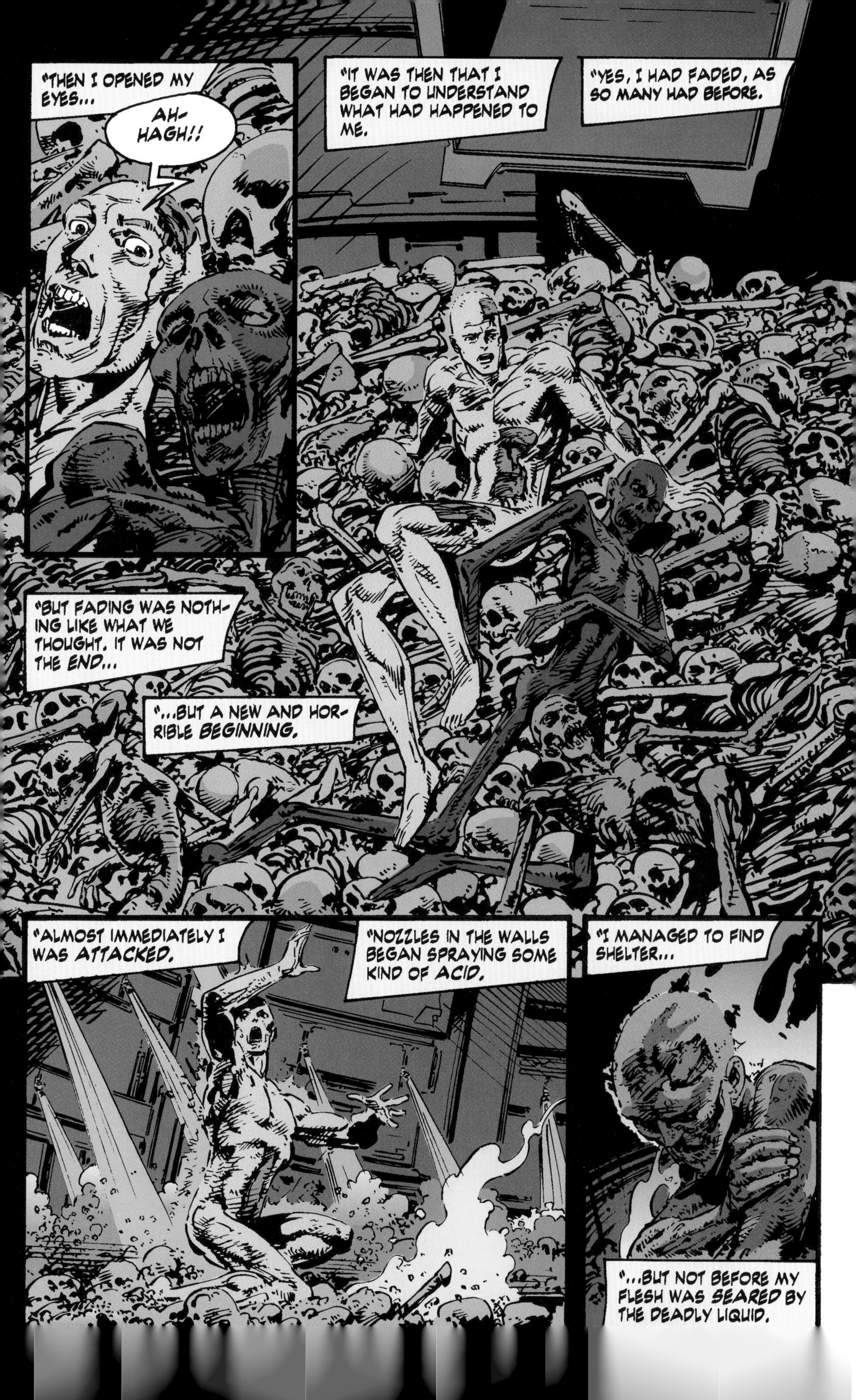
"THEN I OPENED MY EYES...
AH-HAGH!!
"IT WAS THEN THAT I BEGAN TO UNDERSTAND WHAT HAD HAPPENED TO ME.
"YES, I HAD FADED, AS SO MANY HAD BEFORE.
"BUT FADING WAS NOTHING LIKE WHAT WE THOUGHT. IT WAS NOT THE END...
"...BUT A NEW AND HORRIBLE BEGINNING.
"ALMOST IMMEDIATELY I WAS ATTACKED.
"NOZZLES IN THE WALLS BEGAN SPRAYING SOME KIND OF ACID.
"I MANAGED TO FIND SHELTER...
"...BUT NOT BEFORE MY FLESH WAS SEARED BY THE DEADLY LIQUID.

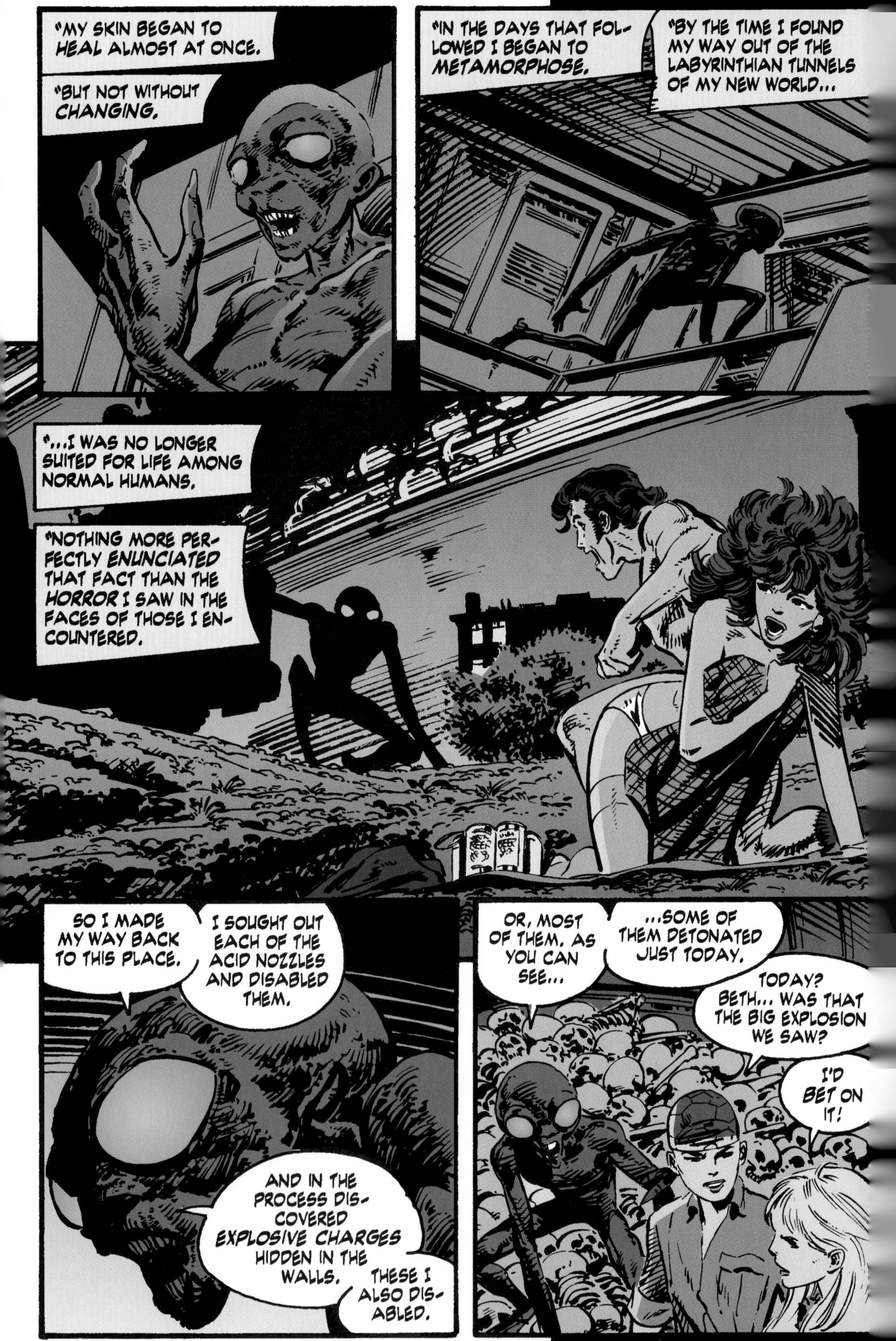
"MY SKIN BEGAN TO HEAL ALMOST AT ONCE.
"BUT NOT WITHOUT CHANGING.
"IN THE DAYS THAT FOLLOWED I BEGAN TO METAMORPHOSE.
"BY THE TIME I FOUND MY WAY OUT OF THE LABYRINTHIAN TUNNELS OF MY NEW WORLD...
"...I WAS NO LONGER SUITED FOR LIFE AMONG NORMAL HUMANS.
"NOTHING MORE PERFECTLY ENUNCIATED THAT FACT THAN THE HORROR I SAW IN THE FACES OF THOSE I ENCOUNTERED.
SO I MADE MY WAY BACK TO THIS PLACE.
I SOUGHT OUT EACH OF THE ACID NOZZLES AND DISABLED THEM.
AND IN THE PROCESS DISCOVERED EXPLOSIVE CHARGES HIDDEN IN THE WALLS.
THESE I ALSO DISABLED.
OR, MOST OF THEM, AS YOU CAN SEE...
...SOME OF THEM DETONATED JUST TODAY.
TODAY? BETH... WAS THAT THE BIG EXPLOSION WE SAW?
I'D BET ON IT!

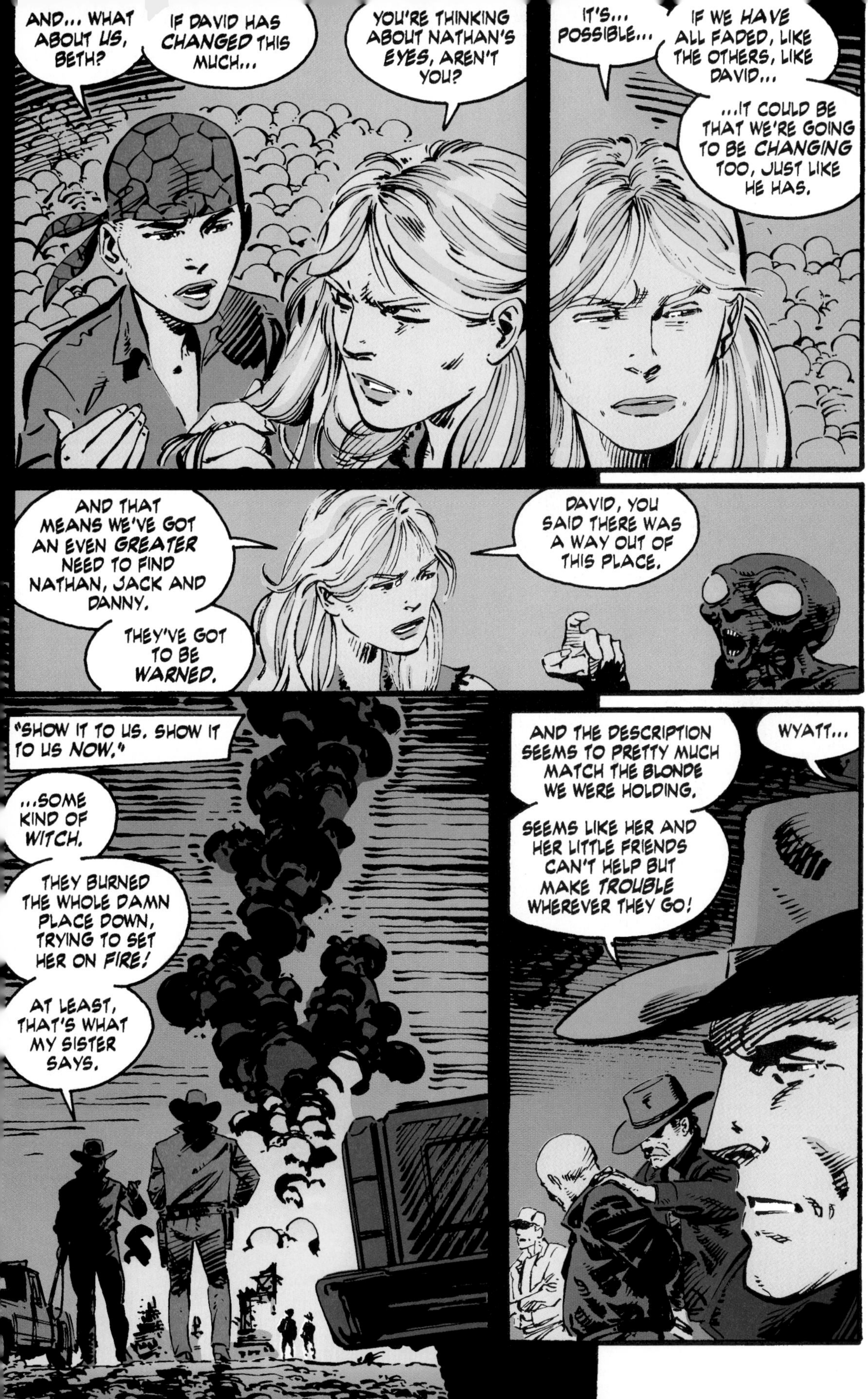

AND... WHAT ABOUT US, BETH?
IF DAVID HAS CHANGED THIS MUCH...
YOU'RE THINKING ABOUT NATHAN'S EYES, AREN'T YOU?
IT'S... POSSIBLE...
IF WE HAVE ALL FADED, LIKE THE OTHERS, LIKE DAVID...
...IT COULD BE THAT WE'RE GOING TO BE CHANGING TOO, JUST LIKE HE HAS.
AND THAT MEANS WE'VE GOT AN EVEN GREATER NEED TO FIND NATHAN, JACK AND DANNY.
THEY'VE GOT TO BE WARNED.
DAVID, YOU SAID THERE WAS A WAY OUT OF THIS PLACE.
"SHOW IT TO US. SHOW IT TO US NOW."
...SOME KIND OF WITCH.
THEY BURNED THE WHOLE DAMN PLACE DOWN, TRYING TO SET HER ON FIRE!
AT LEAST, THAT'S WHAT MY SISTER SAYS.
AND THE DESCRIPTION SEEMS TO PRETTY MUCH MATCH THE BLONDE WE WERE HOLDING.
SEEMS LIKE HER AND HER LITTLE FRIENDS CAN'T HELP BUT MAKE TROUBLE WHEREVER THEY GO!
WYATT...

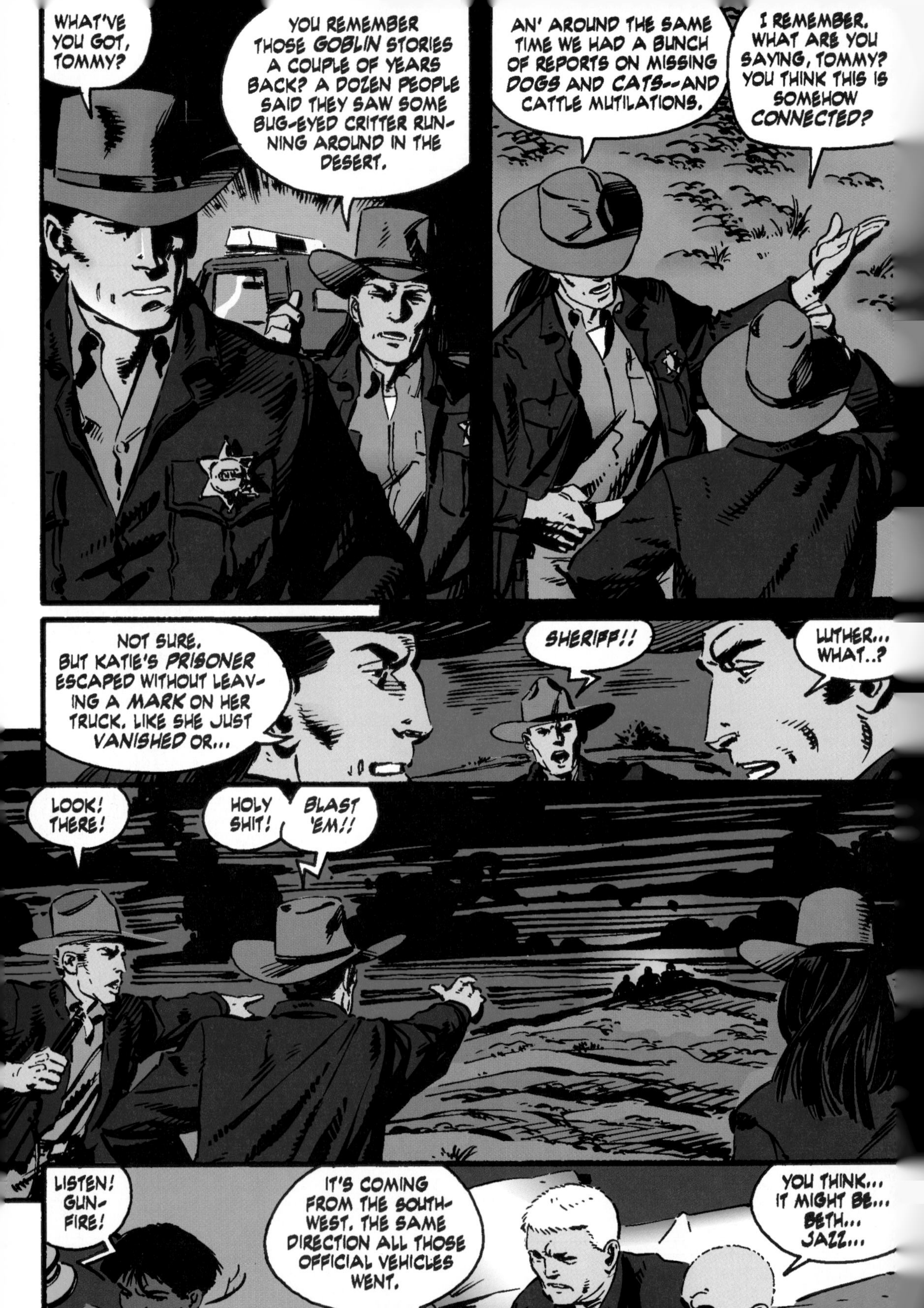
WHAT'VE YOU GOT, TOMMY?
YOU REMEMBER THOSE GOBLIN STORIES A COUPLE OF YEARS BACK? A DOZEN PEOPLE SAID THEY SAW SOME BUG-EYED CRITTER RUNNING AROUND IN THE DESERT.
AN' AROUND THE SAME TIME WE HAD A BUNCH OF REPORTS ON MISSING DOGS AND CATS--AND CATTLE MUTILATIONS.
I REMEMBER. WHAT ARE YOU SAYING, TOMMY? YOU THINK THIS IS SOMEHOW CONNECTED?
NOT SURE. BUT KATIE'S PRISONER ESCAPED WITHOUT LEAVING A MARK ON HER TRUCK. LIKE SHE JUST VANISHED OR...
SHERIFF!!
LUTHER... WHAT..?
LOOK! THERE!
HOLY SHIT!
BLAST 'EM!!
LISTEN! GUNFIRE!
IT'S COMING FROM THE SOUTHWEST. THE SAME DIRECTION ALL THOSE OFFICIAL VEHICLES WENT.
YOU THINK... IT MIGHT BE... BETH... JAZZ...

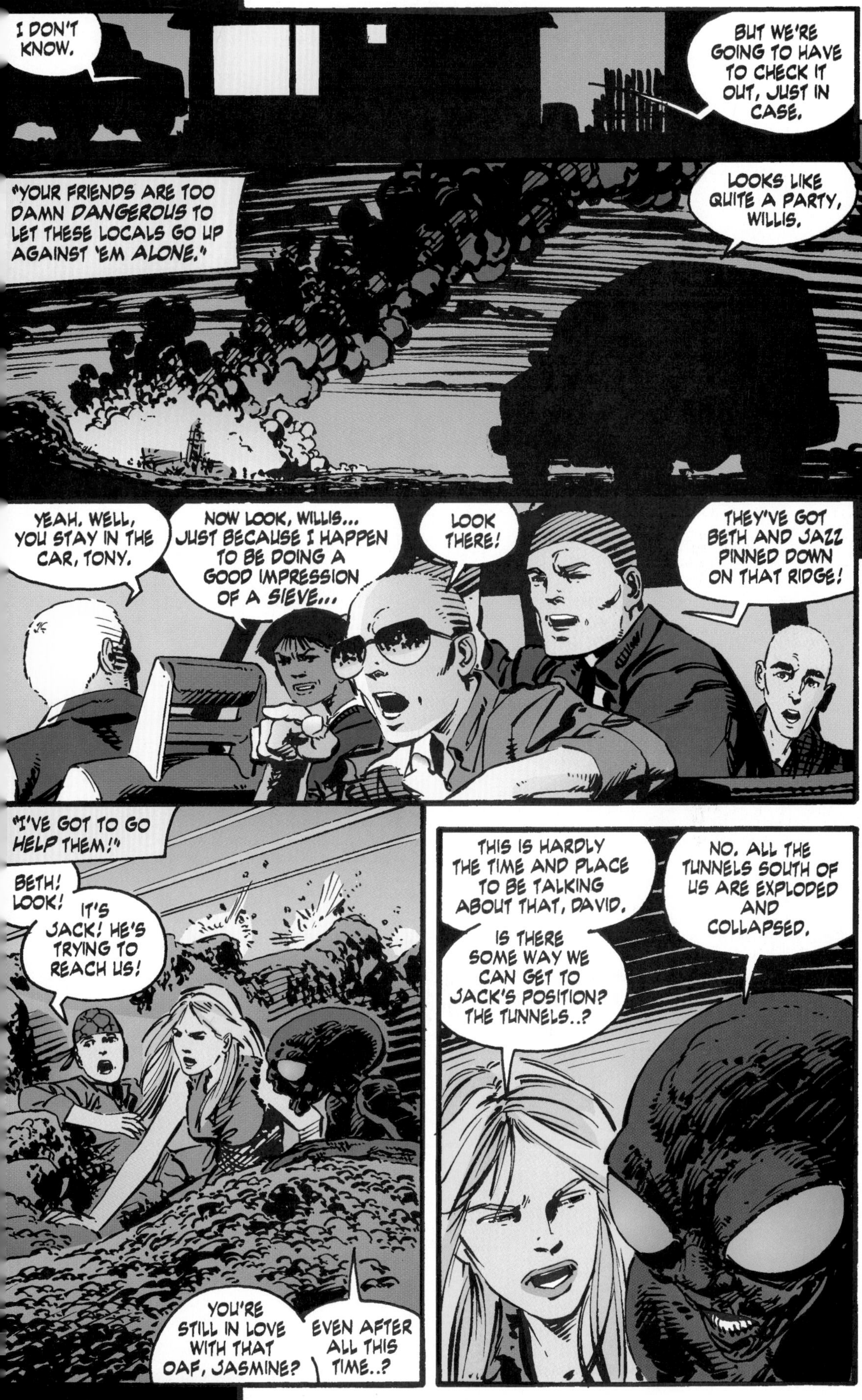
I DON'T KNOW.
BUT WE'RE GOING TO HAVE TO CHECK IT OUT, JUST IN CASE.
"YOUR FRIENDS ARE TOO DAMN DANGEROUS TO LET THESE LOCALS GO UP AGAINST 'EM ALONE."
LOOKS LIKE QUITE A PARTY, WILLIS.
YEAH. WELL, YOU STAY IN THE CAR, TONY.
NOW LOOK, WILLIS... JUST BECAUSE I HAPPEN TO BE DOING A GOOD IMPRESSION OF A SIEVE...
LOOK THERE!
THEY'VE GOT BETH AND JAZZ PINNED DOWN ON THAT RIDGE!
"I'VE GOT TO GO HELP THEM!"
BETH! LOOK!
IT'S JACK! HE'S TRYING TO REACH US!
YOU'RE STILL IN LOVE WITH THAT OAF, JASMINE?
EVEN AFTER ALL THIS TIME..?
THIS IS HARDLY THE TIME AND PLACE TO BE TALKING ABOUT THAT, DAVID.
IS THERE SOME WAY WE CAN GET TO JACK'S POSITION? THE TUNNELS..?
NO. ALL THE TUNNELS SOUTH OF US ARE EXPLODED AND COLLAPSED.

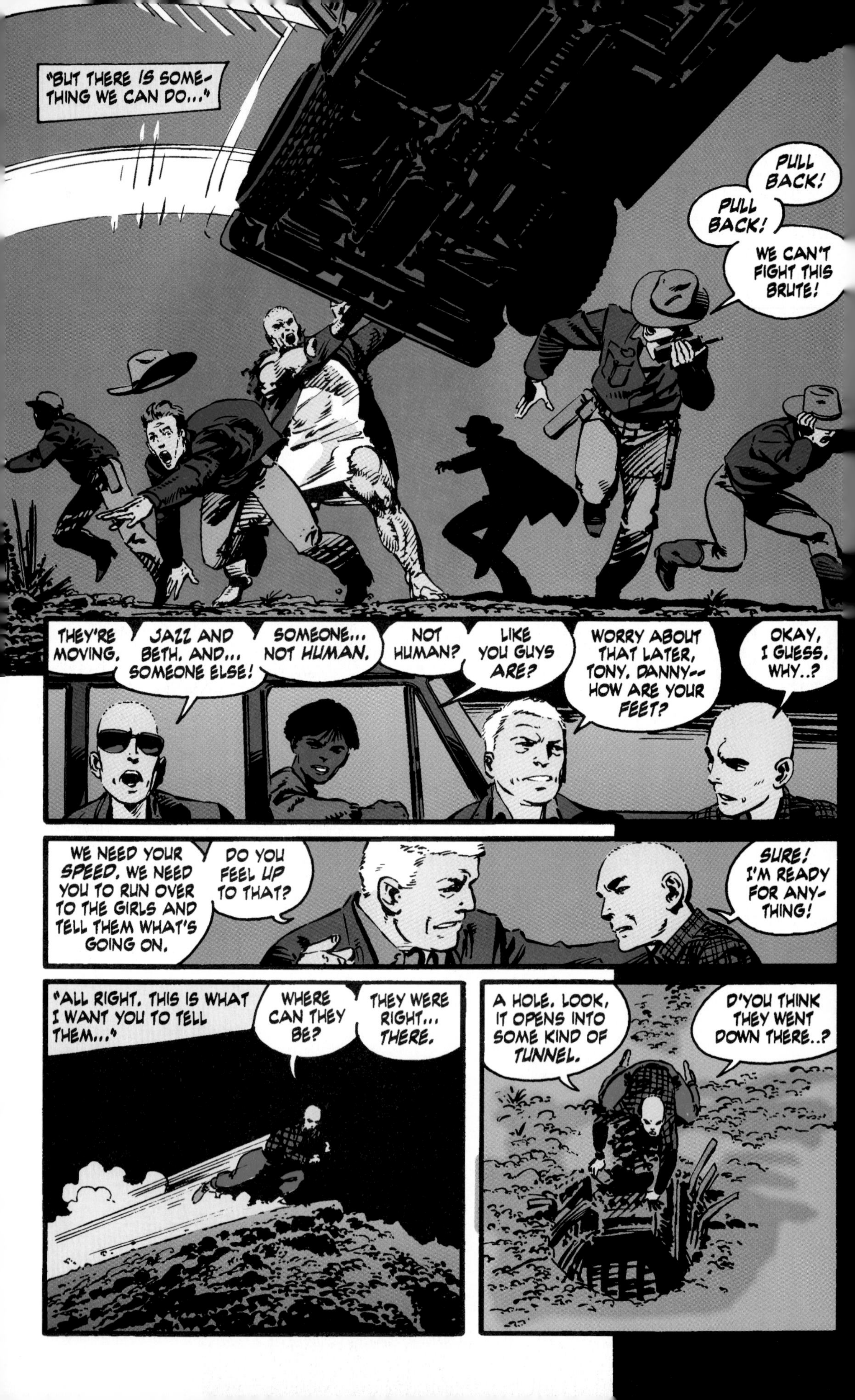
"BUT THERE IS SOMETHING WE CAN DO..."
PULL BACK!
PULL BACK!
WE CAN'T FIGHT THIS BRUTE!
THEY'RE MOVING.
JAZZ AND BETH. AND... SOMEONE ELSE!
SOMEONE... NOT HUMAN.
NOT HUMAN?
LIKE YOU GUYS ARE?
WORRY ABOUT THAT LATER, TONY. DANNY-- HOW ARE YOUR FEET?
OKAY, I GUESS. WHY..?
WE NEED YOUR SPEED. WE NEED YOU TO RUN OVER TO THE GIRLS AND TELL THEM WHAT'S GOING ON.
DO YOU FEEL UP TO THAT?
SURE! I'M READY FOR ANYTHING!
"ALL RIGHT. THIS IS WHAT I WANT YOU TO TELL THEM..."
WHERE CAN THEY BE?
THEY WERE RIGHT... THERE.
A HOLE. LOOK, IT OPENS INTO SOME KIND OF TUNNEL.
D'YOU THINK THEY WENT DOWN THERE..?

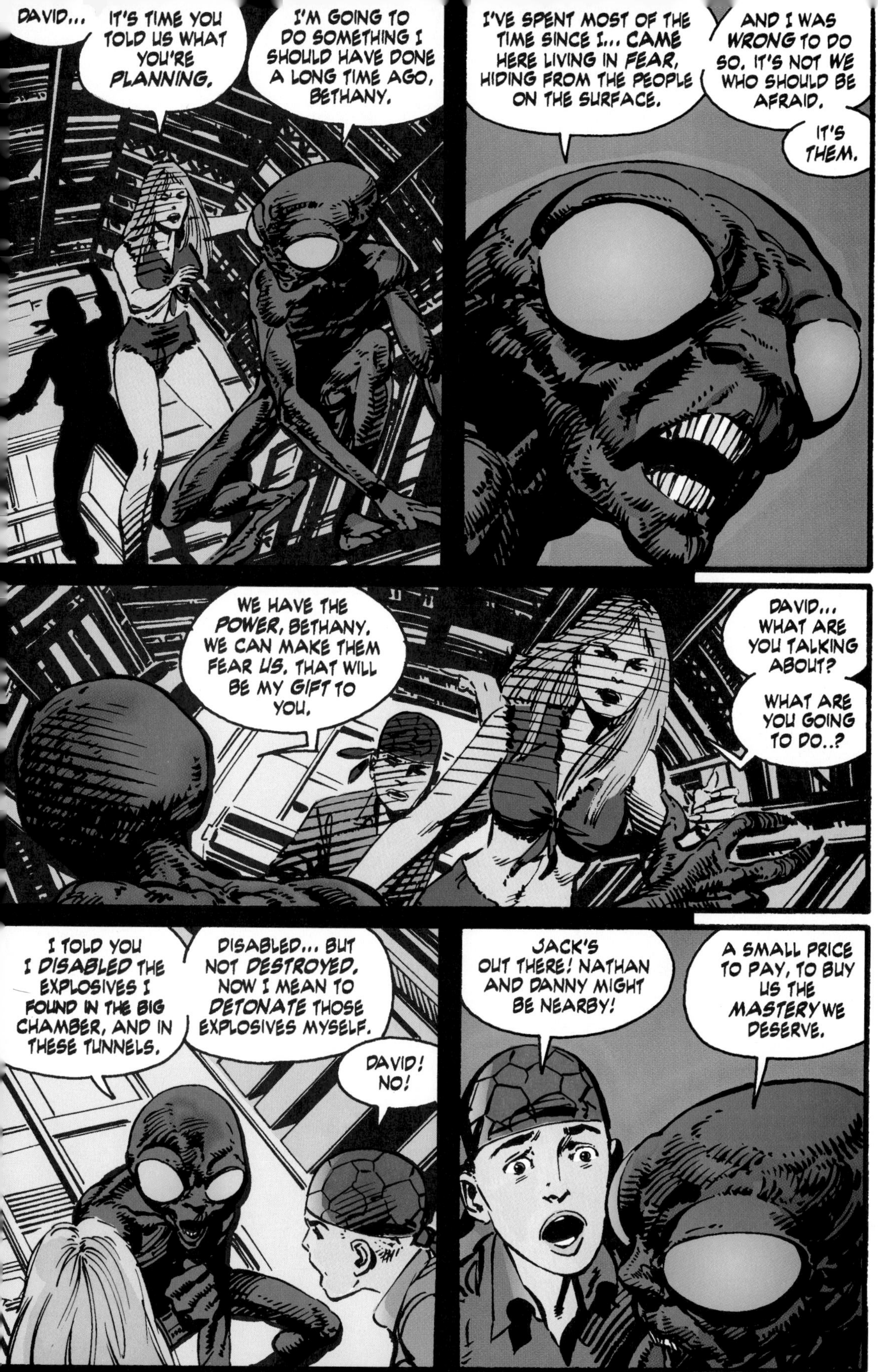
DAVID...
IT'S TIME YOU TOLD US WHAT YOU'RE PLANNING.
I'M GOING TO DO SOMETHING I SHOULD HAVE DONE A LONG TIME AGO, BETHANY.
I'VE SPENT MOST OF THE TIME SINCE I... CAME HERE LIVING IN FEAR, HIDING FROM THE PEOPLE ON THE SURFACE.
AND I WAS WRONG TO DO SO. IT'S NOT WE WHO SHOULD BE AFRAID.
IT'S THEM.
WE HAVE THE POWER, BETHANY. WE CAN MAKE THEM FEAR US. THAT WILL BE MY GIFT TO YOU.
DAVID... WHAT ARE YOU TALKING ABOUT?
WHAT ARE YOU GOING TO DO..?
I TOLD YOU I DISABLED THE EXPLOSIVES I FOUND IN THE BIG CHAMBER, AND IN THESE TUNNELS.
DISABLED... BUT NOT DESTROYED. NOW I MEAN TO DETONATE THOSE EXPLOSIVES MYSELF.
DAVID! NO!
JACK'S OUT THERE! NATHAN AND DANNY MIGHT BE NEARBY!
A SMALL PRICE TO PAY, TO BUY US THE MASTERY WE DESERVE.

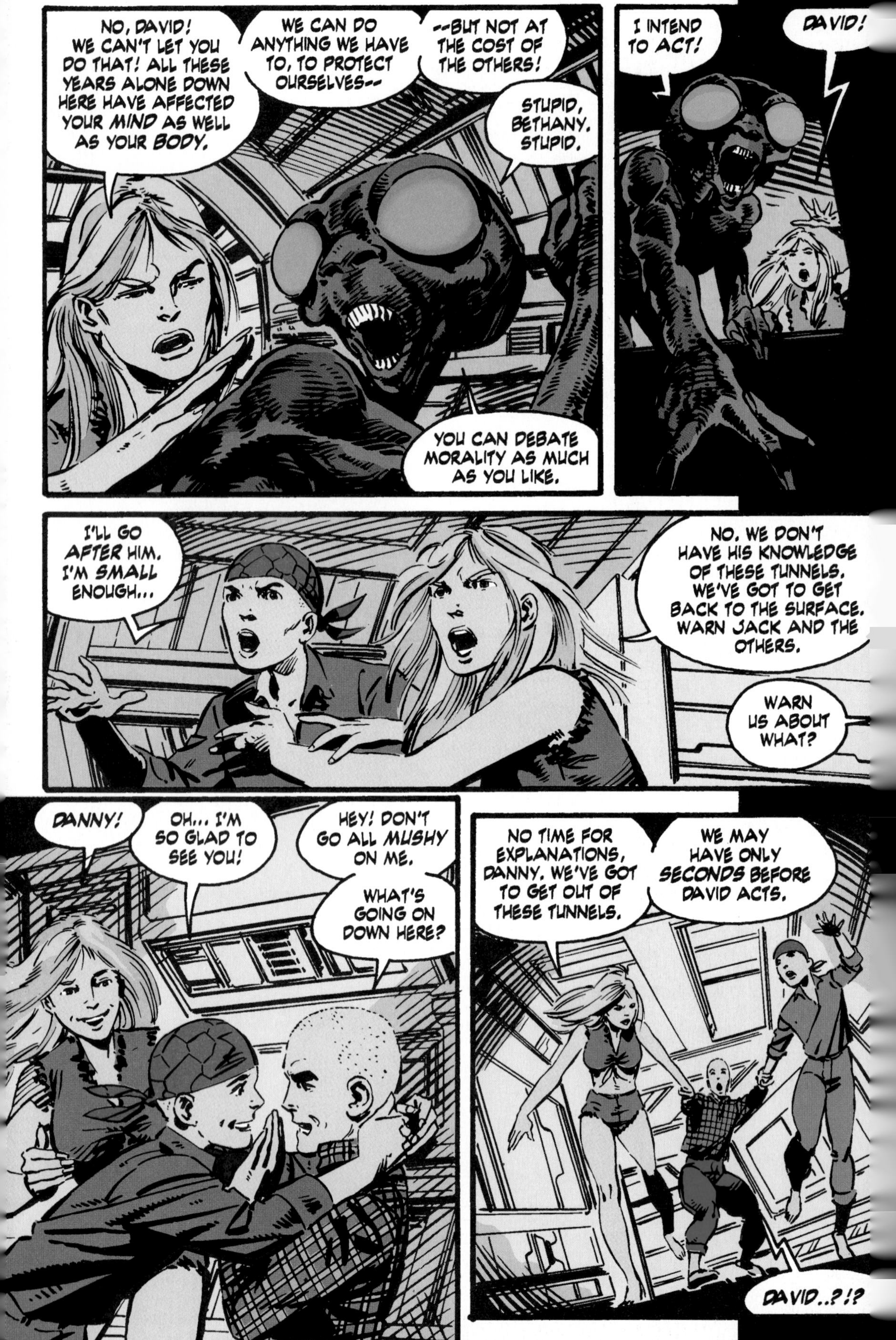
NO, DAVID! WE CAN'T LET YOU DO THAT! ALL THESE YEARS ALONE DOWN HERE HAVE AFFECTED YOUR MIND AS WELL AS YOUR BODY.
WE CAN DO ANYTHING WE HAVE TO, TO PROTECT OURSELVES--
--BUT NOT AT THE COST OF THE OTHERS!
STUPID, BETHANY. STUPID.
YOU CAN DEBATE MORALITY AS MUCH AS YOU LIKE.
I INTEND TO ACT!
DAVID!
I'LL GO AFTER HIM. I'M SMALL ENOUGH...
NO. WE DON'T HAVE HIS KNOWLEDGE OF THESE TUNNELS. WE'VE GOT TO GET BACK TO THE SURFACE. WARN JACK AND THE OTHERS.
WARN US ABOUT WHAT?
DANNY!
OH... I'M SO GLAD TO SEE YOU!
HEY! DON'T GO ALL MUSHY ON ME.
WHAT'S GOING ON DOWN HERE?
NO TIME FOR EXPLANATIONS, DANNY. WE'VE GOT TO GET OUT OF THESE TUNNELS.
WE MAY HAVE ONLY SECONDS BEFORE DAVID ACTS.
DAVID..?!?

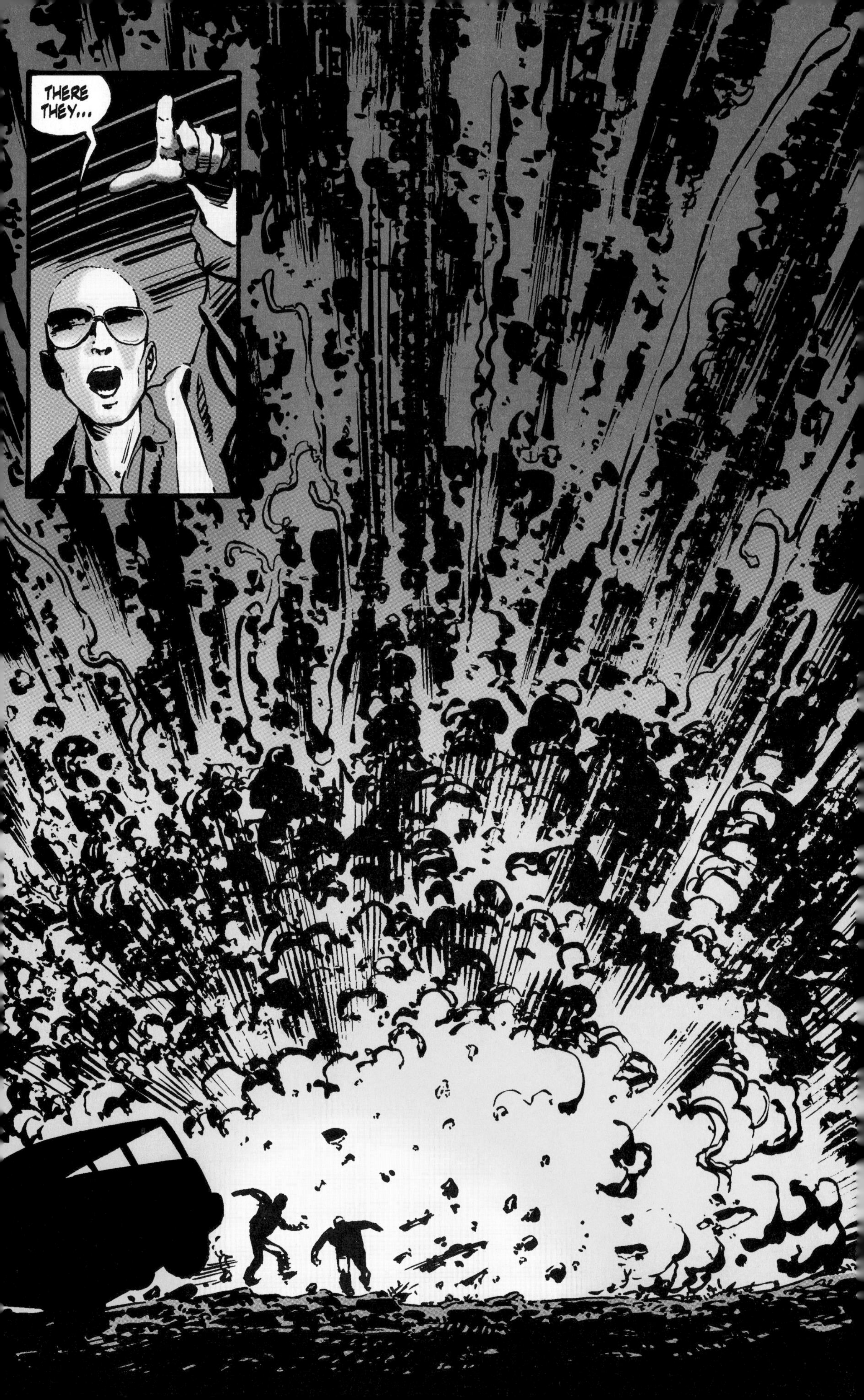
THERE THEY...

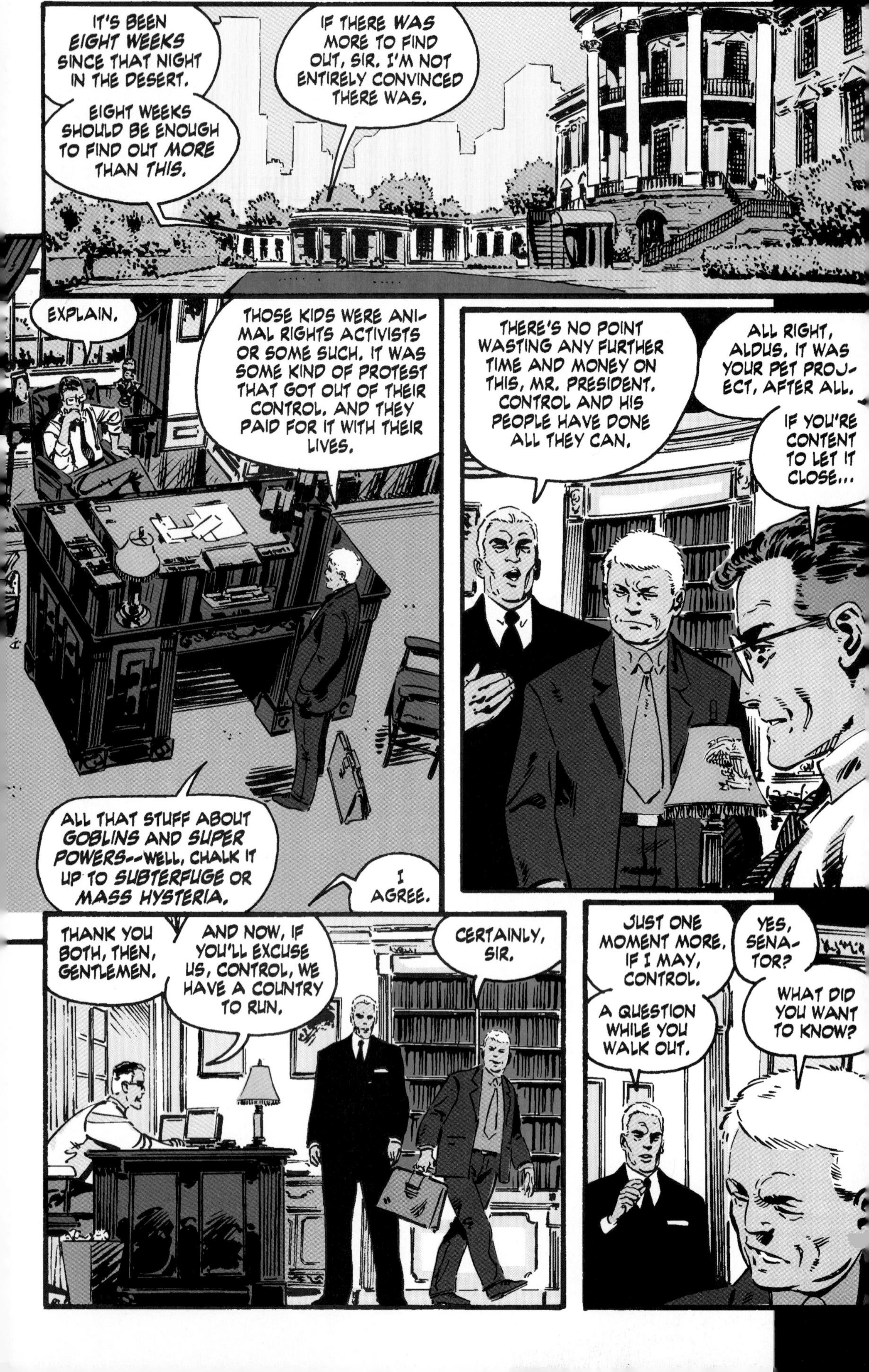
IT'S BEEN EIGHT WEEKS SINCE THAT NIGHT IN THE DESERT.
EIGHT WEEKS SHOULD BE ENOUGH TO FIND OUT MORE THAN THIS.
IF THERE WAS MORE TO FIND OUT, SIR. I'M NOT ENTIRELY CONVINCED THERE WAS.
EXPLAIN.
THOSE KIDS WERE ANIMAL RIGHTS ACTIVISTS OR SOME SUCH. IT WAS SOME KIND OF PROTEST THAT GOT OUT OF THEIR CONTROL. AND THEY PAID FOR IT WITH THEIR LIVES.
ALL THAT STUFF ABOUT GOBLINS AND SUPER POWERS--WELL, CHALK IT UP TO SUBTERFUGE OR MASS HYSTERIA.
I AGREE.
THERE'S NO POINT WASTING ANY FURTHER TIME AND MONEY ON THIS, MR. PRESIDENT. CONTROL AND HIS PEOPLE HAVE DONE ALL THEY CAN.
ALL RIGHT, ALDUS. IT WAS YOUR PET PROJECT, AFTER ALL.
IF YOU'RE CONTENT TO LET IT CLOSE...
THANK YOU BOTH, THEN, GENTLEMEN.
AND NOW, IF YOU'LL EXCUSE US, CONTROL, WE HAVE A COUNTRY TO RUN.
CERTAINLY, SIR.
JUST ONE MOMENT MORE, IF I MAY, CONTROL.
A QUESTION WHILE YOU WALK OUT.
YES, SENATOR?
WHAT DID YOU WANT TO KNOW?

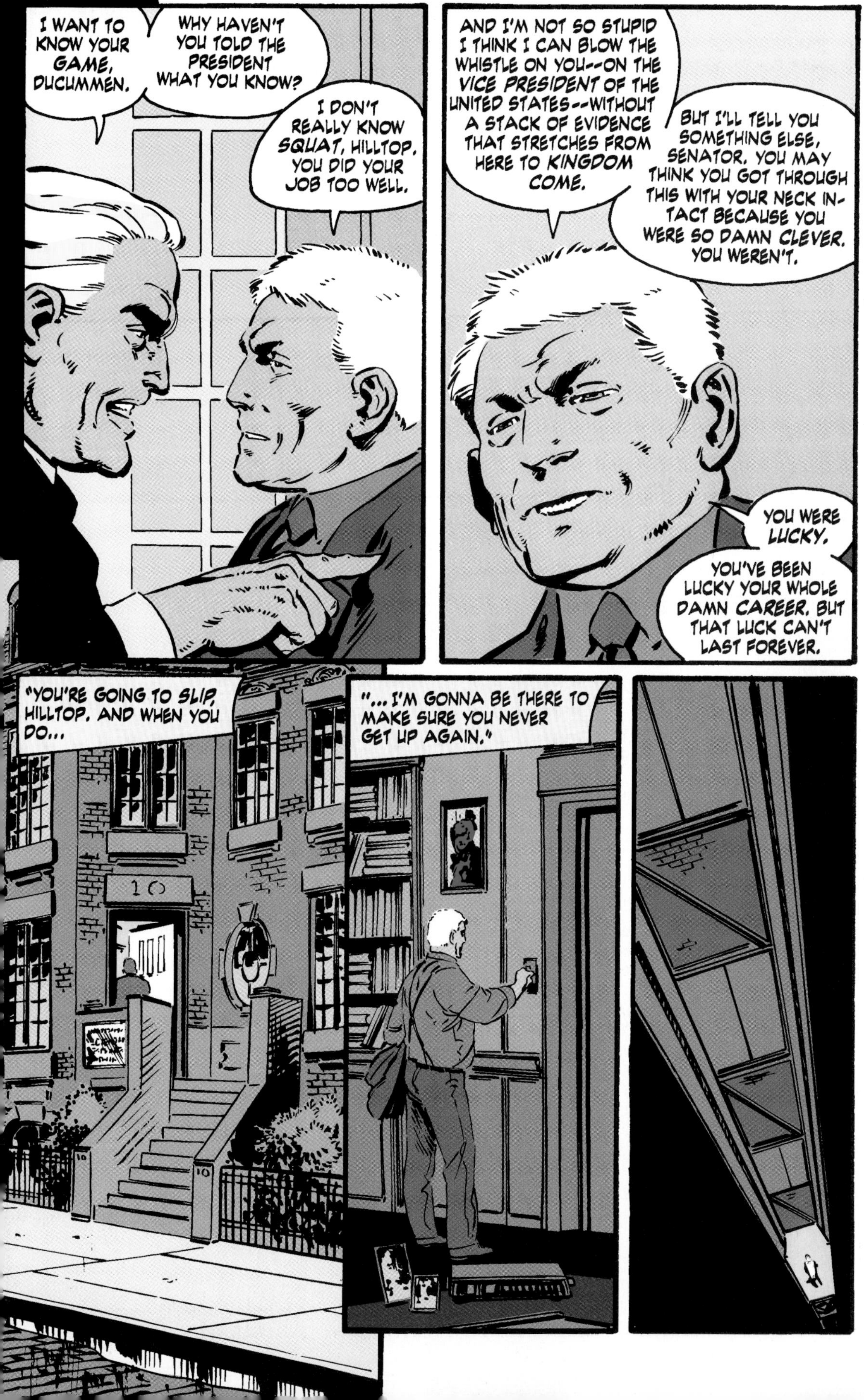
I WANT TO KNOW YOUR GAME, DUCUMMEN.
WHY HAVEN'T YOU TOLD THE PRESIDENT WHAT YOU KNOW?
I DON'T REALLY KNOW SQUAT, HILLTOP. YOU DID YOUR JOB TOO WELL.
AND I'M NOT SO STUPID I THINK I CAN BLOW THE WHISTLE ON YOU--ON THE VICE PRESIDENT OF THE UNITED STATES--WITHOUT A STACK OF EVIDENCE THAT STRETCHES FROM HERE TO KINGDOM COME.
BUT I'LL TELL YOU SOMETHING ELSE, SENATOR. YOU MAY THINK YOU GOT THROUGH THIS WITH YOUR NECK IN-TACT BECAUSE YOU WERE SO DAMN CLEVER. YOU WEREN'T.
YOU WERE LUCKY.
YOU'VE BEEN LUCKY YOUR WHOLE DAMN CAREER. BUT THAT LUCK CAN'T LAST FOREVER.
"YOU'RE GOING TO SLIP, HILLTOP. AND WHEN YOU DO...
"...I'M GONNA BE THERE TO MAKE SURE YOU NEVER GET UP AGAIN."
10

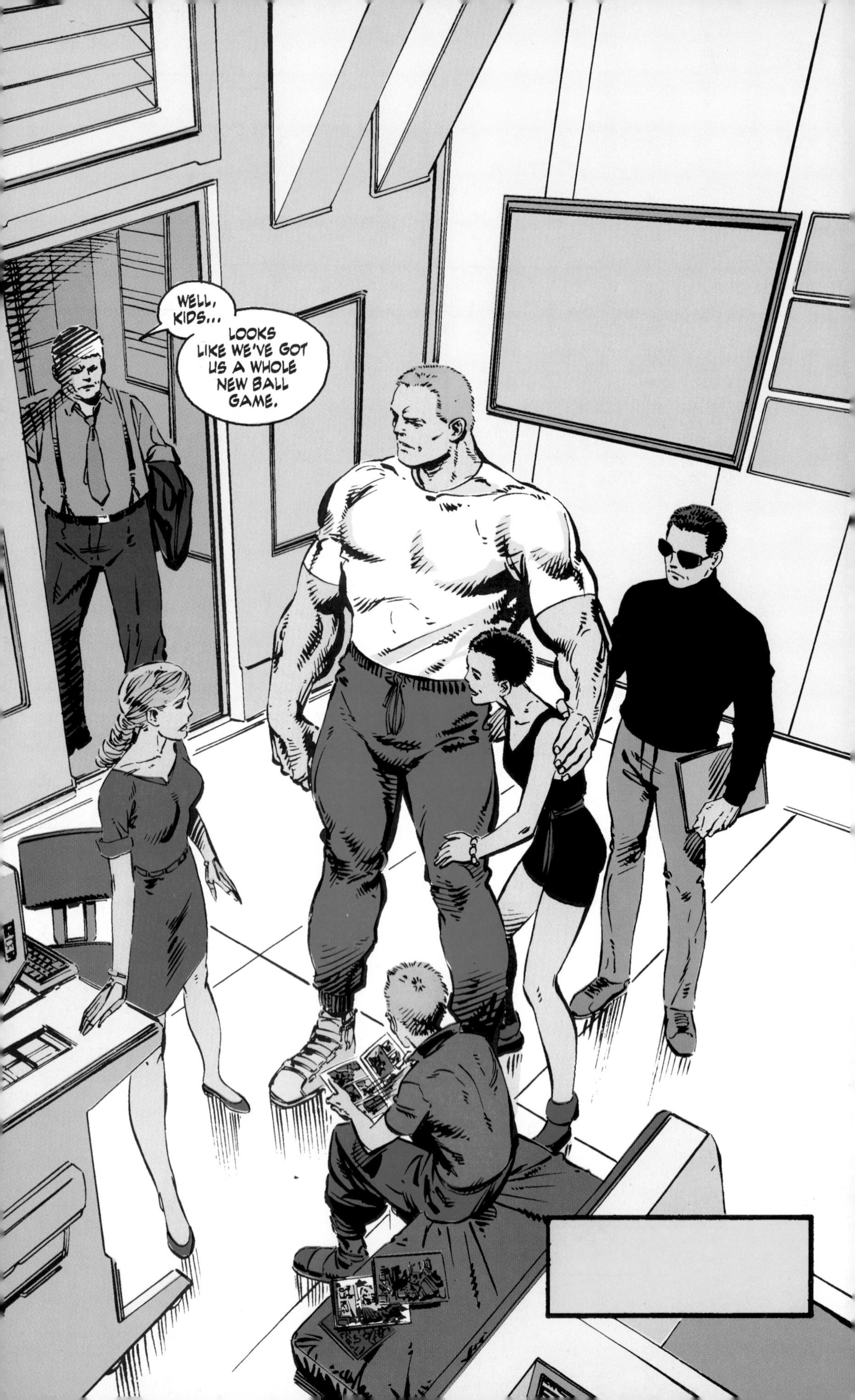
WELL, KIDS...
LOOKS LIKE WE'VE GOT US A WHOLE NEW BALL GAME.